2-6/22

MAJOR DETOURS

ZACHARY SERGI

RP|TEENS

PHILADELPHIA

Running Press Teens
Hachette Book Group
1290 Avenue of the Americas, New York, NY 10104
www.runningpress.com/rpkids
@RP_Kids

Printed in the United States of America

First Edition: September 2021

Published by Running Press Teens, an imprint of Perseus Books, LLC,
a subsidiary of Hachette Book Group, Inc. The Running Press Teens
name and logo is a trademark of the Hachette Book Group.

The Hachette Speakers Bureau provides a wide range of authors for speaking events.
To find out more, go to www.hachettespeakersbureau.com or call (866) 376-6591.

The publisher is not responsible for websites (or their content)
that are not owned by the publisher.

Print book cover and interior design by Marissa Raybuck.

Library of Congress Cataloging-in-Publication Data has been applied for.

ISBNs: 9780762471416 (hardcover), 9780762471386 (ebook)

LSC-C

Printing 1, 2021

To Mom, Dad, Kyle, Louis, Amanda,
& Everly, unconditionally.
To Grandma Florence, forever flo.

This novel was written for two kinds of readers:
Those who love control and those who love to lose control.

So, go ahead, read every page like a novel straight through if you want;
this was written with you in mind.

However, if you really want the full experience, follow the interactive
brick road and honor your choices while reading.

You might just find following the rules is the fastest way to break them . . .
Either way, this story now belongs to you.

INCLUDED IN THE back of the novel is a Reading Guide to help keep track of your most important decisions. You can easily read without using this guide, but it's there for you if you need it.

Once your Reading Guide is complete, you can also use it to compile two Character and Tarot Personality Profiles. These determine what kind of reader you are and sort you into your unique tarot corner.

PART ONE

WANDERERS

CHAPTER ONE

AMELIA

SODA BUBBLES FIZZLE on my tongue and french fry salt coats my fingertips. Vintage Mariah plays on the stereo and white lines fly by underneath the van. There's nothing around but steep mountains and open road and my three best friends in the whole world.

The next two weeks stretch ahead of us like a highway, the last two weeks before we all head off in different directions. The best two weeks of our lives, we promised. I can already feel how good it's going to be now, just two hours in, with junk food in my gut and a sugar rush buzzing in my veins. With my eyes set on the vivid blue sky and the dry green brush, on the puffed white clouds slung above the red hills.

Blue and green, white and red. The colors of the tarot. Or at least the colors of this tarot, our most prized possession. I really shouldn't be holding it with my fast-food fingers, but I want to keep it close. This tarot deck, well-worn and beloved, was the inspiration for our road trip. It contains multitudes: histories and memories, mysticism and mysteries—the exact kind we hope to solve on this trip.

"Amelia," Chase says.

I know what he really means: *Don't touch the deck with grubby fingers.* I may have inherited the cards from my grandma, but they mean just as much to Chase.

"Is that thing really going to beep for the entire trip?" Logan asks from the driver's seat.

"That thing has a name," Cleo answers from the front passenger side. "And Toky is our official trip mascot, so you should learn to love them now."

Cleo dangles her keychain beside Logan's face and the rainbow-glitter egg nearly brushes his cheek. She got that Tamagotchi back when we were freshmen, when she cracked it open and configured it to live forever. Cleo never met a rule she didn't love to bend.

"You'd better give Toky a kiss before they throw a tantrum."

"Now, now, I thought we agreed tantrums are only allowed in Charvan on Wednesdays," I say, watching Chase bristle. His parents gifted him this ancient Volkswagen van when he turned sixteen, and he has since meticulously transformed it into our happy place. We both decided to name this mobile headquarters Charvan, after the tarot's Chariot card. Chase would prefer we keep Charvan curbside forever, but I'm thrilled we finally get to take it out on this long-overdue adventure.

"Remind me why I agreed to come on this trip again?" Logan sighs.

To answer that, Chase leans forward and kisses him on the side of his neck. At first glance, it'd be easy to question how buttoned-up Chase and athleisure Logan go together, but they've been the perfect couple for years.

"Oh, right, my brainiac boyfriend has me under his spell," Logan says.

Chase smiles, settling back into his seat. He then returns to his combination-lock journal, the little leather notebook that's like his permanent appendage. No one, not even Logan, gets to read inside that locked journal, but I bet Chase is going over his plan for the front end of our trip. Personally, I'd rather see where the road takes us, but that's why Chase and I work so well as best friends. He plans, I deviate. He thinks, I act. He writes, I talk:

"Okay, I think the next junction is coming up pretty soon. Which means you all know what time it is."

Cleo groans from the front, but Chase snaps his journal closed.

"It's tarot time."

"I can't believe we're actually going through with this," Cleo says, her short black hair swinging as she turns to face us. She sports a pair of sunglasses with green triangular lenses, one of my favorites in her legendary collection.

"This is a perfect idea and you know it," I answer. "Chase plans our general route, but we let the tarot cards decide the specifics. It's perfectly balanced."

I reach my hand over and squeeze Chase's. He is more like a brother to me than a best friend. Really, he is my NRLP: my nonromantic life partner. Plus, a sometimes-maddening reminder of my complete lack of an actual romantic life partner. The two of us separating for college is still a thought I cannot process, so I focus instead on pulling the tarot cards out of their faded cardboard box. All these years later, they still have that fresh cardstock smell, with just a hint of lavender.

"I researched two occult shops on the way out to Joshua Tree," Chase begins, flipping through his journal. "They're on alternate routes, so we need to decide where to stop."

"No, we need to let the cards decide," I add. "Which reading configuration do you think we should use?"

Chase furrows his dark brows, his brain thrumming like an engine.

"Obviously we need one of the simpler configurations," he begins. "I'd say the two-card Yin and Yang, but a classic One Card Pull will probably do."

"Couldn't agree more," I answer, beginning to shuffle the cards.

As usual, I can feel our added homemade cards brushing my palms, their laminated edges slightly thicker than the rest. Grandma's deck has always been missing four cards, ever since she bought it at a yard sale years ago. This deck is full of gorgeous, seemingly hand-painted images, so when Chase and I were kids we crafted our own far-inferior replacement cards. We've been obsessed with the tarot for as long as we can remember, likely because Grandma taught us everything we know about it.

One thing we've never learned, however, is where this deck really comes from. We haven't been able to find any mention of anything like it online. Growing up, Grandma always said she'd take me and Chase on an adventure to find the missing cards once we were older, a kind of mystic road trip where the tarot would be our guide. Grandma might not be able to take that trip with us anymore, but when Chase and I were deciding how to spend the last two weeks before college, our answer was clear.

"Any key differences between the two shops?" I ask.

"The first is called Eastern Light Tarot and the second is Mother Earth Occult and Antiques. That gives us plenty to go off."

"Perfect. Cut the deck and draw the first card?" I say, holding out the stack toward Chase. "Everyone ready to see where the tarot takes us first?"

"Am I the only one who finds this spooky?" Cleo asks, craning to watch.

"Spooky or not, that junction is coming up in a few miles," Logan says, glancing at the GPS. "Please let the tarot proceed with some speed."

Not wasting another moment, Chase pulls the top card from the freshly cut deck. He looks down at it and grins for a few seconds. When he finally lays the card down, I see why. I gasp out loud when I glimpse her green goddess eyes staring up at me.

The Empress.

"Well that couldn't be clearer," Chase says. "The Empress stands at a doorway to transformation, beckoning us to take action. But most importantly, The Empress is the Mother Nature figure. So, Mother Earth Occult it is?"

I sigh. Chase always reads the cards like an encyclopedia, analyzing their symbols historically and isolating their meanings from context. It's not that he's wrong. It's more that, deep down, I've always felt the tarot is more personal than that.

Not to mention, it's just like Chase to overlook the fact that The Empress is my personal tarot card expression.

◊ "Since The Empress is my card representation," I say, "I think I should be the one to decide where we go next. She is a **Queen** in charge, after all."

Turn To Page 5

◊ "I couldn't agree more," I say. "The Empress is **Mother Earth**. It's the obvious direction based on the intention we set."

Turn To Page 6

"Is this how it's going to be every time?" Chase whines. "I lay the foundation and you make the decision, like always?"

"That's not how it always is. The Empress just happens to be my card. And, for your information, I was going to choose Mother Earth Occult anyway."

I watch as Chase resists the urge to respond, especially since he got his way in the end. Sometimes I feel like he pushes back on purpose, just for the sake of arguing. Then again, I am indeed an Empress at heart. *Spontaneous. Commanding. Demanding.*

One of the first things Grandma taught us was how to find our expressions in the Major Arcana, adding up the digits in our birthdays and combining the sum. Mine is August 1, 2001, which equals twelve. With a number that low, I then had to choose to keep twelve, The Hanged Man, or add the one and the two to make three, The Empress. For little-girl me, this choice was easy. Chase's own birthday is October 27, 2001, which brings his final sum to four, making him The Emperor.

It seemed so fitting back then, proof that we were the perfect complementary pair. However, the older we got, the more we realized this really meant we were more like balanced opposites.

"The Major strikes again," Cleo says. "Not that you two tarot wizards care about third opinions, but I agree with Mother Earth Occult as the outcome."

"Then it's unanimous," Logan adds, "because that one is closer and I really need to pee."

I can feel Chase bristling once again at Cleo's comment, but he keeps quiet. *Amelia and Chase, The Empress and The Emperor. Major Amelia,* named after the bold and chaotic personalities of the tarot's first half. *Minor Chase,* named after the precise and numbered second half, structured like a traditional deck of cards.

Grandma always believed what really makes the tarot so universal is the way it draws strength from two opposing halves that make up a whole. Thankfully, Chase and I have always understood that our differences only make us stronger.

At least, most of the time.

Turn To Page 7

Chase smiles, hearing me agree. Part of me wants to challenge him with an opposing interpretation just to keep things interesting, but we have many more miles—and many more readings—to go.

"The Empress leans into her giving side, resisting the urge to become possessive," Chase adds. "Pulling your card is a very good sign we are exactly where we're meant to be."

"Sounds like round one goes to The Minor," Cleo says, a devilish smile on her face. Poking at any underlying tension is a never-ending source of amusement for her.

Amelia and Chase. The Major and The Minor.

Grandma gave us these nicknames, way back when. *Major Amelia*, named after the bold and chaotic personalities in the first half of the tarot. Then there's *Minor Chase*, named after the numbered and precise second half of the tarot, structured like a traditional deck of cards.

Grandma believed what really makes the tarot so universal is the way it draws strength from two opposing halves that complement a whole. She also believed it's what makes the bond between Chase and me so unbreakable. Lucky for Chase, when his instinct is to be the commanding and authoritative Emperor, I embrace the thoughtful and nurturing side of my Empress essence.

Still, that's only half the story.

Turn To Page 7

"Okay, it's four p.m. sharp," Logan says, pulling my attention. "You know the drill. You all get five minutes of phone time before they go back into the box."

I try to restrain myself from immediately reaching for my phone like some rabid animal. It was Logan's idea to keep everyone's phones in a shoebox during the trip so that we all remain present. The idea of detoxing off the grid for a couple weeks actually sounded lovely at first, but that was before I knew we'd be making a special stop in the hometown of my number one crush of all time.

Chase hands out our phones and, once I get mine in my grip, my thumb scrolls furiously through the stacked notifications. I hold my breath until, finally, I find the exact DM I was hoping for.

I swipe right and Anwar's chiseled face lights up my screen. Everyone always says he could be a model, the tall-dark-handsome hybrid of Zayn Malik and James Dean. But Anwar is much too serious to ever consider modeling. His nose is always in a philosophy book or underneath the muscle car he restored himself. At least, that's what social media leads me to believe.

I had the biggest crush on Anwar growing up, but he moved up north before high school. I nearly fainted the first time he DM'd me this year, commenting on one of my stupid stories about watching horror movies. Since then we've become kind of like social media pen pals, flirt messaging about our favorite horror classics. At least, I hope we've been flirt messaging. The line had been pretty blurry up until a few days ago when Anwar suggested we swing our road trip through his town for an in-person visit.

At first Chase balked at the idea of deviating from his preciously calculated plan. However, when I reminded him that he's the one in a stable, intimacy-filled relationship and I haven't even kissed anyone in . . . well, far too long, he finally agreed to find room for the added stop.

As I read the latest messages from Anwar, my heart begins to pound.

I see your road trip has started. Which means we get to hang soon.
Hope you packed a sweater, it gets colder here at night than you're used to.
And we have lots of seaside star-gazing to attend to.

I immediately picture Anwar lying on a blanket in the sand beside me, the sound of waves crashing in the background. Just the two of us and the salt spray and the stars. His steady hands pointing out the constellations, his shirt unbuttoned just enough to see the curves of his tan chest. Me staring at his full, round lips when he talks, the lips that would eventually connect with mine.

I snap myself out of this daydream, however, because time is short and I need to write a response.

◊ I never get to see enough stars back home. Or the **ocean** for that matter.

Turn To Page 9

◊ Why would I pack a sweater when I could just use you for **body heat**?

Turn To Page 10

It's not exactly the most romantic thing I can say, but it's the truth.

I hit send and the familiar nerves begin to collect in my chest. Gripping my phone, I know I should use my precious remaining minutes to check my other notifications, but my eyes remain fixed on the screen, willing Anwar to answer.

Sometimes I wish I could care a little less, that I could turn down the dial on how intensely I feel most things. Everything always seems so heightened in my world, like my emotional valleys can sometimes be bottomless.

Then again, once I see the three flashing dots by Anwar's photo, I remember that my peaks can also be sky high. Exhaling, I welcome the flush of warmth that replaces my nerves.

Oh, I remember. But trust me, you're going to love it here. This is my solemn swear.

I smile at the screen, my mind racing to compose a good response.

Well, I plan to write a yelp review on your tour guide experience, so you better bring your A game.

For you? Always.

I fight the urge to melt into a warm puddle right here in this seat. Instead, I write back:

5 Stars, here we come.
Gotta go, but will text when we settle in for the night.

Turn To Page 11

Screw the blurry line.

I hit send and immediately feel a swell of nerves. Sometimes I really wish I had more of a filter. Then again, what fun would that be? I just hope Anwar doesn't mind my bouts of bravado.

I look around the car to distract myself, but Chase and Cleo are equally absorbed by their phones, and Logan seems fully focused on the road. With nowhere else to turn, I glance back down at my phone. Mercifully, the three dots appear, indicating that Anwar is already typing.

**Body heat on the beach? Way too much sand
for that.**

My heart promptly sinks into my stomach. I twirl a strand of hair between my fingers, my thoughts pulsing. How could I have ruined the vibe so quickly? Why do I have to be so damn eager all the time? Now Anwar is going to think I'm a total—

**But the heater in my car is broken. That's a much
better place to keep each other warm?**

I exhale, letting the rush of anxiety melt away. Maybe being forward has its advantages, after all. I smile as I tap out my response.

**Look at you, always thinking ahead.
Gotta go. Will text tonight when we settle in
for the night.**

Turn To Page II

"All right, the phone five is over," Logan announces. "You all should've seen yourselves. You looked like a bunch of zombies getting your next brain fix."

"In that case, was anyone else's fix as delicious as mine?" I ask, dropping my phone into the shoebox first.

"My mom told me to say hi to everyone," Cleo answers. "So, not particularly."

"I think Amelia meant to say 'salacious,'" Chase replies. "Judging from the dopey look on her face, I think someone got a love note from her brooding vampire boy."

"I know you mean that as a negative, but I'd let him nibble my neck any day."

The walls of Charvan immediately echo with a series of grossed-out groans.

"On that unnerving note," Logan says, "we'll be arriving at our first destination in ten minutes."

I laugh and don't fight the massive smile that spreads across my face.

There's just so much to look forward to, I don't even know where to begin.

◆　◆　◆　◆

It turns out that Mother Earth Occult and Antiques is appropriately labyrinthine, a collection of narrow rooms filled with all kinds of oddities and accursed items. We decided to split up and explore before converging on the tarot reader's room at the back of the shop, so Cleo and I wander from space to cramped space.

We walk around a pile of dusty books and come face to face with a wall of framed paintings based on the tarot. I see Cleo's eyes light up. She's our resident artist, always doodling colorful, one-frame snapshots of events from our days.

"Gran Flo would've loved this one, huh?" Cleo says, adjusting the straps of her mini-narwhal backpack, which is always filled with charcoal pencils and flare pens.

The painting is a wheel of the tarot's most iconic symbols, linking them to their world cultures and religions of origin. My eyes well up because Cleo is right. Grandma should be here to see this herself, but I press my eyes shut before any tears can escape. This trip is supposed to be a celebration and a tribute, a step forward in the journey, not back into the past.

Still, before moving on, I reach into my pocket and run my fingers over the locket I carry with me everywhere. It holds a picture of Grandma when she was in her twenties on one side and a current picture of me on the other, the two of us looking very much like sisters. I trace the grooves of the symbol engraved into its enamel surface: the Hebrew letter Dalet, which represents a door opening to

11

potential. Grandma gave me this locket because Dalet is traditionally associated with The Empress. After all, there are twenty-two characters in the Hebrew alphabet and twenty-two cards in the tarot's Major Arcana.

Just as this thought settles, I notice a particular symbol on the painting.

"Yep. Especially that symbol for The Fool," I say.

"Really?" Cleo asks. "Why The Fool?"

"In the tarot, The Fool is the first figure, embarking on a journey to learn an essential lesson," I begin. "She steps into the unknown blindly, ignoring potential dangers in order to learn from the guides of the Major Arcana. This journey might seem naive or reckless to others, but The Fool knows if she takes the harder path—the one lined with uncertainty and self-reflection—she'll learn something vital. Grandma always said we should all be lucky to find that brand of foolishness."

"In that case, Gran Flo was right," Cleo says, rubbing my shoulder with a soft smile.

I nod and offer a smile in return, because forward we must go, just like The Fool. So I peer around the fronds of a fake purple palm tree beside us, finding a hall that leads to two adjoining rooms.

♦ Earlier, I decided to lean into my **Queen** side, so I lead us left.
Turn To Page 13

♦ Earlier, I decided to lean into my **Mother Earth** side, so I lead us right.
Turn To Page 14

We head left, pushing through hanging beads into a darkened room.

"What do you think this . . . Oh, it's just a storage room."

I agree with Cleo's conclusion once I see the walls are lined with shelves of boxes. We turn to leave, until something catches my eye. I turn and see there's a curtain covering the back wall. At least, I think that's what it is.

"Can you make out what's back there?" I ask.

Cleo shakes her head beside me. Now curious, I shuffle through the room in the semidarkness and my hand taps against the dusty curtain. I start to pull it aside, until something brushes against my hand. I can't see it, but it feels like an enormous spider skitters across the tops of my fingers.

I gasp, pulling away and accidentally moving the curtain along with me. I stagger backward, clutching my hand.

"Are you okay?" Cleo asks, rushing to my side.

"Yeah. I think it was just a spider," I shudder. "Let's get out of here."

"Wait. Amelia . . ."

Cleo points back up at the wall, at what has now been revealed in the dim light of this room. Hanging there are six framed paintings, all of them recreating images from our tarot deck. From Grandma's deck.

My eyes widen, seeing the gorgeous renderings. I've never seen this tarot artwork anywhere other than our own set of cards. Seeing them expanded in such detail like this is—

I lose the thread of this thought, however, as a hand clamps down on my shoulder.

"You shouldn't be in here."

Turn To Page 15

We head right and enter a large room with a counter and a cash register, which must be the winding shop's lobby. The register is unoccupied, but my eye is drawn around the room anyway.

Cleo wanders up to a wall full of crystals and glass vials, but my focus is pulled by two bookshelves across the room. One houses a veritable library of volumes on the tarot, while the other is filled with dozens of different variations of tarot card decks.

I step up to the bookshelves and examine the colorful spines and deck sides, searching for anything familiar. I dig out our tarot deck from my bag and glance at it, then back to the shelves a few times, but nothing seems to resemble the unique look.

"Oh my god."

Hearing this new voice, I spin around to find an old man emerging from a doorway on the other side of the room. He doesn't look at me, though.

Instead, he stares at the deck in my hand—Grandma's deck.

"Where in all perils below did you get that?"

Turn To Page 15

CHAPTER TWO

CHASE

MY EYES DON'T know where to settle.

After we split from Amelia and Cleo, Logan and I drifted in separate directions. I was drawn into this dimly lit room, which feels like a pocket where unwanted things collect. The shelves are cluttered with antique and occult things as expected, but somehow everything still seems out of place.

I find myself focusing on one shelf that holds a whole horde of items: a crescent moon tea set, a cloth sack full of jade marbles, a speckled white feather. I run my finger along the objects, leaving a faint trail in their dust. I feel unsettled. It's like, in this room, I can somehow sense the energy each object has trapped inside.

Amelia always insists it's just my imagination, but I've always felt objects are like people. They can carry their history inside, bottled and brewing just underneath the surface. Standing here, I feel like the history of all these objects is somehow fraught. Like they've all been trapped here too long, or that they're . . .

Haunted?

I take a step back, and that's when I hear it: a creaking sound from across the room. I snap my head in that direction, but there's nothing there.

I tell myself to calm down, even though my pulse flutters in my neck. I don't know if it's just being around these storied items, but I can't fight the feeling that someone is watching me.

"Come here."

I feel the whisper against my cheek as one long arm wraps around my chest from behind. A scream starts to form in my throat, but then another hand clamps down over my mouth. Panic bursts open inside my veins, sending charges of adrenaline throughout my body.

"You're way too cute to be wandering this store all alone."

Next, something wet connects with the skin at the base of my neck. Something that feels like lips.

"Logan, I'm going to kill you," I sputter, spinning around to find the grinning face of my boyfriend.

"But if you kill me, then who are you going to make out with in this creepy place?" Logan says, pulling me against him. I'm pretty tall, but Logan is taller. And more muscular. And, honestly, way hotter than me. I still can't understand how I was lucky enough to find him, or lucky enough to have him fall for me.

This thought dissolves, however, once Logan kisses me. There are very few things that can pause the eternal forge of thoughts burning in my brain, but feeling Logan's hands travel up my back is one of them. Even after two years, he leaves me breathless.

I still can't believe that in two weeks moments like these are going to be in short supply. The idea of Logan and me leaving to go to college on opposite coasts still causes a sting so deep, I try to avoid thinking about it altogether.

"Chase!"

I step away from Logan because that was definitely Amelia's voice shouting my name from somewhere deeper in the shop. Suddenly all of Logan's warmth leaves my body. I'm used to Amelia being somewhat dramatic, but I am not used to her sounding distraught.

I spin and begin sprinting toward her voice, barely sideswiping the packed shelves as I go. I rush into some checkout space, filled with tarot decks and astrology charts and quasi-mystic paraphernalia. Finding Amelia there, I stop in my tracks so quickly that Logan nearly crashes into me.

I exhale, seeing that Amelia isn't hurt or in danger. Still, something isn't quite right. She looks stunned and Cleo stands at her side, fists clenched.

"Welcome to Mother Earth Occult and Antiques," the man standing in front of Amelia and Cleo says, turning to face us. "It appears your friends have stumbled into a rather deep well of discovery."

"And you are?" I ask, walking to join them.

"Why, I'm the owner," the man says.

Given the name of this shop, I expected a flowing goddess type, but this man is made of ridges, thin as a twig and dressed in black. I can't quite explain it, but I immediately sense he is a person of absence, not abundance. My guard flies up.

"Chase, he recognized our deck," Amelia says, her eyes wide. "He says he knows where the cards come from."

Disbelief ripples through me. We've never found anything about Gran Flo's deck over the years, not even on our deepest research dives. How could we be lucky enough to find answers on our first stop? I then remind myself that anything trading in truth—spirituality, religion, psychics, the tarot, and all the rest—is always riddled with scam artists.

"'He' goes by Maggie," the man says. "And are you four telling me you really don't know what that deck is?"

"It was my grandma's," Amelia blurts out. "She bought it at a yard sale years ago and we never—"

"We'd love to hear what you know about the deck," I interrupt, stepping beside Amelia. My first rule of tarot engagement? Never give yourself away.

"It really means the world to us. It's why we came here on this trip," Amelia adds. She can't help herself, because her first tarot rule? Open the floodgates.

"Well, I'd certainly like to meet this grandmother of yours, because there's no way she bought that deck at a yard sale. May I see it up close?"

"Amelia's grandma passed away earlier this year," I say, placing my hand over Amelia's. Thankfully it doubles as a gesture of affection, while also keeping her from giving over the deck. "But why do you say that?"

Maggie passes his cloudy blue eyes over me with a mix of annoyance and respect. He then walks behind the register counter, trying to gain some authority.

"That right there is a genuine Carson Perilli tarot," Maggie begins, once settled. "He only made a handful of decks in his lifetime, each one unique. And he only gifted them to people he deemed very special."

"Who was this Perilli person?" I ask, still grasping Amelia's hand. I feel an electric hum begin to charge my veins, sparking something new. I can only imagine how Amelia must feel. Maybe we somehow are that lucky, at least today?

Then I remind myself what Logan would say, that luck is only the surface awareness of a person meeting their purpose. Either way, Maggie now has my undivided attention.

"Carson Perilli was a respected artist and an even more respected spiritual leader, at least in certain Californian circles," Maggie explains. "He never reached mainstream popularity, nor was he interested in doing so. But he did amass a rather . . . occult following."

"And he made this deck?" I ask. "How do you know?"

"Well, I must admit, I'm a bit of a Perillian myself. All of his decks have been accounted for since his passing. All except his final work, that is."

Maggie's eyes flick down to our deck for just a second, but it's enough for me to clock the pang of collector's lust he tries to mask.

"If I'm right, then that deck is missing four cards," Maggie says. "The Prince of Wands. The Princess of Cups. The King of Pentacles. The Queen of Swords."

"That's . . . that's absolutely right."

I don't stop Amelia from answering this time, because even I'm surprised.

"Perilli always withheld the same four cards from every deck he made," Maggie continues. "He hid each one in a treasured place and peppered unique clues to find these hidden cards in his artwork. The only way to uncover the missing cards is to use the signs in the corresponding deck."

A sense of awe ripples over me. That's eccentric, at best, but also maybe . . . deeply cool?

"So, this dude made personalized tarot scavenger hunts?" Cleo jumps in. "Uh, that's a little much."

"Genius always looks like foolishness to the uninitiated," Maggie says, his chin raised. "But you can imagine the kind of enthusiasm this practice garnered among his followers. All of Perilli's decks have long been accounted for and the missing cards have been found. Again, all except one last, lost set."

A pulse of realization snaps across the room. As we begin to understand, the energy suddenly shifts.

"The masterpiece you hold in your hands is quite valuable, to the right eye," Maggie says. "I'd be happy to buy it from you."

"It's not for sale," Amelia says automatically. "To us, it's invaluable."

"Yet you knew nothing of its true value moments ago," Maggie snaps, his cool exterior cracking a moment. He takes a breath to gather himself. "You'll always have your memories, my dear. But that deck belongs in a museum for all to enjoy."

"If all of this is true, then why is there no mention of Perilli or his decks anywhere on the internet?" I ask, hoping to keep Maggie engaged. Something tells me that the further our interests diverge, the less forthcoming he'll be.

"You young ones and your internet," Maggie sighs. "We Perillians pride ourselves on earning our knowledge. Hunting down any easy public mentions is as time-honored a tradition as finding the missing cards."

"Then when you say 'in a museum,' you really mean in the private hands of some cultish following?" Logan says, taking the words right out of my mouth.

"Museums exist in many forms," Maggie answers. "Perilli himself had a favorite saying: *Rules are for peasants, but context is for royals.* I've told you nothing but the truth. I could have tried to swindle you out of the deck, but I didn't because I can tell those cards mean something to you, in a different way than they do to me. That's the beauty of the tarot, isn't it? The way its meanings adapt to the individual. For the honor of preserving that beauty properly, I would pay. I would overpay."

"But without any mentions online, how could we even know what overpaying us means?" Cleo asks, putting on her sweetest voice.

Maggie sighs again, sensing checkmate.

"We'd never sell it, period," Amelia repeats, tears welling in her eyes.

Never is a strong word, I think. After all, as Cleo said, we don't know what kind of money Maggie is talking about here. Besides, if the deck is already valuable in partial form, then it has to be worth much more if completed. And I bet Maggie knows more about finding these missing cards than he is letting on.

◇ "I think it's clear we're not giving up the deck, certainly not before we've had the chance to verify all you've said," I begin, thinking over my next words carefully. "You're our first tarot shop stop of many. So, what **guidance** can you offer that others can't?"
Turn To Page 20

◇ "We understand how special this deck is," I say. "What if we keep in touch and try to work together for the sake of the deck? We could use the **help** of an expert."
Turn To Page 21

Maggie sizes me up with another glance. I bet he thinks I'm too cerebral and impatient for my own good. That's fine, because I'm well acquainted with Maggie's type, as well. One of the first things Gran Flo taught us is that each person has a Major Arcana expression tied to their birthday, like a tarot astrology sign. If I had to guess, Maggie seems like a classic Magician type.

After all, Magicians teach us to be open to the unknown, but also to be wary of deception. They use fiction to lead us to fact, illusion to reflect the real. That makes Magician types full of life and truth, but also captivated by the prettiest lies. I can also spot a Magician type anywhere, because I happen to be very in love with one.

"Sorry, my guy can be a little intense," Logan says, as if on cue. "We'll get out of your hair. Thanks for all your help, Maggie."

Logan grabs my hand and turns to leave, knowing exactly what he's doing.

"Wait," Maggie calls out. He closes his eyes as if fighting off a sudden migraine. When he reopens them, his eyes set on us with intensity.

"Any halfway decent reader knows the tarot only provides answers if you're able to read the cards properly," he says. "So whatever answers you're looking for in that deck, you're going to need these."

Maggie then reaches into a drawer, pulling out a small homemade booklet and a compass.

"You'll need these to read the cards properly," he explains. "One is the final deck guide written by Perilli, the other is a uniquely tuned Perillian compass. If you're really meant to find the missing cards, you'll discover how to use both."

"Wow, fantastic," I say. "How much for them?"

"Free of charge," Maggie answers, holding out the items. "Perilli intended they go to the holder of his decks, so please accept this as a gesture of good faith . . . offered in the hopes it may someday be returned?"

Amelia breaks away from the group and steps forward. She snatches the toolset without hesitation.

"Deal."

Turn To Page 22

I might not always be the most decisive, but I am good at reading people, just like the tarot. And my intuition tells me that Maggie is a classic Major Arcana Magician type.

Magicians believe in things they cannot see, like the faithful, but they're often wary of deception, like skeptics. They tend to be wells of deep complexity behind seemingly simple surfaces. I can also spot a Magician type anywhere, because I happen to be very in love with one.

"Maggie, I have a feeling you can relate to what we're saying," Logan says, as if on cue. "We're all on the same side here, aren't we?"

Maggie closes his eyes, rubbing them with his forefingers. When he reopens them, his eyes set on us with a restored warmth.

"Any halfway decent reader knows the tarot only provides answers if you're able to read the cards properly," Maggie says. "So whatever answers you're looking for, you're going to need these."

Maggie reaches into a drawer and pulls out a small homemade booklet. He also pulls a keychain of large charms: a wand, a sword, a pentacle, and a cup—the four suits of the Minor Arcana.

"You've already been given a great gift, possessing that deck. But you'll need these to use the cards properly," Maggie explains. "One is the final deck guide written by Perilli. The other is a set of specific Perillian charms. If you're really meant to find the missing cards, you'll discover how to use both."

"Wow, fantastic," I say. "How much for them?"

"Free of charge, my friend," Maggie answers, holding out the items. "Like you all said, we're on the same side. We tarot lovers have to be. Besides, Perilli intended for these to go to the holder of his final deck. I only hope that, whatever you decide to do, you share the particulars of your journey with me?"

Amelia steps forward and snatches the toolset without hesitation.

"You have our word."

Turn To Page 22

"I've now given you all I can to get you started," Maggie says. "Perillians believe the cards end up where they're meant to be, in the worthy hands Perilli himself intended. I suppose we'll all know whose hands those are soon enough."

"Right. Okay," Cleo says, clearly feeling ready to get out of here. "Thanks."

"My business card is in the booklet, should you need to reach me," Maggie says. "I do hope to hear from you all again."

"You will," I say as cheerfully as I can manage. Like Cleo, I am ready to go. My brain feels crammed full of new information screaming to be unpacked.

"One last thing you must know," Maggie adds as we make it to the doorway. "I'm a decent man. I wouldn't dream of taking anything from anyone by force. But fair warning, my fledgling Perillians. The world is not made of the decent alone."

Back in Charvan, I try to let its familiar comforts soak into me. I've done a lot to make this van our safe space: repainting it navy blue and white, refurbishing two rows of bucket seats up front, commissioning a built-in bench and table as a reading room in the back. There's a plush rug and several crammed bookshelves under the bench, but both are currently blocked by mounds of luggage. I'd be lying if I said this clutter didn't stress me out a little, but at least the linen curtains remain visible, tied with ropes and lit warmly by the string lights hung inside the roof's rim.

Charvan is indeed the ideal chariot for our trip, but after what we just learned, even its familiar interior feels foreign. I'm not sure where to begin.

"Is everyone thinking what I'm thinking?" Amelia says first. "That we have to find the missing cards? I mean, what if my grandma had this whole secret tarot life?"

"Let's not get carried away," I reply. "Even if Maggie was telling us the truth, Gran Flo could still also be telling the truth about where she bought the deck."

"Maybe, but how likely is that? This has to be a way to get to know her more," Amelia says. "Besides, learning more about the deck was the whole point of this trip."

"I thought the point was us spending time together before college?" Cleo says.

"Of course, and we can still do both," Amelia replies. "But, come on! This turned out to be so much more interesting than we ever could have hoped! A real-life tarot mystery adventure?"

"Amelia, no offense, but this sounds like a wild goose chase more than anything else," Cleo says. "We have no idea what we're really wading into here."

"What could possibly be dangerous about looking for some missing cards?"

"Uh, the people who think it's so special. They sound intense. I mean, didn't that Maggie guy kind of straight-up threaten us before we left?"

"Now who's being dramatic, Cleo?"

"I never said you were being dramatic, Amelia!"

"Well, I'm sure this comes as a surprise to no one," Logan interjects, "but I'm always down for an adventure. Besides, how can we argue with the signs here? I think we're meant to at least try."

I brace myself for Amelia to engage with Logan on his reasoning. These two disagree about some pretty fundamental stuff when it comes to what's *meant to be*. Amelia believes that life is random, but Logan just as firmly believes there are signs pointing us where we need to go.

"Then that makes the vote two to one," Amelia says, turning directly to me—and leaving me dead in the middle, as usual. "Chase?"

When I don't respond immediately, Amelia leans toward me. I've been listening to this exchange, but I've also been thumbing through the booklet Maggie gave us, which has simple quotes corresponding to each card. Naturally, I gravitated first to The Emperor, my own Major Arcana expression. According to this Perilli person, The Emperor represents one key question: *When you lead, do you contribute more than you require?*

It's a compelling interpretation, if not a little simplified. Still, it applies. Being the tiebreaker isn't my favorite, but that's where I so often find myself. I'm further reminded as Amelia drops the actual Emperor card into my lap. His impassive eyes stare up at me, representing a leader who can inspire courage and determination—or just as easily abuse his power to feed his ego.

Feeling fueled by The Emperor, I already know I'm going to vote for us to look for the first missing card. Still, looking between Logan and Amelia, I know it won't be enough to simply agree. They want to know who I agree with most.

◊ "The only way we really **learn** is when we see things for ourselves," I finally say. "I think we owe it to ourselves to embrace this detour, like Amelia said."
Turn To Page 24

◊ "Whatever reason this deck came into our hands, I think it's our **responsibility** to try finding the missing cards," I finally say. "Maybe it's something we're meant to do, like Logan said."
Turn To Page 25

I can hear Amelia's voice in my head, saying that blind chance might have brought us here today, but that human minds are designed to bring order to chaos—the same way tarot cards were designed to do.

"If we have the chance to answer some lifelong questions, we have to choose that path," I finish.

Amelia smiles, hearing my answer. She may have gotten her way, but it's probably more important to her that I agreed with her over Logan. Though it's not like I disagree with either of them outright—it's more that I'm not fully sure what I believe yet. I love facts and proof, but neither really applies to life's unanswerables. And if I'm being really honest, I'm not as convinced that one truth can apply to every situation as Logan and Amelia.

Unfortunately, I'm the only person I know who seems to think that way. This probably makes me seem weak, but is it so wrong that I don't feel compelled to choose a side? I still don't know exactly who or what I want to be when I grow up . . . but the older we get, the more being undecided just feels like being left behind.

Looking to Logan, I find him faking a smile. As much as I want to, I can't please him and Amelia all the time.

"Then it's settled," Amelia says, smiling even wider. "Sincerest apologies to Cleo, but you know what this means."

Turn To Page 26

I guess after all these years, Logan must be rubbing off on me. Luck, coincidence, déjà vu, serendipity—he believes all these things are just signs that you're headed where you need to be. I'm not as convinced that destiny rules over human agency, but right now it's hard to argue. How many stars had to align to bring the four of us here today, on this path?

"We can't ignore the signs," I finish. "I think we could all be here for a reason. If that's true, we need to find out what it could be."

Amelia smiles hearing my answer, but her eyes betray the gesture. She may have gotten her way, but she hates it when I don't side with her reasoning, too. It's not that I disagree—it's more that I'm not fully sure what I believe yet. I love facts and proof, but neither really applies to life's unanswerables.

Though if I'm being really honest, I'm also just not as convinced that one truth can apply to every situation as Logan and Amelia. It's kind of ironic, actually. Logan isn't into organized religion, but he believes in his own version of God, or "the universe" as he calls it. Meanwhile Amelia is Jewish, but she doesn't believe a higher power holds any sway over our individual actions. Even Cleo is self-assured in her near-universal skepticism. But then there's me, the lapsed Catholic, still sorting out what I believe.

I guess this maybe explains why I'm so drawn to tarot cards as their own spiritual system. The tarot asks all these same questions, but it never defaults to one truth for every situation. Instead, the cards constantly shift their meanings depending on the context. Just like me, forever shifting and debating, side-kicking to the bigger beliefs around me.

So even though Amelia doesn't say it out loud, I can still tell she takes this as some kind of invisible sign that I value Logan more than her. Sadly, this is still one gap I have no idea how to bridge. I just wish there wasn't so little time left to do so.

"Logan clearly has you brainwashed," Amelia says, rolling her eyes. "Nevertheless, that's a majority. Sincerest apologies to Cleo, but you know what this means."

Turn To Page 26

Cleo sighs, folding her arms across her chest. Still, I spot a glimmer of curiosity in her eyes. We all feel the pull of this deck, even our most skeptical.

Amelia then rumbles her fingers across the back of her bucket seat, building a drumroll before finishing her announcement.

"Our road trip just turned into an intrepid tarot scavenger hunt! A 'taroad' trip, if you will!"

"Oh no," I say. "We will definitely not be calling it that."

I smile and make sure to look Amelia's way. I take in her familiar sight, her mane of frizzy curls and signature pastel clothes. Really, only Amelia can understand what I'm feeling underneath it all—how special this moment is, despite its baggage. I might still be terrified of what life is going to be like at college without my partners in crime, but that worry washes away as we share this private look.

For now, we have this one last perfect adventure to pull off.

CHAPTER THREE

AMELIA

I **KNOW I'LL PROBABLY** get sick of it soon, but right now diner comfort food still seems like the best thing on the planet. So tonight I am having banana pancakes with a side of hash browns for dinner and I refuse to feel guilty about it.

Once the waitress finishes stacking our menus, I clear the middle of our table to lay out the purple, moon-patterned reading cloth Chase got me a few birthdays ago. Though right now Chase only has eyes for his journal and his owl-tipped pen, taking furious notes on the Perillian booklet. He's been at it since we left Maggie's shop, obsessing over every detail to see if he can decipher any clues that lead to the hidden cards. I've always envied Chase's ability to pour every ounce of himself into an intellectual task, like his brain is a funnel. His dark eyes sharpen as they flicker from line to line and he looks perfectly polished, his brown hair curled left and his button-down pressed straight.

I, on the other hand, probably look like a tornado, wild and wrinkled. Still, I have more important things to focus on. Chase might believe the clues we seek will be embedded in facts and histories, but I think the most important answers are always found by looking within.

"Why are you reading me specifically?" Logan asks. "Shouldn't we just examine the cards for clues?"

"Detective Chase Rubino over there already has that covered," I answer, nodding toward a still-focused Chase. "I think we need to try letting the cards guide us a bit."

"Right, but why focus on me?"

"Because your Major Arcana expression is The Magician, which has the closest connection to the Minor Arcana Wands suit," I answer. "Since we're near Joshua Tree and in the middle of the desert, Wands is probably where we start, because they stand for red and fire and east."

Logan considers this a moment. "And faith meeting action, right?"

"Someone has been spending way too much time around these two," Cleo says, pulling her phone out of the shoebox nestled beside Logan. "I'm using my next five minutes to do another search on Perilli. The sooner we get some answers, the sooner we can give up this tarot ghost."

It's a noble effort on Cleo's part, but not a single one of our searches on the drive here turned up anything useful. It's like Carson Perilli never existed, at least according to the internet. A follow-up call to my parents proved equally unhelpful—Mom had never heard Grandma mention anyone by that name.

I shuffle the cards, anticipation crackling in my limbs. How on earth did Grandma come to possess this deck? I suppose it's possible she really didn't realize its true origins, but if I know Grandma, she probably had some inclination it was special. My heart aches once again, thinking about how much I wish she were here. I try to choose another thought instead, like how lucky I am to have this chance to learn more about her, even after she's gone.

Before I start on Logan, I remind myself of the most important thing Grandma ever taught us about reading the tarot. I can almost hear her voice in my head, speaking these foundational words: *Tarot cards have nothing to do with predicting the future. The tarot's true power resides in using ancient symbols, drawn from every corner of history and mythology, to unlock the secrets we keep from ourselves. You see, a chance drawing of cards is meaningful not in what the symbols predict, but in the personal reflections you find in them.*

As I prepare myself to read, I try to clear my mind of everything else, ready to become reflective. Then, for good measure, I run my fingers over the engraved surface of the Dalet locket in my pocket.

"Okay, Logan, what intention do you want to set for this reading?"

"That's easy, my dear Amelia. How do we follow the clues to find the closest missing card?"

"I couldn't have said it better myself," I answer, handing Logan the shuffled deck to cut. While waiting, I decide what reading configuration to use, since the placements can change the interpretations of each card dramatically. For this reading, I quickly realize I should use Grandma's favorite: The Seeing Square.

Logan hands me back the deck and I lay out the top four cards face down on the cloth. We are faced with the same symbol on the card backs: a unique geometric shape that looks like a Hebrew letter Mem connected to an inverted number four. Seeing it now, the shape is unmistakably an altered letter P—which, I now realize, must stand for Perilli. My heart then skips another beat once the cards are dealt, because one of our homemade replacement cards has appeared in fourth position. A chill runs up my spine, seeing a representation of one of the four missing cards turning up in the final placement.

Shaking this off, I reach out to begin.

"The card in first position represents your current situation, the place you begin to achieve your goal," I explain, flipping over the first card.

My eyes light up as they fall on the Ace of Cups.

"That's an excellent sign," I continue. "The Ace stands for one, the number of new beginnings, but also indivisibility. And Cups are the suit of emotions and flow. Definitely an auspicious place to begin, perhaps a sign this goal is worth obtaining."

I glance over at Chase, but he is still absorbed by the booklet and his journal scribbles. That's fine, since this next phase of my reading is the part he never likes. He thinks any personal touch dilutes the tarot's meaning, but I believe it only enhances it.

"Now, Logan, can you tell me what you're drawn to most in the Ace of Cups?"

Logan considers my question a moment. "Visually speaking? I guess my eye is pulled to the central cup in the card."

That tracks. Others might be drawn to the heart symbols or the flowing ocean background, but Logan has always been one to cut to the heart of the matter. Knowing I now need to read this Cup symbolism to Logan, I stare down at the card and try to tap into my inner Empress.

"The Cup in this card traditionally stands for a central source of life," I begin.

◊ "In this case, I'd say it represents the **fountain of life**. A source of abundance, but something equally elusive and difficult to grasp."
Turn To Page 30

◊ "In this case, I'd say it represents the **holy grail**. A source of strength, but also of mystery and great danger."
Turn To Page 32

"If the fountain of life represents the goal we seek, then achieving it will require intuition and courage," I conclude.

"Says the nurturing Empress mother," Logan replies, smiling.

"That brings us to second position," I carry on. "This card represents potential obstacles that could stand in your way."

I reach forward and flip the second card to reveal the Queen of Pentacles.

"Oh, wow. In the material Pentacles suit, the Queen represents the duality of a mentor. She can spin her wheel of creativity just as easily as she can spin a web of entrapment. She has great gifts of protection and bounty, but she is also prone to corruptible wealth and luxury.

"So, Logan," I finish, "which part of the card speaks to you most?"

"If we're looking for obstacles, I think the message is clear," he begins. "We shouldn't be seduced by material wealth. We'd also better be wary of the answers to our questions, because they might trap us just as easily as they might inspire us."

"Yes," I respond, even though I hope that idea isn't remotely true. I want to say our obstacle will be someone who will take advantage of us to obscure the truth, someone who will do us harm in the name of helping. But this is the danger of reading a person whose intention you're invested in: letting your own feelings inform the reading.

"Very good," I say, keeping my thoughts to myself. "Let's move on to third position, the card that represents qualities needed to overcome this obstacle."

I then flip the third card to reveal the Four of Wands.

"Okay, fascinating," I begin. "The number four calls for balance and the stability of a square. The way the wands are arranged, it shows that faith in one wand can be easily broken, but a bundle of four is unbreakable."

"Then the message here is pretty straightforward again," Logan says. "We're going to need to use teamwork to overcome obstacles and achieve our goals. Four of Wands, four of us. Those signs couldn't be clearer."

Logan looks pleased with himself, but I have to bite my tongue once more. I know he thinks this pull is a fateful sign sent from on high, but I don't think his interpretation is serendipity. Really, it's nothing more than his human mind making connections. Of course, this is what the tarot is for—letting the subject realize things about themself and their situation—which is the only reason I let it be.

I'm so preoccupied with silencing myself as I reach for the final card, I forget it's one of our homemade cards until my fingers actually touch its laminated edges. A spark of anticipation lights up my chest, feeling it there.

"In fourth position, this final card represents achieving your goal. It's both a sign of what you stand to gain and a 'be careful what you wish for' message."

My fingers twitch with excitement as I turn over the final card, finding our homemade representation of the Prince of Wands.

Silence falls over us. Obviously, this is one of the hidden cards we hope to find, showing up in the outcome position. On some level we all knew this was coming, but still, seeing it actually lying there feels charged. Like the card might burst into flames on the table, coursing with magic and meaning.

I'd say something, but my throat has suddenly gone dry.

"Okay, now that is downright freaky," Cleo says, putting down her phone. "Anyone else just get the chills?"

"That's wild," Logan says, leaning in to examine our homemade card. "Hey, why did you and Chase draw the centaur Prince holding a flaming wand in your version?"

I take a sip of water and try to remember our childhood thought patterns, hoping this will also calm my hammering heart.

"The flaming wand represents the Prince of Wands' need for protection on an adventure filled with danger, especially since his courage makes him impulsive."

"Right. If we're pulling a message from that, it might be that if we follow through, we will actually find the card," Logan extrapolates. "But is the Prince of Wands warning us not to lose ourselves in pursuing this task? Or is he telling us to avoid danger and chaos, even if it's tempting?"

"That's all well and good," Chase interrupts, his attention suddenly shifted. "But whatever direction we're looking for probably really has something very specific to do with this."

♦ Earlier, Maggie's **guidance** got us the **compass**, so Chase puts that toolset half on the table.

Turn To Page 34

♦ Earlier, Maggie's **help** got us the **charms**, so Chase puts that toolset half on the table.

Turn To Page 35

"If the holy grail represents the goal we seek, then achieving it will require bravery and sacrifice," I conclude.

"Says the demanding Empress mother," Logan replies, smiling.

"That brings us to second position," I carry on. "This card represents potential obstacles that could stand in your way."

I reach forward and flip the second card to reveal the Eight of Swords.

"That's not great." I pause. "Swords are the suit of rationality, and eight is the number of infinity. However, when representing obstacles, this card can be super ominous. To reach a point of realization, you must endure a terrible ordeal, one riddled with self-doubt and rife with misinformation. The temptation will be to turn back, but the only way out will be through."

"Well, I think that message is pretty clear," Logan sighs, evidently feeling the weight of this card.

"Yeah, let's move on to third position," I say, also feeling it. "This card represents the qualities you'll need to overcome the obstacle."

I then flip the third card to reveal the Four of Wands.

"Okay, much better," I begin. "The number four calls for balance and the stability of a square. The Four of Wands represents versatility, how faith in a single wand alone can alter reality, but combining the possibilities of four diverse wands is limitless."

"Definitely better," Logan says. "It probably means we're going to need to use teamwork to overcome obstacles of doubt and deception. Four of Wands, four of us. Those signs couldn't be clearer."

"Well, the connections you just made yourself couldn't be clearer, at least," I reply as gently as I can manage. Part of me knows I shouldn't say anything to interfere with Logan's conclusions—letting the subject realize things about their situation is the whole point of my tarot readings. Then again, not speaking my mind isn't exactly what I'm most known for.

I return Logan's weak smile with one of my own, reaching forward to flip over the final card. I'm so distracted, I actually forget it's one of our homemade cards until my fingers touch its laminated edges.

"In fourth position, this final card represents achieving your goal. It's both a sign of what you stand to gain and a 'be careful what you wish for' message."

My fingers twitch with excitement as I turn over the final card, finding our homemade representation of the Prince of Wands.

Silence falls over us. Obviously, this is one of the hidden cards we hope to find, showing up in the outcome position. On some level we all knew a missing card was coming, but still, seeing the Prince of Wands specifically lying there feels charged. Like the card might burst into flames on the table, coursing with magic and meaning.

"Okay, now that is downright freaky," Cleo says, putting down her phone. "Anyone else just get the chills?"

"That's wild," Logan says, leaning in to examine our card. "Wait, why did you and Chase draw the Prince as a centaur wandering the desert with a flaming wand?"

"Most cards we researched showed the Prince of Wands being pulled in a chariot by horses or lions, so we made him pulling his own chariot as a centaur."

Logan gives me a look, but I just shrug.

"What? We were kids."

"Hey, centaurs are still completely awesome," Cleo adds.

"Agreed," I continue. "As for wandering the desert, the Prince of Wands is a courageous and gifted hero, but he risks losing his way if he becomes too headstrong."

"Right. Well, if we're pulling a message, it might be that we will actually find the card," Logan extrapolates. "But is the Prince warning us to beware of someone betraying us? Or is he telling us to be wary of focusing only on our own needs in our search?"

"That's all well and good," Chase interrupts, his attention suddenly shifted. "But whatever direction we're looking for probably really has something very specific to do with this."

♦ Earlier, Maggie's **guidance** got us the **compass**, so Chase puts that toolset on the table.
Turn To Page 34

♦ Earlier, Maggie's **help** got us the **charms**, so Chase puts that toolset on the table.
Turn To Page 35

"Here's the Perillian booklet quote on the Prince of Wands," Chase continues. "*Can looking behind bring you forward, can looking within broaden your horizons without?* I figure that has to have something to do with the compass, but—"

"Oh my goddess."

The words tumble out of my mouth. Logan and Chase's questions spark an idea in my brain so brightly, I reach across the table and snatch up the compass.

"Hey, what are you . . . ?"

Ignoring Chase, I examine the compass. It's a little bigger than my hand and made of intricately carved bronze pieces. Its face appears simple enough, but the front isn't what I'm interested in. Right now, I only care about *looking behind.*

On the back of the compass, I see a little barcode sticker in the lower left corner. I use the tip of my nail to scrape it off, and once I do, I gasp at what I see underneath: a small button set into the back of the compass, too small to press with my finger. Looking around the table, I grab Chase's pen.

I then insert the pen's tip into the button slot. First, a small compartment opens in its back, revealing a miniature flashlight, the tiny kind you'd keep on a keychain. Then something clicks into place on the surface of the compass. Flipping it over, I gasp again at what I see.

Something on the face has shifted, revealing new letters in previously covered grooves. Where the letters N E S W once stood for compass directions, new letters now replace them: P W S C. It takes me a few seconds, but I then realize these letters must stand for the Minor Arcana suits: Pentacles, Wands, Swords, and Cups. Then, even more astonishingly, I see that beside each letter, there are corresponding symbols. I instantly recognize these symbols, because each Major Arcana card in our deck is painted with a unique one. Looking first at Wands, I recognize the symbol for The Magician: a tree branch wand.

While the others take turns looking at the compass, I rifle through the tarot deck until I find The Magician. Looking over the card, I spot the familiar symbol.

"Amelia, the flashlight?" Cleo suggests.

Nodding at her, I grab the mini-flashlight that was hidden inside the compass. Squeezing it to shine on The Magician symbol, I gasp all over again.

Turn To Page 36

"Here's the Perillian booklet quote on the Prince of Wands," Chase continues. "*Can looking behind bring you forward, can looking within broaden your horizons without?* I figure that has to have something to do with the charms, but—"

"Oh my goddess."

The words tumble out of my mouth. Logan and Chase's questions spark an idea in my brain so brightly, I reach across the table and snatch up the keychain to examine it. Each charm is a large three-dimensional shape, and the wand stretches across the palm of my hand. It appears simple enough, a wand made of red metal, but its surface isn't actually what I'm interested in. Right now, all I care about is *looking within.*

Turning the wand over, I notice a seam splitting it up the middle. I use my fingernail to pry between the seams and, sure enough, the wand pops open easily. Looking inside, I gasp at what I see: a long, thin key hidden within.

"Oh wow, what do you think that's for?" Cleo asks, leaning forward.

Looking next at the Sword charm, I see it has the same splitting seam. One quick pry later, I unearth a second key.

"Amelia, the other charms," Chase begins, but I already hold the Cups charm in my hand. Looking it over, I am somewhat stunned to find a little keyhole. Within seconds, the Wand key opens the Cups charm, splitting it in half. Next, the Sword key opens the Pentacle charm in the same way.

Inside the Cups charm we find a miniature flashlight, the tiny kind you'd keep on a keychain. Then, inside the Pentacle charm, we find a folded piece of paper listing the four Minor Arcana suits, with corresponding symbols. I instantly recognize these symbols, because each Major Arcana card in our deck is painted with a unique one. Looking first at Wands, I recognize the symbol for The Magician: a tree branch wand.

Feeling set on fire, I rifle through the tarot deck as quickly as I can until I find The Magician. Looking over the card, I spot the familiar symbol.

"Amelia, the flashlight?" Cleo suggests.

Nodding at her, I grab the mini-flashlight that was hidden inside the Cups charm. Squeezing it to shine on The Magician symbol, I gasp all over again.

Turn To Page 36

I quickly learn this is no ordinary flashlight—it's a black light. Shining it on The Magician symbol on the card, it suddenly reveals writing that must have been printed in invisible UV ink. Then, looking closer, I see this writing is actually two sets of numbers. No, not numbers . . .

GPS coordinates.

Once I fill the others in on this finding, it only takes Cleo a few seconds to search the coordinates on her phone. Sure enough, she pulls up a general location: the Joshua Tree Inn, which happens to be only a few miles from this diner.

I could scream, I'm so excited. I wonder if Maggie knew about this hidden function when he gave us this toolset, but I suppose it doesn't really matter—the clues hidden inside would be useless without our Magician card. I then realize we can repeat this process to find the locations of the other three missing cards, using the toolset and the card symbols that they designate in our deck.

I raise my eyes to look at Chase grinning. I might have been the one to make this discovery, but his research led us down this path. Complementary halves.

"Okay, now I am legitimately freaked out," Cleo says.

"There's no reason to be freaked," Logan responds. "We're obviously meant to find this card. The universe's signs are just particularly clear in this case."

"Well, I don't think we're meant to do anything," I finally say. I'm no longer reading Logan's cards, so enough is enough. "I think us seeing signs everywhere really just shows how much we all want to search for the cards."

"Amelia, come on," Logan deadpans, as if already expecting this reaction. "The Empress pull leading us to Maggie's shop. The Four of Wands in the qualities required position. The Prince of Wands, the closest missing card, in the achievement position. Us already heading east to Joshua Tree. How can that not all be somehow connected, somehow meant to be?"

Listening to Logan, passion explodes in me, shooting sparks across my mind.

"Easy," I answer. "We would have learned about our deck at some point, given all the tarot shops we were planning to visit. The number four and the Prince of Wands hold significance to us we always would have emphasized, in any position. We got other suits and numbers, too, but you don't see those as 'signs.' Because this is all just human synapse, us making meaning of coincidence as we decide where we really want to go."

"You think this is all meaningless?" Logan pushes back. "That there's no higher power at work? I'd think you of all people would understand the significance behind the tarot's spiritual roots."

You of all people. For some reason, it's like invisible kerosene soaking my skin suddenly ignites. I become a woman inflamed, my words ready to burn.

"What I understand is that the human mind is powerful and that the tarot draws from its roots in psychology. So, yes, this is all deeply meaningful. But not because we're trudging along some predestined plot penned by an omnipotent man in the sky."

"That's so reductive," Logan counters sharply, "and not at all what—"

"Could it be both are true?" Chase interrupts. "That we choose our way walking down many planned paths? That it's up to us to learn the right lessons?"

Chase is smart to try to defuse this conversation, even if I'd rather just have my best friend side with me. With literally just one moment to cool down, I realize Logan and I have been talking *at* each other instead of *to* each other. Still, the coded "Does God really exist?" debate has been bubbling below the surface between us for too long. We usually have the space to let it breathe, but today's road tripping has pushed us together a little too tightly.

"Well, we can at least agree on one thing: we need to go stay at the Joshua Tree Inn tonight," I say, standing. "Now if you'll excuse me, Mother Nature now truly calls."

Washing my hands in the sink, I try not to stare too hard at my reflection in this fluorescent-lit mirror. My earlier suspicions were correct—I look like a hot mess of a wreck.

Once my hands are dry, out of habit I pull back my wild tangle of curly hair to see if the stress spots are finally growing back. I inadvertently pulled out entire strands when my panic disorder got particularly bad last year, but now most of the visible patches have grown over. Once finished, I then press a pastel-nailed finger on the underside of my jaw, flattening out the layer of fat there. I've always had a double chin and I've always wanted to know what my face would look like without one.

"I don't know why you do that," Cleo says, suddenly beside me.

I nearly jump because I didn't hear Cleo come in. She really can be as silent as a ghost when she wants to be.

"You're an ancient Roman statue of freaking beauty."

"Old habits die hard," I sigh, very much wanting to get the focus off me. "Hey, you sure you're cool being in here?"

Cleo takes her turn to sigh back at me.

"Before this road trip, I made peace with the fact we'd probably encounter very few gender-neutral bathrooms. I figured, while I'm sorting stuff out and sticking with female pronouns, I might as well use the women's stalls, too. Besides, no part of my potentially nonbinary self is ready to learn what men's restrooms smell like."

I smile at Cleo. She may be uncomfortable in this predefined space, but no amount of bad lighting could make her cheekbones any less high, her skin any less flawless, or her short black hair any less glossy. How could she ever feel uncomfortable looking like that? Then I remind myself, we all have our own stuff, and my surface struggles have nothing to do with Cleo's internal ones.

"Hey, I'll still guard the bathroom door for you whenever you want, just like when we were kids," I say.

Cleo laughs.

"Yes, we Yamashiro-Gustins were born with a deep fear of pooping. My sister still can only go in our own bathroom with the white noise machine cranked up to ten. I may take you up on that generous offer in the future, but I actually braved the bathroom to make sure you're okay. Things got weirdly heated back there."

"Yeah. Blame it on the mysterious excitement. And lack of sleep."

"And the amount of sugar consumed. Do not forget the sugar consumed."

"Quite right, quite right," I say. "But sugar rushes aside, I'm jealous you can stay tuned out of this tarot stuff. It just means so much to me. Maybe too much?"

"There's no such thing as caring too much," Cleo replies. "And it's not that I'm tuned out. It's just, most spiritual systems don't make space for people like me, so I don't make space for them. But still, spirituality is really just trying to make sense of the questions we can't answer yet. So I figure, for all we know, that means no one could be right, or everyone could be right? If you look at it that way, deciding what to believe only really matters because it drives our actions. So, then, what Logan believes really only matters for him, right? It doesn't have to affect what you believe, or how it makes you act."

Cleo shrugs her shoulders and stares back at me like she was just telling me about her day, not delivering a whopping dollop of wisdom. I could physically crush her with the hug I want to give her.

"You know, for a maybe-atheist, you can be pretty freaking profound."

"Still waters run deep," Cleo says, smiling. "But you shouldn't be surprised. What Major Arcana weirdo are you always saying I am?"

"The High Priestess, a keeper of hidden knowledge."

"Yeah, that. Minus the 'ess' part, maybe?" Cleo grins.

Then she gives me that look, the one that reminds me she might be the only person to really see me. The realest me, underneath all the emotion and the mess, the one not even Chase really sees.

And for one perfect moment, I feel completely at ease.

I'm about to give Cleo that limb-busting hug when my phone buzzes in my pocket. I almost forgot I snuck it out of the shoebox when we sat down. When I pull my phone out, my eyes light up along with the screen.

"Ah. That's your Anwar face," Cleo says, frowning a little. "I'll leave you to it."

=====

◇ Anwar can wait. I give Cleo that **hug** before she can escape.

Turn To Page 40

◇ I smile at Cleo before crafting a **response** to Anwar's latest DM.

Turn To Page 4I

"Hey, what's this for?" Cleo asks, her words constricted by my mega-squeezing arms.

"For just being you."

"Aw," Cleo answers, hugging back.

Sometimes Chase and I spend so much time together, it's easy to overlook how special Cleo is—and how much her friendship means to me. Or maybe it's because Cleo and I are both going to colleges in New York. I know I'm going to see her more often, even if I'll be downtown at NYU and she'll be all the way uptown at Columbia. Either way, it's no excuse to take Cleo for granted.

She must feel the love right now, though, because she nestles her face into my wild curls, squeezing me back.

"Hey, while I've got you alone, I have a new doodle for you," Cleo says, reaching into her pocket.

She hands me a ripped-out piece of sketchbook paper. Looking down, I see it's a flare pen doodle of Cleo and me inside Maggie's shop. She has us drawn in simple black and white, but we then both wear jester hats striped with every color possible.

Cleo has drawn us to look like The Fool.

I couldn't love it more.

"This is some of your finest work yet," I say, hugging her again. "I'm obsessed."

"What can I say?" Cleo replies. "We look good in silly hats."

"That we do," I laugh. "So good, I'm going to need to make a little album of all your doodles from this trip. Who needs phone cameras or photo albums when you have a resident Cleo?"

"You know, Amelia," Cleo says as she hooks my arm to exit the bathroom together. "I ask myself that same question nearly every day."

Turn To Page 42

"Thanks for checking on me, Cleo," I say with a smile.

"Anytime," she says, turning to leave.

The moment she does, I turn my eyes down to devour Anwar's DMs.

**So how far did you intrepid road-trippers end up
making it?
Me, I haven't left my couch. Watching a Brit Marling
triple feature of Another Earth, Sound of My Voice,
and The East.**

I have seen exactly zero of those movies, but judging by Anwar's taste so far, I imagine I'd love all three. I start tapping a response as quickly as my fingers will fly:

> **Must hear about those movies at some point, but I
> have a pressing update first.
> You are NOT GOING TO BELIEVE what happened
> on our first tarot shop stop.**

The three dots appear next to Anwar's name until his responses appear.

**You were chased by a serial killer.
You were cursed by an ancient psychic.
You learned your future self was going to hang with
a very cool guy soon.
You joined an underground tarot coven.
Am I getting warm on any of these?**

Smiling down at my phone, I cannot wait to tell Anwar how warm he's getting.

Turn To Page 42

CHAPTER FOUR

CHASE

AFTER FINISHING AT the diner, we drove over to the Joshua Tree Inn and decided to stay the night there. We realized we were going to need the time, since we still have no idea where to find the Prince of Wands on the grounds. We tried to eyeball the place as we checked into our rooms, but nothing in particular stood out amidst the kitschy decor. The inn is a one-story motel with a sidelong stretch of rooms colored mauve and terra-cotta against the desert sand and sky. Perilli's Prince of Wands could really be hidden anywhere—in one of the maroon and stone rooms? Buried in the sand on the grounds? Placed near the cactus-lined pool?

Before we left the diner, we used the Perillian toolset to find the coordinates for the three other missing cards as well. These coordinates now point us to general locations all up the California coast. Unfortunately, I've had no luck finding any clues in the toolset or the deck about where each missing card is hidden at these locations. I should be rereading the booklet right now to see if I can find any hints I missed, but there's one thing that can break my focus. Right now, he happens to be sitting cross-legged on the bed with his eyes closed and his shirt off.

No matter how hard I try, my gaze will not budge from the sight of Logan's stomach muscles crunched together or the curve of his biceps against his chest. The light shines across his brown skin with a warm glow, and his lips part just enough for him to breathe—just enough to drive me crazy. I pour my eyes over Logan St. Genstead and I want to tackle him where he sits. I want to rip off his gym shorts and press my skin against his until we both sweat through the sheets. Instead, I push my glasses farther up the bridge of my nose and try to take a deep breath.

"You're staring again," Logan says, peeking at me through one open eye.

"Was I?" My ears flash with heat.

"You know, it's hard to meditate with an audience."

"Then in the future you should be sure to meditate with a shirt on."

Logan laughs, his white smile gleaming as brightly as his brown eyes. A small rocket ship blasts off somewhere deep inside of me, flooding my brain with thrust and smoke. I try breathing again.

"Well, I cleared my head enough to come up with some ideas on how to start searching for the Prince of Wands," Logan says, standing from the bed to stretch.

He tosses down his fidget spinner, the one he carries with him everywhere as a reminder of his meditative practice. Logan's parents passed down their tradition of Transcendental Meditation, which includes a secret mantra. Logan modified the practice by adding the fidget spinner, which physically represents his mantra. The spinner is actually quite pretty, a stainless silver triangle spinner inside a perfect golden circular base.

"Amelia's going to love that," I sigh.

"Yeah. We both got a little carried away back at the diner, didn't we? She can just get so intense."

"That's Major Amelia for you."

"Well, Magician Logan can stick to his guns, too. Especially since we're starting this search in Wand territory."

"Right. And actually, if we follow from there, next comes the Minor Arcana Cups suit, which is most related to The High Priestess, Cleo's tarot expression," I say, my brain ticking like clockwork. "Then there's The Empress, Amelia's expression, whose Mother Nature vibe relates to Pentacles. Then finally The Emperor, my expression, whose symbol is the Sword. I guess I never really considered how neatly all of that lines up in a row for us."

"I suppose Amelia would want us to believe that's also completely meaningless?" Logan sighs. "She'd argue the four of us are just drawn together because of our complementary personality types. And that making this connection is our minds telling a good story, spinning fiction from fact. But I don't know. That seems so clinical. And unlikely. What do you think?"

"I think, if you can inspire all this insight after just ten minutes of meditation, I really should have let you be."

"Well, I keep telling you how much you'd benefit from it," Logan smiles, walking over to my chair. "You don't even have to do TM."

I smile at Logan in the absent way I always do when he tries to get me to meditate. The part I've never told him—or anyone, for that matter—is that I've developed my own practice. The first half of my journal is filled with the most meaningful quotes and wisdom I've come across. I copy this section and add to it in every iteration of my journal, like my own custom Bible. Most mornings, before I get out of bed, I make sure to read a portion to center myself.

"Well, I can think of a few mind-clearing ways to spend those last ten minutes," I say, hooking my arm around Logan's waist.

I know I should focus on finding clues for the missing Prince. I know I shouldn't be purposefully dodging Logan's spiritual-prodding question. However, I also know my time to spend uninterrupted with him is running out. So instead, I pull him close.

◊ I just **hold** Logan for now. Being intimate doesn't always have to mean sex.
Turn To Page 45

◊ I **kiss** Logan. We're definitely putting those ten minutes to good use.
Turn To Page 46

There would be nothing wrong about getting physical with my loving, committed boyfriend—I've untangled enough of my Catholic guilt to know that much. It's just, every so often, I like reminding my body that my mind is the one really in charge. Besides, sometimes I feel closest to Logan when we're doing nothing at all.

And sometimes delaying the things we want makes them so much better. Logan and I do have this room to ourselves all night, after all. Why spend ten minutes now on something that could take much longer later?

I stand and wrap my arms around Logan, my hands gripping the warm skin of his back. It still causes me physical pain, the thought of living across the country to go to Penn while Logan stays here to go to UCLA. At least I'll be able to persuade my parents to cover some extra flights home during breaks so we can see each other, but every part of me is terrified of this looming separation.

I'm reminded of this as Logan nestles his face into my neck and takes a deep breath. He has never said it out loud, but I can tell he loves the way I smell. Sometimes it's like he can't get enough.

I know the feeling.

"Love you," I whisper in his ear.

"Love you, too," he says back.

For now, I try to let go of my future fear long enough to enjoy this present moment. For now, it's so much more than enough.

Turn To Page 47

I take a second to reflect that I'm in an empty room with my committed boyfriend of two years. How lucky am I to be here? There's a reality where this privilege would never have existed for us. Hell, that reality still exists in many places. There's also a reality where my inherited Catholic guilt would make me feel ashamed of my body and my sexuality, but that's one benefit of being queer—if you let yourself, you learn to throw away some of the old expectations earlier than most.

The way I see it, Logan and I are respectful and responsible. We are beyond lucky to have each other. Really, it'd be a sin *not* to be with each other, instead of the other way around.

Especially since it still causes me physical pain, the thought of moving three thousand miles away to go to Penn while Logan stays here to go to UCLA. At least I'll be able to persuade my parents to cover some of the extra flights home during breaks so we can see each other, but every part of me is terrified of this looming separation.

I banish this thought as we make our way to the bed, leaving a trail of discarded clothes in our wake. I fall on top of Logan and feel myself tumble into wonderland, where suddenly everything else melts away. All I want to do is make him feel as good as I do. Luckily, I know all the right moves.

My hand travels up his abs and over his chest to grip his cheek while we kiss. Then I reach into the tight curls of his hair and pull slightly, breathing into the stretched curve of his neck. Logan moans and I fall deeper down in the swirling wonder, my every thought evaporating like raindrops on a summer sidewalk.

Steam fills my body as lips keep moving over skin, until time stands still and races by at the same moment. Some corner of my mind knows the real world will come rushing back soon, but until then, Logan and I sink deeper into this warmth, this fire burning out of control.

Turn To Page 47

Too little time passes before a knock comes at the door. Mildly annoyed that Amelia can't leave us alone for a while, I take a few seconds to pull myself together before I open the door. I'm very glad I took this beat once I do, because it is not Amelia who stands there.

Instead, it's a guy I do not recognize. He appears to be our age, or maybe a few years older. He wears only shades of maroon and dark green, the palette of the desert itself, but it's his utility belt that really draws my attention. It's where a phoenix-shaped lighter and a wooden baseball bat both hang.

Fear churns in my stomach. As a kid, I didn't have nightmares about monsters in the closet and boogeymen under the bed. Instead, from the moment I understood I wasn't like other boys, I had nightmares about a life trapped in the closet and "faithful" men coming to take away the things that matter most. Men who look quite a bit like this.

One second later I feel Logan at my side and remember to exhale.

"Sorry to interrupt," the guy begins, "but you all have something I've been searching for for a very long time."

Before I can utter a word in response, the door to the adjacent room opens and Amelia and Cleo poke their heads out. Their eyes widen when they see the guy before me. Upon second inspection, he looks not unlike a wand come to life, between his reedy clothes and lean limbs.

"Who are you?" I ask. "What do you want?"

"My name is Cain. I might be the first one here, but other Wanderers could start arriving soon. There's no telling how many others Maggie called. He is offering a pretty penny for your Perillian deck, along with the missing Prince of Wands and the toolset he loaned you."

I glance over at Cleo and can tell she's fighting the urge to break out an "I told you so" look. So Maggie sold us out after all. Suddenly, the pieces come together. He needed the coordinates written in our deck to find the missing cards. Since we weren't handing that over, he must have given us the toolset to find the coordinates on our own, then he sent his people to follow us. And we played right into his hands.

A hot feeling radiates up my spine. How long has this so-called Wanderer been following us? How many more like him are coming? My instinct tells me to slam the door shut, but then we'd just be trapped in this room and separated from Amelia and Cleo, who have the deck. I need to keep this guy talking to learn as much as possible, as much as I hate the idea.

"I'm sorry, but Maggie never meant for you to leave the desert with everything he gave you," Cain continues. "But you're lucky I got here first. Ancient Maggie and his one-track mind, thinking all of us would only want the money."

"If you don't want the money, then what do you want?" Amelia asks.

"Some of us place a higher power in these cards than just money," Cain answers. "I learned about Perilli's decks from my dad. He taught me how to be a Wanderer. All he ever wanted was to find one of Perilli's missing cards before he died. He . . . didn't get to do that."

Grief then plays across Cain's face, raw and unmistakable.

"When I got the call today from Maggie, only days after my dad . . . Well, it felt like a sign. Especially when I heard you all were so close to my age. And that you inherited the deck from someone you loved, too."

Cain's eyes turn to connect with Amelia, next. He can probably see it in her just as strongly, the desire to honor a legacy left behind.

"I came here to help you find the Prince of Wands, as a tribute to my dad."

As moving as these sentiments might be, I try to remain skeptical. "How do we know you won't just take the card from us once we find it?"

Cain turns back to me, looking like I've asked an offensive question. In response, I glance down at the lighter and bat on his belt. Cain understands.

"Perilli believed in finding physical expressions of our deepest beliefs. These were my dad's," he explains. "Baseball and phoenixes were his favorite things. I've carried these both with me everywhere since he gave them to me."

"Is the phoenix part of this whole Perillian Wanderer thing?" Logan asks.

"Phoenixes fit, but being a Wanderer is about more than that," Cain answers. "Perilli taught that the reverent throughout history have wandered the desert seeking—"

Cain then stops himself, looking around as if he has somehow said too much. I suddenly picture the phoenix painted on the Death card in our deck, its fiery wings unfurling as it rises from a mound of ashes. The card scared me when I was younger, but eventually I began to find comfort in the Death phoenix. It symbolized that death could always be about rebirth, in a way.

It wasn't until recently I learned that phoenixes always burn themselves out, agents of their own demise.

"I'm sorry. Perilli believed knowledge worth having should be earned," Cain says. "I can tell you more if you find the Prince."

Staring back at Cain, I think: *Of course, we have to pass some kind of test to be let inside the circle.* It's unclear whether this all smacks more of the occult or an actual cult, but I do know this: the most dangerous people on the planet can be the reverent, if properly armed and improperly motivated.

Just then I hear the sound of a car pulling into the inn entrance up front. No, more like two cars, both probably bringing more Wanderers. I suddenly realize we may have no choice but to accept Cain's help, now. Depending on who these others are, we might not just be at risk of losing the missing Prince. We might be at risk of losing the entire deck.

"I have a hunch where the Prince of Wands is hidden," Cain then says. "But all Wanderers do. If we go now, we might be able to beat them to the right room."

"The only thing we should be doing is getting in Charvan and leaving," Cleo says. "I mean, we didn't even unpack. We can grab our bags and go right now."

I turn to Amelia. She looks just as conflicted as I feel, but then a look of determination settles onto her face.

"I have to try to find the first card while we still have this small head start," Amelia says. "But Cleo, you're right. While I look, someone should pack up Charvan so we're ready to leave the second we can."

"I'll stay with Cleo," Logan says. "Chase, you go with Amelia."

We all look at one another, not sure this is the best version of the plan. But we also know we just have to go with our gut instincts here.

"Splitting the party is never the best idea," Cleo says, "but I'll make sure we get the bags to Charvan without being seen."

"Great. Let's go," Cain says, already moving.

Amelia spins and grabs something from inside the door—Cleo's art backpack. We all agreed to keep the deck in there, since it has a secret compartment in the interior lining. Amelia and I then step to follow Cain, turning to give Cleo and Logan pleading nods to be careful. They return the gesture before we're off.

Cain strides deeper down the stretch of rooms ahead of us, thankfully in the opposite direction of the front parking lot. I look over my shoulder as we follow, not seeing anyone coming for us. Yet.

"Perilli was a big Gram Parsons fan, and Gram actually died here in room eight," Cain whispers as we walk. "They keep it open for tourists to visit. Honestly, I've gone there before and searched the room for the Prince, but I never found anything. It's pretty hopeless trying to find the final missing cards without the clues in your deck."

"How do you know so much about Perilli?" I ask. "How does anyone?"

"He had some collections of his teachings, but they're mostly owned by Perilli's biggest benefactors," Cain answers, revved like an engine. "They own a place called Azure Tarot in Summerland. I bet that's your next stop, when it comes to the other missing cards."

As Cain promised, the door to room eight opens and we step right inside. Once we do, Cain locks the door behind us—hopefully to keep others out and not to keep us in.

"Okay, great," Amelia says, "but right now we need to focus on the Prince."

"Yes," Cain says. "There has to be a clue on the card that led you here."

As Amelia pulls the deck out of Cleo's bag, I do a quick survey of room eight. It looks just like the others, with its classic terra-cotta tones and wood-beamed ceiling, except there are little colorful guitar tributes nestled everywhere. The paintings hung in this room are also slightly different, more vibrant and abstractly symbolic.

"Oh my goddess," Amelia suddenly exclaims, holding up The Magician as she pulls it from the deck. "That wand symbol in the bottom corner of that painting, it's exactly the same one Perilli drew on The Magician, where he wrote the coordinates."

We huddle to examine Amelia's discovery and quickly realize she is correct. We then walk into the bathroom, where there's a painting that takes up nearly the entire back wall. It's made of abstract shapes and colors, so The Magician wand symbol fits right in. It would be nearly impossible to distinguish without Perilli's card.

"I've checked behind all the paintings in this room, they're bolted to the walls," Cain says, excitement vibrating in his hushed voice. "But that Magician symbol— Perilli taught that Wands are about magic, which is really about faith. He believed all of it just represented hidden truth. And Perilli said that nothing obscures truth like perspective, because perspective shapes our reality."

"*Can looking behind bring you forward, can looking within broaden your horizons without?*" Amelia whispers the Perillian quote, almost in a trance. "If we shift our perspective . . ."

Then, as if by instinct, Amelia reaches forward and touches the surface of the painting. I gasp as she does, but not because touching a painting is a forbidden act by most standards. I gasp because, as Amelia's fingers press against the Magician's symbol, the painting indents, clicking like a button. It reminds me of the way Amelia opened the toolset, which must be how she thought to press it in the first place.

The wall around the painting then comes forward, opening a hidden door . . . which reveals another small room, hidden behind the bathroom.

Our attention is pulled from this incredible discovery, however, as the doorknob to room eight suddenly begins to rattle, followed by a very loud banging on the door.

"Let us in!" a man's voice shouts, full of force. "You can't keep us out for long!"

Obviously, Cain was right about not being the only Wanderer with a hunch about this room. My bones buzz with dread. Suddenly I feel like I'm in one of Amelia's horror movies, lost in an abandoned place while some furious assailant chases after us.

Turning back to the secret room, I see it's more like a large closet. I also realize it has a second back door, one that appears to lead to the rear of the inn.

"Chase, that exit," Amelia says, on the same page. "We can use it to sneak out."

"If we go inside and close the painting-door behind us, it'll buy us some time," Cain adds. "No one has ever found that hidden button before, so we should be safe hiding in there."

I breathe a sigh of relief, because this is a huge break. The feeling quickly fades, however, as we enter the secret room. Suddenly the idea of trapping ourselves in a cramped, dark room with a total stranger doesn't feel quite as comforting.

But the moment to change our minds vanishes as Cain closes the door behind us with a quiet click. The tiny room goes dark, so Cain sparks his lighter to life. Looking around, I find the walls are painted a deep maroon color and trimmed with sand-colored molding. Abstract brown lines cover the walls, a mural pattern of wands that wraps around everything. I wonder if every room in the inn has a back exit foyer like this, or if Perilli somehow had this one custom-built behind the painting trapdoor.

The only other thing in this room rests on the floor: a clear container. Crouching down, we see there are phrases painted across it, in a neat and lean font:

Perspective is all that matters.
If you learn to master your perspective, you unlock personal power.
To give birth to the new self, you must set your former self ablaze.
And shed a light that leads the way for others.

Could this message have been left behind by Perilli himself? This thought burns away, however, when we all see what this clear container holds. Inside lies a face-down card, printed with the same back design as our own deck.

I look up and see Cain first, hovering over the container with tears in his eyes, reflecting the little flame flickering.

"I can't believe I really found one," he whispers in awe.

Amelia appears equally awed beside him. Not wasting another moment, she then reaches to open the container. As she unearths Perilli's first lost card, an involuntary chill shivers through me. We may not know everything about the true origins of the deck yet, but we've always appreciated its power and beauty. Amelia must be feeling this also, because tears shimmer in her own eyes as she takes in the long-lost Prince of Wands.

She then hands the card to me, knowing I'll want a closer look, too. From what I can see in the flickering lighter light, the Prince is painted in the same style as our deck. It depicts a young man dressed in red and holding an elaborate golden wand. He is led by a large black bird, its wingspan spread fully over a fiery desert.

Holding the card, it does really feel like we've found a piece we've been missing our entire lives. The sensation of discovering something so coveted, so special—it's intoxicating.

Suddenly I begin to understand these Perillians a bit better.

We all then freeze as we hear a muffled voice through the hidden door we came through. The Wanderers obviously found a way into room eight . . .

But after several seconds of holding our breath, the indistinct voices dissipate. Whoever is searching the room, they don't know how to access this secret room—and it turns out neither side can really hear much through the wall, mercifully. Still, that doesn't mean we should linger much longer.

Though I'm distracted once again as Cain bursts into quiet sobs.

"I'm sorry," he whispers, trying to compose himself. "I just can't believe my dad isn't here to see this."

"I understand," Amelia whispers back, patting his shoulder. "These cards mean a lot to us, too. But we should really get going before—"

"I can stay behind and cover long enough for you to drive away," Cain says, tear stains now creasing his cheeks. "But I need to ask something of you, first."

Amelia and I both tense. Cain has helped us, but the idea he was doing it for nothing never quite sat right with me. I brace myself to finally hear his price.

"My dad always said he'd never rest until he found a card like this," Cain begins. "I can still feel him all around, like he really is restless. There's this Perillian belief, that only a reading with cards of your Corner can grant completion. I tried with a replica deck, but it didn't . . ."

Cain pauses, sniffling and taking a breath. He then focuses his full gaze on Amelia.

"I don't want your deck, that belongs with you. But is there any way you'd let me bring the Prince of Wands to my dad's grave? That way I can do the reading and close his chapter."

My brain spins. I can only imagine how Amelia must be feeling, hearing this request. It's all too much, so fast. And we still don't have any idea how much time we have before we are potentially discovered. The sentimental side of me wants to believe Cain—after all, every religion is made of rituals like the one he describes. Then again, my skeptical side thinks Cain could just be lying to get the card.

"You can still sneak out of here with the deck and find the other missing cards," Cain tries. "All I want is the Prince. And I promise I'll return it to you once it serves its purpose."

"These cards are my last connection to my grandma," Amelia whispers. "I just want to know more about her and why she had it."

"Then you understand why the Prince means so much to me," Cain says.

Doubt blazes in Amelia's eyes, paralyzing her. I can tell she wants to keep the Prince, but she also isn't sure that's the right thing to do. At the same time, the card feels like it burns a hole in my palm.

With a sudden jolt of clarity, I realize I'm going to have to be the one to make this decision. Amelia will never be able to live with herself, whether we keep the card or give it away. But do I trust Cain for what he's done to help us? Will he refuse to cover our exit if I don't give him the Prince—or worse?

Phrases race through my fragmented mind, faster with each fraught second. What was it Amelia and Logan said we needed to beware most, during their diner tarot reading? Do I really believe the Prince holds the power Cain claims?

Making this decision based on just one of these questions would be hard enough . . . but then again, I'm uniquely prepared to make a choice from the middle.

◊ "If the card is meant to be with us, it'll find its way back. So we'll **give the Prince** to you, Cain."
Turn To Page 54

◊ "I'm sorry, we have to **take the Prince** with us, until we know for sure who to trust."
Turn To Page 56

The words leave my mouth, and with them I know so many implications will follow. Ultimately, I have faith this card will end up exactly where it's meant to, as valuable as it might be. Besides, giving the card to Cain is the kind thing to do.

Still, I turn to Amelia before delivering on my promise, to give her the opportunity to stop me. She stares back at me with wide eyes . . . but she does not tell me she disagrees.

So I turn to Cain and hand him the long-lost Prince of Wands.

He clutches the Prince and I watch the relieved look that warms his face.

"I can't thank you both enough," Cain whispers. "I promise to return it to you when the time is right. Until then, let's get you out of here."

Cain then treads lightly over to the exit door and hands me his lighter to hold. I keep my eyes on Amelia, willing her to send me some signal of approval, but she keeps her eyes fully focused on Cain. He uses his entire body to push the door as he turns the knob, hoping to be as quiet as possible. The door sticks at first and my heart stops, thinking we're now trapped in this dark room. However, after some finessing from Cain, the door swings open and I finally exhale.

Amelia and I follow him out into the night air, finding ourselves in the back of the inn. A quick check confirms we're alone out here. So, hoping the Wanderers are still occupied searching through room eight, we creep along the back of the inn toward the front parking lot.

"Well, you've earned the right to learn the true power of the Wanderers, if you still want to hear it," Cain whispers as we stride forward.

Obviously our priority needs to be making a clean getaway, but I figure it also couldn't hurt to learn as much as possible before we escape. Amelia seems to think the same, since neither of us protest.

"Perilli made his decks as an artist and a teacher, but also a prophet," Cain continues. "He believed his cards could unlock hidden potential within those who read with them. He also gave each Corner different wisdom, so only we faithful Wanderers know this: Perilli made his decks and hid cards to seek out the worthy, who must be called to face a time of sharp growth. Wanderers believe Perilli's cards provide the answers to grow through struggle, through an age of peril."

Hearing Cain, half of me thinks this just sounds like the stuff of mythology, or science fiction. Or the kind of charismatic fear-mongering that breeds loyal followers. However, the other half of me recognizes an idea Gran Flo herself always repeated:

The fluid truth of the tarot is a tool to unlock what you truly think of yourself—and what you need to do next. Looking to Amelia, I can tell she senses all of this as well. And that she has something to say, finally.

"Cain, do you really believe your dad is—" Amelia begins, before pausing to change tack. "Do you really believe this card will change anything?"

Cain looks over at Amelia, trying to maintain as much eye contact as possible as we reach the end of the inn's sidelong stretch.

"My dad taught me to have faith in things I can't see, that can't be proved yet. He believed the tarot holds power we don't understand," Cain whispers. "And Perilli's decks are obviously special. You see the influence they hold over people. So, yes, I do believe that card will bring my dad peace. But I also hope it will help bring me some purpose. That's the hidden potential I hope to find, using the lost Prince."

I can't see Amelia's reaction as Cain finishes, because we round the corner into the front lot. I don't know if she believes any of this or if this makes her feel differently about the choice I made on her behalf. But I do know Cain believes all of this, to his core. To me, right now, that's what counts.

We don't say another word as we cross the parking lot, knowing we've entered the most dangerous stretch of our escape. Every step back toward Charvan feels like a mile, like we're prey crossing the path of a lurking predator. But not only do Amelia and I make it back unseen, we also find Cleo and Logan waiting for us inside.

Once we've taken down Cain's number, it only takes a second for Logan to start the engine and roll Charvan out into the desert night. As we leave, I turn back to take one last look at Cain. I see him standing in the driveway, watching us go with a fiery determination burning in his eyes. In this moment, I really do believe he will repay us someday, however he can.

At least, I really hope that's true.

Turn To Page 61

The words leave my mouth, and with them I know so many implications will follow. Ultimately, I don't believe the missing Prince will help Cain the way he hopes. Besides, it's now our responsibility to protect the value of these cards, for so many reasons.

Still, I turn to Amelia before delivering on my promise, to give her the chance to disagree. She stares back at me with wide eyes . . . but she doesn't say anything.

Which means it's beyond time to exit this cramped room and sneak back to Charvan. I step toward the door, but the second I do, Cain lunges toward me. He reaches out his hand, aiming to grab the Prince I still hold.

Reacting on instinct, I tighten my grip and try to pull away. Whatever happens next, Cain must drop his lighter, because suddenly the room goes dark. I can feel Cain's fingers on the Prince, pulling as he struggles against me.

But I do not let go.

In the next second, light pours into the small room. I turn and see Amelia has gotten the exit door open. In that same second, however, I hear a sound that cracks my heart.

I hear the sound of the Prince of Wands ripping in two.

Cain then falls to the ground in the room, banging against the far wall with a loud thump. Fury blazes in my chest like a furnace. All I can think about is rounding back on Cain to pry the half-Prince from his treacherous fingers.

"Chase," Amelia hisses, trying to keep her frantic voice low. "Let's just go!"

All of my instincts tell me to charge Cain, but I realize Amelia is right. The Wanderers inside must have heard that crash. They'll be after us now.

There's no more time to think.

So I run, following Amelia as she sprints along the backside of the inn. I run, even when I hear the shouts coming from behind us in room eight. I run, fueled by fear and anger and fiery determination.

It's only a few more seconds before Amelia and I reach the front lot. Every churning step back toward Charvan feels like a mile, like each newly parked car in the driveway could be a booby trap. I can't shake the thought that more unseen Wanderers might spring from the shadows to steal from us again.

But when Amelia and I make it safely to Charvan, we find Cleo and Logan waiting for us inside. They both stay silent, but they look just as simultaneously frantic and relieved as we must.

It only takes another few seconds for Logan to start the engine and roll Charvan out into the desert night. As we leave, I turn to take one last look out of the back window. Mercifully, I don't see any Wanderers flooding the road to chase us.

All I see is the Joshua Tree Inn disappearing into the darkness.

I finally exhale, very ready to leave this deserted land of Wanderers behind.

Turn To Page 61

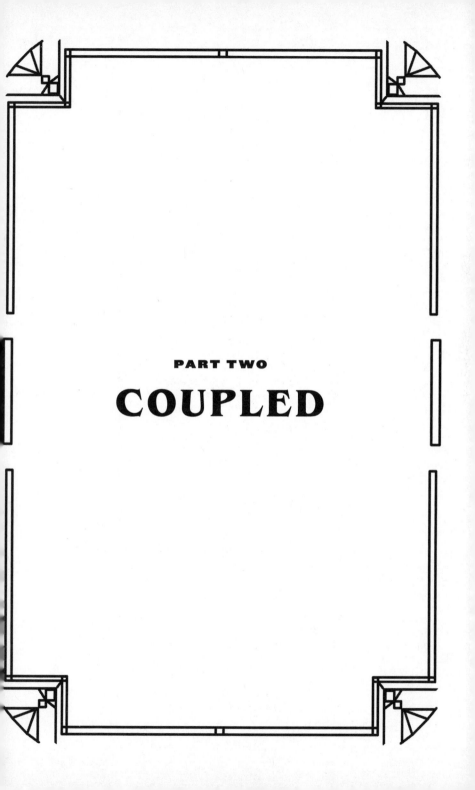

PART TWO

COUPLED

CHAPTER FIVE

AMELIA

IN THE TAROT, every ending is a new beginning. If that's true, I hope this next beginning won't be anything like our last ending.

My heart never hammered harder than it did on our way out of the Joshua Tree Inn. It wasn't until we were miles away that I felt I could breathe. Even then, I knew what was coming next, at least for me.

I learned last year that my body doesn't work quite like everyone else's, that it stores anxiety like a bathtub. It might take a while to fill up, but once it does, all I need is a shot-glass worth of stress to overflow. Ever since a string of nasty panic attacks last year, I do everything I can to keep my anxiety from accumulating—but last night's events didn't exactly decrease my stress levels.

Once we were far enough away from the inn to be sure we weren't followed, Chase and I filled Logan and Cleo in on what happened with Cain and the Prince of Wands. Well, Chase mostly did. I could still feel the emotions and the nerves rattling my veins, jumbling everything. I didn't actually speak much, but I figured Chase had already taken it upon himself to act on my behalf . . .

After that, Charvan fell eerily silent. It was like we were all drains, opened and emptied. The only conversation we had was agreeing to drive all night to our next destination, in case any Wanderers picked up our trail. This pointed us toward Solvang, a tourist town near where Anwar moved. I then pulled my phone out of the shoebox to check the location of the shop Cain mentioned, Azure Tarot, the supposed hub of Perillian knowledge. One quick search confirmed Azure Tarot is located in Summerland, a town just south of Solvang.

This new town sounded familiar to us, so we rechecked the coordinates for the next missing card, the Princess of Cups. Sure enough, we pinpointed its location off the coast of Summerland, on the chain of Channel Islands. Those islands are supposed to be uninhabited, but this was another mystery we filed away for later. For that moment, it was enough to know our next steps all converged in one place.

I knew we should keep talking about what happened, but I just felt so exhausted. I kept trying to process things, but every time I grabbed hold of anything, my thoughts seemed to evaporate. I knew I was in no condition to talk to Chase about the choice he took from me.

Everyone must have felt the same way, because our silence stretched deep into the midnight drive. Chase and Cleo eventually managed to doze off while Logan drove, fueled by podcasts and gas station coffee. But I certainly didn't doze. Residual adrenaline supercharged my limbs, making my heart pound long after our departure. I tried to tell myself that this was normal, at least for me. That it was just my fight-or-flight reactions lighting up long after they were actually necessary.

Still, I spent much of the drive warding off a panic attack with breathing exercises, pulling my hand away from my hair every time I began twirling strands. I learned the hard way that tugging at my hair was one of my automatic coping mechanisms. To their credit, both Cleo and Chase woke up at some point and checked to make sure I was okay, knowing the deal with my panic disorder. But I just nodded at them both—there wasn't much anyone could do once I got like this.

The only thing that ended up calming me down was going over the tarot cards, sitting in Charvan's back bench under the warm glow of the string lights. I focused on The Lovers for what must have been hours. This was one of the cards the toolset singled out, the one marked with invisible coordinates for the missing Princess of Cups. But really, I fixated on this card because The Lovers was Grandma's Major Arcana expression, standing for relationships and love and flow—just like she did. I couldn't stop asking myself: What would she make of all this, if she were still here?

Right now, as we drive through the mountain pass behind Santa Barbara, everything feels collected into a pool stagnating in my brain. The panic has finally dissipated from my system, but in its wake I feel flattened.

The sun just begins to rise over the peaks around Charvan. Our surroundings are stunning on this winding valley road nestled between the steep hills. All around there's craggy brown and leafy green and even the shimmering blue of a hidden lake, dazzling in the morning sunshine. Still, all I can think about is our night in the desert. I now sit in one of the back seats beside Cleo, willing myself to finally start speaking.

"Okay, I know we're all tired," I say, my tone dull and cool. "But we should really talk before we get to Solvang."

♦ "Chase, I really need to know how you could **give the Prince** away without even asking me first," I say, the words practically tumbling out of my mouth on their own.
Turn To Page 64

♦ "Chase, I'm not sure it was right to **take the Prince**. And we paid the price for your decision," I say, the words practically tumbling out of my mouth on their own.
Turn To Page 67

Maybe a better-rested version of myself could temper my reaction, but this version is majorly depleted.

"Right, because how could I ever make an independent decision without clearing it with you first?" Chase snaps from the front seat.

I know Chase. So I know he only gets defensive like this when he thinks he might have screwed up. But right now, that's not enough.

"No, don't do that," I return. "You know what you did was selfish. You know what this deck means to me."

Chase turns in his chair to face me.

"Of course I do. Why do you think I let you off the hook that way, not having to make that kind of impossible choice?"

"Is that what you think you did?"

"You have every right to be upset that I gave away the card without asking you first," Chase answers. "But I only did it because I could tell how conflicted you were. You care so much about other people and about Gran Flo's cards, I knew either choice would have torn you up. There was no time to think, so I did a very not-Chase-like thing and followed my gut. And I thought you'd stop me if you disagreed."

Anger flushes my exhausted muscles. Am I just looking for someone to blame for losing the card, for losing what feels like another important piece of Grandma? It doesn't matter.

"It's not like I was going to take the card back from Cain once you gave it to him," I say. "You didn't leave me much choice."

"I . . ." Chase takes a breath, looking out the window instead of at me. "You're right. I should have let you decide."

Chase delivers these words with an annoyed-sounding edge, but I know that's only because he hates being vulnerable.

"So you would have kept the card?" he asks, turning back to me.

I freeze. This is the part where I know I lose any high ground.

"I honestly have no idea," I finally answer. "So maybe it was best you were the one to make the call? I don't know."

Chase processes this a moment.

"Maybe. But how likely is it that Cain will actually return the card?"

"I know we weren't there," Cleo suddenly jumps in. "And if it were me, I probably would've kept the card. I don't think it has any power to give him peace. That said, giving Cain the card was the kind thing to do. That can't be too wrong."

"For what it's worth, I agree," Logan adds. "Besides, that card will find its way back to us if it's meant to be."

Hearing Logan's words surges back my emotions. I can accept a lot, but I can't stomach his destiny fantasies right now. Before I can say anything else, Chase reaches his hand out to place on mine, sensing the tides turning under my skin.

"If you'll indulge me a minute, I spent some of our drive sorting something out," Chase begins.

I remember he did spend some time scribbling away in his journal early this morning, transcribing more secret thoughts. Despite myself, I'm always eager to hear those.

"I know giving the card to Cain, on some level, makes it seem like I agree with Logan about the cards being fated. But coming so close to those Wanderers, then getting out of the desert and focusing on The Lovers, it reminded me of my favorite thing Gran Flo always used to say when we did readings. *The tarot is meant to be fluid. There is truth to be found in the cards, but you must interpret the truth for yourself. The thing mostly everyone gets wrong about every spiritual system is the idea that there's just one truth. Wouldn't that be easy?*

"So, really, disagreeing with each other doesn't mean we're choosing sides. It's probably better that we disagree, because it just means we get to see more angles of the same fundamental thing."

I take a few moments to digest Chase's words. Once I have, I nod—but not because I think he is completely correct. Really, Chase is saying a version of what Cleo did in the diner bathroom, but this time his actions directly affected me. Part of me still isn't really okay with the way he handled things with the Prince, but I'm hoping some actual sleep and distance will change that. Another part of me believes splitting the middle doesn't count the way Chase hopes it does, but I don't want us to spend our last few weeks together arguing. So I stuff these feelings down and hope they will also disappear with time. And I muster a smile for Chase, who has tried so hard to express himself just now.

"You know, you're really annoying when you get all 'much older soul' on us," I say, meaning some of it.

"Lies," Chase laughs. "But actually, we can thank Gran Flo for that one, by way of this mysterious Perilli guy."

"Yeah, okay," Logan says, turning to wink at me. "But Chase, who do you love more, me or Amelia?"

I force a laugh, this time for Logan's sake. "Very funny."

Not funny at all.

"Easy," Chase says. "I obviously love Cleo most of all."

Turn To Page 69

I'm not sure this reaction is entirely fair, but holding the half-ripped Prince of Wands in my hand, part of me needs to blame someone for its destruction.

"I know you, Amelia," Chase says, turning in his chair to face me. "I could tell how conflicted you were. You care so much about other people and about Gran Flo's cards, I knew either choice would have torn you up. But mostly I know if you thought giving Cain the card was the right thing to do, you would've stopped me."

"That's not the point," I try, knowing this is probably exactly the point.

"It's not my fault Cain ripped the card, Amelia," Chase says quietly.

Again, he is right. But that doesn't feel satisfying. The satisfying thing would be to blame him for tearing this lost piece of my grandma we finally found.

"I think we all have the right to be freaked after last night. It was more intense than any of us expected," Chase continues. "I didn't mean to take the decision from you. I honestly just didn't want anyone else to have to be the bad guy."

I reach out my hand and place it on Chase's, hoping the gesture will speak the volumes I currently can't. Usually I'm the one to lead the charge while he thinks everything through, but last night was quite the role reversal. On top of everything else, something about this shift doesn't sit quite right in my gut. Like this might be first tangible sign of the waves of change barreling our way.

"For what it's worth," Cleo suddenly jumps in, "I think you did the right thing. That card won't give Cain any peace. That's something he needs to give to himself."

"Well, if we're sharing," Logan adds, "I would've given the card to Cain."

I look to Logan in the driver's seat, feeling that familiar flush of animosity rear its ugly head. However, I then catch a glimpse of Logan's face in the rearview mirror and I can see it—he feels left out. He wasn't there for the action last night, and then Chase keeping the card honors my way of thinking over his, in some ways. Seeing Logan's reaction manages to soften some of my edges.

"While we're at it, Logan, I want to apologize for getting so fired up at the diner yesterday," I say. "I know we believe in pretty opposite things, but that's no excuse."

"Actually, if you'll indulge me a minute, I spent some of our drive sorting something out," Chase interrupts.

I remember he did spend some time scribbling away in his journal early this morning, transcribing more secret thoughts. Those, I'm always eager to hear.

"Especially after studying The Lovers quote in Perilli's booklet: *Could things that appear to be opposites really be two versions of the same source?* I know on the surface you two seem to believe in very different things, but let me ask you something. Amelia, why does it matter you believe there's no such thing as fate?"

I'm not sure where Chase is going with this, but I answer anyway.

"I think relying on some 'grand design' is an excuse people can use to act however they want. Exactly the way Cain acted, as a matter of fact. I think we all have to be accountable for our actions, because what we do matters."

"Right, yes, I thought so," Chase says, turning to Logan next. "And why do you believe in destiny?"

Logan thinks for a beat. Then, to my surprise, he grins widely.

"Because if life is random and meaningless, it's an excuse for people to live only for themselves and act however they want. I think if we believe we all have a purpose, if we're all connected somehow, then we know our actions really matter."

Logan's eyes then find mine, glancing up into the rearview mirror.

"Maybe someone like Cain uses that kind of purpose to hide behind when he does something selfish," Logan says directly to me now. "But if he really believed in a higher power, he wouldn't need to act that way."

Logan's final sentiment does more to prove my point than convince me otherwise, but thanks to Chase, I suddenly realize that's beside the point. What he just laid out reminds me of exactly the kind of thing Grandma would say—and what Cleo said in the diner bathroom, actually.

So I smile at Cleo first, and she gives me a private little wink. Then I turn to offer Chase the same smile, because he has earned that much, despite everything else.

Turn To Page 69

"I'm glad you three are all resolved, but I think you're missing the real point," Cleo says next. "Looking for that card put us in actual danger last night."

Leave it to Cleo to cut to the core. I purposefully didn't want to start the conversation in that place, but Cleo is right—we do have to talk about this.

"Not to be the party pooper, but I think we need to ask ourselves if we really want to keep looking for these missing cards," Cleo finishes.

I sigh. I still don't know how to process our close encounter of the Wanderer kind. Sure, we managed to make it out of the inn safely, but what could have happened still hangs over us. We don't know the full extent of what we're dealing with here yet, but if last night was any indication, then maybe Cleo is right.

Then again, I can't help but wonder if maybe the other suits—these other "Corners" as Cain called them—will be less intense than the fiery desert Wanderers? After all, Cups are so much more about love and light. Or am I just telling myself what I want to hear because I can't imagine giving up the search, no matter the risk?

"I actually have an answer for that one, if I may," Logan jumps in. "To be reminded there are people out there who will attack you for what you believe, or what you possess—that's the worst. I know it feels safer to protect ourselves and run away from that kind of thing. But I don't think living in fear is really living at all. So I say we stay sharp and smart and we absolutely do not go looking for trouble. But I also say we don't let anyone else stop us from having this one last adventure together, now or ever."

Logan's words reverberate through all of us for several beats, gaining more power with each second. At least, that's how it feels to me.

"Jeez, this is some insightful stuff we're cranking out this morning," I finally laugh. "Maybe we should get stalked and chased every night?"

"No thank you," Cleo also laughs, but it's more of a nervous release. "And Logan, I hear what you're saying. I do. I just don't want us to get so wrapped up in the excitement of what we might gain that we don't think about everything we could lose, you know?"

"I think you're all right," Chase says, because of course he does. "I don't think we should be intimidated away, but I also don't think we should go rushing in as blindly as we did last night. So we need to keep our eyes wide open.

"But I was also thinking, if we are going to keep looking for the cards, maybe we should pinpoint exactly why we want to find them? I know for me personally, I'm dying to learn more about Perilli. And if I'm being really honest, I want to find out how much this deck is really worth."

"Well, I'm still just along for the ride with you weirdos," Cleo answers next. "But Chase's thoughts are all good ones. It sounds like we'll definitely learn something at this Azure Tarot place. A lot more than we did with Maggie, anyway. I'm glad we are under no obligation to ever call that guy again, after he sold us out. Plus, once we get past this spot, which they must all know about, maybe the Wanderers won't have any idea where to look for us next?"

"Don't worry, I've been keeping an eye out the entire drive. No one has been following us," Logan says. "But if we're talking purpose, personally I think we're at this giant juncture of change in our lives. Everything is inevitably going to feel more intense. I mean, look how much we already learned in just one day of this trip? If we keep going, there can only be more growth, right?"

Hearing everyone else's answers, I realize there are many reasons to keep looking for these missing cards, despite the potential dangers we might face. I'm relieved everyone else agrees, because continuing to look for the other missing cards was already a foregone conclusion, for me.

Still, I take my turn next, because no one pinpointed my own reasons for wanting to keep the search alive.

◊ "Something tells me Grandma had an adventure with this deck, whether or not she really knew where it came from. And even if she didn't, I believe learning more about the cards will be the best way to **honor** Grandma's **legacy**."
Turn To Page 71

◊ "I don't think we can argue that there's something special about these cards—fortunes, cults, the occult, the arts. So I think if we assemble the deck, we really will unlock some kind of hidden potential. Some new **personal power**."
Turn To Page 72

"I know we still can't be sure whether my grandma really knew anything about these hidden Perillian origins," I continue. "But if she was involved in some deeper way, I need to know. And if so, I definitely need to know why she kept it from us."

"Well, if she did," Cleo begins, "I'd imagine it was to protect you from exactly the kind of experience we had yesterday."

"And even if she did come into the deck by blind chance," Logan offers next, with a knowing smile, "these cards are your inheritance. Discovering more about their mysteries can only enhance that legacy."

"I totally agree," Chase adds. "Moving forward, we definitely need to keep our eyes peeled for any clues potentially relating to Gran Flo."

I smile at my friends, finally feeling some energy and peace return to my body. It might seem like a small thing at first, naming my intention this way. But if our encounter with Cain taught us anything, it's that our intention always rules the outcome—if only because our intention also rules our perspective.

And now I know exactly what perspective I hope to gain from this unexpected adventure.

So even if this intention I just set doesn't affect much in the present, I have a feeling it may still prove to be my biggest decision yet.

Turn To Page 73

"I think we need to stay attuned to exactly what kind of power these cards can wield," I continue. "Psychologically, financially, spiritually, and maybe even . . . supernaturally?"

"Who knows," Logan responds first. "If there really are all different kinds of followers behind Perilli who believe in his work so fervently, then they must be on to something."

"Let's not get carried away," Cleo interjects. "Having followers is more a credit to Perilli's charisma than anything else. But I do promise to keep an open mind."

"No, it'll be good to have a skeptical eye on all this," Chase says. "We have to remember, it's our job now to figure out what's fake and what's real—and what's really so special about these cards and their creator."

I smile at my friends, finally feeling some energy and peace return to my body. It might seem like a small thing at first, naming my intention this way. But if our encounter with Cain taught us anything, it's that our intention always rules the outcome—if only because our intention also rules our perspective.

And now I know exactly what perspective I hope to unlock from this unexpected adventure.

So even if this intention I just set doesn't affect much in the present, I have a feeling it may still prove to be my biggest decision yet.

Turn To Page 73

◆ ◆ ◆ ◆

The air in Solvang already feels lighter. It's not just that the sky here is filled with sunshine and crisp ocean air, it's the actual spirit of this little town. Joshua Tree felt reverent and powerful, sure, but also unforgiving and foreboding. Here in this quaint faux-Dutch village, the roofs are angled with wooden beams, and every other storefront sells homemade fudge or local wine or craftsman toys. The people here smile as if the festive spirit has soaked right into their very skin. After last night, it's a welcome change.

Once we arrived at the adorable B&B Anwar recommended, we all fell into naps like the dead. Waking up midafternoon, I actually started feeling way more like myself. We all then set out in search of food. Thankfully, Cleo, our resident foodie, prepared extensive research on where to eat along Chase's tarot-lined route. Despite yesterday's enormous detour, arriving at our first preplanned stop allowed Cleo to unleash her first culinary curation.

"You can direct all of your rave reviews to my forthcoming travel blog," Cleo announces proudly, finishing the last bite of her Danish. "I'm thinking of naming it *CleoCraft: Food So Good It's Magic.*"

Cleo's killer opening restaurant pick has been an excellent reminder of all the things we looked forward to doing on this road trip, before the tarot scooped us off our feet. In fact, my feet still feel thoroughly scooped, since I'm due to meet Anwar any minute.

"Solvang may be my new favorite California town," Chase says.

"I absolutely have to doodle us in front of every windmill we come across."

"Cleo, that would take all day," Logan laughs.

"Well, we need to occupy ourselves somehow while Lady Piccolo entertains her suitor," Cleo replies, rolling her eyes.

"Yes, but Chase only allotted Amelia an hour before we go to Azure Tarot."

"Indeed I did," Chase says. "So when is Sir Anwar slated to arrive?"

"He's on his way from Los Olivos, the next town over," I answer.

"Correction, he has arrived," says a new voice from beside our table. "I was impressed when Amelia messaged that you were here. Only locals are supposed to know about this spot."

I look up to find Anwar standing there, all six feet of his chiseled self. He looks like a curated social post come to life, wearing a linen button-down, dark jeans, and a jade-gemmed ring. Seeing him in the flesh, I could physically die, just cease respiration and float out of my body into the cloudless heavens.

"That's all thanks to Cleo," I say by some miracle. "She's a sniper with a search bar."

Introductions are made. Laughs are shared. Anwar and I are given leave. Not too long, Chase reminds. Just enough time for a stroll around the village.

I know all of this happens, but it feels like I watch it from a place hanging somewhere above my head. I don't sink fully back down into my body until Anwar and I settle on a park bench. It faces a lily pond, one with a white walking bridge stretched over its blue surface. We each hold a paper tray of some jelly-topped pancake-donut things called *aebleskiver*, an authentic Dutch dessert Anwar insisted I try. But eating again is the last thing on my mind.

Anwar is just so goddess-damned gorgeous. Despite my best efforts, only one thought keeps repeating in my head: *Why on earth is he potentially interested in me?*

"I have a somewhat radical proposition," Anwar says, wiping powdered sugar off his lips. Radical proposals of my own race through my mind.

"It's been an unusual couple of days," I answer. "Try me."

"Why don't we skip the whole awkward small talk thing and skip right to the fun stuff? A lightning round, three questions each, which we have to answer on instinct. No long pauses allowed."

"Sounds dangerous," I say. "I'm in."

"Excellent." Anwar then turns to me, his eyes two amber pools. "I'll start. I'll even go easy on you. What's your favorite scary show or movie?"

"There is nothing easy about that question."

"First instinct. No thinking. Go."

"*The Haunting of Hill House.* Close second would be *The Birds.*"

"Amelia Piccolo, I did not take you for a cheater. One answer only."

"Okay, fine," I say, angling myself toward Anwar. "Then here's my first question. If not a cheater, then what kind of girl do you take me for?"

Anwar grins. "The best kind: lionhearted and unabridged."

It's my turn to grin.

"Wow, does the brooding poet thing always work for you?"

"Usually," Anwar answers. "That's two questions, for the record. My turn. What keeps you up at night?"

Another impossible question because, really, what doesn't?

"The thought of losing people I love," I answer on instinct, as instructed. "Or the thought of love lost in general."

"Who's the poet now?" Anwar says. "That was a rhetorical question; it doesn't count."

"Sneaky. In that case, my last question is a big one," I reply, pausing for dramatic effect. "You know we're headed back over the hill to Summerland today. Since our time is limited, want to come with us?"

"I do," Anwar answers right away. "Assuming you promise to return me home at a reasonable hour. Period there, not a question mark."

"Sorry, I can make no such promise," I say, knowing he was only joking. "Okay, what's your final question? Better make it a good one."

Anwar sets his paper plate of pancake balls down on the bench and turns toward me, his arm now resting against mine. The contact gives me a jolt, like a flint strike. He beams his full smile, and looking at him feels somewhat blinding.

"If you could do anything right in this moment, without fear of consequence, what would it be?"

Anwar's last question turns out to be a dangerous one.

Still, I know the answer.

◊ "I would ask you for one more **bonus question**," I say, knowing that bonus round would definitely include a first kiss, if I have my way.

Turn To Page 76

◊ "I'd bring you to hang with my friends. Mostly because Cleo would never forgive me if I didn't **bring** her **back** some of this pancake-ball magic."

Turn To Page 78

"Then consider us entered into a bonus round," Anwar answers.

I put down my mostly untouched dessert on the bench to try to catch my breath. My heart pounds so loudly in my ears, I swear Anwar must be able to hear it. *Don't think!* I yell in my head. *Just ask.*

"Why did you really ask me to come visit you?"

"Because you have really good taste in classic and contemporary horror," Anwar begins without hesitation. "Because every girl up here seems to be preoccupied with social media influencing, but you don't care about perfectly curating anything. Because I look forward to our pen-palling every night. Because I think you're brave and sensitive where most are timid and guarded. And because I think you're beautiful."

Well, damn.

Damn.

"While we're asking bonus questions," Anwar continues over my stunned silence, "why did you go out of your way to come visit me?"

I smile back at Anwar, standing from the bench.

"Well, this is embarrassing now," I say. "But I came for the *aebleskiver.*"

Anwar laughs, standing to join me. "In that case, glad I could be of service."

"Well, I might have come for something else . . ." I say, angling my body toward Anwar. "Something . . . well, you know."

Anwar looks down at me, puzzled. "Do I?"

Embarrassment flushes through me, steaming my insides. What in the world was I thinking? We're sitting in broad daylight on a park bench, and I'm a relative stranger to this boy. Of course Anwar is not going to kiss me here, if he even wants to kiss me in the first place.

I put down my paper tray to give my hands something to do. When I turn back toward Anwar, I'm surprised to find him leaning in closer. His hand suddenly reaches out and holds my cheek, steadying my face. Electricity shoots out of his fingertips, shocking me into place.

Anwar's lips come close to touching mine, but he hangs there for a few seconds. His eyes flicker up and down and I feel his breath on my lips. I have to fight the urge to gasp out loud.

"I've been wanting to do this for quite some time," he finally says, holding himself back for another second. It's just enough time for me to place my hand on the solid muscle of his chest.

Then Anwar kisses me.

And I am reduced to a puddle of a person.

This kiss might last a second or an hour, I cannot tell. But what I can already tell, without a shadow of a doubt?

Today is going to be an absolutely above-average day.

Turn To Page 80

"Then let's get moving," Anwar says with a smile.

If he's at all disappointed I asked to cut into our alone time, he certainly doesn't show it. He just seems so . . . enthusiastic. It makes me wonder, as we start walking, if I owe him another warning about the detours our trip has taken.

"I know we've messaged about it a bit," I start, "but if you're really coming with us for the next leg of the trip, you should know—"

"Amelia, are you trying to talk me out of joining you?" Anwar asks. "Because if I'm intruding on your friend time, I don't—"

"No!" I blurt. "It's not that at all."

"Then trust me when I say I couldn't be more excited to meet your friends and get to hang a bit. With them . . . and especially with you."

My cheeks feel flush, warming from the heat of Anwar's words. "Then it's settled. But don't say I didn't warn you."

We round the next corner and end up finding Chase, Logan, and Cleo strolling toward us.

"Miss us already?" Chase asks, surprised.

"Anwar let me in on a local dessert secret, so I needed to report back. Cleo, you're going to faint over how good these pancake balls are."

Cleo gives me a smile, but it feels slightly dimmed. Or maybe distracted? She seems preoccupied studying Anwar, like she's searching him for something.

"Well, I can actually propose a trade," Cleo says, snapping herself back. "I just finished a fresh doodle of the four of us in front of that windmill over there."

Cleo holds out the sheet of ripped sketchpad paper, and indeed she has drawn us all in full cartoon color: Logan in his standard athleisure, Chase in his young professor uniform, Cleo in her romper, and me in my pastel linens. We stand on either side of a bright windmill—Chase with Logan, and Cleo with me. As usual, the doodle feels perfect, capturing something essential about our afternoon here.

"Wow, that is deeply awesome," Anwar says, taking in the doodle. "Think there's room for one more in the middle there?"

Anwar smiles at Cleo, and she returns the gesture, but something about it feels . . . hollow? Or am I still just being paranoid about Anwar fitting in?

I already invited Anwar along, so there's no backing down now. Besides, the others will really like him once they get to know him. And we came all this way, we can't just leave it at twenty minutes. I want to get to know Anwar better myself, after all.

Still, I make a little mental note to keep an eye on Cleo, to make sure she doesn't feel left out. The last thing I'd want is for her to feel like a fifth wheel, because as far as I'm concerned, she's the whole damn car.

Turn To Page 80

◆ ◆ ◆ ◆

When I told the others Anwar was joining us for the day, the only one to protest vocally—and predictably—was Chase. But one stern glance reminded him that he owes me a command decision or two, after last night. Besides, our first detour pulled me out of my usual Empress ways, so I was due for her to reemerge.

I had to agree to sit on Charvan's back bench to make room for Anwar, but I don't care. I don't care about the lingering fast-food smell or the unanswered questions still left at our feet. I don't care about Cain and the Prince. I don't care about wandering the desert or my night soaking in panic. Right now, I let it all go.

Because right now, we are simply all princes and princesses, riding our chariot over the great hill. We have just come through the mountain pass out of Solvang and now drive down the winding road to the coast. The ocean sparkles miles below us in the distance, glistening in an endless blue stretch of possibilities.

I remind myself that despite whatever challenges we still face, we are blissfully young and free. And right now we all sing at the top of our lungs to Logan's music selection. Journey's "Don't Stop Believin'" blares at top volume, the perfect song for this super-shot of road tripping. Cleo's pick, Carly Rae Jepsen's "Run Away With Me," will come next. Then for my turn I will insist on Taylor Swift's "Cruel Summer," my favorite sing-along anthem of all time.

I know Chase will then insist on his own favorite karaoke epic, Celine Dion's "It's All Coming Back to Me Now." It wouldn't make my own list, but I have to admit, I'm quite curious to see how Anwar handles this particular ballad.

Almost as curious as I am to see what this glorious chapter of overflowing cups and shimmering beaches has to offer us next.

CHAPTER SIX

CHASE

WE MAKE SURE to park Charvan around the corner from Azure Tarot, just in case any Wanderers do come looking for us here. Amelia's new companion seemed amused by our trend toward caution, so we had to waste another fifteen minutes walking him through the details of our trip so far. Absolutely zero part of me thinks a stranger like Anwar should be joining us on a day this important, but as Amelia silently reminded me, I owe her one. At the very least, Anwar seems kind and respectful enough not to interfere too much.

We find Azure Tarot on a corner of Summerland's main street, a sleepy stretch of beach town paradise. Inside, everything is cast in cool tones and smells of fresh soaps and salt spray, with doors kept open to ocean views. It's like we've entered another reality, yet again. Where Maggie's Mother Earth Occult was all dust and decay, Azure Tarot is all bright and breezy. The shop is uncluttered, offering only a few products: healing crystals, assorted turquoise jewelry, and several copies of The Azure Tarot—an original deck, advertised for readings with the creator herself.

Lauren "Lady Azure" Baxter stands behind a glass counter wearing an aquamarine caftan and a necklace that bears Perilli's signature symbol, recreated with sapphires on a platinum cup. Being in Lady Azure's shop I feel a deep resonating calm, paired with an even deeper sense of illusion. It's like we've suddenly dived into an ocean trench, our surroundings both serene and filled with the unknown.

As usual, Amelia feels no similar instinct for caution, seeming immediately at ease with Lady Azure. Then again, perhaps Amelia is working her just as hard with her burst of openness, retelling select details of our past day's encounter. Either way, I can't blame Amelia. Lady Azure radiates maternal warmth, like she stepped right out of a Nancy Meyers movie with her perfect blond hair and blue eyes.

"My dear children, what an absolutely outlandish ordeal you've endured!" Lady Azure says once Amelia finishes. She speaks with an accent that feels affected by wealth, like maybe she studied abroad in London or has watched *Grey Gardens* one too many times.

"You simply must allow me to set things suitable once more. While the power of Perilli's teachings resonate with many, I'm afraid not all interpret them with the proper intent. I'm sure those Wandering heathens would speak similarly of us Coupled, but let me assure you, not all Perillians are of their kind. Not remotely!"

"Coupled?" Amelia asks.

"There's so much to explore, where to begin?" Lady Azure says, shifting her gaze upward to the gem-speckled ceiling. "Yes, Coupled is the name of the Perillian Cups Corner."

Lady Azure points to a Cup charm inside the counter, which rests beside a Perillian toolset, just like the one Maggie gave us.

"The final Perillian toolset is special, but not entirely rare," Lady Azure explains. "It's just like that old coward Maggie to use it as bait."

"Hey, Mom," a new voice speaks from behind us. "I can come back later if you have customers to read."

We all turn to find a teenage boy about our age in the doorway, standing with a surfboard and a half-unzipped wetsuit. My eyes don't know where to start: On the water dripping down his visible six-pack? The sun reflecting off his flawless, light brown skin? The smattering of freckles across the bridge of his nose? Every one of us tenses seeing him—well, maybe not Anwar, but I still don't think he belongs here in the first place.

"Seidon!" Lady Azure coos. "These aren't just any customers! These are the sojourners I predicted would come in the waning days of summer! Those possessing the last, lost Perillian deck!"

Seidon blinks at his mother and I can practically smell his skepticism from here, along with the saltwater and sunscreen.

"Oh, wow," he says. "That's a big deal, right?"

"Positively enormous," Lady Azure answers. "I was actually just going to offer our new compatriots a complimentary reading so that we may all align ourselves in the same Corner. Why don't you stay before we retire for dinner?"

Seidon nods, waving hello to us as a group.

"It's true, we have waited eons for your arrival," Lady Azure continues, turning back to us. "Might you allow me the honor of imparting my gift upon you, so that we may commune with a reading?"

Out of the corner of my eye, I swear I see Seidon roll his eyes. I also notice Logan still stares at Seidon a little more intently than I'd like.

"While I have divined my own unique deck, The Azure Tarot, I'm marvelously desperate to try reading you with your deck, if you'll allow it. I believe your deep history with the cards will help my own cosmic clairvoyance come through. Though I admit, I'm also quite eager to glimpse Perilli's final masterpiece. You must know, I was his most loyal benefactress before his untimely passing."

"I think that'd be all right," Amelia says in a voice that lights up my instincts.

"I needn't even lay hands on the cards," Lady Azure offers. "You can deal for me and I can read from afar."

Astute, I think. Unlike Maggie, Lady Azure might actually be charming enough to play on our emotions here. Amelia can clearly sense it, too.

"Would you mind if I got the reading instead?" I ask, putting my hand on Amelia's shoulder. "I have some questions I need answered."

My favorite part of having one best friend my whole life? Amelia and I don't always need words to understand each other. She nods at me with relieved eyes, knowing I'm probably better equipped to get what we need from Lady Azure, given my detached and rational approach to the cards.

Taking note of this exchange, Lady Azure then nods herself.

"Marvelous! Let our reading resound into the great beyond!"

Once we're set up at the cozy reading booth, I try to tune out the audience at our side and focus only on Lady Azure. Despite her grand and breezy facade, I have a feeling this reading is going to be not unlike a game of poker. Lady Azure agrees to let me deal the cards in the Celtic Cross Spread, a configuration I know well. However, she counters by insisting I only use the Minor Arcana Cups cards. All the better to orient ourselves appropriately, she claims. Or all the better to conveniently orient her "gift," I think now, as I deal out the five face-down cards.

"Normally I'd ask you to set an intention for this reading," Lady Azure begins, "but I sense your intention is already clear. Where is your missing Princess of Cups, and why have you been brought here today?"

I nod at Lady Azure and flip the first card, trying to keep the pace fast enough that she won't have much time to think. Usually in a Cross configuration, this first card stands for the current situation or the potential obstacles faced.

"Ah, the Ten of Cups," Lady Azure says, her eyes focused on the upturned card. "As always, exquisitely drawn by my darling Carson! Oh, how his art and his intuition evolved near the end of his days! But enough about us."

Lady Azure then closes her eyes and sways, as if accessing some sixth sense.

"The voices are particularly clear here," she continues. "This is a card of completion, of a cup fully filled. You are summoned to rely on the selflessness of others to complete a great journey."

Lady Azure opens her eyes, and I can't help but think how well this "from the beyond" act must work on casual walk-ins. Luckily, there's nothing casual about me. This is the part when most others would open up, hooking into something they heard and expanding upon their connection to it. I know, however, Lady Azure's Ten of Cups reading was factually accurate—just cast in a shade favorable to her.

So I simply nod and continue. As I flip the second card, I remind myself that this position usually represents the qualities needed to answer the question posed.

"My King of Cups!" Lady Azure cries when she sees the next card, with a mix of drama and enthusiasm. "Heavens beyond, but does he look like my Jamie! Seidon, don't you see the resemblance to your father?"

Seidon steps forward, his stomach muscles crunching together through his open wetsuit as he leans over to examine the card. The King of Cups is a handsome black man riding a winged horse across a shoreline of crashing waves.

"Yes," Seidon says. "But Uncle Carson knew him before he went bald, huh?"

"Too true!" Lady Azure replies, gripping Seidon's shoulder.

Uncle Carson? I fight the urge to look at Amelia to clock this new nugget of information. I don't want to give Lady Azure any advantages, so I force myself to keep my focus on the cards in front of me.

"Might you turn the third card?" Lady Azure asks, now matching her pace to mine. "I prefer to read cards two and three in tandem, for balanced duality."

I flip the third card and Lady Azure gasps as the Queen of Cups is revealed. The rest us finally react as well—even me. On the card, the Queen of Cups rises from the ocean holding a dripping bouquet of water lilies and looking every bit the mirror image of Lady Azure. Suddenly this familiar card takes on new meaning.

I watch closely as Lady Azure wipes at her eyes. When she looks up at me, her voice sounds tight with sadness.

"You must forgive me, but we're still not quite over the loss of our dear Carson. To see ourselves reflected in his final deck this way . . . It's thanks to Carson we all came to understand our gifts more keenly."

"However, this reading is meant for you," Lady Azure says, shifting gears. "And the meaning is clear. To find what you seek, you must rely on the Family Baxter."

This is another very convenient interpretation of the King and Queen of Cups, but then again, the cards do literally depict Lady Azure and her family.

"Might you flip the final two cards together?" Lady Azure then asks.

I nod and next, the final two cards revealed are the Ace and Five of Cups.

"Fascinating," Lady Azure exhales, closing her eyes and bobbing once again. "These cards speak to me of loss. A great disappointment prompted this trip for you. The five of you gathered together to solve a mystery—one left to you by someone very important. I sense the answers you seek lie in the unfolding of this grand journey. Only assembling all the missing pieces will grant a clear portrait."

Lady Azure opens her eyes, blinking as if emerging from a dream. "Tell me, do I speak truly?"

My mind whirrs as I fight to keep my face expressionless. There are certainly parts that Lady Azure got right, but then some parts she got completely wrong. So how much of this reading has been divined and how much has been designed?

The only way to answer this question will be to coax as much information out of Lady Azure as possible. So as I gear up to ask more, I decide to honor the intention Amelia set for our journey earlier this morning. I might be the one getting read here, but I can't forget this trip is about Amelia, at its heart.

♦ Amelia made it clear she wants to try to **honor** Gran Flo's potential **legacy**, so I should ask about Perilli's background and history.
   Turn To Page 86

♦ Amelia made it clear she wants to unlock potential **personal power** from the deck, so I should ask specifically about Perillian mythology.
   Turn To Page 88

"We came here because there's so much about Carson Perilli we want to learn," I begin, "but honestly, it's been hard to discover much about him at all."

"I'm afraid that's by design," Lady Azure says. "While we Perillians might differ greatly in our four Corners—Wanderers, Repentant, Sworn, and Coupled as we are—we all agree on keeping Carson's teachings guarded. But as far as I'm concerned, possession of that deck entitles you to all the knowledge I have."

Lady Azure then stands and disappears into a small back room for a few moments. When she returns, she holds a beautifully handbound book with a cover bearing the signature Perillian symbol.

"What's this?" Amelia asks, leaning in to examine the homemade tome. Behind her, Cleo and Logan lean to look as well.

"This is one of the only gathered collections of Carson's teachings," Lady Azure begins. "He preferred to share his knowledge in readings and conversations. He detested that we could summon answers at a technological whim. He thought that ease was making us all dimmer, not brighter."

"May we?" Anwar asks, his eyes set on the volume. We all turn to him, surprised—including Amelia. I guess no one knew he was interested in the tarot.

Lady Azure nods. "Carefully, please."

With Amelia and Anwar close at one shoulder and Logan and Cleo at the other, I take a deep breath and open the book to the first page:

> **The tarot is not a fortune teller.**
> **The tarot is a doorway.**
> **One that leads to many worlds.**
> **To ancient history, through cultural symbolism.**
> **To depths of your own consciousness,**
> **through the revelation of secret desires.**
> **A chance drawing of tarot cards does not predict the future.**
> **Rather, it illuminates the inner reflections you find**
> **in its endless representations of truth.**

As we read, I hear Amelia's breath catch in her throat. The wording might be different, but this passage also captures Gran Flo's own teachings on the tarot. Reading this, it feels less and less likely she could have happened into this deck by chance at a yard sale.

"Carson believed the tarot was the most precise spiritual tool on earth," Lady Azure says. "He believed every human soul was a unique reflection of the same source, much like tarot cards themselves—walking contradictions, bound and fused in one unique expression. He knew the cards, like humans, contained multitudes. If you were ever lucky enough to be read by Carson, he had a gift for using his decks to illuminate who you were. And even more keenly, what you have to offer the world."

"I can see how that would be a compelling thought," Logan replies, "that Perilli could reveal your deepest talents and truest purpose."

"'Compelling' is certainly the right word for it," Cleo adds. "I mean, was Perilli really just a benevolent spiritual teacher and a gifted artist? Or did he think of himself as some kind of prophet? He sounds a lot like a charismatic leader, to me."

Lady Azure turns her gaze to Cleo, her blue eyes cooling over.

"Could it be that Carson Perilli was all of this at once?" she asks. "Just like the complex figures of the Major Arcana themselves?"

"Well, on some level that's always been part of what draws Chase and me to the tarot," Amelia jumps in, obviously trying to defuse. "It has inherent expressions of our talents, mine for empathy and his for analysis."

"I'm not surprised one of Carson's decks would bring this out in you," Lady Azure offers. "It's what they were built for, even if you never received a proper Perillian reading."

My mind churns. As fascinating as this discussion is, we need to get back to the central question of this unraveling mystery: Why did Perilli's final deck really end up in our hands? Flipping through this book, I see it's just more quotes—which means Lady Azure must still keep the deepest well of knowledge to herself.

Something tells me that if she does possess more answers, pulling them out of her might require a subtle touch. So I need to dress this question up with a hook she can't resist.

◊ "Something about our possession of this deck feels fated, like some kind of **calling** being fulfilled?" I say.

Turn To Page 91

◊ "There must be a natural explanation rooted in fact and history—or maybe even in sheer **coincidence**?" I say.

Turn To Page 93

"How is it all of you Perillians came to be organized?" I ask. "I mean, how did you all find one another?"

"I dare say we're not quite as organized as I always pressed Carson to be," Lady Azure answers. "Still, he did believe there was a natural order to humanity, just like the tarot."

Lady Azure stands, her caftan brushing the floor as she paces toward a specific spot on the shop's far wall.

"Carson believed the tarot was the most precise spiritual tool on the planet," Lady Azure continues. "If you were lucky enough to be read by him, he had a gift for using his own decks to illuminate who you were and where you belonged."

Lady Azure then unfolds a chart hanging on the wall. Glancing at Amelia, we both stand to see it. Logan, Cleo, and Anwar follow closely behind.

"Carson taught that the Major Arcana represents archetypal lessons, covering the inner world of the mind and the spirit. Meanwhile, the Minor Arcana were suited to cover the physical world of bodily action and environment. Accordingly, Carson believed all of humanity could fit into one of four Minor Arcana tribes. After all, the foundational number four appears in so many other sacred systems."

"Like winter, spring, summer, fall?" Amelia asks. "West, north, east, south?"

"Or water, earth, fire, air?" Anwar adds. We all turn to him, surprised—including Amelia. I guess no one knew he was interested in the tarot.

"Indeed," Lady Azure answers. "And thus, Cups, Pentacles, Wands, Swords. Carson's greatest joy was to sort those he read into one of his Four Corners."

Standing in front of the chart, we study the information written within a large Perillian symbol. I'm first drawn to the Wands Corner, where our journey began.

WANDS: Fire. Red. East. Summer. // Aries. Leo. Sagittarius.
Spiritual. Passion. Faith. Action. Growth. Goals. Intention.

"There are the Wanderers, the seeking and the faithful," Lady Azure narrates, evidently following my gaze. "In reality, they are mostly conspiracy theorists obsessed with some nonsense vision of an age of peril."

"I don't know," Logan replies. "Something about the desert just burns to the truth. We all know there's nothing stranger, or harsher, or more maddening."

Leave it to my Logan to find the good, even after our own Wanderer experience. However, Lady Azure seems less enthused.

"Next we have the Repentant, the toiling and the scientific," she pivots.

PENTACLES: Earth. Green. North. Spring. // Taurus. Virgo. Capricorn.
Elemental. Physical. Senses. Transaction. Material. Health. Body.

"Hustlers and hard workers, they tend to be drawn to grounded nature. They're a touch overly practical and transactional if you ask me, but to their credit, they believe in healing the ills of the world with physical magic, namely science."

My eyes slide to Empress Amelia. Predictably, she lights up at this.

"Does psychology count there?" she asks.

"Indeed," Lady Azure says. "My own husband is drawn there, as a therapist. Though I'd say Seidon here belongs with the Sworn, rational and commanding."

SWORDS: Air. White. South. Autumn. // Gemini. Libra. Aquarius.
Rational. Logic. Warrior. Planning. Analysis. Clarity. Change.

"If Carson ever sorted an actual Sworn, I never heard of them. Grounded in reality and lifted by mindfulness, they are the monks on mountaintops. Thought to be lions of leadership, they are rumored to be some kind of 'Perilluminati.' Personally, I believe they're an ideal Carson devised, one that can never be fulfilled."

"That's actually awesome," Anwar says.

Lady Azure frowns in return. "Perhaps. But of course, I'm most partial to the Coupled, emotional and loving."

CUPS: Water. Blue. West. Winter. // Cancer. Scorpio. Pisces.
Emotional. Love. Relationships. Intuition. Connection. Tides.

"Valuing relationships above all else and drawn to bodies of water, we consider ourselves lilies, fronds floating on ponds, flowing with the tides. We are the most organized Corner, partially because of the value we place in human connection. Though if I'm honest, it's mostly because of my efforts. I organize meetings here every month, to carry on my Corner of Carson's tradition."

Hearing all this, half of me thinks it's fascinating. Then the other half thinks it's completely indulgent, especially the bits using Perilli's name.

"For a secretive organization, you sure do like explaining," Cleo says, smiling sweetly at Lady Azure.

"Well, my dear, as far as I'm concerned, possession of that deck entitles you to all the knowledge I have," Lady Azure responds. "I'd offer to do a Perillian reading to sort you all into Corners, but you've been in possession of Carson's final deck all this time. The power of the cards have likely already imbued you all."

My mind churns. As fascinating as this discussion is, we need to get back to the central question of this unraveling mystery: Why did Perilli's final deck really end up in our hands?

Something tells me that if Lady Azure has deeper answers, pulling them out of her might require a more subtle touch. So I need to dress this question up with a hook she can't resist.

◇ "I believe the tarot—and especially Perilli's deck—does hold **symbolic** power we don't yet understand," I begin. "But why do you think this deck was sent to empower us?"
Turn To Page 91

◇ "I think tarot cards hold only the power we decide to **invest** in them, subconsciously or willfully," I begin. "Which means this deck was sent to us with intention?"
Turn To Page 92

Whether Perilli meant Gran Flo to have this deck or she came to it by chance, there's a deeper reason we must possess it today. The cards have shaped so much in our lives, have offered so much wisdom and guidance and knowledge—now we're only just beginning to understand why.

Of course, all of this means we need to take Lady Azure seriously, and not just as an expert on Carson Perilli. Her readings, however they are devised, tap into the deeper fabric of the tapestry being woven here—into the deeper power these cards have to offer. The power we've already experienced.

But that's not the only reason to take Lady Azure seriously as a Perillian authority. I can also tell, pretty instantly, that she already has an answer to my delicately posed question.

Turn To Page 93

Whether Perilli meant Gran Flo to have this deck or she came to it by chance, there must be a rational reason why we have it today.

Perilli's cards might have shaped so much in our lives, might have offered so much wisdom and guidance and knowledge—but that's only because we have turned to them for such answers time and time again. Just like Lady Azure's tarot readings likely deal in facts instead of some cosmically divined intuition.

However, even if I don't believe Lady Azure possesses the kind of psychic gifts she claims, we still need to take her seriously as an expert on Carson Perilli.

Especially because I can tell right away she already has a clear answer to my complicated question.

Turn To Page 93

Lady Azure stares back at me, oceans seeming to brim behind her crystal blue eyes.

"Carson always said knowledge is like an onion. It's best peeled back in layers, each one better protected than the last—and each one more likely to bring you to tears." Lady Azure grins. "And I do believe you've all earned your next layer.

"Before he died a decade ago, I gifted Carson the guest house on our property, as a live-in studio to produce his tarot artwork and cultivate his teachings. It is there, at Coupled Cottage, where Carson spent many of his final years, creating the very deck you've brought here today."

"Wait. If you've never seen our deck before, how do you know he created it there?" Amelia asks.

"Perilli was famously secretive, even the times he lived as our guest," Lady Azure answers. "Indeed, I wouldn't have known about this final deck had he not asked to have it mailed to someone."

This revelation drops a silence, thick and icy, into the shop. The same question must occupy all of our minds.

"Do you have any records of where Perilli mailed the deck?" Logan asks, speaking the heart of the matter, as usual.

"Carson kept a file with this information, one he made us swear not to open until the deck finally returned. My husband keeps this file under lock and key so we're not tempted."

"You never opened it?" Cleo asks. "And you never tried to find this deck?"

"If you can believe anything about me, it's that I have complete reverence for Carson's ways," Lady Azure answers. "Besides, Carson assured me his final deck would return to Coupled Cottage. He also left very specific instructions for whoever did appear with it, to help them find the missing Princess of Cups."

"Does this location mean anything to you?" Amelia asks next, stepping forward with her phone. We all agreed keeping our phones on us would be smarter than leaving them in the shoebox, just in case. "This is supposed to be an uninhabited island."

"Yes, my parents paid handsomely to ensure it seems that way," Lady Azure says, glancing down at Amelia's phone. "They were perhaps even more secretive than Carson, so Baxter Manor isn't supposed to exist. Actually, its complete seclusion was precisely why it appealed so greatly to dear Carson."

"Wait, these coordinates point to your home?" Amelia asks, surprised.

"More precisely, they pinpoint Coupled Cottage, where the missing Princess of Cups is hidden," Lady Azure answers. "So, my dearest darlings, would you like to sojourn to the Isle of Baxter?"

Lady Azure then raises her arms, stretching them out so her caftan blows with the breeze. Chills run up my arms, despite myself. I look to the others and can tell they all feel the same. If we really are invited to the secret island estate of a wealthy family of Perillian patrons, what long-buried secrets might we unearth there?

"Well, my fair lady, we accept your invitation," Cleo answers first. "Because I spy with my little eye some Wanderers on their way here."

I turn, along with the others, to see a rusted red car turn down the street—one of the same cars we saw parked outside the inn when we left. Adrenaline bursts into my veins. Our hunch about the Wanderers checking for us here was right.

Suddenly a remote island getaway feels even more impossible to resist.

◆　◆　◆　◆

The next hour becomes a blur of some of the most surreal moments of my life, including yesterday's desert danger. We sneak out of Azure Tarot's back entrance into Charvan, then follow Lady Azure as she and Seidon drive to a private dock. We marvel as wrought-iron gates swing open for us, then we split up to board two luxury motorboats. I then find myself speeding off into the sunset with Seidon and Logan across the Pacific Ocean, riding the choppy waters without any clue where we're really headed.

When we finally arrive at the Isle of Baxter, we find it is indeed nestled within the chain of Channel Islands. As we approach, we separate from the boat carrying Lady Azure, Amelia, Cleo, and Anwar. Seidon says it's to reach a secondary dock, but Logan and I eye each other, sensing there must be a different reason.

Still, it's hard to feel anything other than amazed once Seidon piles us into a golf cart and drives us up a winding path to Baxter Manor. It turns out to be a sprawling Victorian mansion, complete with turrets and stained-glass windows.

Right now, as Logan and I step out of the cart and up to the mansion's grand staircase, we share another awed glance.

"Shouldn't we be meeting the others?" I ask, despite my excitement.

"We will," Seidon answers. "But Mom said I should take you to Dad's office first to unlock Uncle Carson's final deck file."

That's logical enough, but it still doesn't feel quite right. Could there be a deeper reason Lady Azure wants us separated, or am I just being paranoid? Either way, I remind myself we are guests here. Which means, for now, we have to play by the Baxters' rules—at least until we know what game is really being played. It'll be tempting to get caught up in the grandeur of this place, but I need to remember that we are also now effectively trapped here.

"So, Seidon," Logan says, pacing beside him a little cozier than I'd like, "I thought the Channel Islands were all national parks?"

"Most of them are. My family likes everyone to keep believing they're uninhabited," Seidon answers as we climb the central staircase. "You'll find that, here, fortune makes the impossible possible. Just like my mom's precious tarot."

"Forgive me," Logan says, "but it doesn't sound like you buy into all this."

"'This' being all the money, or the tarot?"

"Both."

Seidon sighs, looking at each of us—though the full weight of his gaze falls on Logan. I suddenly feel invisible, a sensation I've grown used to standing beside Logan all these years. What I'm not used to, however, is feeling like a third wheel.

Seidon and Logan probably have way more in common, at least on the surface. Logan is Trinidadian of African, Indian, and French descent, and from what we've seen of Seidon's parents, he has African and European genes as well. Logan and Seidon also both appear outwardly athletic—actually, I bet someone seeing the three of us would assume Logan and Seidon are the couple.

"I've never really known what to make of my family," Seidon says. "But doesn't everyone feel that way?"

"I hate to break it to you, but I don't think your family is much like anyone else's," Logan laughs.

By now, I can tell Logan has turned on the full wattage of his charm. I can't help but take it personally, but I also can't seem to bring myself to say anything. It's like the deeper we venture into this island, the further I fade.

"Fair enough," Seidon replies. "So how long have you two been together?"

"Just about two years," Logan answers, smiling over at me.

"I'm jealous," Seidon says, glancing at me before returning his attention to Logan. "I didn't even kiss a guy until I got to college last year."

"We're both off to college soon, too. This trip is a bit of a last hurrah."

"Why is that?"

"Well, we'll be on opposite coasts, and we've never done long distance."

Reaching the front door, I ponder whether I should insert myself into this conversation, but my footing feels a few steps behind. All my intellectualized confidence feels suddenly deflated. As if on cue, a blustery snap of wind rattles across the staircase, making me feel particularly thin and frail.

"Impressive that you're staying together," Seidon says, that longing tone returning to his voice.

"Well, we love each other," Logan answers, smiling at me again.

As always, it manages to warm me, despite everything else.

"We'll figure out how to make it work as we go," he finishes.

"Ever think about trying—" Seidon opens the front door and his eyes flicker between us once again "—I don't know, an open thing?"

My cheeks flush. I don't know what Seidon is poking at here, but no, we certainly have not thought about being with other people.

"Maybe," Logan answers. "I mean, we've talked about being flexible about what feels right as we go."

Hearing Logan's words, my insides freeze. Suddenly I am brittle again, liable to shatter.

"Wait," I finally manage. "What?"

CHAPTER SEVEN

AMELIA

EVER SINCE WE learned the prestigious origins of Grandma's deck, it has felt like we've fallen down a rabbit hole. Our latest tumble has brought us face to face with a stone-walled cottage—though "cottage" feels like the wrong word, since it's twice as big as my house. Coupled Cottage is many shades of weathered slate and covered in twisting vines. Something about it feels even more remote than this private island, like it's a shrine preserving an era long gone.

A gust of wind tears across the island, and I fight a chill by taking a sip of tea. Lady Azure brewed it for us on the arrival dock, claiming it was for the "arduous" golf cart ride across her property. Of course, there has been nothing arduous about this experience so far, except for this wind whipping up as the sun sets.

"I am so glad you invited me along today," Anwar whispers as we approach.

"Not too much for you?" I whisper back.

"Are you kidding? I might not know anything about the tarot, but spooky island mansions?" he says, grinning like a kid. "This is spectacular."

I smile up at Anwar. Spectacular is certainly one word for it, despite how far out it feels like we've sailed. I'm not thrilled Chase and Logan got separated from us, but Lady Azure promised that Seidon will bring them to Coupled Cottage after finding Perilli's locked file. I look over to check on Cleo, holding her still-full paper cup of tea, and she nods. Whatever she thinks, her poker face is on.

"If you don't mind, I'd like to wait for my daughter to join us," Lady Azure says. "She's an equally devoted Perillian."

"Perilli really must have meant a lot to you if you let him work and live here," Cleo begins. "It's kind of surprising you haven't offered to buy the deck."

"That offer stands, for the record," Lady Azure replies, turning to me. "But I assumed you'd never part with the deck, not after all you told me of your grandmother. After all, some things in life are far more valuable than money."

I look to Cleo—easy for Lady Azure to say, standing on her private island. Still, I don't disagree.

"Just how many wealthy Perillians are out there?" Cleo then presses.

"Not many. Which has worked to my advantage," Lady Azure says. "I see your encounter with Maggie left you cautious, but let me assure you, that old coward couldn't actually afford the deck. He probably offered a lowball bounty to get his paws on it, then planned to sell it for what it's really worth, to my infuriating competitor."

"Wait, you have a competing collector?" I ask. "Who?"

"I know their name, but not who they really are," Lady Azure continues. "This buyer has only surfaced recently, gobbling up every Perillian scrap they can, often over the price I offer. They always operate through proxies and go by the name 'Page Zain,' the Hebrew letter symbolizing the sword. Since Pages and Knights sometimes replace the tarot's Princesses and Princes, the name is a deep reference."

"While we're on the subject, what exactly does overpaying mean?" Cleo asks.

"Young Cleo, that deck is priceless," Lady Azure says. "Still, if we're talking brass tacks, I'd probably pay a few million for it, as a work of contemporary art alone."

I have to physically stop my jaw from dropping. Anwar has no such luck, choking on a mouthful of hot tea beside me. My heart starts racing. That is a lot of money. Not that I care about the price—I just know how much others do.

"If this deck is so valuable, why help us?" I ask.

"An astute question." Lady Azure pauses, sipping her own tea. "I hope, in return, you might allow me to spend some time with Carson's final deck. Conducting a reading and perhaps taking some pictures for my collection. It was Carson himself who declared me Coupled and fostered my clairvoyant talents. Any tools that might sharpen these skills and connect me deeper to Carson is all I am truly after."

Looking at Lady Azure, I'm not sure I believe a devotee like her would really settle for only that. Still, this answer seems fair enough.

"But truly, I am helping you because it was the express instruction Carson left us. I dare not dishonor him, for Carson's eyes are always upon the Isle of Baxter."

"You mean in the form of Coupled Cottage?" Anwar asks, still looking at the place like it's a carnival funhouse. I really hope his enthusiasm isn't misplaced.

"In a metaphoric manner, yes," Lady Azure says. "But also literally. Carson's spirit still resides here, because Coupled Cottage is where he drew his final breath."

My blood chills in my veins, slowing and sloshing.

◇ I **don't believe** in ghosts or hauntings, even if Perilli did pass away here. Lady Azure needs to know that.

Turn To Page 100

◇ I **do believe** in spirits of the deceased leaving traces here in our world, so I think what Lady Azure suggests is entirely possible—especially if Perilli actually died in Coupled Cottage.

Turn To Page 101

I understand the appeal of believing in ghosts, just like I understand the appeal of believing in a higher power or fate. But honestly, I think if anyone is being haunted, it's because they're just doing the haunting themselves. The human mind is a vastly powerful thing.

"Well, then, it's a good thing we don't believe in ghosts," I say, looking to Cleo.

"We most certainly do not," Cleo affirms.

I turn to Anwar next and am surprised to see him hesitate. I know we both love horror movies, but does he actually believe some of that stuff could be true?

"Then I suppose you're in for quite the awakening," Lady Azure says, letting Anwar off the hook. "At any rate, the time has come to tell you why we're awaiting the arrival of Lily, my eldest. Carson himself divined Lily's talent as a medium when she was just a child, so their connection from beyond the veil is particularly strong."

My eyes find Cleo's again. *Of course this family would claim to have a medium.* I admit, I've always found the idea of mediums to be compelling. I never believed they actually talk to ghosts, but I can't argue that they do seem to have some ability to perceive exactly what a person needs to hear from a deceased loved one, somehow.

"That is so cool," Anwar says. "I've always wanted to meet a medium."

Lady Azure smiles and Cleo rolls her eyes. I feel more like Cleo in this moment, but I try to give Anwar a smile. After all, part of me is also fascinated to meet a self-proclaimed medium for the first time . . .

Especially if we are about to enter an allegedly haunted house.

Turn To Page 102

To me, the idea of an afterlife is so different than the concept of a higher power. Death is simply a reality of life, and one of our most fundamental physical principles is that energy cannot be destroyed. We may not know where our energy goes when it leaves our bodies, but I think it's actually pretty rational to believe it's recycled somehow. I've always held reverence for the idea that spirits might still have ties to our physical world, as resonant energies transferring . . . somewhere.

Ghosts, to me, are an entirely separate manner. We all live half inside our memories, their reconstructed truths always shaping our perspectives. And what are memories, if not ghosts of a time past? I've always believed ghosts are all around us in the form of photos and videos and stories—and now smartphones.

Looking to Cleo, I already know she buys none of this ghostly stuff. Anwar, on the other hand, has turned a shade paler than normal. I know we both love horror movies, but does he actually believe some of that stuff could be true, too?

"Are you saying we're about to enter a real-life haunted house?" Anwar asks, staring at Lady Azure.

"I'm not sure I'd use those words exactly," Lady Azure answers. "But the time has come to tell you why we're awaiting the arrival of Lily, my eldest. Carson himself divined Lily's talent as a medium when she was just a child, so their connection from beyond the veil is particularly strong."

Once again, a wave of emotion passes through me. Not just because I do believe mediums exist, at least a few of them in the sea of scam artists. Mostly, I feel woozy because I've never actually met a real-life medium before . . .

And if Lady Azure's daughter is the real deal, then maybe she'll be able to deliver a message from Grandma?

Turn To Page 102

As if on cue, a twenty-something woman comes walking down the path from the main mansion, bracing against a fresh burst of wind. Lily is as striking as her brother and mother, with light brown skin and deep brown eyes. Unlike them, however, Lily appears completely modest, sporting simple clothes, a short pixie haircut, and no makeup.

"I came as soon as you called, Mom," Lily says, her voice low and melodic. "I can't believe this day has finally come. We're so happy to have you all here."

Introductions are made as Lily gives each of us a hug, smelling of lavender and jasmine. She seems to linger when hugging Cleo—long enough that Cleo steps back, seeming justifiably uncomfortable. What was that about?

"Now that Lily has arrived, we can begin," Lady Azure says. "Carson was sick for months before he died, so he had time to plan. He made us promise to help facilitate the discovery of his missing Cups royal when this day inevitably arrived. Carson always said Lily was our very own Princess of Cups, so he decided she alone must be the one to guide you to the missing masterpiece. Now knowing he drew us as the royal Cups in his final deck, this instruction makes even more sense."

"I was pretty young when Uncle Carson passed away," Lily picks up, "but I remember him promising that whoever came with his final deck would be special. And that they'd be worthy of passing the tests to unearth his final Princess."

Lily then pauses, perhaps for dramatic effect, but also because a particularly large wave batters the island's rocky shoreline nearby.

"So shall we?" Lily asks. "Into Perilli's Hall of Cups?"

I'm tempted to ask what kind of tests we'll face, but Lily simply strides forward. Lady Azure gestures for us to follow, a longing look occupying her face as we leave her behind.

Entering Coupled Cottage, the lights turn on, but it remains to be seen if anyone is truly home. Entering the quaint living room, which looks plucked right out of the English countryside, nothing feels haunted or abandoned about this house. It feels more like a museum, eerily clean and preserved—and somewhat generic, actually.

"First, we're supposed to visit Uncle Carson's studio space," Lily says, leading the way deeper into the house. "He left instructions locked away for you there."

"And all these years, none of you ever tried to unlock them?" Cleo asks.

"No, we didn't," Lily says. "Uncle Carson made us swear not to when he was alive, and then . . . in other ways since. Besides, Mom and I know we wouldn't get very far without the final deck. All the important clues are embedded in there, as you probably already know."

"So is Perilli here now?" Cleo asks. "I doubt he'd want to miss this."

"Do you mind if I ask your birthday?" Lily replies instead, ignoring Cleo's sarcasm. "Yours too, Amelia and Anwar."

Hearing our names spoken together like this somehow flushes me with a warm feeling. *Amelia and Anwar.* It does have a nice ring to it—but there will be time for that thought later. Instead, I answer Lily first, giving Cleo and Anwar the green light to follow with their own birthdays. I know this is probably part of Lily's medium routine, but I'm also pretty sure I know exactly what information she can pull from the tarot using our birthdays.

Lily then leads us through the back of the house to a great room. I quickly forget everything else as I take in this space. It's as if we've entered a tarot fever dream, one with charts and maps and diagrams everywhere. Volumes of tarot histories line the many bookshelves, along with dozens of different decks and guidebooks. Hand-painted artwork by Perilli hangs on every wall, and spiral sketchbooks sit piled all over the floor. Crystals and keychains and charms hang from the ceiling, all in the recognizable shapes of tarot symbolism. Now, this space definitely screams den of tarot occult masterpieces.

"Welcome to Perilli's Workshop," Lily begins. "Uncle Carson, please meet Cleo The High Priestess, Anwar The Hanged Man, and, of course, Amelia The Empress."

Just then, the lights in the workshop dim as another gust of wind barrels around the cottage. It only lasts a moment, but it's hard not to note the timing. I look to Cleo and Anwar for reactions, but find completely opposite expressions on their faces. Anwar looks freaked out and awed, while Cleo's skepticism seems to have boiled over into . . . something else.

"Actually, I don't really do the whole Priestess thing," Cleo says. "I don't buy into how the tarot is built to be so binary."

"Oh, I'm sorry," Lily replies. "What pronouns do you prefer?"

"*She* and *her* are fine," Cleo answers. "I just don't like being put into boxes."

"I could tell that about you from the moment we met," Lily says. "So if you don't mind my asking, why not use less binary pronouns?"

"Because pronouns don't define her," I say, feeling instantly defensive. It was only this past year Cleo started exploring her most authentic identity, experimenting with a more androgynous and evolving presentation of her gender. Sometimes I worry Cleo keeps female pronouns because it's easier than correcting everyone all the time, but I'd never presume to push her on this the way Lily just did.

"It's okay, Amelia," Cleo says, turning to Lily. "Pronouns might not define me, but I respect every individual's right to choose identifications that feel right."

Lily pauses before responding. "I totally understand. I'm a trans woman myself, so female pronouns mean everything to me. I sometimes forget my experience doesn't translate to everyone else's."

Cleo looks like she wants to respond but doesn't know what to say. We've had a few conversations about how she hasn't really had the opportunity to connect with anyone else who identifies outside the binary gender poles, at least not in person this way. We might be getting a little sidetracked here, but I know this is too important to Cleo to brush aside. Anwar must also sense this, because he begins to wander off, pretending to look at the compiled objects to give us some space.

"Still, The High Priestess might suit you more than you think," Lily says. "She embodies the truth that, to make personal progress, we must reconcile oppositions within ourselves—including the spectrum between the masculine and feminine pillars of the tarot. But The Priestess's reversal is failing to make proper use of her knowledge, blinded by the privilege of possessing it."

Lily says all this with a melodic lilt in her voice, almost as if singing. As she does, the entire house creaks from the wind, the walls themselves seeming to groan. The lights do not dim this time, however—a detail I note while paying close attention to Cleo. I know she can handle this on her own, but I want her to know I have her back. Always.

"I'm still not sure what you're trying to insinuate, but while we're imparting unsolicited wisdom," Cleo begins, "I just think it's human nature to box things in, because we think it makes them more reliable. But when we accept that everything eventually changes, that's when we learn to rely only on ourselves instead of any labels."

"Yes, the tarot captures this fluidity beautifully, just as you do," Lily replies. "That's all I meant to say. Forgive me if I overstepped. I tend to do that. Often."

"Well, thanks for the apology," Cleo responds. She looks at me next and I can tell she's very ready for this conversation to end.

"My grandma had a mantra," I jump in. "*Flowing will get you places forcing never could.* It fit because her name was Florence and everyone called her Flo, but it also encapsulated her outlook on life. And her outlook on reading the tarot."

"Your grandma sounds like she was a smart woman," Lily says, taking the hint. "Anyway, I suppose that brings us to our first moment of truth."

Lily points to a small chest in the center of the studio and moves toward it. I turn to Cleo before following, but she just takes a deep breath and nods at me again.

"This chest holds the instructions on how to use the deck to find the missing card," Lily explains. "Before you open it, I'm told there's something you must know."

Lily clears her throat, closing her eyes for a moment. It's almost like she listens to the wind whining around the house, but maybe she's just gathering her thoughts? Either way, the sight reminds me distinctly of Lady Azure.

"Are you listening to your Uncle Carson?" Anwar asks.

"I can't always tell," Lily sighs. "Uncle Carson understood how this felt. He didn't like to talk about his gift either, because of how it made him sound. But he said he began having visions later in life. He described them as flashes, glimpses into a deeper world of the tarot. He believed that this world might be coming—and he began painting his decks to capture these visions."

Suddenly I think of Cain the Wanderer, who believed in baptismal rituals and perilous tidings. Do the Coupled believe the same about Perilli's decks?

"What Uncle Carson meant by this new world is a matter of debate among the Perillian Corners," Lily continues. "But most agree there could be answers in his final deck and their missing cards. Many also believe these will somehow identify The Arcere, the one meant to follow in Uncle Carson's footsteps."

I tense. As if the perceived value of this deck wasn't enough, now it's also the key to decoding some lost Perillian prophecy? I look over at Cleo once again to ground myself. Sure enough, she still looks completely skeptical, believing this to be a rehearsed act. Meanwhile, Anwar looks like he hangs on Lily's every word.

"Do you really believe all that?" It's the only question I can think to ask.

"I used to think my mom and the others were just eccentric," Lily answers, looking me right in the eyes. "But then getting to know Uncle Carson before he died, despite being so young—I could tell he was just so genuine and earnest in his passion for the tarot. If nothing else, I believe in him."

"But if Perilli was so earnest and genuine, why did he operate with such secrecy?" I try. "Could it also be that he was intentionally trying to draw people in?"

"I don't know," Lily sighs again. "But I do know he always said the tarot that channeled through him scared him a little. He was never so sure it was really all his to share. I can understand that much, at least.

"But really, it doesn't matter if you believe any of this. My mom and I have been waiting years to see if this final deck ever returned home, as Uncle Carson promised. Amelia, as the deck's owner, it must be you who opens the chest. To do so, you must make your intentions known. So I ask you now: Inside this chest, what is it you really hope to find?"

Finally, a question I have a very clear answer to.

♦ "I seek the missing tarot to **honor** my grandma's **legacy**."
Turn To Page 107
♦ "I seek the missing tarot to understand my own **personal power**."
Turn To Page 108

As I say these words out loud, I do my best to conjure a clear memory of Grandma. I close my eyes and see her in my mind, her tidy gray hair and bright eyes. When I picture her, she's always greeting me as I come home from school, most days with Chase at my side. That was our time, the first hour after school, when Grandma would sit smiling with some prepared snack, asking how we were doing. She always smelled of flowers and would have some insightful words to offer.

This image brings tears to my closed eyes. Really, Grandma always reminded me of the person I want to be: warm and supportive, but firm and honest. If any part of this tarot trip can strengthen those parts, then it'll all be worth it. But I can't resist the idea that this trip might also bring me closer to Grandma in other ways, that it might teach me something about this woman I thought I already knew inside out.

"Keep walking through, little Dalet."

Lily says these words and my stomach flips over. Suddenly there's a buzzing in my ears, a rushing sound that grows louder with each second.

"Does that mean anything to you?" Lily asks. "It's the only voice I can hear coming through. It keeps repeating that same phrase."

Opening my eyes, I find it impossible to summon words. Instead, I reach into my pocket and pull out the Dalet locket, the one Grandma gave me.

"Oh," Lily replies, looking awestruck herself.

"Amelia's grandmother gave that to her, which you must have known somehow," Cleo says, taking her turn to rush to my defense. "Amelia, didn't you always say Dalet was traditionally associated with The Empress?"

I nod, still unable to muster words. I can see where Cleo is headed, suggesting Lily made this clever connection knowing my Major Arcana expression. It's a leap, but it's possible. A greater leap still—is Lily really communicating with Grandma?

"Is there . . . anything else?" I manage.

"I'm sorry, that's all I hear," Lily answers, frowning. "But I've stared at this chest there long enough to know Dalet is on it. It's one of the lock button options."

My insides freeze again. I know what I believed about mediums before, but hearing Lily's latest words, I don't know if it muddies the waters or clears them.

Turn To Page 109

As I say the words out loud, another gust of wind batters the cottage's walls, causing the lights to flicker violently. They come on and off in bright bursts, so I close my eyes to press out the flashing. When I do, I see a vision so vivid, I gasp.

In the blackness I see a globe with four half-hemispheres: flaming, flowing, growing, and sweeping. I open my eyes to make it stop, but the globe imprints on the workshop wall, like a projector blinking. The colors bleed as the lights flash again, then I see figures on the globe. Cleo appears in a color-blocked tunic holding a flowing cup. Chase appears wielding an ice-white sword, then Logan waving a fiery wand. Finally, Anwar swings upside down from a tree. The lights flicker one last time and I see myself under this tree, holding a green coin that bears one symbol:

Dalet, the Hebrew letter on the locket Grandma gave me.

I see all of this, but do I really see none of it? As the wind stops and the lights stop flickering, this vision on the wall disappears—if that's what it was.

"Amelia, are you okay?" Cleo asks, suddenly at my side.

I don't know how to explain what I just saw. Nothing like that has ever happened to me before. Is my imagination playing tricks? Is exhaustion setting in from not sleeping last night? Or did I just have some kind of haunted tarot vision?

"You saw something, didn't you?" Lily asks, pressing forward.

"Were you expecting her to?" Cleo says, taking her turn to rush to my defense. "Helped along by the lights routine and Lady Azure's dockside tea?"

Wait, is Cleo . . . Does she think maybe there was something slipped in my tea? Is that why she never drank any? But everyone else was drinking the tea, Lady Azure included. I turn to Anwar and he shakes his head as if to say he feels fine.

"I won't even dignify that with a response," Lily says, anger flashing through her for the first time. "Amelia, that chest has three Hebrew letters on its lock. Is there any chance you saw one of those?"

Looking down, I am once again stunned to see Dalet as one of the lock options. My heart races so fast, all I can hear is it pounding in my ears. I know what I believed about all this psychic stuff before, but could Perilli's tarot, his house, his cards— could they really be affecting me somehow?

Turn To Page 109

"Uncle Carson claimed only one button will open the chest," Lily offers. "He also said pressing the wrong button will lock it forever."

"Well, that explains why you haven't tried opening it," Anwar replies. "Though I guess you all never heard of hammers or crowbars?"

Anwar releases a nervous burst of laughter, but the rest of us are too—whatever we are—to join in. Still, I offer him a small smile.

"Uncle Carson said the person who came with the deck would know which button to press," Lily continues. "And it sounds like you do, Amelia?"

Standing in front of the chest, I see it has three buttons, each one bearing a different Hebrew letter: Gimmel, Tau, and Dalet. Suddenly, I don't care what's real or fake, what's prophetic or set up. All I care about is finding what we came here for.

So I step up to the chest. Without hesitation, I then press the Dalet button on the lock. I move so quickly, Lily tries to warn me against being too impulsive. But it turns out she doesn't need to.

The moment I release my finger from the button, the chest swings open.

In the next second, the lights sputter out, leaving us in complete darkness.

Minutes later, after Lily tries and fails to reset the circuit breaker, we follow her up a narrow flight of stairs using the flashlights from our phones. My heart skips another beat as something loud bangs in the walls of this darkened staircase. I can already feel the panic stirring in my chest. I'm tempted to tug at my hair to calm the nervous energy, but instead my hands clutch what we found inside the chest: a scroll, which Lily said we needed to read upstairs, in the "Hall of Cups."

"Does the heat always make this much noise trying to come back on?" Anwar asks, sounding genuinely spooked. I don't blame him.

"No," Lily says, perhaps predictably.

At the top of the stairs I expect to enter another grand floor of Coupled Cottage. Instead, we are met with a solid blue wall set with two wooden doors, each boasting an intricate carving.

"Mom had the upper floors modified for Uncle Carson to protect the Princess of Cups," Lily explains. "None of us have ever seen the design, but Uncle Carson said it's a maze inspired by The Sephirot, the Kabbalistic Tree of Life. Ten circles joined by twenty-two crossing pathways, which line up neatly not only with the ten numbers of the Minor Arcana and the twenty-two Major Arcana, but also the twenty-two letters in the Hebrew Alphabet."

"Wait—the Princess of Cups is hidden in a mystic Jewish labyrinth?"

The words fly out of my mouth. I instantly think of Chase. I still can't believe he's not here for this, because he'd definitely be nerding out over these historical puzzles.

"Beyond this wall, the layout is a simplified version of The Sephirot," Lily explains. "And before Cleo can ask, no, we've never gone inside. Uncle Carson made it very clear that only the person possessing the deck may enter. If they succeed, they will find the card. But if they fail, the Princess of Cups will be destroyed."

I know the impact Lily's latest news is meant to deliver, but I find my reserves of shock and awe have been depleted.

"I'm ready," I say, stepping up to the first door. "How does this work?"

"Unroll the scroll," Lily instructs.

Doing as she says, I find the scroll has two parts. The first is a list of symbols. Next to it is an empty column titled "Major Arcana Codex." Instantly, I realize we need to use the symbols on the deck to match the Major Arcana.

"Cleo, can I have a pen and the deck?" I ask.

Cleo opens her backpack to give me both. Then, by the phone flashlight and with everyone gazing over my shoulder, I fill in the codex:

0		The Fool
1		The Magician

2		**The High Priestess**
3		**The Empress**
4		**The Emperor**
5		**The Hierophant**
6		**The Lovers**

7		The Chariot
8		Justice
9		The Hermit
10		Wheel of Fortune
11		Strength

12		The Hanged Man
13		Death
14		Temperance
15		The Devil
16		The Tower

17		The Star
18		The Moon
19		The Sun
20		Judgment
21		The World

Once I finish, I stuff the pen and deck back in Cleo's backpack, then turn to the second part of the scroll. It's a list of questions, the first reading: *Door One: Where do you find life's most important wisdom?*

"The symbols that answer the questions are on each door," Lily says. "You'll need to use the scroll codex to translate the symbols into the Major Arcana card, then decide which one best answers each question. You'll follow that process until you reach the end of the maze."

As Lily finishes, I turn my flashlight to the two symbols mounted in bronze metal. One door has a lighthouse, while the other has an ornate key. Looking to the scroll codex, I see the first symbol corresponds to The Tower, the tarot card that represents a crisis of faith. The Tower's lightning and fire can destroy the existing, but they can also illuminate an escape. Meanwhile, the second symbol corresponds to The Hermit, which represents a call for solitary contemplation. The Hermit signals a more demanding phase of a journey, implying we only have ourselves to rely on.

"Once you enter the maze, Amelia, you'll be on your own," Lily says. "But since we're here with you for this first step—"

Just then, a loud noise groans from the floor beneath us, and the lights flicker back on. In the same moment, I swear I see the writing on the scroll float off of the page and onto the wall, melting and swirling into its deep blueness. In the next second, the lights flicker back out and the writing all disappears. Blinking, I convince myself this was just my eyes playing tricks on me . . .

"As I was saying," Lily continues, "I'm told the answer lies in The Tower."

I turn to Lily, our flashlights casting sharp shadows across her face. I didn't expect such direct guidance from her, given the whole "you must enter alone" routine. Nor does she offer the source of her "advice."

"I still don't know much about the tarot," Anwar jumps in. "And I'm not sure my opinion should matter here, but I think we can trust Lily after all she has done to help, right?"

"And I think you should go with your gut, Amelia," Cleo immediately adds. Her eyes pour into mine in the semidarkness, communicating the subtext behind her words: she still does not trust Lily.

Great. As if there wasn't already enough riding on this decision, now it will also be about choosing between Lily-Anwar and Cleo. Looking at them all, I curl a thick strand of hair between my thumb and forefinger, nerves jangling all the way through me. But then, suddenly, I force my hand away and make a decision. If I can't fight the adrenaline, then I might as well use it.

Because if anyone is equipped to interpret or channel Perilli's deck, it's me.

Where do you find life's most important wisdom?

Strapping Cleo's backpack on and clutching both the scroll and my phone's flashlight, I make my first choice.

◊ I open the 🗼 door.
Turn To Page 117

◊ I open the 🗝 door.
Turn To Page 118

I walk through this first door and it closes behind me with a heavy thud. I don't check the knob to see if it has locked, because if I am trapped in here, I don't particularly want to know. Instead, I raise my phone's flashlight and find myself facing a narrow hallway. My breath catches in my throat—small spaces aren't my favorite. The darkness doesn't help, pressing in thickly all around me. Still, I step forward, because I already decided my anxiety has to charge me forward, not hold me back.

The hallway soon opens into a new room, which has another set of doors on its far wall. I move to examine these doors, but as I walk farther inside, I suddenly notice this room's ceiling is covered with glow-in-the-dark stickers. Pinkish fiery suns and yellowish lightning bolts create a shining sky of faded stars. I pause to take them in and quickly realize they're shaped like . . .

A tower.

The floorboards creak loudly as I rock back and forth on my feet, absorbing the blurred image above me. I wonder when was the last time anyone looked at these shapes—and who were they really intended for?

Letting these questions roll away, I illuminate the symbols on *Door Two*, then I find the corresponding prompt on the scroll: *In what force should you trust?* Finally, I look up their Major Arcana meanings on the scroll's codex.

◇ I open the 🦌 door.
Turn To Page 119

◇ I open the 🌐 door.
Turn To Page 120

I walk through this first door and it closes behind me with a startling quickness, like it's spring loaded—which it very well might be. After all, once you enter a maze, you shouldn't be able to go backward.

Holding up my phone's flashlight, I quickly find this room is filled with a large tent—one I'm going to have to move through. Taking a deep breath and bracing myself, I really wish I didn't have to do this in the semidarkness. Still, I reach for the zipper to open the tent's entrance. I already decided my anxiety has to charge me forward, not hold me back.

Stepping inside, the flashlight illuminates thick strokes of paint covering nearly every inch of the tent walls. Tallies and symbols are written everywhere, looking like the scrawlings of a prisoner. The tent walls also billow back and forth, either from my movement or some unseen draft, making the writing look like it comes alive. Immediately I feel overwhelmed, like I might get trapped in here. All I want to do is find my way out.

Trying not to grow too frantic, I paw for the zipper at the other end of the tent. Climbing out, I find it opens into a short hallway. The hallway soon opens into a new room, which has another set of doors on its far wall marked *Door Three*.

I then look to the corresponding prompt on the scroll: *What moves you forward fastest?* Finally, I look up their Major Arcana meanings on the scroll's codex.

◊ I open the ⚙ door.
Turn To Page 120
◊ I open the ⚐ door.
Turn To Page 121

I walk through this door and find myself in another hallway, this one much longer and narrower than the last. And much . . . hotter? Suddenly it feels like I've entered an inferno. Could that be by design? Or is this hallway just conveniently set over some ancient boiler, which would also explain the loud banging coming through the floorboards?

Either way, it feels fitting, given that this is The Devil's room. Looking up, I also see this hallway is painted an ominous, warning-sign red. Most think of The Devil as being evil, but nothing is ever that one-sided in the tarot. The Devil reminds us that sometimes we need negativity to inspire us, because we can't ever really appreciate the light without the darkness. Clearly, I decided to trust in this force, especially given my current situation.

But as I reach the next room, I think maybe I shouldn't have. Something in here suddenly smells ungodly. As I enter this room at the end of The Devil's corridor, I realize what: there's a dead raccoon in here . . .

One crawling with wriggling maggots.

I fight the urge to vomit, instead turning to the next wall of doors. Is this rotting carcass here because no one has been through these rooms in years? Or was it somehow left here on purpose? Not really wanting to know the answer, I realize there's actually only one door set into this next wall, painted purple.

◇ I walk through this singular **purple door**.
Turn To Page 126

I walk through and find myself in another long room. I also notice there happens to be a second door beside the one I entered through, which means multiple symbols must lead in here.

My eye is immediately drawn to a small sculpture in the center of this room. Looking over its smoothed curves more closely, I realize it's a chariot carrying a globe—two of the most clearly defined tarot figures.

The World completes the Major Arcana journey, signaling that every ending is a beginning. Meanwhile, The Chariot represents movement and reflecting on the distance traveled in a journey. Taken together, I realize these cards actually represent a reconciliation of opposites: the journey and the destination, descending and ascending, ending and beginning—which are all really the same thing in the universe of the tarot.

Taking in this sculpture, a sense of serenity washes over me. It's a very welcome sensation, given the couple of days we've had. If only I could dwell in here a little longer, to calm my racing nerves.

But I know it's time to answer the question for *Door Four*: *Who are you?*

◊ I open the ▮ door.
   Turn To Page 122
◊ I open the ✦ door.
   Turn To Page 123

Walking into the next room, I actually find it's much more of a hallway, curving into an unseen bend. I hope this is a good sign, considering I'm supposed to follow the path that leads me forward. Really, I chose this door because Grandma's Major Arcana expression was The Lovers. How could I not honor her by choosing her doorway?

As I make my way in the semidarkness around the curving hallway, I find it leads to another wall with doors. But I also spot something that freezes me in place: two figures standing on either side of the doors, elongated and misshapen. At first I'm convinced someone is standing there, some incorporeal form . . .

Until I realize the figures are just painted, abstract outlines of two humans.

Feeling somewhat haunted by these looming figures, I focus instead on the scroll question for *Door Five*: *What matters more?*

◇ I open the ⚖ door.
   Turn To Page 124
◇ I open the 🏕 door.
   Turn To Page 125

Who am I? I am The Empress, of course.

As I walk through the doorway of my expression, my only question is whether Perilli was just as taken with The Empress, or if he somehow intended for me to be the one walking these maze halls?

Whatever the truth is, I do feel at home in this next twisting room. It's full of fake plants, since theoretically no one would be allowed in to water real ones. Still, the point is taken. I've entered Mother Nature's transformative doorway, walking through representations of her green grandeur.

As I do walk though, the lights flicker violently once again, trying to come back on. I close my eyes, waiting for the flickering to pass. After a few moments it does, returning me to darkness. Using my flashlight, I find the next wall . . .

Which has only one door set into it, painted blue.

◊ I walk through this singular **blue door**.
Turn To Page 129

Who am I? Just like I felt at the start of this journey, I fancy myself The Fool. I am one who seeks the road less traveled, one who will ask the hard questions to find the answers I seek. Perilli's own booklet quote on The Fool snaps into my brain, one of the few I committed to memory on our sleepless overnight drive: *The Fool is dissatisfied with the superficial things that please most people, seeking something deeper.*

I find that, in this room, seeking something deeper will mean doing something I'd really rather not. Just ahead of me in this dark room is a plastic tube tunnel, the kind children play inside. It leads through a wall into the next room.

Anxiety pings in my brain again as I think of how eerie and silent, how insulated and cramped that tunnel will be. I reach my hand up to play with my hair, but then force that feeling away again.

After all, I chose this hard path, fool that I am.

The crawl into the next room is indeed tight, but it's also fast—and oddly freeing. Once through the tunnel, I examine this next room from the floor. Once I do, I find there's only one door left for me to walk through, painted purple.

◇ I walk through this singular **purple door**.
Turn To Page 126

What matters more? That answer is pretty simple—what matters more than anything, really? Justice.

The decision to walk through this doorway was an easy one. The tarot's Justice card calls for a careful examination and good judgment, not just of others, but also of ourselves. Appropriately, this entire room is painted half in pitch black and half in stark white, while the path through the middle remains gray.

This feels especially fitting, as more gusts of wind bash against the walls outside. After all, the only path forward we usually have is the solitary gray one.

Walking this path leads me to the next wall, where I find only one final door, painted blue.

◇ I walk through this singular **blue door**.
Turn To Page 129

What matters more? That answer is pretty simple—what matters more than anything, really? Strength.

The decision to walk through this doorway was an easy one. Especially because the tarot's call for Strength doesn't require brute force. Instead, it suggests that sometimes the truest strength comes from being gentle and kind. Which is probably why, in the center of this next room, a giant open palm is painted on the floor, covering a clenched fist.

Since Strength stands for unexpected solutions to a problem, I figured this might be the cleverest path forward. However, crossing this particular room, the house seems to come alive all around me, banging and clanging louder than ever. It almost feels like I really have entered some kind of horror house, as if the walls themselves are cautioning me to turn back.

Then again, perhaps this is just another sign that I require unique strength to continue forward.

Coming to the next wall, I find only one final door, painted purple.

◊ I walk through this singular **purple door**.
Turn To Page 126

I press my hand to the purple painted wood and see it also has an inscription printed in bronze. It's not just one symbol, though, like the other doors. I recognize this writing as half of the quote for the Princess of Cups listed in Perilli's booklet. It reads: *Rise above jealousy, manipulation, and possession.* Beside each emotion, the symbols for The Devil, The Fool, and Strength appear. Whatever else this means, it must mean I'm close.

I walk through the door and I am faced with another room, one that has several other doors leading inside along the near wall. On the far wall, however, is another single purple door—which must make this some kind of funneled outlet. Approaching the final door, I wonder if I'm about to find treasure or ruin.

I enter another darkened space and hear a metallic shift and a soft clunk. Shining my flashlight around, I see there's no new door in here, just a set of stairs that must lead out of the maze and into the attic. Then I see something that makes my heart stop. Positioned in the center of the room . . .

A fish tank filled with water. There's a compartment above this tank, one that has a wire leading back to the door I just entered through. Then, shining the flashlight down, I see the Princess of Cups card floating in the water inside. Then I realize it can't be just water, because the card disintegrates far faster than it should.

I rush up to the tank, looking for some way to save the drowning Princess. But I realize the trigger-switch on the purple door I entered through not only dunked the card, it also locked the tank lid in place. Looking back, I see a second blue door also leads into this room—without any trigger. Somewhere, according to Carson Perilli, I must have chosen the wrong path. The Princess will now be destroyed in a matter of seconds, and there's nothing I can do about it.

I pore my eyes over the disappearing card while I still can. I find the Princess has been painted to resemble Lily, just like the rest of the Baxter Cups royals. Instead of her usual flowing femininity, this Princess has Lily's simple style and short hair. She holds a cup on her stomach as she floats face up on the surface of the ocean. This is the last thing I see before the Princess of Cups vanishes, lost in the water forever.

Part of me wants to linger beside the tank as an act of grief, or reverence, or maybe both. But a far larger part of me wants to get the hell out of this fraught maze.

So I stride forward across the room and climb the stairs, feeling heavier with each step. Once I reach the top I find myself in a vaulted attic that smells of cedar and sawdust. Moonlight spills in through windows, making it slightly less dark, but I still shine my flashlight across the space. First I see another staircase at the opposite end, one that must lead back into the house. I let out a scream, however, when I see what waits between me and that exit.

Lady Azure stands and stares at me, looking almost like a ghost herself.

"Did you secure the Princess of Cups?" she asks, her voice low and steady.

I shake my head, raising my hand to cover my mouth. That's when I hear a banging coming from across the attic, traveling up the second set of stairs. I also hear muffled voices and a doorknob rattling. Could that be Lily, Cleo, and Anwar?

"Oh, thank the goddess," Lady Azure then cries out. I shine my flashlight back on her and it's only then I realize she seems to be crying tears of . . . joy?

"Carson's beloved Princess, the source of our powers. It's ours forever."

My heart sinks. Suddenly I feel like the drowned Princess myself, plunged into unexpected waters against my will.

"But the card," I try, "it's destroyed."

"Dead things don't really die, little girl." Lady Azure speaks almost in a chant, her head down. "Here in the Isle of Baxter, the energy resides."

My skin prickles cold. Suddenly I feel sick.

"You . . . this is what you wanted all along?"

"Our talents sharpened after Carson hid this card on our island. I would never disrespect Carson's wishes. I never entered the maze below our feet, but I sat up here often, soaking in the presence of Carson's hidden card. We did follow his instructions to the letter, but you are correct."

Lady Azure raises her face then, her tearful eyes connecting with mine.

"This is indeed the outcome I desired."

A wave of realization crashes over me. Details soak into my skull, running through our time with Lady Azure. Her tarot readings. Our group's separation. Her "herbal" tea. The flickering lights. Her presence here in this attic outlet, blocking the others. Where does the line between Carson Perilli and Lady Azure lie?

I don't know the answers to this question. All I do know, with a sudden surge, is that we have to get off of this tragic island as fast as possible. I clutch the scroll in my hand against the straps of Cleo's backpack, because who knows what else Lady Azure wants to take from our visit.

Just then, there's a bang across the attic as the exit door flies open.

"Amelia, are you all right?" Cleo asks, rushing to my side.

"We came up here to try to meet you, but the door was locked," Anwar adds. "It took me forever, but I picked the lock."

"We need to go," I whisper back to them. "Now."

"Mom, what are you doing?" Lily asks. "Why did you lock us out?"

"It's done. The Princess of Cups is ours, floating in the flow of the Isle forever," Lady Azure answers.

"What?" Lily responds. "You're not making sense."

"The card is destroyed. Which means it can never leave. Don't you see what this signifies? These cards really belong to us, Lily."

Lily stares back at her mother, looking horrified.

"No," Lily says. "They don't."

Lily's eyes then flutter, like she is putting the pieces together. Or . . . listening? Either way, she turns to us next.

"Take the stairs to the basement, then use the exit down there. I texted Seidon to meet you. He'll take you and the others back."

"No!" Lady Azure cries. "We have to see the final deck! Now that—"

"If you love me," Lily interrupts, turning back to her mother with icy intensity, "you will let them go."

Lady Azure appears thunderstruck. In the same second, Cleo takes my hand and walks forward. She knows this is our window, while Lady Azure is uncertain.

"You have to let this go now," Lily adds. "It's enough."

We make it to the stairs before we can hear Lady Azure's response, or before we can say anything to Lily. As we rush down through the levels of Coupled Cottage, I can only hope that Lady Azure doesn't try to follow us.

Turn To Page 132

I press my hand to this blue door and see it also has an inscription printed in bronze. It's not just one symbol, though, like the other doors. I recognize this writing as half of the quote for the Princess of Cups listed in Perilli's booklet. It reads: *It's time to awaken to something new.* Whatever else this means, it must mean I'm close.

I walk through and am faced with another room, one that has several other doors leading inside along the near wall. On the far wall, however, is another single blue door—which makes this some kind of funneled outlet. Approaching the final door, I can't help but wonder if I'm about to find treasure or ruin.

I enter another darkened space and shine my flashlight. There's not a door in here, just a set of stairs that must lead out of the maze and into the attic. Then I see something that makes my heart stop. Positioned in the center of the room . . .

A fish tank filled with water. There's a compartment above this tank, one that has a wire leading back to a second purple door that leads in here. Shining the light on that compartment, I see the Princess of Cups hanging above the tank.

With a sigh of relief, I realize that I chose correctly, at least according to Carson Perilli. If I had somehow entered through that purple door, it would have dunked the Princess into the tank. Understanding how thin this line remains, I rush forward to grab the card before anything tragic can happen to it.

Holding the lost Princess of Cups in my hands, I see she has been painted to resemble Lily, just like the rest of the Baxter Cups royals. Instead of her usual flowing femininity, this Princess has Lily's simple style and short hair. She holds a cup on her stomach as she floats face up on the surface of the ocean. I then make out a symbol painted lightly on this cup: the Hebrew letter Mem.

Part of me wants to linger beside the tank and soak in my success, but I know it's time to leave. I stride forward and climb the stairs, feeling lighter with each step. At the top I find a vaulted attic that smells of cedar and sawdust. Moonlight spills in through the windows, making it slightly less dark, but still I shine my flashlight across the space. First I see another staircase at the opposite end, one that must lead back into the house. I gasp, however, when I see what waits between me and that exit.

Lady Azure stands and stares at me, looking almost like a ghost herself.

"Did you secure the Princess of Cups?" she asks, before her eyes travel down to see the card grasped in my hand. That's when I hear a banging coming from across the attic, traveling up the second set of stairs. I also hear muffled voices and a doorknob rattling. Could that be Lily, Cleo, and Anwar? Why would Lady Azure block them from meeting me this way?

"Carson's Princess, the source of our powers. The heart of the Isle of Baxter," Lady Azure begins, tears sliding down her cheeks. "You weren't supposed to . . ."

My skin prickles cold. Suddenly I feel sick.

"You must understand, the Princess belongs here," Lady Azure pleads, her watery eyes boring into me.

"You . . . you never wanted me to find the card, did you?" I ask.

"Our talents sharpened after Carson hid this card on our island. I would never disrespect Carson's wishes. I never entered the maze below our feet, but I sat up here often, soaking in the presence of Carson's hidden card."

Lady Azure looks away from me then, her eyes falling to the floor. "But I cannot let go of this final gift. I would have preferred it destroyed, its energy resonating here forever."

A wave of realization crashes over me. Details soak into my skull, running through our time with Lady Azure. Her tarot readings. Our group's separation. Her "herbal" tea. The flickering lights. Her presence here in this attic outlet, blocking the others. Where do the plans of Carson Perilli end and the plans of Lady Azure begin?

I don't know the answer to this question. All I do know, with a sudden surge, is that I'm trapped in a dark attic, at the end of a locked maze, with a resourceful fraud, stranded on her desolate island. I flatten the card in my hand against the strap of Cleo's backpack, because who knows if the Princess is the only thing Lady Azure wants to take from me.

"You know what I expected in return for my guidance," Lady Azure says, turning from flowing to icy as she creeps forward. "You trust I know what Carson would've wanted, don't you? You know this was his home, his final resting place."

I recoil backward, trying to get away from Lady Azure. Then, suddenly, there's a loud bang from the exit door flying open.

"Amelia, are you all right?" Cleo asks, running up and rushing to my side.

"We came up here to try to meet you, but the door was locked," Anwar follows. "It took me forever, but I picked the lock."

"We need to go," I whisper back to them. "Now."

"Mom, what are you doing?" Lily asks, placing herself between us and Lady Azure. "Why did you lock us out?"

"Lily, she has your card in her hands, the source of our gifts," Lady Azure answers. "Amelia must understand that card belongs to you. To us."

Lily stares back at her mother, looking horrified.

"No," Lily says. "It doesn't."

Lily's eyes then flutter, like she is putting the pieces together. Or . . . listening? Either way, she turns to us next.

"Take the stairs to the basement. Then use the exit down there. I texted Seidon to meet you. He'll take you and the others back."

"No!" Lady Azure cries. "We have to see the final deck! Now that—"

Lady Azure freezes, however, as Lily grabs her wrist. She sets her eyes on her mother with a glare so intense, it gives me a chill. "Uncle Carson would be ashamed."

Hearing these words, Lady Azure appears thunderstruck. In the same second, Cleo takes my hand and walks forward. She knows this is our window, while Lily has Lady Azure filled with doubt.

"You have to let this go now," Lily adds. "Not everything is yours to own."

We make it to the stairs before we can hear Lady Azure's response, or before we can say anything to Lily. As we begin to rush down through Couple Cottage, I can only hope one thing:

That Lily can keep her mother from haunting us any further.

Turn To Page 132

CHAPTER EIGHT

CHASE

IF I WERE in my right mind, I'd be enjoying the hell out of this. I'd be giddy, winding through the gilded halls of a secret Victorian island mansion. I'd be marveling at the stone statues and curved wooden staircases, the high ceilings and golden frames. I'd be awed entering Seidon's father's double-oak-door office, with its floor-to-ceiling bookshelves and library ladder, its mahogany desk and rich red rugs. I'd even enjoy the gusts of ocean wind that currently tear across the island, making the house creak and groan like an ancient living creature.

But I am most definitely not in my right mind.

Logan's words still ring in my ears, echoing inside my seized skull. *Open relationship.* We talked about how things might change going long distance, promised we'd make adjustments to stay together. I thought that meant figuring out the rhythms of how often to talk or visit each other. The idea of being with anyone else never entered the conversation.

Open relationship. The words don't make any sense to me. All they conjure are questions, each one more painful than the last. Answering any of them feels like pulling at a loose thread that might unravel the fabric of my life.

So I don't speak. I don't let myself think. All I do is follow Seidon and dare not look in Logan's direction.

"This office is even more unbelievable than the rest of the house," Logan says.

On the surface this sounds like a compliment, but I know Logan—he believes inherited wealth is one of America's greatest evils. Suddenly, intuiting this simple thing about Logan feels like a buoy in an ocean. It also hurts, because a new thought enters the equation: *Do I really know Logan the way I think I do?*

An entire chunk of myself drifts off at the thought, iceberg I've become.

"My dad is a psychologist," Seidon explains. "He's at his main office now, but he uses this space for recordkeeping and research."

"Is his research on the tarot, too?" Logan asks, eyeing the stack of histories and texts on the enormous desk.

"Right now, yes," Seidon answers. "He's researching the historical link between the tarot and clinical psychology. It's a bit of a challenge to my mom, if I'm honest. To get her to see the more practical side behind all of her mysticism. It can all be a bit . . . much, sometimes.

"Anyway, Dad says there's so much to unpack there. A lot of the symbolism used in the tarot appears in the archetypes devised in Freudian and Jungian psychology, to access the unconscious. There are also parallels to Rorschach's inkblot tests, which analyze what we see instead of what's really there. Dad's toying with titles like 'Taropy'— he actually makes a pretty compelling argument that tarot card readers are really the world's oldest therapists."

Hearing this, I suddenly wish Amelia were here. Not just because she'd find the idea of "Taropy" fascinating—she has grand plans to study psychology at NYU, so she'd probably light up at linking the tarot to therapy. Really, I wish Amelia were here so she could tell me what to do about Logan.

"Interesting," Logan says. "I never thought of it that way. Though I did always respect the tarot's link to so many world religions, the way its symbolism connects to their foundations."

"Well, symbols capture truths hard to relate in words, right?"

Seidon's eyes connect with Logan, and suddenly I feel as if I am watching their first date. The floodgates inside my head buckle, so I drain all my disdain into some deep, internal pool.

"Should we find that file so we can rejoin the others?" I ask, my voice leaden.

"Right, of course," Seidon says. "Dad keeps Uncle Carson's files in a safe, so my mom can't go snooping. I have the code saved in a password keeper on my laptop. You two hang here while I go get it?"

"Thanks, that's perfect," Logan says, smiling back at Seidon.

Perfect.

As Seidon holds Logan's gaze, I see just how *perfect* they both are. Effortless and easy and sturdy, unburdened and beautiful. Captivating. Men—queer, sure, but *men* through and through. All of that used to be mine, with Logan by my side. But now I suddenly see how stupid I've been. How could I think I'd ever be enough for Logan? Me, twig-thin and brainy. Reserved me, who isn't fun or funny or charming. I always hoped if I appeared intelligent enough, it'd make up for the rest of me. Being smart is what everyone likes about me. Reliable, useful Chase. No one wants to see how complicated I feel all the time, how undecided. I used to think no one would love me if they really knew. But Logan *knows*. He does.

So maybe I was right? Maybe that's why he wants someone else? Someone bright and simple and clean like Seidon.

Luckily, Seidon leaves the office by the time the first tear splashes down my cheek. I try to hold them back, my throat searing, but I can't stop myself. The calm surface, the one I meticulously maintain, ripples. Logan has never seen me cry.

No one has.

"Chase, what's wrong?"

I wipe my face and look at Logan, razor sharp.

"I know. I'm sorry," he says. "It just came out. I wasn't going to tell you until the trip was over."

Tell me. As if his mind is already made up. How long ago did Logan decide . . . whatever this is?

"Wow," I say. "Thanks."

"I meant, bring it up, talk about it," Logan tries. "I just wanted this trip to be perfect. I know how much it means to you."

Logan reaches out his hand to touch my arm, but I recoil. Suddenly he is a stranger to me, limbs of a foreign body.

"What, before you break up with me?" The words hurt, boiling in my chest.

"No, no," Logan says. "Chase, I still love you."

"But?" I respond. "You still love me, *but . . .*"

Logan sighs.

"But we're barely eighteen. I've never even kissed anyone else and we're going to be so far apart. I just thought—"

"You thought you want to hook up with other guys?" I interrupt, even though I nearly choke on the sentence. The entire earth seems to tilt around me, like some fundamental axis has shifted.

"I think I need to go into college open to experiencing a lot of new things. And yes, maybe even that," Logan says. "But I don't want to lose you. Besides, who says we have to do things the old way? Straight people break up all the time for a reason, because of these unrealistic expectations of lifelong devotion, of never accounting for change. I've been doing some reading, and it's pretty common for older gay men to have some degree of openness in their relationships."

It's like Logan speaks another language. I recognize the words, but the meaning is lost on me.

"I don't want us to become bitter and resent each other," he goes on. "I want us to grow in the same direction, to experience all this together. And if we're really meant to be, don't you want to know for sure there's no greener grass and all that?"

Logan takes my hand and I let him, limply.

"Besides, if we really love each other, nothing—no one—can keep us apart."

I can't speak.

Our entire relationship suddenly casts itself in a different light. What was once steady and safe begins to warp; it becomes unsure and dangerous. How long have I not been enough? How did I miss the signs? When did Logan take this turn without me? Logan is a pillar. *I'm gay and I'm with Logan.* It's a fact of my life. But now the entire foundation of that life feels like it's crumbling.

Logan looks distraught. I wish it helped me feel better.

"You were just going to drop this on me before I left for school?"

"I wasn't even sure this is what I wanted," Logan answers. "I thought maybe we could see when you came back for our first break. But then something settled along the way, while I was waiting. And then . . . then I just wanted us to be us, as long as possible."

"That's . . . that's so . . ."

Selfish, is what I want to say. All of this is just so damn selfish.

"I don't want to hurt you," Logan pleads. "And I don't want to lose you."

Tears now brim in Logan's own eyes.

"But I can't ignore this other feeling, Chase. Doing that will only end us. And I can't bear that thought."

My mind is a riptide. Everything feels upside down. Could I even do an open relationship? The thought of Logan being with someone else makes me feel physically ill. I've never felt like I needed anyone else that way, but could I find a way to do this for Logan? I don't know . . . it feels impossible to decide how I feel about any of this when I'm so overwhelmed, when I feel like I have so little time. Did Logan really wait this long to save me suffering? Or was this all some way to try to force my hand?

I don't have the chance to answer, because Seidon walks back into the office. Seidon, with his irresistible dimples and flawless everything. Will Logan call him the second I get on a plane, their muscled bodies inevitably joining together right here, on the sprawling rugs . . .

"I've got the—" Seidon starts, then stops. "—Oh, sorry. Am I interrupting something?"

"No," I answer immediately. "We're ready."

The sooner we find what we came for, the sooner we can get off this island. This godforsaken place where everything has changed. *Here lie Chase and Logan, ghosts haunting each other forevermore.*

I turn my head away to compose myself and my eye catches on a single tarot card laid on the desk, from the Rider-Waite deck: the Wheel of Fortune. I nearly laugh out loud. This card represents a reversal, reminding you to examine who is responsible when a turn for the worse arrives. Seeing its spokes and creatures, it feels like a cruel joke.

Turning back to Seidon, I see that he looks unsure, but he keeps walking anyway. He leads the way to a palatial closet where the safe must be kept. Following him, I have an unfathomable urge to hit him.

"Why are you helping us?" I suddenly ask, my tone pointed.

Seidon pauses and turns to face us.

"The great Lady Azure would probably say it's because I'm the Prince of Cups, well-intentioned and supportive, but prone to the unexpected," Seidon says. "Just like my dad is the King of Cups, guardian of secrets and mental strength."

"But what would you say?" I press.

"I'd say I led you here because my mom asked me to, but I know her. She's only appearing to help you so she can get what she really wants. Which is why I'm going to make sure you leave with everything you came for, despite her wishes."

"Why would you do that?" I ask.

"Because ever since I left for college, I see her much more clearly. And I see how stuck she is." Seidon sighs. "All the money she inherited, this house—it seems like a blessing, but I think it's a curse. It's a golden prison, one my mom will never leave. So she obsesses over Uncle Carson and his tarot because she feels like it gives her purpose, instead of doing anything actually good with all she's been given."

"Jeez," Logan says. "Your dad really must be a psychologist."

"Yeah, tell me about it," Seidon laughs. "Mom has convinced herself she deserves all this wealth because of her tarot practice, so she started believing her own hype. Her intensity settled down a bit over the years, but this final deck is going to pull her right back in. I don't want to live like that. And I want more for her. So maybe if she is forced to let go of this last deck, we can all move on. Really move on."

I look to Logan and he appears impressed. It guts me.

"So you don't believe in the tarot?" I ask instead.

"Not the way my mom does," Seidon answers. "She wants to believe the cards literally give her a psychic connection. My sister thinks the same thing, though she's far more in tune with reality—and far less attached to material things. They both believe Uncle Carson's ghost lives here. Me, I'm with my dad—I don't really believe the psychic stuff and fortune-telling and visions are much more than uncharted psychological—"

Seidon stops himself. Instead of continuing, he sets his eyes on mine.

"Actually, I should really be asking: What do you believe, Chase?"

◊ "I think your entire family is toying with **forces** you couldn't possibly understand." **Turn To Page 138**

◊ "I think you're right. Whatever mess is collecting here, it's all of our **own making**." **Turn To Page 139**

"You all seem to revel in claiming things you haven't really earned," I continue, viscerally.

Seidon stares back at me, no doubt hearing the anger in my voice.

"If you really believe that, then it's all the more reason for you to take your cards away." Seidon sighs. "Because I'm sick of this Perillian stuff haunting us."

Staring at Seidon, I realize I'm not the only one who believes there's something bigger happening here. I think we'd all be foolish not to have some reverence for the forces at work on this frigid island. I also realize I'd better shut my mouth if all that's going to spew out right now is venom.

"Why do you still live here, then, if you disagree with it all so much?" Logan asks, shooting me a look: *What was that?*

"Family is family," Seidon answers. "But really, I'm just home for the summer before heading back to UCSB."

"Oh, I'm headed to UCLA next—" Logan begins, but then must feel the steam rising off my skin.

Anger might be all I'm capable of projecting, but really, I feel like I might vomit.

"Let's just see what's in the records," Logan finishes instead, unable to look at me.

Which is fine, because I already feel unseen as all hell.

Turn To Page 140

Seidon stares back at me. It's an odd stare, like he's somehow trying to figure me out.

"Then we agree," he finally says, perhaps ignoring—or perhaps embracing—the subtext of my answer. "And getting this deck away from my family is the best way to prove that."

"In that case, all three of us agree," Logan says, stepping beside me.

Logan believes in a higher power, but I know he doesn't believe in "powers." He'd just call it psychic energy tapping into universal flow. I'm sure he thinks all of this is spiritual, not supernatural. Human, not superhuman.

I still might not be sure exactly what I believe, but in this case, I can definitely agree. This all feels particularly, painfully *human*.

Seidon looks back at us, at Logan and me standing together, and suddenly it's as if a charge opens up in the room. There's silence for a few more beats.

"You know, I didn't only bring you boys up here because my mom asked," Seidon begins. "I kind of knew the house would be empty . . ."

Seidon's eyes slide from mine to Logan's and a stone forms in my stomach.

Oh. No. There's no way I could . . . I mean, I'm not ready to . . . Oh god, what if Logan wants to . . .

"That's very flattering," Logan answers. "But we're not there yet."

Logan puts a hand on my shoulder and Seidon stares at it, intensely.

"Shame," Seidon says, shrugging his shoulders. "Well, you know where to find me if you ever change your mind."

If Seidon feels embarrassed or rejected, he doesn't show it. Though he maybe seems to feel somewhat . . . left out? He turns to the safe and I flush with relief, but not much.

Because I'm the one who really feels left out. At best, I'm the wet blanket of his scenario. At worst, I'm the consolation prize.

Turn To Page 140

Seidon opens the safe and rifles through the files piled inside. I'm so lost in my thoughts, I have no idea how long he does this. It could be seconds or it could be minutes, but next thing I know, Seidon turns and stands again.

"Here it is," he says, opening the file. "There actually isn't much in here, mostly photos of Uncle Carson working on the deck. But this was at the top."

Seidon then hands me a UPS tracking receipt from a decade ago.

"He must have wanted whoever showed up with the deck to know exactly where he mailed it. Does the name there mean anything to you?" Seidon asks.

Indeed it does.

And seeing it, I know only one thing: we need to get back to Amelia and Cleo. Now.

Wonders refuse to cease.

We asked Seidon to take us to Coupled Cottage to meet the others, but after checking his phone, he said he was getting texts from his sister—and there was a change of plans. So we follow Seidon into the basement of Baxter Manor. Once down here, he pulls on a seemingly ornamental trident set into the wall, which reveals a secret door leading into an underground tunnel. Seidon explains that this tunnel reaches across the island to both docks, serving as an old panic-room escape route. The escape tunnel is very cool, just like everything else on the island, but I've endured one too many surprises to enjoy it much.

Halfway through the tunnel, we finally meet Amelia, Cleo, and Anwar. Spotting Amelia, I don't think I've ever been more relieved to see anyone in my entire life.

"Oh my goddess," she says as she grabs and hugs me. "You're never going to believe what just happened."

I hug Amelia and feel like melting. Her presence is like a lighthouse shining.

"We only need to take one boat back," Seidon says. "But we should keep moving, just in case . . ."

Seidon doesn't finish, so I turn to Amelia. From the look on her face, I can tell what must have happened with recovering the Princess of Cups. What I can't tell, however, is what happened with Lady Azure to make us need to "keep moving." Obviously, we'll need to discuss all this later, because now is not the time. My pulse picks up in my harried veins. It feels like some big bad looms behind us in this darkened tunnel. Anything feels like it could come for us, after these last two delirious days.

"For the record, I texted Lily when we first got here," Seidon says as we all half-jog through the tunnel. "I only went through with separating you so we could help you get what you need faster and get off the island. I didn't know what my mom really wanted either, but I knew it wouldn't be as . . . selfless as she seemed."

"I can vouch for Seidon," I say, even though I hate speaking the words. "It's a long story, but let's all talk about it back in Charvan."

"Wait," Amelia says, grabbing my shoulder as we move. "Did you find out who Perilli mailed the deck to?"

"Yes," I answer directly.

I then hesitate a beat. I know what this news will do to Amelia, the impact it will have. Though really, at this point, is there any other way to say this?

"Perilli sent his final deck to Gran Flo, at your home address."

Amelia's jaw falls open. I have to pull her along a little to keep her from stopping. I can tell her brain then begins to brim, just like mine. Obviously Carson Perilli must have known Gran Flo. And she felt the need to lie to us about where the deck came from. But why? And why teach us so much about it, then leave it to Amelia?

"See, the cards are meant to be with you," Seidon says. "Lily and I will make sure they stay with you, no matter what Mom wants."

"Did Perilli ever say anything about a woman named Florence Piccolo?" Amelia asks.

"Not to us, no," Seidon answers. "But we were still pretty young when we knew him. I think you've gotten all you will from here."

On that note, we fall into a rushed silence. We just keep moving through this labyrinthine tunnel hidden underneath the Isle of Baxter, our own cups feeling both drained and overflowing at the same time.

◆ ◆ ◆ ◆

As much as we all have to talk about, we found we couldn't speak much over the roaring of the ocean wind on the boat ride back. My heart still pounds in my chest, despite how weary it feels. I couldn't shake the feeling our boat might capsize in the middle of the windy sea, lost in the raging Pacific winds. Amelia kept looking over her shoulder, like Lady Azure might be right behind, speeding in the second boat to ambush us. I have a feeling these fears are going to linger, along with some other parting gifts from our very own Haunting of Baxter Isle.

We now stand back outside Charvan. I just want to run and hide, but Seidon has insisted on saying goodbye for some reason.

"Well, best of luck finding the other missing cards," he tries. "I doubt you'll want to after today, but I can give you my number if you need help with anything?"

Seidon steps forward then, but not toward Logan. Instead, he steps to me.

"What?" I blurt out. "Don't you mean to give that to Logan?"

"Oh, sure," Seidon says, scratching his head. "Either way. You're great, Logan."

He smiles over at Logan a beat, then turns back to me.

"But if I'm being honest, you're way more my type, Chase."

Shock seizes my body. What the actual hell?

"But you've barely looked at me," I say. The words seem to vomit themselves. This isn't possible. There must be some mistake, some joke being played.

"Yeah, well, I get nervous around—" Seidon's face flashes with embarrassment for the first time all night. "You guys are great together, though, obviously. I don't mean to—"

"Dude, maybe read the room?" Cleo interrupts. I could kiss her.

Seidon indeed steps away, but I just spin around.

"Thanks for the ride," I say, my back turned. "Logan, can we talk?"

Logan and I sit in Charvan's front seats, alone. We both look out the windshield, too afraid to look at each other. But the others are waiting, and we've already sat in silence too long. We need to get this over with.

"I have to admit," Logan says, beating me to it, "I did not love seeing Seidon hit on you like that, as entertaining as it might have been."

I don't respond right away, because I'm pretty sure I feel another *but* coming on. Besides, I'm still not sure what to make of this whole Seidon thing. It just does not compute: Who would ever be attracted to me over Logan?

"But still, it was kind of exciting, wasn't it?" Logan finishes.

Considering this question, something suddenly shifts. There are still mountains of mess to sort through, but in this moment, I know there's only one way for me to begin doing so. Turning to Logan, I know . . .

◊ I'm furious about how Logan kept this from me, about not being enough for him. So I **need some space** to sort through what I want next.
   Turn To Page 144
◊ I'm not really okay with how Logan handled this, but I don't want to lose him. So I **tell him it's okay**—at least until I decide maybe it's not.
   Turn To Page 145

"I don't want to say anything I'll regret," I say, my voice chillier than I intend. It just feels like right now if I give an inch, a mile of myself might collapse. "I think I need some time to sort through all this on my own."

"But, Chase . . ." Logan tries. "It's me. We can talk about anything."

"Can we?" I ask, my implication clear. "You already told me what you want. So this isn't about us anymore. It's about deciding what I want, isn't it?"

Logan appears crushed, like I'm suddenly a stranger to him.

Good. Now he knows how it feels.

"It wasn't an ultimatum, Chase," Logan says, his tone pleading. "We don't have to do this if you don't want."

"You don't mean that," I say, my voice nearly cracking. "You can't just take it back and make it disappear."

It occurs to me that all I want to do in this moment is bury myself in Logan's shoulder. He's the one who tells me it's all going to be fine when something goes wrong. He's the safe place I go when things aren't right. So what do I do now that he's the cause of the wrong?

"Really, Logan. I just . . . I need to think. And I can't do that with you here."

Logan looks like he doesn't want to accept this. I don't know if I mean the words, but right now pushing Logan away feels like the only option to save myself.

So push I do, right into this uncharted territory, where everything feels numb and explosive at the same time.

I push right into this next chapter, where nothing feels certain . . .

And where Logan maybe doesn't belong anymore?

Turn To Page 149

The words leave my mouth, but I'm surprised by how hollow they sound.

"Chase, do you really mean that?" Logan asks, his hand falling on my knee. "Or are you just saying that?"

I turn away from Logan, my head falling.

"I don't know."

It might be seconds or it might be minutes, but eventually Logan's hand leaves my knee.

"Well, maybe I should give you some space?" he tries. "So you can decide?"

"No." I react on instinct, turning to Logan. "I don't want that."

"Neither do I," Logan says, looking pained once again. "But I also don't want to force you into something you're not sure about."

All I want to do is tell Logan *no* again. Tell him not to leave. That I don't want to figure anything out without him. That I'll do whatever it takes. That I love him.

So then why do I say nothing at all?

Turn To Page 149

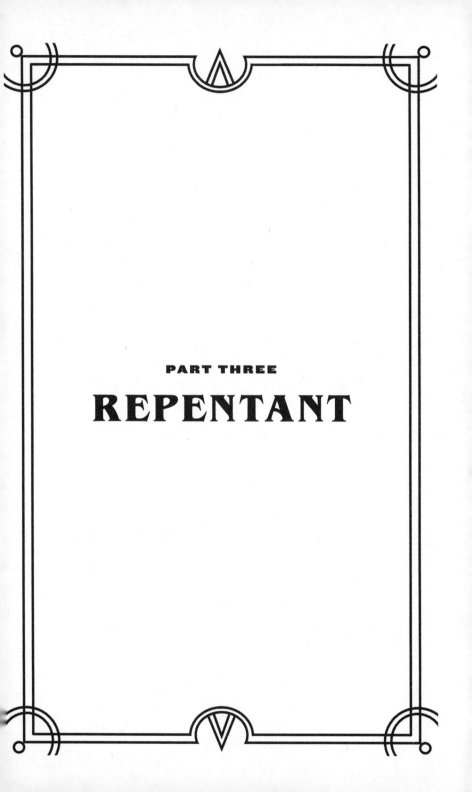

PART THREE

REPENTANT

CHAPTER NINE

AMELIA

I SIT ON THE deck overlooking the dark forest and try to let the greens and browns soak into me. I try to let the trees remind me who I am, remind me why it's still important to take this journey. For good measure, I also hold several tarot cards in my hand, hoping they'll speak to me if the woods won't.

It's only been one day since we left the Isle of Baxter, and the experience has most definitely stayed with us—especially since not all of us actually stayed. Last night we spent a pretty sleepless night at a nearby motel, because Anwar claimed his home was too far and winding a trip to make that late. Then first thing this morning, Logan insisted on taking the bus home. I tried to talk both him and Chase out of it, but he and Chase barely spoke five words between them.

Which is why, unbeknownst to Chase, I stole a secret moment with Logan when we dropped him at the nearest bus station.

"Listen, I don't know what happened, but I just need to say this before you go, because someone needs to," I began. "You're one of us, Logan. No matter what."

Tears had formed in Logan's eyes then. I knew what this would mean coming from me in particular.

"Thank you, Amelia," Logan said. "This actually—"

Logan had to stop himself from finishing, for fear of breaking down.

"I still love him," Logan tried finally. "And I never meant to hurt him. The fact that I did . . ."

Logan couldn't finish this sentence either, so I just pulled him into a hug.

"I know. He knows," I offered. "Just give him some time to do his Chase thought hurricane thing. You'll sort it out once his brain-storm dies down."

I wasn't so sure Chase's brain was really the part of him in turmoil, but I had to say something. Thankfully, wiping at his face, Logan actually laughed.

"Well, I hid something of mine in Chase's bag," he said. "He'll know what it means when he sees it, hopefully."

I left Logan, having no idea what he hid for Chase. Even now, I'm still not sure if Chase knows. He hasn't exactly been bursting with communication. I still can't believe Logan isn't going to be with us for this final part of the road trip. Almost as much as I can't believe Anwar decided to join us.

I was weirded out at first when Anwar kept us away from his home. Could there be a reason he also wanted to meet us in Solvang and not closer to his house? However, once he asked if he could join us to help find the next missing card, my doubts started to melt away. I'm impressed our detour to Coupled Cottage only seemed to fascinate Anwar instead of scare him off. I'm also impressed by how respectful he remained while still trying to engage. Maybe that's why Cleo and Chase didn't protest when I pitched the idea of Anwar filling our fourth seat. I wish Logan were still here, but I'm also happy Anwar is joining.

After Logan left, we drove from Summerland up to Carmel by the Sea. We stopped for lunch at one of Cleo's superb restaurant picks, where I was finally able to pry a few words out of Chase about what happened with Logan.

"So . . . are you broken up?" I chose my question carefully, since Chase seemed not unlike an overheated computer.

"I don't know, honestly. I was too afraid to ask."

The words seemed almost impossible for Chase to muster, like speaking them was a Herculean task.

"Well, maybe don't go calling Seidon right away, in that case?"

I meant it as a joke to help Chase smile, but it had the opposite effect. Ever since, Chase seems to have shut himself down, entering some kind of low-power mode. As much as I'm worried about him, I can't say I blame him. Seidon had a lot of nerve, hitting on Chase in front of Logan that way. I can't fathom what it must be like for Chase to feel a rift form with Logan. It's upsetting even to me, seeing what I thought was an inseparable couple buckle under sudden pressure.

After lunch, we stopped to buy Anwar some clothes for the next leg. Then we made our way through Monterey and fulfilled a solemn oath to Cleo to stop at the famous aquarium, which was a much-needed break. We also now have an excellent Cleo doodle of me, her, and Toky posing in front of a tank of glowing jellyfish.

After that, we finally arrived at a rental house on the northern outskirts of town. Chase found this cozy log cabin last minute, choosing it because it's closest to our next missing card: the King of Pentacles. The King's coordinates pinpoint in the neighboring forest, so we plan to "camp" here before heading out first thing in the morning.

Which means Anwar and I might actually get to share a room for the night. Chase and Cleo already went to bed, but Anwar was game to hang on the back deck and gaze at the stars a bit. He's currently brewing us some of his "signature hot chocolate," which has left me out here for a merciful moment to gather myself. Despite all the driving, I still haven't had much time to process what happened in Coupled Cottage. Perhaps I've avoided doing so on purpose, if I'm being honest. I've evaded a panic attack so far, but after last night I know my anxiety tank is rising far too high— it's bound to spill over if I don't manage it.

So I try to sift through the images that remain tattooed on my brain. The first is the sight of Lady Azure's face, frozen with tears, gaunt and ghostly. I don't really want to sort through what she might have deliberately done to us, to me . . .

So instead, I dwell on a different moment imprinted on my mind.

◊ Back at Coupled Cottage, I **recovered** the Princess of Cups.
   Turn To Page 152
◊ Back at Coupled Cottage, I **did not recover** the Princess of Cups.
   Turn To Page 153

I look down at the Princess of Cups, which I have placed at the top of the card stack. It's surreal holding it in my hands; it's like another small piece that has been missing my entire life is now found. The Princess feels like she overflows with meaning, given all I had to endure and overcome to save her.

And I really do feel I saved her from Lady Azure's clutches. I found a way to set the Princess of Cups free—and hopefully, in the process, I set some of the Baxters free as well.

Especially because, staring down at the Princess, I now see only Lily's face gazing back up at me. I know what I believed about hauntings and psychics and mediums before Lily led us into Coupled Cottage, but nothing could prepare me for what happened inside. I'm not sure if what I believe has actually changed, but how I *feel* about all of it? That has become a beast of an entirely different color.

Of course, nothing truly compares with the revelation that Perilli mailed his final deck to Grandma—and that both of them went to such great lengths to keep it a secret. All I can really settle on is that it all obviously can't have been a complete coincidence. So maybe if I can find the through line connecting these threads in the final two missing cards, then maybe I can finally solve some of these lingering mysteries?

Turn To Page 154

I can only see the Princess of Cups drowning in that horrible tank.

Part of me feels devastated to have lost the card this way, but another part feels like this might actually be a blessing in disguise. If coveting these Perillian cards is a path that inevitably leads to being like Lady Azure, then maybe it's best I learn to let some of the cards go now?

Then again, I did get a good look at the Princess before she was dunked. Which meant I could work with Cleo last night to recreate as much of the card as possible. She reminded me that we could technically make the card whatever we wanted, but I just felt it was right to do the original some kind of justice.

So I now hold Cleo's replacement card in my hands, at the top of the stack of Perillian cards. And Lily's floating face gazes back up at me, drawn in Cleo's signature style. I know what I believed about hauntings and psychics and mediums before Lily led us into Coupled Cottage, but nothing could prepare me for what happened inside. I'm not sure if what I believe has actually changed, but how I *feel* about all of it? That has become a beast of an entirely different color.

Of course, nothing truly compares with the revelation that Perilli mailed his final deck to Grandma—and that both of them went to such great lengths to keep it a secret. All I can really settle on is that it all obviously can't have been a complete coincidence. So maybe if I can find the through line connecting these threads in the final two missing cards, then maybe I can finally solve some of these lingering mysteries?

Turn To Page 154

Right now I hold a stack of specific cards in my hands, hoping something will come to me: The Magician, The Lovers, The Empress, The Hanged Man, The Emperor, and Death—the six cards designated by the Perillian toolset.

In particular, I find myself focusing on The Empress and The Hanged Man. Unlike The Magician and The Lovers, which held the complete coordinates in their symbols, Perilli split the numbers for the missing King of Pentacles between the symbols of The Empress and The Hanged Man. My best guess is that these two cards are tied to the nature vibes of Pentacles, in addition to being tied together numerically: the one and two that make up The Hanged Man's twelve also add up to three, The Empress.

Could this be part of why I feel drawn to Anwar, this connection between our own expressions? Is this why I've trusted him joining this journey? Or is this just my mind assigning meaning to another coincidence, however powerful it might be?

"Hey, isn't that my tarot card alter ego or something?" Anwar asks, reappearing on the deck with two steaming cups of cocoa.

"Indeed it is," I answer, putting the cards down to accept my mug.

"He seems kind of . . . I don't know, messed up?"

Anwar looks down at The Hanged Man, and I understand this initial reaction. I used to be spooked by this card, too, until I learned the true depths of its meaning.

"Actually, The Hanged Man is one of the more sophisticated cards," I begin. "It represents a resolution, using your circumstances to open up to a new world. His hanging upside down isn't ominous; it actually represents a pivotal moment in a journey between worlds, looking to both."

I finish speaking to find Anwar staring back at me with a strange expression on his face. Some mix of pain and maybe . . . adoration? Looking him over, his strong nose and wavy black hair and liquid eyes, I can't help but feel like he could maybe be a turning point for me, a gateway into a new perspective. Goddess knows he already flips my stomach upside down.

I hate to say it, but Anwar's interest finally makes me feel like I am someone to be interested in. I know I should feel that way on my own, but I just never have.

"That's fascinating," Anwar says, meaning it. "I can't believe I never got into the tarot before. It's so much deeper than most people know."

"That's what my grandma always used to say. Turns out, she was talking about something even . . . deeper."

I feel an angry stab in my chest. The truth, the one I don't want to admit, is that I'm mad at Grandma for lying to us. This anger, in turn, makes me feel horribly guilty, which then makes me miss Grandma even more. I find myself constantly trying to reconcile these emotions, to ball them up into one thing. Then I remind myself that, like the tarot, all of these emotions can exist in me at the same time.

These feelings must play across my face in some way, because Anwar reaches out and places his hand on my shoulder.

"You probably have so much on your mind," he says. "What can I do to help?"

Staring back in Anwar's earnest eyes, I feel the warm glow of his concern. Suddenly I don't want to dwell anymore on tarot mysteries or questions, if only for a little while.

So I return the cards to the deck, careful not to bend the edges. Then I stuff the deck in the secret compartment of Cleo's backpack, which I now keep with me when Cleo doesn't need her art supplies. Then, with the tarot put to rest, I turn back to Anwar.

Except behind him, a light goes on in the kitchen, and I see Cleo through the window at the sink. It's not like her to get back up once she has gone to bed—she usually sleeps like the dead. Maybe she's just getting some water or something?

◇ I return my focus to Anwar, because all I want to do is gaze at the stars with him on the back lawn. Then I want us to finally **get intimate**.
Turn To Page 156

◇ "Do you mind if I **check on** Cleo inside for a minute?" I ask Anwar. "I just want to make sure she's all right."
Turn To Page 161

"What are the chances we could lie down in the yard and just stare at the stars for a while?" I ask, leaning toward Anwar.

"Chances are high, on one condition," he answers. "We get to cuddle up under some blankets?"

We. I know this is absolutely not the word to focus on in Anwar's response, but I can't help it. *We.* It sounds nice, bouncing around in my brain. So I smile, because this is one condition I can most definitely agree to.

Once we assemble the perfect blanket spread on the back lawn, I feel myself relax into the soft nook beside Anwar. This close, I can smell his comforting scent, somewhere between pine and sea breeze. I then turn my head up and take in the starry sky, spread out before us like a glittering canvas.

For what might be minutes or even hours, I lie beside Anwar in the soft grass of the backyard, feeling his warm body beside mine. We stare up without speaking for so long, it feels like I've entered a trance. All that remains is the rustling of the leaves and the glow of the moon and Anwar's chest rising and falling with every steady breath.

This feels like the most intimate thing two people could possibly do. To be at ease not talking, not moving—to just be together. It requires a special kind of connection, a rare breed of magic. Right now, Anwar and I are wrapped in it.

But it only makes me crave more.

Feeling ready, I turn my head back toward Anwar. I see his gorgeous face smile for just a second before he leans toward me. The second I kiss Anwar, my entire body begins to buzz. His lips are just so soft and taste rich and full, almost like wisps of smoke and cherries. His stubble brushes against my cheek, and suddenly I think I'm kissing a man—a real-live, fully grown man.

I feel Anwar's hands reach forward and brace against my hips, which is not my favorite feature, so I roll Anwar onto his back and position myself on top of him. I then feel his hands travel to the small of my back—much better.

My chest presses against Anwar's and I feel him gasp a little, but a good gasp. So I press a little harder, reaching my own hands toward Anwar's stomach. I don't mean to, but I manage to slip my hands under his shirt and my fingers find warm skin. I almost pull back, but he just feels so soft. And as I grasp tighter, all I feel is the solid muscle underneath.

Then it's my turn to gasp.

Anwar turns and buries his lips into my neck, sending a shudder through my body. His hands travel down lower to the arch of my butt, one of my best assets, and I can feel how turned on he is by it. By me.

"I have thought about doing this for a very long time," Anwar whispers, his breath in my ear.

"Then let's not wait any longer," I answer, kissing him again.

This time there's more passion in the kiss, more urgency. It becomes supercharged, frantic—like we have to have each other.

So we do.

◆ ◆ ◆ ◆

Once again, I have no idea how much time passes. All I know is I now lie in the curve of Anwar's arm back in our bedroom for the night, my head resting on his chest. We did exactly what I wanted to do—what I was ready to do—and nothing more. And we were safe. With Anwar, that's how I seem to feel, like the anxiety melts out of my body somehow.

"Why, oh why, did you have to move away all those years ago?" I ask, tilting my head up to face him. When I do, Anwar looks far away, like he's troubled. "Hey, you okay?"

"Yeah. But can we have another question lightning round?"

"Sure," I say.

"What do you think happened back at Coupled Cottage?" Anwar asks. "I mean, what really happened. With the lights and the cards and everything else?"

◇ I wish Anwar's asking this question would **magically sprout** an answer in my head, but it doesn't.
Turn To Page 158

◇ "Honestly? I don't think there was just one thing happening there, not just **one truth** unfolding."
Turn To Page 159

"Honestly, I still don't know what I think happened," I sigh. "Everything happened so fast in that strange place, I have no idea how to begin sorting through what was real and what was imagined."

I pause, not sure what else to say. "I'm sorry, I know that's a dissatisfying answer."

"That's not a dissatisfying answer at all," Anwar says.

"Oh. Good," I reply. "What do you think really happened?"

"I think we were straight-up haunted," Anwar answers without hesitation. "I think we got exactly what we were asking for, going there. I mean, regular tarot cards tap into something way bigger than us, right? So it makes sense your extra-special deck would supercharge that kind of connection."

"You really think it was all real?" I ask, unable to hide the surprise in my voice.

"Not all of it, no. I think Lily proved herself to be much more genuine and trustworthy than her mom," Anwar says. "But it sounds like Lady Azure was more like those Wanderers you met back in Joshua Tree."

"I guess I'm going to have to get used to these Perillians trying to manipulate me," I say. "Hiding behind their secrets."

"Maybe," Anwar begins. "But if I've learned anything about people who go out of their way to tell you they're ultra-secretive, it's that they're usually eager to spill their guts out. Especially devotees like the Perillians. They can't help themselves."

Turning this thought over in my mind, I realize Anwar is absolutely right. The Perillians we've encountered have claimed to open up to us because we possess the final deck. Sure, they keep the internet scrubbed, but they've all been tripping over themselves to share with us how special their knowledge is. Could it be the way they see themselves and the way they actually act are two different things?

If that's true, it's something we can use to our advantage on these next two legs of the trip.

Turn To Page 160

"Lady Azure. Perilli. Lily. Seidon. The five of us. Everyone had their own agenda, their own version of events," I continue. "Some of it could have been true, some of it could have been faked. Some of it might have meant to help, some to manipulate. We could probably spend a lot of time untangling that experience. A large part of me really wants to."

"I sense there's a *but* coming, isn't there?"

"Sure is," I reply. "A very smart friend told me this recently: Sometimes it doesn't matter what's real. What matters is how you let things define your intentions and drive your actions."

"So how are you going to let this experience drive you, then?" Anwar asks.

"That's the question of the hour, isn't it? I'm not sure I know yet, except for this: whatever Lady Azure stood for, I'd like to stride in the exact opposite direction."

"That seems very wise to me." Anwar smiles. "Out of everything that might have been true on that scary island, I think she was the most fraudulent."

"That, we can definitely agree on," I say. "But does that mean you think there was actually some truth there?"

"Yes," Anwar answers without hesitation. "I'm not saying I understand it, but those tarot cards definitely have some major mojo. And if nothing else, Lady Azure and Lily were pretty willing to share their 'secret Perillian knowledge' with us. Maybe it's because they have respect for that final deck, or because they wanted to take it from you. Or maybe . . ."

"What?" I ask, when Anwar doesn't finish.

"Maybe all these Perillians just can't help themselves," he finally finishes. "Maybe they're not really quite as secretive as they'd like to think they are?"

Hearing Anwar's words, it makes me think of Maggie and Cain, too. So far, all these Perillians like to say they're only revealing themselves to the worthy. That might be true, but either way, holding this final deck seems to deem us universally worthy. That's definitely a privilege we can use to our advantage when finding the last two missing cards.

Turn To Page 160

"Can I ask you another big question?" Anwar says, running his fingers through my curls.

"You know you can."

Anwar pauses, his eyes scanning like he is trying to find the right words.

"Is there a world where maybe it might be a blessing in disguise if one of these Perillians happened to get the deck?"

This question jolts me. I prop myself up, needing to see Anwar's face clearly.

"No," I say plainly. "Why would you ask that?"

"I mean, think of all the turmoil it has caused. What you told me about Joshua Tree. What the Baxter siblings said about Lady Azure. The rift between Chase and Logan. You doubting your grandmother. That deck just seems to stir up trouble."

Anwar locks eyes with me then, looking deadly serious.

"I don't know, do you think maybe Perilli's final deck is . . . cursed?"

That's a wild thought. I'm not sure I believe such a thing is even possible, but it's hard to argue that this deck does seem to have some kind of chaotic quality— a disruptive force, once it enters your life. Then again, every one of us involved has made the choice to empower the deck this way. To idolize this physical thing made by another person, an artist with intentions of his own.

"No, I don't think the deck is cursed," I answer. "But your point is taken—I need to remember it for what it is: cardstock and ink and paint. The powerful thing about it is the ideas it represents, the relationships and the history it carries."

"If you say so," Anwar says, settling his head back down. "Really, I was only thinking that because it'd be nice to have an excuse to never leave this bed."

I smile at Anwar, because that last thought is a nice one. His other thought, however, lingers like a mud stain. I decide, quickly, to let it go. Anwar is new to this and he means well, but he doesn't fully understand how deep this deck goes for me. There's so much left to do, so many more miles to travel and questions to answer—I could never let the cards go before it's finished. That said, right now this respite also feels very necessary.

So, kissing Anwar again, I resolve to enjoy it for every second it lasts.

Turn To Page 166

"Oh, of course," Anwar says.

"Great, be right back," I say, standing up.

A few steps later I enter the kitchen to find Cleo rummaging for a midnight snack.

"I stashed the sour gummy worms in that cabinet," I say, pointing.

Cleo turns and smiles at me. "Am I that obvious?"

"Rarely. You also usually sleep like you really mean it."

"I know," Cleo sighs, pulling out our candy stash. "I just have a lot on my mind after yesterday."

"Glad I'm not the only one," I reply. "Well, not glad. But you know what I mean."

Cleo sits at the table and opens up the bag of gummies, when she sees the back deck light on.

"Did you leave Anwar out there to come check on me?" she asks, a warm grin spreading across her face.

"Of course I did," I answer.

Cleo looks at me with that familiar expression. Like she sees all of me somehow, and every bit is magical.

"So while I'm doing the checking, want to tell me what's up?" I ask.

Cleo chews away at a gummy worm, her lips puckering before answering.

"Just thinking about all the new friends we made yesterday. And how little I trust any of them."

◊ My **stomach drops**. "Wait, are you talking about Anwar?"
Turn To Page 162

◊ I **tilt** my **head**. "Do you mean everything with Lady Azure and Lily at Coupled Cottage?"
Turn To Page 163

"Well, if you really want to know . . ." Cleo answers, hesitant.

"I do!" I say, not really sure I actually mean it.

"So, don't you get this feeling like . . ." Cleo tries. "Like he's always playing a version of himself, instead of just being himself?"

This question jars me. That's not at all how I've seen Anwar.

"I mean, aren't we all doing that?" I respond.

"No. Actually, that's what I love about you, Amelia," Cleo says. "You don't know how to be anything other than yourself at all times."

I find a way to smile, even though my brain branches to process Cleo's words.

"I don't know, it's like at Coupled Cottage when I didn't trust the Baxters," Cleo continues before I can respond. "I just don't get the right vibe from Anwar."

Cleo says the words and I feel my entire body react.

I really, really like Anwar. Which means I really, really want my best friends to like Anwar, too. But what if they're seeing something I'm not? Is there some disingenuous reason he is here? Or is my instinct that someone like him couldn't possibly be into someone like me totally correct?

Just minutes ago, I felt somewhat calm, finally. How can Cleo topple that in the span of seconds, with just a few words?

"Amelia, are you okay?" Cleo asks. "Should I not have said anything?"

"Of course not," I respond immediately. "You can always tell me anything."

I mean the words, I do. At the same time, I have no idea where to put this new storm of emotions Cleo has whipped up. I feel a pulse of frustration, against my will. Chase and Cleo are always telling me to be more cautious, but what if they should both be more open, more inviting? I try not to give in to this impulse, however, because I know anger is always the surface expression of some deeper emotion. I'm probably feeling hurt by Cleo's disapproval. Or wounded by her implied judgment of my own judgment. And maybe part of me is terrified that Cleo is actually . . . right?

Then there's this feeling, a voice in my head I can't ignore. It still feels like there's more Cleo wants to say on this subject. Could there be some other reason she doesn't want Anwar around?

Turn To Page 164

"Yes, of course," Cleo answers, after a slight pause.

"It turns out you were totally right to be skeptical of Lady Azure," I sigh. "Whatever else she might believe or possess, she only brought us to that island to try to manipulate us."

"I'm not as surprised by that," Cleo replies. "I mean, she screamed fraud to me from the jump. I'm more conflicted about Lily."

"Really? Why's that?"

"Well, I want to write her off as an accomplice to her mom, but the way she stuck up for us in the end . . ."

"It makes you believe she was being honest the whole time?" I ask.

"Honest at least about honoring Perilli's wishes to help us find the card," Cleo answers. "The rest, I don't know."

"You mean the whole medium thing?"

"No. I mean, I believe Lily wasn't lying about that. She believes she is a medium. What that means in reality, we can't really know."

"So you mean the conversation she forced on you?" I finally say, feeling silly for not getting there sooner. "That unsolicited gender advice she offered?"

"Yeah," Cleo says, pulling another worm loose. "She might have been overstepping, but once again, that doesn't mean she was wrong."

Suddenly, all I want to do is wrap my arms around Cleo and tell her everything is going to be okay. The impulse is so strong, it takes me completely by surprise. I've never felt this protective of anyone, not even Chase. And certainly not Anwar.

And suddenly, I have no idea what that means, underneath it all.

Turn To Page 164

Just then, the door to the back deck opens and Anwar enters.

"Hope I'm not interrupting?" he asks. "Was just getting lonely out there."

"Of course not!" I reply a little too loudly. I clear my throat, course correcting. "We were just talking about yesterday."

"Yeah, I figured," Anwar says. "I was actually going to ask you about something I've been thinking all day."

Anwar shifts his eyes from me to Cleo. She holds up her hands.

"Don't let me stop you," she says.

Anwar pauses, his eyes scanning as if he's trying to find the right words. Then he returns his focus to me, looking serious.

"Do you ever think maybe . . . you'd be better off without the deck?"

The question jolts me.

"No," I say plainly. "Why would you ask that?"

"Sorry. I was just thinking, from a total outsider's perspective, owning that deck is starting to seem more like a burden than a privilege," Anwar begins. "All these Perillian followers wanting things from you. The stuff they're claiming about your grandma. I don't know, maybe some things are just meant to stay buried? Or maybe digging it all up could be someone else's problem?"

"But it isn't someone else's," I answer. "It's mine."

"I know. All I'm saying is that you have a choice here, even if it doesn't feel like it. I mean, this deck has become the center of your universe, at least for this trip. If it weren't yours anymore, what would this trip—what would your life— look like?"

"You think I should sell the deck?" I ask. "That I'm becoming obsessed with it, like the Perillians?"

"If you don't mind me jumping in here," Cleo says, continuing off my nod. "We're nothing like the Perillians, not really. Who they claim to be and who they really are don't line up at all. They say they want people to work for their knowledge, but spill their guts at the first sign of interest. They say they want to be private, but that's just their way to draw people in. Their obsession with the deck makes them feel special, like queens and kings of their own mountain. Luckily, that mountain is just a little hill to us. We see things for what they really are. Right?"

"Right," I say, even though I wouldn't necessarily have thought of our Perillian experience this way. Leave it to Cleo to have a totally fresh perspective.

"I totally get it. Just figured I'd play devil's advocate," Anwar says. "It's all pretty exhausting, as you already know. Think we can pass out?"

I look back at Anwar—so much for our romantic night. Then I think it's just as well. I don't really think I can do anything with him until I process what he just said.

And, more important, until I process the conversation I just had with Cleo.

Turn To Page 166

◆ ◆ ◆ ◆

When I wake up the next morning, Anwar sleeps soundly in the main bedroom. I allow myself a few seconds to stare at his still-ridiculously-good face, then leave him behind in pursuit of coffee and carbs. Walking downstairs, sunlight pours through the windows of our cabin, and the green of many trees can be seen in every direction. I exhale, feeling at home. Despite anything and everything else, I think I am exactly where I belong, as I breathe in the sappy freshness of the air.

Entering the kitchen I am surprised to find Chase sitting at the table, looking distinctly like he doesn't belong. His hair is all rumpled, there are bags under his eyes, and his usual focused intensity seems to have curdled into a permanent frown.

"You're up early."

"I didn't sleep much to begin with," Chase answers.

"Wanna talk about it?" I try.

"I don't think I can yet."

I give Chase a sitting-down side hug as I pass him, hoping it will help. I know it's probably normal for someone with a maybe-broken heart to act this way, but I'm still worried about him. Chase has barely spoken or eaten or done much besides breathe since yesterday.

"Can I at least make you something to eat?" I ask.

"I already made coffee," Chase says, suddenly standing. "I'm gonna shower before we head out."

With that, Chase exits the kitchen. I don't have much time to dwell, because Cleo enters soon after. She wears another pair of her signature glasses—hot neon pink today—and a loose-fitting pair of overalls covered in custom patches.

"Morning sunshine! You just missed Chase."

"I hope that's him in the shower?"

"Indeed it is."

"Good," Cleo says, making a direct line for the coffee pot. "Charvan was starting to smell like his breakup funk."

"At what point should we be launching an intervention?"

"Just give him time," Cleo answers, reaching for the inhuman amount of sugar and creamer she puts in her coffee. "I remember sharing a wall with my sister during her first breakup. Broken hearts are no joke, but they heal. Eventually."

There's a beep from Cleo's pocket, then she takes out Toky, who must require feeding and poop-clearing. It makes me reach for my own pocket, where the Dalet locket rests. I haven't felt ready to touch it since Coupled Cottage. Part of me doesn't want to open it again, not until I can see Grandma fully, with clarity. Who was that twenty-something girl in the photo, really? And was she anyone to Carson Perilli?

"Besides, I think it's obvious we all came out of that Isle a little changed," Cleo adds, sitting at the table. "I know I have. I was actually up most of the night thinking about it."

"Oh, really?" I say, settling down at the table next to her. Rummaging for pots and spatulas can wait. "Do tell."

"I actually told myself I was going to wait until we got back to say anything," Cleo begins. "There's so much else going on, I don't want to distract."

"Impossible," I say. "You're on this strange journey just like the rest of us. And you could never be a distraction. To me, you'll always be a main event."

Cleo blushes, hearing this. Then she smiles at me in that way I'm so used to, with that warm beam of sunshine.

"Even though that was a hot mess being made in Coupled Cottage, I still can't stop thinking about my conversation with Lily," Cleo continues. "She might have been out of line, but I also think she might have had a point. I think maybe I've stuck with certain things because they're easier for everyone else. But reacting to Lily, I realized it's not my job to shrink to make anyone else feel comfortable. So I think . . ."

Cleo pauses a second, gathering herself.

"No, I *know* I want to start using nonbinary pronouns. I'm going to start with *they, them,* and *their,* to see how it feels."

I know Cleo means this as a statement, but it still comes out sounding like a question. Cleo looks to me imploringly, almost as if for . . . approval? Or if not approval, then some sign that this is okay with me, as one of their best friends. Well, if Cleo needs my support and my acceptance, they have it. Unconditionally.

"If that's what feels right to you, then I am so here for it," I say. "I think it's great, Cleo. Really great."

Cleo exhales, their smile brightening once again. "It does feel right. This has always been who I am. It's just, given the way our world works, it took me some time to fully understand it. I've learned so much about myself this past year, how much I like embodying ends of a spectrum. I like remaining fluid. I like balancing incongruous things. So I think my outward sense of self needs to embody that, too?"

"You know you kind of sound like a walking tarot card right now, just a little?" I say, grinning.

"I know," Cleo sighs. "Who knew I'd actually learn something grounded from these cloudy cards of yours?"

"Welcome to the club," I say. "But hey, two opposing things can be true at the same time, right? I've been trying to get that idea into my thick skull, too."

I smile at Cleo and they widen their own smile one more time. I take a beat to really soak in this conversation. Even though it was short, something tells me it'll be a moment Cleo and I both remember for the rest of our lives.

"Shouldn't we get going?"

Chase appears in the doorway looking freshly scrubbed, but definitely still exhausted. Despite his dubious appearance, he actually is correct—we've taken more time than we should getting to the next missing card. We all needed a beat to collect ourselves, but the moment to scale the next cliff has arrived. After all, we haven't come across a single Perillian since we left Summerland. Somehow, I can't tell if that's a blessing or a bad omen.

"I'll go see if Anwar is awake."

Upstairs I find him still in bed, definitely sleeping. He looks so peaceful, his full lips slightly parted and his hand strewn across the curves of his chest. I hate to disturb a picture so pretty.

Instead of dwelling, I dress myself in lilac shorts and a mint green t-shirt, because it feels like this day is in need of some bright, flowery vibes. Somewhere during this process Anwar stirs, stretching like an enormous grumpy cat.

"Is it morning already?" he asks. "I feel like I could still sleep for hours."

"Morning it is. We're getting ready to head out."

"Oh, damn," Anwar says, looking overwhelmed suddenly. "Hey, do you think maybe it's okay if I stay behind for this one? I'm not feeling my finest or freshest."

"Oh. Sure," I say, trying to hide my initial burst of disappointment.

"Besides, this hidden tarot thing is for you and your friends. I'm sure they'll be happy not to have me intruding again."

"You're not an intruder."

"I am," Anwar says. "But I'm also an intruder who can make a mean meal, cooked for whenever you adventurers return from your latest journey."

Thinking this over, the next set of coordinates is only a short trail through the woods from here. So chances are we'll be back at the house sooner than later, one way or another.

"I request an eternal breakfast when we return."

"Your wish is my command."

Anwar leans across the bed to squeeze my hand before I go. He then looks up at me, his amber eyes suddenly brimming with feeling.

"Thank you, Amelia."

"For what?" I ask, a little unnerved by this sudden rush of emotion.

Anwar doesn't respond. He just squeezes my hand again, like I already know the answer. Perhaps I do, I think, as I step away. Grabbing Cleo's backpack, I give Anwar one last look from the doorway . . .

But he has already nuzzled his face back into his pillow.

♦ ♦ ♦ ♦

The walk through the woods takes longer than any of us expected. Not necessarily because of the distance, but because there was no actual "trail" to follow. We had to forge our own path every step of the way, over rolling roots and around enormous trees and through rocky dirt. Somewhere along the way all three of us lost cell service, but luckily Cleo's map app still got us where we needed to be.

We now stand in front of a wooden structure in the woods, built in a low valley between two hills. It's not big enough to be a cabin, but it's probably too big to be a shed, plus it has windows and a greenhouse-style roof. Not that we can see anything inside—the entire structure is completely unkempt, overgrown with moss and vines. It looks not unlike something out of a fairy tale, warm and inviting but likely hiding something grim inside.

"Well, the door is ajar," Cleo says, pointing. "But I so do not want to be Hansel or Gretel in this scenario."

Chase looks equally hesitant, so it falls to me to lead the charge.

"It doesn't look like anyone has been here for a long time," I say, striding forward. I force myself to take a breath as I approach the door because, truth is, I have zero idea what I'll find on the other side. After all we've been through, literally anything feels possible.

Still, with Chase and Cleo standing behind me, I slowly push open the door. Unexpectedly, my first thought is that it feels weird being only three of us—unbalanced somehow without a fourth. My next thought washes this away, however, as the door swings open.

Inside the shack, we see only color. My eyes struggle to take it all in. Nearly every inch of the space is filled with flowers. One corner is devoted to roses, thick-thorned stems with white and red blooms. Another corner houses a hydrangea bush blooming light blue and pink. To our left, I'm stunned to find an actual pond, brimming with lilies.

The middle of the shack has a wooden beam that stretches across it, but it's barely visible. Pots of flowers and succulent bulbs hang from the beam, which is also covered with twisting vines and rows of herbs. Perhaps most breathtaking, however, is what sits underneath this beam, in the center of the room: an arrangement of flowers and plants in tiers, like something you'd see at an opulent wedding. Just behind this floral altar I spot a platform that is shaped, rather appropriately, like a pentacle.

Taking this place in, I feel its energy coursing through me, its floral and earthy smell hanging thick in the air. Suddenly I feel like an Empress who has found her throne room, deep within the heart of Mother Nature. It's like my senses come alive in this place, like this space somehow belongs to me.

Or rather, like I belong to this space.

Though I doubt it's as abandoned as I first thought. Plants might do well on their own, but they don't stay this manicured. Which means the next Corner of Perillians must know about this location, even without our deck. My heart starts pounding. What exactly do these so-called Repentant Perillians have in store for us?

"Look, in the center of the pentacle platform."

Chase points as he speaks, so Cleo and I look closer. I immediately see it, in the center of the platform—the seams of a secret door.

As much as I really want to soak in the wonder of this secret garden, I walk straight up to the platform. Finding the other hidden cards involved such difficult processes, but could it really be that finding the King of Pentacles might be more straightforward?

Examining this door, I see there's a hidden panel in its upper corner. Opening this panel, we find it houses a keypad lock, its numbers replaced with simple tarot symbols. My hope crumbles like dirt, however, when I realize this keypad has already been unlocked, along with the formerly locked door. Lifting open this door, my hope then shatters entirely when we find an empty compartment inside—which means whatever was once here must have already been taken.

Someone got to the King of Pentacles before us.

I suppose it was naive to think all the Perillian Corners would have the same reverence as the Baxters. Or that all Perilli's puzzles would be equally unsolvable. But then I think: these hidden cards are supposed to be unobtainable without our deck. That rule has proved to be true so far, so could there be something more than meets the eye here?

I look to Chase to find him already staring at me. He nods—we're obviously both thinking the same thing.

"Hey, wonder twins," Cleo says. "Not everyone understands your freaky unspoken language. What are you thinking?"

"That these hidden cards can't be found without the deck," I say, reaching around to open Cleo's backpack. If we're looking for clues, surely the cards will help. "Which means someone either got very lucky, or the King of Pentacles is still hidden here somewhere."

"You think this is all a decoy?" Cleo asks.

Chase just shoots Cleo a look: *Stranger things have happened.*

I zip open the narwhal backpack's secret compartment, the one hidden in its inner lining. My fingers reach for the deck, but with a sudden lurch, I grasp . . .

Nothing.

My breath catches in my throat.

"The deck isn't here."

Even as I speak the words, I refuse to believe they're true.

However, even after I've emptied the backpack, handing it over to Cleo to double check—even after we turn the entire damned thing inside out—still, we find nothing. The deck is gone, just like the emptied pentacle platform. My hands reach up into my hair, tugging in exasperation as buds of panic begin to flush my skin.

How can that be? I just put the deck in here last night. How could—

"Amelia," Cleo says, their eyes filled with dread. "Did you . . . Did you ever put the deck away in front of Anwar?"

My heart suddenly sinks. It slides out of my body and buries itself in the coarse earth below.

Oh goddess. Please, no.

CHAPTER TEN

CHASE

BACK AT THE rental house, we find Anwar has gone without a trace.

I wish I could say I expected something else. Just like I wish I could say I expected Anwar to pick up any of the dozen times Amelia tried calling him. Wherever he has fled, two things are clear: One, he took the Perillian deck with him. Two, we're never going to hear from him again.

I suppose we could track down Anwar's home near Solvang, but by then he will no doubt have sold the deck—it's the only reason I can fathom he stole it in the first place. There would be no point to that empty confrontation, showing up at Anwar's door to fight over something long gone. It wouldn't undo what he has done, or make his betrayal sting any less.

These words scroll through my head and sear as they settle, because they can obviously apply to Logan. Though really, since he left, I find myself applying most things to him. Almost everything reminds me of Logan and nothing makes me feel better about potentially losing him. Food just makes me nauseated, and I have no appetite anyway. I can't sleep, instead playing over every single thing Logan has ever said to me. I don't have energy for anything except this loop, agonizing in my own rut. Missing Logan feels deep, like my roots have been severed. Instead, there's only rot left, wet and bleeding.

The one thing that distracts me also disgusts me, but right now disgust feels like a welcome relief. So, sitting alone in the kitchen while Amelia and Cleo ransack the bedroom for a third pointless time, I do the disgusting thing: I open Instagram on my phone and search for Seidon's page.

I haven't messaged or followed him, but I have spent many sleepless hours poring over his photos. No matter how much I stalk and stare, I cannot resolve how someone like him could be interested in me. Am I allowed to be flattered? Am I allowed to want to sleep with him? It feels like Seidon's interest could be a bridge to some other world, a ledge that dives into uncharted valleys.

Mostly, I just end up feeling angry. The anger is so easy, I let it bloom in my chest like a flower. He loves me, he loves me not. *Screw you both, with your casual attractions. You did this to me, you made me this way.*

How can I ever trust Logan if he wants someone else? How can I trust anyone ever again, if they can turn on a dime like this? Then comes the scariest cycle in this repeating track: How can I ever trust myself if I didn't see this coming? I keep writing in my journal, like dumping my thoughts in there and locking them up will make it all go away. I keep rereading the lessons and quotes I keep copied in my personal bible section, but all the words feel hollow.

This is when I descend into the darkest pit, because this doesn't feel like something I'll recover from. This feels like it will leave a permanent, ugly scar. Suddenly every song I've ever heard makes more sense, like I've been let into this great human club of heartbreak. So I sit here like so many before me, tangled up, pining over the glossy photos of a boy I'll never truly have. Who I'll never truly be.

I'll always just be me. Critical, riddled Chase.

"You look as bad as I feel."

Amelia speaks from the doorway, indeed looking equally terrible. Of course, now all I can think is that Logan would know what to do next. He'd know what to say to make Amelia feel better. But what can I say, aside from welcoming her to the business of misery? I'd love the company.

"Chase, what's that?"

Amelia points to the center of the table in front of me. Shifting my gaze, I find a plain white piece of paper there, folded neatly in three.

"I don't know," I answer, hating myself. Of course I was too absorbed by my thoughts to notice the letter sitting right in front of my face. I'm so terrified that if I stop moving, I'll unravel. I'm a tightly wound ball of twine—tensing up and rolling along is the only way I'll stay in one piece.

Amelia rushes to the table, with Cleo following close behind. She opens the letter, and I don't need Amelia to say a word to know it's from Anwar. So we all read together:

Amelia, this letter is much less than you deserve, but I had to leave something behind. Some explanation that would maybe excuse the inexcusable thing I've done.

My mom is sick. We have no money. We live near Los Olivos because my mom cleans rich people's houses off the books. She and I, we live in a trailer—which is why I didn't want you to see it. Mom can't work anymore and I don't know how we're going to pay for her treatments. So when I found out how much your deck is worth from Lady Azure . . . Well, I think you know what I've done by now.

I tried to sell the deck to Page Zain, but in such a short time, I could only find someone online who claimed to know them: Rosa Resfriado, owner of Chills Coven Shop. As collateral, I gave her the clues on the Empress and Hanged Man cards to open some compartment, because she already knew where the King of Pentacles was hidden. By the time you read this I'll have also sold her the deck. I know she's not giving me as much as I could get if I kept it to sell to Page Zain directly, but the money she promised me will buy us a few months. Besides, I think I was afraid if I held onto the deck, I'd come to my senses and return it to you, like a good guy would. And maybe part of me wanted to sell it somewhere you'd have a shot to get it back.

I'm telling you this so maybe you can go to Chills Coven. I never told Rosa anything about you, so she won't see you coming. Maybe you can take back your grandmother's deck, because I know it really belongs with you.

Just like I know what I did is wrong. I wish I had another choice.

Amelia, you have to know, what we had together, the things I said to you—I wasn't faking that. I promise. I came along with you, knowing nothing about your deck at first. But once I found out what it was worth, I knew what I had to do. And I knew you and I couldn't last, afterward. I just really wish it could be different, because you're every bit as amazing as I'd hoped.

Anwar

I look up at Amelia's face to find it shattered—and torn. I understand.

How do you hate someone who did the wrong thing for the maybe-right reason? And if you can't bring yourself to hate someone who broke your heart, where does that leave you? I want to say these things to Amelia, but I don't say anything at all. Part of me is afraid of breathing reality into any of this. The other part of me is just too tired.

"Anwar asked me if I thought I'd be better off without the deck," Amelia says, still clutching the letter like a lifeline. "I think he was trying to convince himself he was doing me a favor. Like the deck was a burden he was relieving me of."

"Amelia, this isn't your fault," Cleo says, speaking through clenched teeth. "I wasn't exactly a fan of Anwar, but I didn't think he'd do something like this."

"How could he . . ." Amelia tries. "Anwar obviously knew he was going to do this last night. He wrote this letter sometime before today. And he still . . ."

"Why leave the letter at all?" Cleo asks, their words practically quaking.

"Because no one wants to think of themself as a bad person," I answer. "Even when they're doing something they know is terrible. This letter is a justification. It's a window in the cell where Anwar belongs."

Cleo opens their mouth to say something else, but pauses a moment before doing so.

"Maybe this is a sign or something," Cleo finally offers. "This trip stopped being fun the second Logan left, if I'm being honest. Maybe we let it go and cut our losses?"

Amelia sighs, seeming to actually consider Cleo's suggestion.

Well, I won't entertain it for one second. The only thing that feels more unbearable than our current situation is the idea of quitting while we're behind.

"Amelia, you have every right to feel discouraged and frozen. Trust me, I understand," I begin.

◇ "But Anwar did leave us clear tools for **a solution**. Can we really walk away when we still have a chance to recover the deck, this missing piece Gran Flo left us?"
Turn To Page 176

◇ "But think about what Gran Flo would say. If we're at the part of the journey that's the hardest, then we're also about to **learn more** than ever before."
Turn To Page 177

"Just think about The Hanged Man in the Major Arcana journey," I continue. When all else fails, Amelia and I have always relied on the tarot to make sense of the senseless. "It's the place where trials come to test our strength and knowledge."

"Yeah, but then we also have to think about The Hanged Man's reversal," Amelia counters. "Needing to be right. Embracing old ways. Feeling the universe owes you something."

Listening to Amelia's argument, my rusted brain begins to stir. All of a sudden it feels good to have some seeds of motivation planted in me again.

"Sure, but what did Gran Flo always say about trust?" I counter right back. "*If you can't trust a person, then you can at least trust in understanding their motivations. If you can figure out what someone wants, then they become predictable.* I don't think we can close ourselves off from possibility because someone did us wrong. That just means we learn to be smarter for next time."

Amelia raises one eyebrow at me. I can't blame her—this must sound hypocritical coming from me, human-sized off-switch I've become.

"If nothing else, we can try to turn this betrayal into wisdom?" I try. "Besides, if we know now we can't trust any new people on this trip—hell, if we know we can't even trust our own emotions—then maybe that's the exact mindset we need to get the deck back and find the King of Pentacles?"

I feel exhausted from delivering even just this little speech, but maybe that's because I also feel like maybe I've just broken through some internal wall? Unfortunately, Amelia still appears stuck on the other side. Cleo too. Suddenly I feel stupid. Exposed.

Without thinking, I react.

◊ "Fine, whatever. I'm going to this Chills Coven place **with or without** you."
Turn To Page 178

◊ "Or maybe I'm wrong? Maybe we should learn our lesson and not repeat our mistakes by going down the **same road**?"
Turn To Page 179

Amelia still looks unsure. And why shouldn't she? I'm not exactly in a place to be offering advice. Still, when all else fails, Amelia and I have always relied on the tarot to make sense of the senseless.

"Okay, then think of the step in the journey that comes after The Hanged Man," I try. "Think of Death, the card Gran Flo always said was the most misunderstood figure in the entire Major Arcana."

I take a deep breath, trying to recall the seeds of passion Gran Flo always sowed into her own take on this seemingly ominous card. It feels good scraping off some of the rust collecting on my tin brain.

"If Death is about loss, then it's about what you lose when your old self dies. If Death represents the end of an era, then its sacrifice might be what's necessary to bring about a brighter era. Death reminds us that we're meant to flow into challenges. Forcing against them only keeps us stuck in one place. I don't know about you, but I don't want to stay stuck in this place. I need to get some closure on something. Anything."

I feel exhausted from delivering even just this little speech, but maybe that's because I also feel like maybe I've just broken through some internal wall? Unfortunately, Amelia still appears stuck on the other side. Cleo too. Suddenly I feel stupid. Exposed.

Without thinking, I react.

◇ "I'm trying here, Amelia. If I can **push through**, then you can, too."
Turn To Page 178

◇ "I don't know, maybe I'm just running full speed ahead to **keep** myself **distracted**? So I don't have to stop and face reality?"
Turn To Page 179

The moment I say these words, I realize how insensitive they are.

"For someone who hasn't spoken for two days, you suddenly have an awful lot to say," Amelia snaps back. "And for someone whose feelings we've been very sensitive around, you're being pretty freaking selfish right now. Can you just give me a damn minute?"

"I'm always giving you a minute, Amelia," I respond on impulse, without thinking. Another half-truth, another insensitivity.

"Like you gave Logan a minute?" Amelia fires. "I'm sorry if my emotions are too messy for you, or if I trust too big and get myself in trouble. But I'll take that any day over being cold. Over shutting down like a robot."

Suddenly my emotions wither. I can't control it. I know I'm about to spew carelessness, like wind rattling the dying leaves off a tree.

Turn To Page 180

I mean to sound thoughtful, but as soon as the words leave my lips, I can tell they only sound unsure. Insecure.

"Which one is it, Chase?" Amelia sighs, her eyes closing. "Are you going to retreat into yourself or are you going to tell me what's best? Which is most convenient in Chase's world right now?"

These words shift something in me, like plates scraping.

"Do you have a problem?" I ask. "Because I've only tried to support you this entire trip."

"Support me or manage me? I can make my own decisions, you know."

"Yes," I spit, a crater opening in my chest. "We can see where that's gotten us."

Amelia takes my words like a bullet. I hate myself even more for it.

"Well, I'm sorry I know what I want and go for it without apology," Amelia then fires. "But maybe if you got out of your own head for two minutes, Logan wouldn't have left either."

Hearing this, my brain cracks. It's like a tree trunk snapping in half, buckling under the weight of my collected thoughts. Then, for a furious moment, it's not just myself I hate.

Turn To Page 180

"Well, maybe I wouldn't need to consider everything or make myself small if my best friend didn't always take up all the air."

The second I unleash these words, I regret them. I don't even mean them, not really. At least I don't think I do. But Amelia doesn't deserve this, especially with her panic stuff. The last thing I want is to add to her anxiety or push her into an attack. I just feel so . . . everything, all at once. It's too much.

"Amelia, I didn't mean that," I say quickly. "Really, I just . . . I'm so messed up over Logan, I can't see straight."

"I didn't mean what I said either," Amelia offers, her eyes on the floor.

"Well, I was about to tell you both to stop projecting, but it sounds like I don't need to," Cleo adds. "The enemy isn't in this room, that's for sure. And honestly, I changed my mind. I think Chase has a point."

Cleo places a hand on Amelia's shoulder. "We can't quit now, not when we've come this far. So let's just pack up and get the hell out of here."

Without thinking, I stand up and hug Cleo. Coming from them, this means the world. Amelia then stands and hugs me, too. We both know we just got caught in the crossfire because we're the ones here, the ones who showed up, the ones who stayed. I know we took it out on each other because we love each other, not the other way around.

Still, our hug feels a little stiff. Maybe because I don't think what either Amelia or I said was completely wrong? I don't know what that means for us moving forward, but moving forward is all I can think to do right now. So once Amelia releases me, I run up to my room.

I begin to pack on autopilot, my mind still numbed and racing at the same time. Thoughts populate themselves, sprouting like weeds as my hands move. Until I touch something that finally stops me cold in my tracks. I don't know how I didn't find it earlier, but there it is, tucked in a side pocket of my duffel bag . . .

Logan's fidget spinner. His externalized mantra, the piece of him he carries with him everywhere he goes—until now. He must have put it in my bag before he left.

It's only one small thing, the spinner I now hold in my hand, but it contains a multitude of meanings. Just like that first day in Maggie's shop, I feel overwhelmed by the emotional weight of the object. Finding this token of Logan might be a single crack, but it's enough to shatter me.

I cry then, for the first time since Logan left.

I don't stop until I am emptied of everything that had been brimming over. It aches through my body, but when it's done, when my eyes sting and my throat feels raw, I realize that's the thing about being empty. Something in me may have just died . . .

But maybe that just means I'm due for a rebirth?

♦　♦　♦　♦

It's a short drive, but by the time we pull up in front of Chills Coven, Logan is already back on my mind. I thought my little breakdown and breakthrough would extend the relief, but being back inside the familiar walls of Charvan, it's like I can feel Logan's presence in the driver's seat. The thought that I might never get to press my nose into Logan's neck again, might never touch his skin again, it makes my lungs close up. The thought of someone else getting to do all that instead . . .

It's still a notion too painful to touch. I can only test its limits, like probing a fresh cut. I suppose it's true that healing isn't linear, that it happens in fits and bursts. At least the difference, after today, is the radical notion that I might actually be able to heal over time. Still, I know I need to try my best to tuck all of this away for now, because the obsessing isn't helping. And now I'm not the only one traveling with a broken heart.

So as we park Charvan, I let my fingers run over Logan's fidget spinner, which I stashed in my pocket. Feeling its corners, I let myself pretend I am a boy fully healed. After all, we decided that if we had any shot of recovering the deck here, we couldn't reveal our true selves. On the drive over, we actually all discussed our ideal aliases. Cleo immediately went with Janelle, their pansexual, nonbinary, and impeccably styled idol. Amelia went with Jamie-Lee, the reigning queen of Halloween horror. As usual, I couldn't settle on something straightforward. Eventually I decided on Apollo, the Greek god of knowledge and the protector of the young, but also the god of disease and healing. The name stands for an entire contradictory spectrum—just like my brain.

Getting out of Charvan, Amelia and I turn to each other to steal one last private moment. We nod knowingly, probably thinking the same thing: *This is a perfect day to pretend we're not ourselves.*

"How's your panic doing?" I ask. I know Amelia normally hates when I do, because drawing attention to it doesn't usually help. But I'd say our current circumstances qualify as extenuating.

"I'm fine," she answers as we enter Chills Coven. "Let's just get this done."

"Um, is it just me," Cleo begins, "or is this place kind of amazing?"

I take in the space myself, and I can't argue. We found the Monterey location for Chills Coven online, but we weren't sure what to expect. What we find is something that looks like one part trendy coworking space, one part cozy coffee shop, and one part botanical garden. In the back there's a neon script sign that reads: WHERE SCIENCE MEETS SPELLCRAFT.

The Coven is clearly set up to be multifunctional and accommodate lots of patrons, but this early afternoon only three people are present, all huddled together around a long table. They are occupied by a rolling chalkboard, which contains all kinds of numbers and lists—and one phrase written at the top.

The King of Pentacles. Bingo.

"We have customers," one of the three says, breaking their concentration. The other two look our way, and they all stand to greet us.

"Sorry, it's been a slow day," says the first to arrive, a young woman with flowers tucked into her long black hair. "I'm Supriya, and this is Sherwin and Rowe."

Behind Supriya, Rowe offers a smile, and Sherwin just nods. Following our alias trend, I assign each a persona based on their outward vibes: Supriya *Coachella*, Rowe *Lizzo*, and Sherwin *Practical Magic*.

"So what brings you into Chills Coven today?" Supriya asks.

"We're driving up the coast, and someone we met recommended stopping in here," Amelia answers, not missing a beat. We all agreed to keep our lies as close to the truth as possible, without giving ourselves away. "Do you know Lily Baxter?"

I nearly wince—that's quite the opening risk Amelia just took. Luckily, all three of our marks quickly shake their heads, without a trace of recognition.

"Still, love a rec!" Supriya says. "So what do you know about our space?"

"Not much. But it looks amazing."

"It's all the vision of Rosa Resfriado, the founder of Chills Coven," Supriya continues. "She imagined it as a coworking community designed for sisterhood but open to everyone, with a focus in the art of scientific spellcraft. Our members and customers use the space diversely, but we three are the Coven coordinators."

"Though we're better known as the three wicked stepsisters," Sherwin adds without a hint of irony. It's then that I notice Sherwin wears a light layer of makeup, perfectly accentuating his features.

"Forgive Sherwin, he lives for all things *Hocus Pocus*," Rowe says. "But we all have our specialties. Supriya handles the floral shop and essential oils brews. Sherwin is our resident drag night hostess and budding wiccan."

Rowe glances at a small stage in the shop corner, prompting Sherwin to wink.

"And I'm our empress of mathematics," Rowe continues, "but I also run the award-winning coffee counter. Trust me when I say: I mix magic in a cup."

"Science meets spellcraft," Amelia says. "So, like, astrology and the tarot, too?"

"Rosa actually handles that stuff if you're lucky enough to be read by the queen herself," Sherwin says. "She usually only does sessions while she does nails, which are as sharp as her reads."

"Rosa kind of adopted us, her coven of stray children, so to speak," Supriya says. "Everyone is welcome here as long as they have something organic to offer."

"Is Rosa obsessed with Pentacles from the tarot?" I ask, breaking my silence. Amelia tenses beside me, but I know what I'm doing. "It's just, the emphasis on a green and female space. The magical vibes rooted in physical senses."

"Actually, yes," Sherwin answers. "And as Mama Ro would say, collecting them coins. Pentacles are all about the transactional as well. But honey, how do you know so much about Pentacles?"

"Oh, I'm writing a thesis on tarot cards," I lie, surprised by how effortlessly it flows out. "It's why we're on this trip—I dragged my best friends along for one last occult research hurrah before the semester starts. A kind of 'taroad' trip, if you will."

I wink at Amelia, hoping this inside joke makes her smile. I'm not sure I recognize this smoother version of myself, but I don't hate him.

"You might have actually come on the perfect day," Rowe says. "We were just in the middle of solving a tarot equation and we hit a wall."

"Tarot equation?" I feign. "What does that even mean?"

"It's a little bit of a deep dive, if you're really interested," Rowe replies. "And it might seem kind of . . . out there."

"Try us," I say.

Sherwin then shoots Rowe a look: *What are you doing?* But Rowe just shrugs him off: *What? These three are harmless.* Meanwhile, I see Cleo and Amelia exchange a look of their own: *Here we go again with these "secretive" Perillians spilling the tea.*

"Rosa acquired a new tarot deck, a bit of a lost artifact to aficionados like my stepsisters here," Supriya picks up. "It's interesting, but a touch weird for me. The guy who made the deck was some kind of underground artist with a cult following. Apparently he liked to hide some integral missing cards behind elaborate puzzles."

"You're not talking about someone named . . . what was it?" I pause for effect. "Carter Perry? I read a little about him in my studies, but he seemed pretty obscure."

"Carson Perilli," Sherwin corrects. "And yes, he would be."

"Anyway, maybe some fresh eyes would help these two?" Supriya asks, brightening to soften the edges in Sherwin's voice. "I have to admit, I've been pretty useless. Unless you came here for something more specific?"

"I, for one, could stand for a flower crown like yours," Amelia gushes.

"And I could go for some magic coffee, for sure," Cleo adds.

"Well, I forced us to stop in for some research scouting, since we've been visiting notable tarot shops," I say, sealing the deal. "So an obscure tarot puzzle sounds right up my alley. Lead the way?"

Once we've resettled—with what can only be described as truly transcendent cups of coffee—the Coven stepsisters walk us through Perilli's latest puzzle. True to Pentacle form, Perilli hid the King card in a large circular box, one made to look like a coin. On its face, there's a pentacle set with five points. The fifth point at the top is the King of Pentacles, while the other four points have combination-style locks with scrolling numbers from 1 to 14. In the center of the pentacle is a list of instructions on how to open the coin box:

Find the four distinct Pentacle Arcana numbers that add up to the King and tell his story in the correct order. Tampering with the box or locking in an incorrect combination will destroy the card.

Once again, Perilli wasn't kidding around with his homemade self-destruct mechanism—it must have been some kind of secondary, sculptural engineering art form for him. The back of the lockbox does indeed house a canister of some acidic liquid, probably the same kind that Amelia said was in the Princess of Cups maze tank. It makes me wonder why Perilli didn't have a similar mechanism for the Prince of Wands, but then I think that card was far better hidden than the Princess and the King, both of which were also readily accessible by Perillians.

"You're right," I say, trying to seem surprised. "That is pretty out there."

"How did you even find the lockbox?" Amelia asks, seeming innocent enough.

"Well a bunch of us who follow Perilli visit this little treehouse out in the woods. Supriya especially likes to keep it full of her flower arrangement experiments," Rowe explains. "It was one of the places where Perilli liked to paint, so we always expected there was a card hidden there—especially because there's a locked compartment on a platform inside that no one knew the keycode for."

"So what changed?" I ask.

"It was all Rosa, really," Rowe continues. "Some dude called her out of the blue, saying he inherited the final deck from his grandfather. Rosa thought he was a fraud, but then, as collateral, he gave her the coordinates on the cards that led to the tree-house, which also had the code to open the platform compartment."

Anwar may have stolen Amelia's story along with the deck, but at least he had the decency not to sell us out. Otherwise, this visit definitely would have gone much differently.

"Fast-forwarding," Sherwin jumps in, shooting the clearly more loose-lipped Rowe another mean mug. "Rosa agreed to buy the deck and the dude dropped it off this morning. Total dreamboat, but probably not very bright. Rosa bought the deck from him for a fraction of what it's worth, at least to the right buyer. It'll be worth even more if we can unlock the King of Pentacles."

I look to Amelia and am relieved—and proud—to see she holds her face even. Because Anwar getting way underpaid for our deck only adds insult to injury.

"We're all saving to go to college. We have a fund from what we earn here," Rowe says. "Rosa said if we help unlock the King and figure out how to find the other missing cards, she'll split some of the sale between us."

"Rosa went out to see if she could find something called a 'toolset' to determine the other coordinates," Supriya adds. "We're supposed to be solving this four-number sequence while she's gone. We made some headway, but we're stuck."

Sherwin still looks displeased about how much they've told us, but the fact that he hasn't totally shut them down must mean they really do need our help. I also don't see the deck anywhere, so it must be locked up somewhere they think is safe.

"Want to walk us through what you have?" I ask.

"Well, I started us off using my math brain," Rowe says, walking over to the board to explain her work. "We don't know a ton about Perilli, but we know he always believed Pentacles stood for earth sciences. We here at Chills Coven believe science is basically the same thing as casting spells, so we broke it down like a spell equation. The four numbers must be distinct, be related to the Pentacles suit, and add up to the King, which stands for fourteen.

"That leaves us with the numbers one through thirteen. And since our lowest possible combination of numbers is one plus two plus three equals six, that rules out anything over eight, which would put us over fourteen. Then, accounting for the numbers needing to be distinct, that narrows it to just five options that add up to fourteen: 8 1 2 3, 7 1 2 4, 6 1 2 5, 6 4 3 1, and 5 4 3 2. Finally, accounting for every potential combination of the number order gives us twenty-four options per set, so a total of one hundred twenty possibilities."

Rowe points to a part of the board where, indeed, 120 different number combination sequences have been listed.

"Next up, it was my turn to get spooky on it," Sherwin says, taking over. "My darling Rowe misspoke a bit. Existing equations and recipes aren't actually considered spells, because we have mastery over them. We define spellcraft here as any future science, the magic that we don't yet fully understand. Astrology might be considered spellcraft by this definition, but I like to focus on Numerology. Even though numbers have no physical existence, they order every aspect of the universe.

"We all agreed Perilli would probably go with the number set two three four five. It's by far the most sequential, plus it also tells a chronological story. That was just a hunch, but then we tried doing a little tarot reading divination with just the Pentacle cards in the deck. That's when my sisters realized that these four specific Pentacle cards—two three four five—all have special marks the other four don't."

Supriya leans forward to show us her phone, which has pictures of these cards. Instantly, I spot the tiny green star painted on each one, which I never noticed before.

"Sherwin thinks the sequence for these numbers is two three four five," Rowe picks up, "but I think that's too straightforward. It doesn't account for how these four cards and their symbols 'tell the King's story' in the right order."

"So that leaves us with twenty-four possible combinations of two three four five," Supriya summarizes. "We were going to try to figure out how to narrow it down next."

Staring at the chalkboard, my brain begins thrumming again.

"Okay, I actually might have an idea where to look next," I begin.

◇ "I agree that magic and spells are really just possible future science. Just like the tarot, it all has meaning because it's grounded in reality. That's why we need to focus on telling the King's story through **tarot history**."
Turn To Page 188

◇ "I think it's totally possible that magic and spells are real. Like spiritual truth, just because we can't prove it exists, that doesn't mean it isn't real. So we should focus on the **tarot symbols** and how they capture higher truths."
Turn To Page 189

Things like numbers and symbols have only the meaning that history assigns them, just like the fidget spinner in my pocket. To anyone else it would just be an inanimate object, but to me it's a powerful totem carrying so much personal resonance. If we're going to figure out this equation, we need to focus on the thing that seemed to carry the most weight when Perilli created his decks: tarot history. After all, the symbols of the tarot are expressed in almost every historical religion, not to mention astrology, yoga, the chakras, mythology—the list goes on.

"First, should we agree on a definition of the King of Pentacles?" I continue. "From what I know, the King stands for achieving success using common sense, but also the principle that one should never become obsolete and complacent. He also represents reaping what is sewn from steady, hard work."

Starting on this tarot flow feels so good, returning to something I have mastery over. Since Logan left, everything I knew about myself has felt unsteady. Getting back to basics like this reminds me who I am, or at least an important part of who I am.

"Isn't the King of Pentacles the strongest representation of an artist in the tarot, capturing the struggle between inspiration and criticism?" Amelia suddenly adds.

I shoot her a look: *I'm supposed to be the only tarot expert here, remember?*

"I might have gotten into the tarot through my bestie here," Amelia says, winking.

"Don't worry, I'm a tarot newbie, just like Supriya," Cleo chimes in to compensate.

"Right, well that take makes sense to me, too," I say, trying to push us forward past this moment. "Since Perilli was an artist himself, telling the King's story might really mean telling the artist's story?"

Turn To Page 190

Just like objects, I've always believed symbols also carry special meaning, coming in many different forms. Like the favorite objects we brought on the trip: my journal, Cleo's art backpack, Amelia's locket . . . Logan's fidget spinner.

Clearly all the tarot's symbols course with the same kind of power and significance. They might have different expressions in all their varying contexts, but their core meanings resonate—just like numbers. So now our job is to figure out how these numbers, in the right order, symbolize the King of Pentacles.

"First, should we agree on a definition of the King of Pentacles?" I continue. "From what I know, the King represents the reality of nature and the elements: order and chaos, control and abandon."

Starting on this tarot flow feels so good, returning to something I have mastery over. Since Logan left, everything I knew about myself has felt unsteady. Getting back to basics like this reminds me who I am, or at least an important part of who I am.

"Yes, the King of Pentacles is the strongest representation of nature in the tarot, capturing how it always changes with the seasons," Amelia suddenly adds.

I shoot her a look: *I'm supposed to be the only tarot expert here, remember?*

"I might have gotten into the tarot through my bestie here," Amelia says, winking.

"Don't worry, I'm a tarot newbie, just like Supriya," Cleo chimes in to compensate.

"Right, well that take makes sense to me, too," I say, trying to push us forward past his moment. "I think the King also warns against the danger of being left out in the wilderness, especially if you try to tame nature."

Turn To Page 190

Just then, the door to Chills Coven suddenly clangs closed and a new voice sounds from behind us.

"I think Perilli definitely would have agreed with you, young man. But no one knows the King of Pentacles more intimately than . . ."

We all turn and I lay eyes on the woman who must be Rosa Resfriado, chosen mother to the coven of chills, looking every bit the part of her tarot expression:

"The Queen of Pentacles."

CHAPTER ELEVEN

AMELIA

LONG AFTER WE all make introductions, I can't stop staring at Rosa. She is dressed and styled like she's stepping into a music video, or maybe even one of the coven's drag shows. Everything about her seems elongated: false eyelashes, flowing hair extensions, and acrylic gel nails painted forest green with golden stars. She must be in her forties, but it's impossible to tell with the expertly applied makeup contouring her face. She wears a fitted white jumpsuit printed with green palm leaves and gold strappy-sandal heels, which match her full sleeve of gold bangles and pentacle pendant necklace.

Rosa obviously fully embraces the glamorous and generous Queen of Pentacles gig, but if that's true, I also have to remember to beware the Queen's potential reversal: spinning webs and being lured by material wealth. I've already been deceived once today—the thought of Anwar still flashes fury and misery into my veins. I know if I stop too long to think about what he has done, I'll fall deep down into a well of anxiety. So I just try to focus on the present moment, one foot in front of the other.

"You all figured this out in the hour I was gone?" Rosa exclaims, once she is fully filled in. "You chosen children, always making mother proud!"

Rosa smiles and it's like her sunshine beams directly on each of us. She then strides toward the chalkboard, taking point. As she moves I get a whiff of perfume, citrus and golden honey.

"But let me tell you, this queen started searching for her King of Pentacles while most of you were still on playgrounds," Rosa continues. "So gather round. I have a story to tell, now that I know how far you've come."

♦ Just before, Chase had us focused on **tarot history**.
Turn To Page 193

♦ Just before, Chase had us focused on **tarot symbols**.
Turn To Page 194

"I think our new friend Apollo has the right idea," Rosa begins, causing Chase to actually blush. "The artist who made this puzzle believed the tarot carries its history with it in every variation of its cards, just like every specific deck carries the history of those who read it. So maybe 'the artist's story' can be found in the tarot's own herstory?"

Rosa pauses, flipping her hair for dramatic effect before continuing.

"The origins of tarot cards date back as early as the fourteenth century, but the period we probably care most about is the nineteenth century, when artists started creating their own decks. I have a feeling the artist's story we're looking for has to do with the infamous Rider-Waite deck. Perilli was obsessed with the organization it came from: the Hermetic Order of the Golden Dawn."

"Who were they?" I ask. It really is fascinating how each Corner seems to possess a different layer of Perillian knowledge, probably also by design.

"The Golden Dawn was founded in London in 1888, notable for admitting women alongside men. It was a secret society that studied metaphysics and the occult, so they believed the tarot was a path to personal development. As an act of initiation, new members were required to paint their own tarot decks. This was the reason Golden Dawn member A. E. Waite made his deck—a deck that was later published by Rider and Co."

Rosa pauses for another moment, giving me the chance to reflect that this deck-creating practice obviously wasn't the only tradition Perilli followed. Perhaps this Golden Dawn Order was also what inspired his own fledgling secret society?

"As they say, the more personal something is, the more universal it becomes," Rosa continues. "The idea of solving our greatest mysteries with the deeply personal is baked into the very core of the tarot. After all, the word *Arcana* itself means 'mysteries,' or 'secrets.' Major mysteries, minor secrets—both coming from the Latin word *Arcanum*, with roots in the term *Arcere*."

Turn To Page 195

"I think our new friend Apollo is right," Rosa begins. "The key to cracking this code is going to be about symbolism. The artist who made this puzzle believed in the power of symbols. Why the devil wouldn't he? They're the strongest communicative tool we have, outside words. In this hierarchy, first we have signs, which tell us simple directions. Then we have emblems, which capture qualities."

Rosa pauses, pointing to the golden letter on her belt: *H*, for Hermès—a logo as emblem, capturing a brand.

"Symbols, on the other hand, capture the universal truths. Alphabets and numbers might count, but I'm talking icons. Sigils, like the cross. The triangle. The crown. The wolf and the sheep. The sun, the moon, and the star."

Rosa runs her fingers across her own pentacle pendant necklace. "Humans react to symbols on instinct. They stir up our emotions, they conjure images. Symbols tell stories. It's why this equation, this combination of symbols, is about Perilli's story as an artist. After all, artists use symbolism more than anyone—except, of course, for religions. Symbols transcend death, they are sturdier than their creators ever could be. And here at Chills Coven, we know nothing captures symbols quite like the tarot, as a spiritual work of art.

"So, Apollo, I think you're right," Rosa concludes. "If we crack how the numeric symbolism tells the story of how Perilli saw the Pentacle King's nature as an artist, we'll solve the equation."

"I don't know as much about the tarot," I lie, hating every word. "But I am a psych major. Freud, Jung, and Rorschach also used symbols as analytical tools, like archetypes drawn from our collective consciousness."

I finish and Rosa sets her gaze on me, not saying a word. It's unnerving.

"You're right on the money, honey. Jamie-Lee, was it?" Rosa finally responds. "Symbols are about giving shape to the unknowable. This idea is baked into the tarot, too. After all, the word *Arcana* itself means 'mysteries,' or 'secrets.' Major mysteries, minor secrets—both coming from the Latin word *Arcanum*, with roots in the term *Arcere*."

Turn To Page 195

Rosa places emphasis on this last word, scanning her eyes over Chase, Cleo, and me as she speaks it. None of us flinch at its mention, thank goddess, even though we all know *Arcere* is the name Perilli gave his supposed successor, his "chosen one." Clearly, Rosa was using this word was a test.

"My Latin is kind of rusty," Chase says first. "Doesn't *Arcere* mean to conceal? Or to protect?"

"Or to prevent," Rosa answers. "To ward off."

Her voice is all charm and warmth, but we all detect the meaning buried underneath. I can feel us teetering on the edge of dangerous territory. Rosa must be more suspicious of us than her coven "children."

But suddenly in the midst of this, an idea sprouts in my mind, fertile and ripe.

◆ I am walking the path to **honor** Grandma's **legacy.**
Turn To Page 196
◆ I am walking the path to potential **personal power.**
Turn To Page 197

Grandma clearly had sayings she always repeated, but a very specific one unfurls in my head now: *If life is what happens when you're busy making plans, then mysteries are what happen when you're busy missing the details.* It makes me think that we all glossed over that pentacle platform, but what if there are details there we missed, especially inside that hidden compartment?

"Well, if we're taking votes on how to solve this case," I begin, "I say we return to the scene of the crime. From everything we've been exploring, I bet there are more clues hidden there. Especially since we don't seem to have all the pieces to this particular puzzle yet."

Rosa looks at me, holding a penetrating stare. I can't tell if she is buying my little ruse or if she just sees right through me.

"Besides, my grandma always used to say: *If you find yourself stuck, change your perspective,*" I continue, trying not to let Rosa fluster me. "Even if there ends up being nothing where the card was hidden, a change of scenery might help us see things differently, anyway."

Turn To Page 198

Though it's not an idea, really, so much as an image: the platform compartment in the Repentant shack. Suddenly, in my mind's eye, I remember seeing writing inside its shadowed walls.

We breezed over the platform earlier in our rush to find out what happened to the missing King card and . . . Anwar. But I shove all that aside now to try to focus on the image. Unfortunately, I don't remember what the writing actually is; I just can see it's there. I really believe the clues we need to solve this equation must be in that compartment, but how do I maneuver us back to the shack without drawing even more suspicion?

"What if we're thinking about this the wrong way?" I begin. "You said this Carson guy thought of Pentacles as the suit of spellcraft in all its forms?"

Rosa stares me down, eager to hear more. I can't tell if she is buying my little ruse or if she just sees right through me, but I press on anyway.

"Well, doesn't all spellcasting require specific conditions, in addition to specific ingredients? Would it make sense that, to 'cast this spell,' we'd need to be in the right location?"

This idea only elicits thoughtful silence, so I keep going.

"Maybe you missed something in the shed you found this card hidden in? After all, to solve a case, you always have to return to the scene of the crime, right? And maybe if the lockbox is only meant to be opened there, then clues would exist in the physical space?"

Turn To Page 198

Rosa's probing gaze doesn't let up. Even the three stepsisters seem a bit puzzled by her stretch of silence.

"Then again, this isn't really our business," I quickly add. "Sorry if we overstepped. This is all just super fascinating."

"Are you kidding?" Rosa finally says, slapping her knees and smiling excitedly. "You're in on the hunt now, if you want to be!"

I nod along with Chase and Cleo, none of us wanting to seem too eager. Cleo in particular has barely spoken a word. I know they consider themself a terrible liar, so Cleo probably doesn't want to say anything that might give us away.

"Then it sounds like we have a field trip to attend," Rosa exclaims. "And if it's okay, I'd like to ride with our wise new friends?"

"Fine by us," I answer, eliciting more nods from Chase and Cleo.

"Good. I'd love to get to know you all better," Rosa adds. "And there's nothing I love more than taking my Rosa Reads on the road."

I smile, trying to hide my unease. Exactly what is a "Rosa Read"? And by keeping us "wise new friends" close, is she really just keeping potential enemies closer? Well, that's certainly what we're doing, so I'd better remember to keep my guard up around this utterly disarming Queen of Pentacles.

Once we're back in Charvan, I resist the urge to check my phone for an entire thirty seconds. Of course, there's nothing from Anwar, just like there hasn't been the last ten times I've checked. It's stupid of me—it's not like I could actually talk to him with Rosa in the front seat chatting away with Chase about Charvan's charming interior design. What would I even say if I could get a hold of Anwar? What could he say to make his betrayal feel less devastating? Nothing. There's nothing and I know that. As complicated as his situation and his choice might be, Anwar has shown me who he really is. I need to believe him.

So then why do I want so badly, so compulsively, to hear from him? Where do I put all this feeling he left me with? Now I get why people call it emotional baggage. I feel heavy, like I'm lugging a literal suitcase around. Though at the same time I feel a searing absence, this void where something has been ripped out.

The only consolation I can fathom is finding a way to get back the deck that currently rests in Rosa's manicured hands, retrieved from her private office. At the very least, Rosa and her coven have proved to be an effective distraction, getting my mind off Anwar. Honestly, I don't want to think about him ever again, if I can help it.

"So how did you start following Perilli?" Chase asks from the driver's seat. "I tried learning more about him for my thesis research, but I couldn't find much."

"I spent a good chunk of time tracking down anything I could about Perilli," Rosa answers. "I actually got to meet him once, before he died. I was on the waitlist for a reading with him for over a year. When my time came, I drove six hours straight to be there. Perilli was actually the one to divine my connection to Pentacles. It was a real life-changer. He inspired me to quit my job and go after what I really wanted, founding Chills Coven and becoming a surrogate mother to my little house of horrors."

"Wow," Chase responds. "What made the reading so special?"

"Maybe someday you'll earn the right to know," Rosa answers. "But I will say, my own reading style was inspired by Perilli, if you want a glimpse behind the veil?"

"Fire away," Cleo says beside me. Good—I'm glad I'm not the only one dying to see how Rosa reads.

Rosa shuffles our deck and I can tell Chase resists the urge to scream at her not to nick the edges with her nails. I want to snatch the deck just as badly, but short of pushing Rosa from a moving vehicle, we'd never make a clean getaway. Right now, restraint is our only play.

"We can start with you, Jamie-Lee," Rosa begins, jolting me with my alias. "Especially because you look like you're currently holding back an avalanche."

"Boy problems," I manage, figuring it's true enough.

Rosa swivels from the front seat and holds out the deck, also offering a devilish smile.

"Don't I know it, honey. Tell it to the deck," Rosa says. "Just pick a card."

"Only one?"

"It's all I need."

Fascinating. Not just Rosa's potential process, but the fact that she's letting me touch even one part of her invaluable acquisition. Either Rosa trusts us completely or she believes we could never take the deck from her. Both are somewhat unsettling ideas.

As I reach forward, it requires all my willpower to not grab the entire deck and instead just pull one card from the middle: the Three of Swords. Seeing it, I fight the urge to gasp.

"These mother-tucking cards and their tricks are not for kids, are they?" Rosa cackles. "This card represents a trinity being pierced, in the form of a heart being broken. How's that for precise, Jamie-Lee?"

"There's no arguing that," I answer, laughing along nervously.

"Well, if it's a broken heart you've got, then there's only one way to get over it," Rosa goes on. "You've got to be the one who loves yourself, baby. I see you. You've got an enormous heart, one you're eager to share with everyone else. But in this world, that kind of heart becomes a target, a big red bullseye. Especially for someone who probably thinks they aren't beautiful enough to be loved."

Rosa's words crash into me. It's like she has reached into my chest and pierced me with a sword of her own.

"But you can't listen to that voice in your head, that same one we all have," Rosa continues. "The screaming voice that says you're a piece of crap in the center of the universe. You can choose to listen to a different voice, one that says you're worthy and interconnected. And girl, if you find that voice, no boy can ever shatter your heart. Dent it maybe, but never destroy."

I am stunned into silence. Could what Rosa just said really be that simple? Sure, getting played sucks, but it doesn't explain why I feel so discarded, so . . . worthless. Rosa is probably on to something there, but I don't feel stunned because she hit me with this truth bomb so explosively. I'm stunned because, really, I don't have the faintest idea how to start believing in myself that way.

"Janelle, your turn, honey," Rosa says, taking my card of sliced hearts back.

Cleo almost doesn't respond to this name at first, but then quickly snaps out of it. They jump to draw the top card, which turns out to be the Five of Pentacles.

"Worry. Oh worry, worry, worry," Rosa begins. "The cards don't lie, do they? It's obvious you've got lots on your mind, little quiet one. But let me tell you, if you spend too much time thinking about what you should've done before or what'll happen next, you spend zero time where you actually are. Be here. Be now. And maybe don't be so afraid to speak up? The world deserves to hear your voice."

Cleo looks equally shell-shocked listening to Rosa's read. And it's not just because her words resonate—it's because this is suddenly starting to feel like tarot-by-ambush. Where's the conversation, where's the give and take? Is this really Rosa's style, this blunt force insight—or is she just trying to rattle us?

"Apollo, can you spare a hand?" Rosa asks, having already re-collected Cleo's card of worries.

Chase keeps his eye on the road while he pulls a fanned card, but I can tell he'd rather not. Still, Rosa takes his chosen card and reveals the Six of Wands.

"Ah, victory earned," Rosa begins. "A fitting card for someone who clearly thinks so highly of their intellect—and rightly so. But let me tell you, Apollo, if we place all our self-worth on our achievements, that self-worth will always be lost. Eventually we fail and collapse, or if not, we just look for the next mountain to climb. And something tells me you're quite used to defining yourself by outside factors. I bet you define your-self by the things your smarts have gotten you. And probably by your relationships?"

I look to Chase's face and see the same stunned look Cleo and I just wore, like we're prey flayed open by a predator.

"Though I haven't even gotten to the really fascinating thing about the three of you," Rosa continues. "I don't think any of you are actually who you say you are."

It's as if a storm cloud forms inside Charvan next, primed for lightning. None of us dares speak, afraid of being struck first.

"Or I mean to say, none of you are who you think you are," Rosa corrects. "You shouldn't feel bad, it's a condition of being a teenager. I've been one myself, plus I've mentored enough to know. Now I'm sure I must sound a bit harsh, but sometimes a mother's love should be. So I do hope you take this next bit with love."

I exhale hearing this, but only a little. Rosa might not be outing our secret iden-tities, but I don't think any of us are ready for whatever new ground she might shift under our feet.

"Janelle, the strong and silent," Rosa rolls on, turning to face Cleo. "I have a feeling you're more terrified than you let on. And that you play at being unique, but you haven't quite discovered how magical you really are under all these clothes—which are cool as hell, I must say. But being strong isn't just about bold projections.

"Now, Apollo," Rosa rattles on, turning to Chase. "I'd venture to guess you're the type to think of yourself as a beta, the smart sidekick to the leading men and ladies you surround yourself with. But from what little I've seen, you have no problem speaking your mind and acting on it. I hate to break it to you, my dear boy, but underneath those glasses, you're an alpha in waiting. Once you realize that, I fear people will begin to find you quite irresistible.

"And finally, my sweet Jamie-Lee."

My whole body clenches, bracing for Rosa's next rumble.

"You remind me most of myself. At your age, I thought myself large and in charge, the leader of the pack. But really I spent most of my energy silencing myself, not saying what I really thought to spare other people's feelings. I understand. You do it because you feel so deeply yourself, you end up feeling for everyone else, too. Which means you can't bear the thought of causing anyone else pain. But here's the hard truth, love—you'll only be a real queen when you tell people what they need to hear, not what they want."

While words obviously seem to supercharge Rosa, they currently fail me. When she said she'd read us, no one warned she'd be reading us for filth. I want to say something in return, but only one thought fizzles in my head, demolishing everything else.

What if Rosa is completely right?

♦　♦　♦　♦

By the time we park and trek back out to the Repentant shack, I feel like I've pulled out half the hair on my head. I don't even try to stop myself. I know Rosa's reads were only words—spoken by a complete stranger, at that—but I feel wrecked by them. I play her reads on repeat in my mind, where they begin to crystallize alongside the events of this trip. Perilli's deck. Coupled Cottage. Grandma's legacy. Logan leaving. Anwar's deception. Chase's brooding. Right now it all feels so big it could swallow me whole.

"Can we hang back for a second?" Cleo suddenly asks, from my side.

We've been walking for a bit together, neither of us saying anything. Thankfully Chase rebounded enough to maintain some small talk up ahead with Rosa and the others. We've almost reached the Repentant shack, but Cleo is right—I need a minute to stop and think.

"I know you hate me pointing it out, but you're doing the hair thing," Cleo says. "Pretty bad."

"I know," I answer. "But it's only because I'm actively freaking out right now."

"Yeah, that tracks," Cleo sighs. "But you have to know what Rosa was doing back there, right? Either she knows who we really are and was trying to intimidate us, or she just wants us to fall in line behind her. Either way, Rosa is really the wicked one in this equation."

"But that doesn't mean what she said was wrong," I say, feeling breathless.

"So what if she's right?" Cleo challenges. "We're only eighteen. We're not supposed to have it all sorted out yet. And a fully formed adult weaponizing that is bullshit, no matter how . . . insightful she might've been."

Cleo shudders, despite themself.

"But what if I am too much, like Chase said?" I can't help it. I've slid into the spiral and I can't stop until I've circled all the way down. "Or what if I'm not enough, like Anwar made very clear?"

"Anwar literally doesn't matter," Cleo says, now stopping in their tracks. "You know I think you're enough, just as you are. Why can't you see that?"

Then I feel it, roaring in like a runaway truck: panic. It ramps up in my body, readying to tear me apart.

◇ "I'm **too big**. My body, my mouth, my heart. And I make myself big because I know I'm not enough of the things that really count."
Turn To Page 204

◇ "I know. I should **be stronger**. But I'm not like you, Cleo. You know yourself better than anyone I've met. Rosa was wrong about you."
Turn To Page 205

My heartbeat hammers. My hands feel numb. My vision blurs at the edges, because I'm on the edge of a full-blown panic attack. I begin to tug at strands of hair again, hoping the pain will somehow ground me.

"Amelia, listen to me," Cleo whispers, gripping my shoulders. "You have to breathe. Stop for a minute and breathe with me, like you taught me. Inhale four seconds, hold it for six, and exhale for seven."

I do as Cleo says, instantly thankful because I know this will work. Forcing my body to exhale more than inhale is one surefire way to lower my heart rate, which in turn slows the surge of fight-or-flight anxiety.

"All you have to remember is this response doesn't mean your body is breaking," Cleo says, slow and calm. "It means your body is working exactly how it's supposed to—just a little too well."

Letting these words soak in, I take a few more beats of mindful breathing, just Cleo and me. Eventually, I feel the landslide of panic slow.

"You have to listen to me right now, Amelia Piccolo," Cleo finally says, once they can tell I've calmed a bit. "There's no magic spell to recite here, no wand I can wave to make it all better. The world is mean, and people will rip you apart if you let them. And as much as this trip has turned into a very messy detour, I'm actually glad we're here. Because I've learned two things for sure."

Cleo pauses, needing to take a breath themself.

"The first is that no one can really hurt you unless you give them the power to. I know exactly who I want to be, who I am deep down, so all the Cains and Lilys and Rosas of the world can't touch that part of me. I just . . . I wish you could find that for yourself."

A look then comes over Cleo's face—one I'm not sure I recognize.

"Because the second thing I now know for sure is something I've been too terrified to admit for way too long. I'm in love with you, Amelia."

Turn To Page 206

"No," Cleo answers, "Rosa was right about some stuff. I am worried about something all the time, something I'm too terrified to say out loud."

Tears form in Cleo's eyes, but they quickly brush them away.

"What is it?" I ask immediately, my heart straining. Suddenly it's as if, seeing Cleo's pain, all the panic crumbles out of my body like loose dirt. My body somehow understands making sure Cleo is okay matters far more than everything else. "You can say anything to me, Cleo. Anything."

"I don't . . ." Cleo tries, taking a deep breath. "With sorting out my gender, I haven't really even touched my sexuality yet. But . . ."

"I'll love you no matter who you discover you want," I say when Cleo doesn't keep going. Don't they know that they don't have to come out to me by now? Or if they do, that I'll support them no matter what?

"That's the thing," Cleo finally replies. "I might not have a label for it, but I do already know who I love. Who I've loved for a long time."

Cleo raises their eyes to mine, and they don't need to say another word. Because I see it there, written all over Cleo's face.

It's me.

I'm the one Cleo loves.

Turn To Page 206

The thought takes immediate root, grounding me and flooring me at the same time. How could . . . How could I not have known? Or could it be I've always known Cleo feels this way, somewhere underneath it all? Could I ever feel the same? Or is it even possible that I . . . already do?

Cleo's revelation might have swept away the mudslide of panic I was beginning to experience, but now this has only been replaced by an even more complicated emotion: crushing confusion.

"Hey, are you two coming?"

Chase's voice sounds from way up ahead, where he stands at the doorway to the Repentant shack. Seeing the verdant structure again, I can't tell if I want to run toward it or just run away.

"I know my timing is terrible," Cleo says. "But I couldn't keep waiting for the perfect moment anymore."

"Cleo, I don't—"

"You don't feel the same," Cleo mumbles. "It's okay. I don't want to change—"

"No, it's not that," I interrupt. "I'm sorry, I need to say this before we go inside. Honestly, I am surprised. I haven't ever thought of us that way. But I don't . . . I'm not afraid to? Or I mean . . . I just need time to sort out what's even possible for me in that realm?"

"Hey, I get that," Cleo says. "I'm the walking poster child for that."

I release a nervous laugh, and so does Cleo.

"All I know is—" I start to say before catching myself. I want to say nothing will ever change between us no matter what, but I know that's not something I can promise. I want to say I'll love Cleo back, but that's another promise I can't make yet. So instead, I tell Cleo the truth, unfiltered.

"I am so glad you told me. The rest we'll sort out together?"

Cleo looks back at me, more vulnerable than I've ever seen them. Still, they nod. They even smile.

And it melts my overworked heart.

Standing in the Repentant shack, a single seed plants itself in my bones.

Being back here after our coven afternoon, that seed begins to sprout into righteous anger. How dare Rosa mess with our heads the way she did? How dare this false queen lay claim to what doesn't belong to her? Quickly, this fury then branches into purpose.

If nothing else, Cleo just reminded me exactly what matters most. They reminded me that I am The Empress, which makes Pentacles my turf. Finally, this affirmation blooms into determination, flowering out through my limbs: I am reclaiming what's mine.

If I ever felt guilty about taking the deck back from this house of step-witches, that falls away. Now I have a job to do. And nothing will stand in my way.

These are the thoughts that fill my head while the others solve Perilli's tarot equation. It turns out my hunch was absolutely right—the remaining clues we needed were indeed written inside the pentacle platform compartment. Knowing this makes me feel I've done my part, especially because I still can't offer the depth of my tarot knowledge without giving us all away. Besides, Chase is more than capable of working out the details with the coven. This leaves me all the space I need to focus my full attention on getting away with the King of Pentacles once it's unearthed, along with the rest of the deck.

Cleo had an idea they shared, right before we entered the shack. Once the King of Pentacles is either recovered or possibly destroyed, we use the distraction to snatch the deck from Rosa and run like hell back to Charvan. Inelegant, but straightforward.

Luckily, that's my jam.

Now it's up to me to be bold enough to pull this heist off.

Having discovered a Perillian poem written inside the compartment in gold strokes, Rosa, Sherwin, and Chase read it out loud.

THE ARTIST'S DAWN

First, above all else: the work.
Then, the inevitable worry: ineptitude,
    reception, rejection.
Finally, acceptance and success: a perfect
    duality.
Most importantly, once stability is achieved:
    risk it all over again.

♦ We've been solving the Repentant equation using **tarot history**.
Turn To Page 208
♦ We've been solving the Repentant equation using **tarot symbols**.
Turn To Page 209

Given the poem's title, we realize the equation is clearly linked to the Golden Dawn society, as suspected.

Once the others have absorbed the poem, they begin matching this blueprint to the narrowed number set. Quickly, the "King of Pentacles as artist" card story becomes clear: Three of Pentacles, the artist at work. Five of Pentacles, inevitable worry that reminds us to remain present—as Rosa just read for Cleo. Two of Pentacles, flowing forward from balance achieved. Four of Pentacles, stability should inspire risks, not stasis.

Sherwin makes an argument to swap the four and the two, but he is overruled by Chase and Rosa—rightfully so, in my opinion. The initial interpretation just seems to click. It has brought us to this moment, this specific place and time, with the artist's story fully drawn.

Turn To Page 210

Rosa uses a flashlight from her phone to check the rest of the compartment. She doesn't find anything else, but she does illuminate little symbols embedded inside one letter in each line of the poem:

A brush, a frowning mask, arrows of transference, and a raised fist.

From there, it doesn't take the others long to assemble the narrowed number set in order. A brush for the Three of Pentacles, which represents a leader at work. A frowning mask for the Five of Pentacles, which represents inevitable worry that reminds us to remain present—as Rosa just read for Cleo. Arrows of transference for the Two of Pentacles, which represents flowing forward from balance achieved. A raised fist for the Four of Pentacles, which suggests that stability should inspire risks, not stasis.

Sherwin makes an argument to swap the four and the two, but he is overruled by Chase and Rosa—rightfully so, in my opinion. The initial interpretation just seems to click. These symbols capture the different seasons of the King of Pentacles' nature too perfectly.

Turn To Page 2IO

"So who's going to do the honors?" Rowe asks.

"You children have been invaluable," Rosa answers first. "There's no way I could have figured all this out on my own. But if you don't mind, I've been waiting for a long time to take my place in Perillian history. If we're wrong, I'll bear the burden of destroying this priceless artifact. However, if we're right, I'd like to be the Queen who unearthed Perilli's final King of Pentacles."

As expected, no one challenges Rosa. So she approaches the pentacle lockbox, her eyes beginning to sparkle with anxious anticipation.

For once, I'm actually happy to let someone else take the lead. Instead, I find myself in a new position, lurking like some renewed hunter, every muscle in my body primed for action. I watch as Rosa sits on the pentacle platform, placing the deck down beside the lockbox. I glance over at Cleo and they also note this, their own fists clenched in anticipation.

After one last deep breath, Rosa begins scrolling through each combination to lock in the chosen sequence: 3 5 2 4. Once the numbers are set, Rosa looks around at each of us . . .

Then she presses the button set above the King's 14.

For a moment, nothing happens. For a moment, we collectively hold our breath—because we obviously got it wrong. The liquid is about to discharge from the lockbox canister, I just know it . . .

Until the lockbox lid clicks and separates, popping right open. Inside, the King of Pentacles is revealed, nestled into a plastic slot. Above it, a clear tube is suspended, but no liquid dispenses.

We did it.

Rosa gasps, clapping her hands together like a giddy child. I can't make out the details of the unearthed King of Pentacles from this angle, but it doesn't matter. My body swirls, fully charged. It's time to do this.

My eyes find Cleo's and we both nod.

Cleo moves first, darting toward the platform. With all eyes currently on the revealed King, Cleo is able to grab the deck off the platform before anyone realizes what they are doing. By the time everyone does, Cleo is halfway to the door.

"No!" Rosa screams, scrambling to her feet.

"Run!" I scream at Chase. He freezes for a split-second of shock, but then takes off at a sprint after Cleo.

I take advantage of the chaos to make my move. Rosa must expect me to follow my friends, but instead I rush directly at her. I use my momentum to knock her sideways off the platform, sending her falling into a bed of nearby flowers. It's petty, but I have to admit—it feels good.

I then snatch the King of Pentacles out of the lockbox and make a run for it. I don't know if the coven kids are too shocked or too afraid of me after my visible hip-check, but none of them move to stop me.

"Go after them!" Rosa shrieks from behind, just as I slam the door shut.

We have a head start, but not by much. As I begin sprinting, I realize the sun has just begun to set. Which means we don't have to worry about being chased through the woods in pitch darkness, at least. I stride to catch up to Chase and Cleo and suddenly see Cleo topple forward, their foot probably catching on some unseen root. Immediately, I flush with an instinct: I must help Cleo.

But Chase makes it there first. "Are you—"

"Totally fine," Cleo interrupts. "Let's move."

The three of us begin running again, panting as our legs churn. Adrenaline surges in my system, but unlike before, I welcome it—my body should be feeling some urgency right about now. I hear a branch crack behind me and realize the coven kids must be following us, after all. Probably even Rosa herself, since she changed into sensible sneakers before we trekked out here. I think of what she'll do to us if she catches us . . . Far worse than that fear, however, is the prospect of losing this chance to take back the deck.

It's a careful dance, letting the fear fuel me instead of freeze me. Moving as fast as possible, but not so fast that I fall into the dirt. Branches slap against my body as I sprint behind the others, scratching my cheeks and clipping my arms. I clutch the King of Pentacles in my hand, hoping I don't damage it in our chase.

We reach a small clearing and I push myself to run faster, my lungs burning in my chest. Golden sunlight spills across the grassy openness, and I raise my hand in front of my face to glimpse the King of Pentacles. Goddess forbid Rosa catches us, I at least want to lay eyes on this lost creation. Glancing up at the card in punctuated bursts, I am immediately haunted by the King's gaunt face. His head is topped with a crown of leaves and wildflowers and he sits on a throne of twisted thorns. Pentacle coins fall from his outstretched hands, cascading into the grass below and sprouting like seeds.

"I see you!"

I feel doubly haunted as Rosa's voice screams behind us. I turn my head to find her just across the clearing, looking feral. Supriya sprints at her side, joined for the hunt. They've caught up to us quickly—too quickly. And where did Sherwin and Rowe go? Fear trickles into my muscles. We're not going to get away with this.

Just then, a thought bursts into my brain. Cleo has the deck up ahead of me and they are the fastest of the three of us—that's what matters most. But I hold the King, and obviously Rosa cares about that card most of all . . .

The question quickly arranges itself before me: Do I somehow visibly leave the King of Pentacles behind for Rosa and her coven? It would be a consolation prize, giving them the chance to make back some of the money they gave Anwar. More important, stopping to gather the King would maybe slow them down and give us a better shot at making a clean getaway. Or do I continue running forward and keep the King of Pentacles with the rest of the deck, where it maybe really belongs?

Chase made exactly this kind of decision for me earlier with the Prince of Wands, and that has never sat right with me.

So now is my time to make up for that, Empress I remain.

◊ I **leave the King of Pentacles** behind for Rosa and her coven to treasure.
Turn To Page 213
◊ I **keep the King of Pentacles**. Completing more of the deck is a risk worth taking.
Turn To Page 214

As this decision locks into place, I know it's the right thing to do. So, taking one last look down at the King of Pentacles, I say my goodbyes.

However, I find this moment doesn't feel bittersweet at all, because I know now for sure these physical cards are not what really matters. What matters is the journey. The lessons. The truth. What matters is how I become the kind of person Grandma would be proud of.

Scanning my surroundings, I spot a stream nearby, slim but coursing. Instantly, I know how to make this work.

Banking left, I sprint toward the stream. Once I make it there, I stop and turn to find Rosa and Supriya running right at me in plain sight—though Supriya already trails way behind, seemingly running out of steam. Perfect.

I then toss the King of Pentacles into the stream without thinking twice, letting the current pull the card along.

"No!" Rosa shrieks, watching what I've done.

But I just keep running after Chase and Cleo, knowing in my gut that this Queen of Pentacles would never leave her King behind.

Turn To Page 215

As my decision locks into place, I know it's the right thing to do. Anwar and Rosa never had any legitimate claim to this deck, and they never will. Besides, if Rosa and her coven really are devastated over the money they'll lose, they're welcome to track Anwar down to get it back. This feels quite a bit like the right karma to me.

So I don't think twice.

I don't look back.

I don't look down.

I just keep running forward. As I do, I feel more than ever that I was the one chosen to protect these special, coveted, powerful cards. I might not know exactly why this responsibility has fallen to me, but it has.

This one thought carries me forward, moving faster than I ever thought I could. Fast enough to outrun every demon chasing me—including Rosa and her bewitching ways.

Turn To Page 215

I break out of the woods and my entire body feels spent, stars twinkling in the corners of my vision. What I see next, however, seems to glow even brighter. Reaching the street, I find one final wildcard waiting for us, as unexpected as he is welcome . . .

Logan, in the flesh, standing beside Charvan.

I have no idea why he has come back or how he knew where to find us, but I am just so thankful he is here. Because Logan is the best getaway driver we could possibly ask for.

"Cleo, I got your—wait, what's up?" Logan asks.

"We'll explain later," Cleo says, reaching Charvan first. "Are you good to drive?"

Logan just nods, spinning toward the driver's door. Chase unlocks Charvan as he approaches, and I wish I could see the look on his face right now. I'm sure that, as overwhelmed and frightened as he must be, he also must feel the same way I do:

Completely alive.

Once I reach Charvan and climb into the back seat, Logan hits the gas. As we speed away from these dark pentacle woods, I don't know if Rosa or her coven will be able to follow, but I do know this much . . .

I can finally exhale, now that everything is right where it belongs.

PART FOUR

SWORN

CHAPTER TWELVE

CHASE

S ITTING BESIDE LOGAN again doesn't feel real. Maybe it's the surge of adrenaline from being chased through the woods, but everything feels hyper-saturated. Could Logan just be an apparition I've conjured? I want to reach over and touch him to make sure he's really here, but I'm not sure I'm allowed to anymore. I turn myself toward him instead. The act causes a rush of comfort so overwhelming, I almost cry out with relief.

Logan is back.

Suddenly Charvan, still hurtling through the sunset, feels a little bit more like home. There aren't any cars behind us so far, so hopefully Rosa wasn't fast enough to follow. Which means we can focus on this unexpected return.

"Logan, what are you doing here?" Amelia blurts out, still heaving breaths from our sprint. "I mean, how did you find us?"

I know I should be the one asking these questions, but words have been failing me lately.

"I've been texting with Cleo all day," Logan answers. "So much for my phone box rule."

I turn back to Cleo, wondering how I missed this—until I remind myself how preoccupied I've been. Besides, I quickly see that Cleo appears . . . Actually, it's hard to place my finger on their exact expression. Cleo and Amelia seemed to be having a pretty heavy conversation before we entered the Repentant shack, so maybe it has something to do with that? Not to mention, none of us have had a spare second yet to mend the wounds collected from Rosa's reads.

"Obviously, she told me where to find you all, at least until an hour ago," Logan continues.

"Actually, I'm using *they* now instead of *she*," Cleo replies. "I'll fill you in later, but I'm stepping into using nonbinary pronouns."

"Oh, that's awesome," Logan answers, turning for a second to flash Cleo that devastating smile of his. "Well, I bused and ride-shared to the pin Cleo dropped, and when I saw Charvan, I figured you'd all be back soon. From the way you were running, I assume things didn't go well with this Rosa woman?"

Well, Cleo really has been keeping Logan in the loop. I don't know if I should feel betrayed by this, but really it just makes me feel like Logan never really left us. Could this maybe mean the same for our relationship? I hope so, but right now it feels dangerous to hope.

"Why are you back?"

It takes me a few seconds to register that I'm the one who asked this question. It's like my lips speak the words on my behalf.

"A few reasons, actually," Logan answers, his eyes still on the road. "I realized that, no matter what, I needed to see this trip through. It was good I took a little break, but I could never let you all end this chapter without me."

I turn my head to look out the passenger window, even though there's nothing there but blurs of twilight and trees. Hearing Logan's words, a gust of emotion hits so hard, I'm afraid it'll flatten me.

"Also, something happened I needed to tell you about in person," Logan continues. "It's about the hidden cards from before."

I turn back, and from the look on Logan's face, I can tell where this is going.

- Back in Joshua Tree, I decided to **give the Prince** of Wands to Cain.
  Turn To Page 221
- Back in Joshua Tree, I decided to **take the Prince** of Wands with us.
  Turn To Page 222

"When I got home I felt super restless," Logan continues. "I needed to go somewhere, to do something. So I found Cain's address and drove back out to the desert."

Logan doesn't say anything for the next few seconds. Instead, with his eyes still on the road, he reaches one hand into his pocket. Then he pulls out a plastic baggie, one folded over to protect . . .

The Prince of Wands.

"Cain said he was going to get it back to us soon, so he was happy to return it when I showed up at his door."

"Logan, that's—" Amelia begins, finding herself speechless.

I feel the same way.

"I guess we'll never know if Cain would've returned the card if I hadn't found him first," Logan says. "But I think he would have. See, what you put out into the world comes right back to you."

Logan holds the card out to me and I take it, this precious artifact I once gave away. Without hesitation, I then turn and hold the card back out for Amelia, returning it where it belongs.

Amelia's eyes raise from the Prince, and I can see it written all over her face. She doesn't believe in karma, not the way Logan does—or the way, on some level, I suppose I do. Still, she accepts the card with a meaningful nod. In this moment, all that matters is that our resident Magician found our missing Wands card.

"Did Cain say if the card helped him?" Amelia asks, choosing her first words quite well.

"He didn't. And I didn't ask," Logan says. "But it must have helped him one way or another, if he was willing to part with it."

Amelia stares down at the Prince of Wands then, as if still wondering about its truest power.

♦ That's when I notice Amelia **does not hold the King of Pentacles**.
Turn To Page 223

♦ "I guess we can add the Prince back to the deck, along with the **King of Pentacles**," I say, seeing that Amelia grips the new card a little too tightly.
Turn To Page 225

"When I got back home, I couldn't sit still," Logan begins. "So I started looking to find anything useful about Perilli or the cards online. I figured there must be some kind of renewed chatter after the 'final deck' surfaced in their community. But, of course, I couldn't find anything. The Corners really don't seem to communicate publicly, as far as I could find. However, there was one report."

Logan pauses. We all lean in, full of anticipation.

"It was from an auction house based in Santa Barbara, reported by a local paper. Apparently an anonymous Summerland resident donated the proceeds from the sale of a large Californian art collection to a homeless shelter. The resident included only one accompanying quote: 'From a nearby cup, to water our local lilies.'"

Silence falls over Charvan, because we all must be thinking of the Family Baxter.

"There's no way to know if it was Lady Azure or one of the kids. Or none of them, I guess," Logan adds. "But I had to tell you all about this in person."

Immediately, I turn to face Amelia. "Do you think Lady Azure sold some of her Perillian collection after our visit?"

Amelia doesn't answer, though. I suppose I'm in the most unique position to have that question answered, but no one would dare ask me to reach out to Seidon after all that has happened.

Shoving that thought aside, it seems that our Princess of Cups visit might have been a pivotal moment for the Baxters, one way or another. Then I wonder—if Perillian objects were indeed the artworks sold, who exactly were they sold to?

This new question prompts me to look down at Amelia's hands, where our reacquired deck rests.

♦ That's when I notice Amelia **does not hold the King of Pentacles**.
   Turn To Page 224

♦ I see that Amelia also **clutches the King of Pentacles**, a little too tightly.
   Turn To Page 225

"I decided to leave the King of Pentacles behind for Rosa, to slow her down," Amelia explains. "I left it floating away in a stream in front of her."

My jaw drops open, considering the grief Amelia gave me after giving Cain the Prince of Wands. I resist the urge to react, however, because I see the look in Amelia's eyes, lit by the soft string lights hanging above. She appears as overwhelmed by this choice as I once was.

"I didn't just do it to throw Rosa off our trail, though," Amelia continues. "I did it because it felt like she deserved some part of this deck for all her trouble. I understand now why you gave the Prince card to Cain, Chase. So thank you for taking the heat on that one."

I nod at Amelia, not sure what else to do. Especially because she doesn't ask for my opinion on leaving the King of Pentacles behind. She doesn't seem to need it, for so many reasons.

I don't know if that's a good sign or an ominous one, but either way it feels like the winds of change kicking up, pushing us irrevocably forward.

Turn To Page 227

"I decided to leave the King of Pentacles behind, to throw Rosa off our trail," Amelia explains. "I didn't want to tempt fate again, after getting burned by Cain."

Amelia's words hang in the air, her implied judgment of my own decision made clear. I'm tempted to react, but she continues before I can.

"It's not that I think you made the wrong decision, Chase. I just tried to learn from it. Besides, after what happened with Anwar, it felt right to leave the King of Pentacles behind. It would only feel like a reminder of him, of what he did. And now hearing about this potential Lady Azure sale, I think I made the right call leaving the King for Rosa. Maybe it will bring her some peace, like the other missing cards might have."

Listening to Amelia, I still feel the urge defend myself. However, I give myself a second to think it all through first. After everything we've experienced since that very first day of the trip, who's to say I would have made that same decision today? Besides, if Amelia feels right about the decision, I'm in no position to judge.

I nod at her, not sure what else to do. Especially because Amelia doesn't ask for my opinion on leaving the King of Pentacles behind. She doesn't seem to need it, for so many reasons.

I don't know if that's a good sign or an ominous one, but either way it feels like the winds of change kicking up, pushing us irrevocably forward.

Turn To Page 227

"Hey, Amelia, are you okay?" I ask.

"Yes," she answers quickly. "I'm trying to process what just happened."

"Well, I don't think what just happened is over quite yet," Cleo says, their head turned to look out the back window. "We have company."

We've been so distracted by Logan's return, we haven't been focused on our route. Rosa and her coven didn't seem to follow us at first, but we've been driving straight on a relatively remote road. This is the coven's turf, so of course they'd know how to catch up to us. Looking out the back window now, I see two headlights behind us . . .

Growing closer every second.

"Are we sure that's Rosa?" I ask, squinting.

"I can't see through the windshield over the headlights," Cleo answers. "But that's definitely the same Honda the stepsisters drove from Chills Coven."

"Crap," Amelia curses under her breath, looking like she thinks this is her fault. She still clutches the King of Pentacles so tightly, she almost creases it.

"Amelia, whatever happened back there doesn't matter," I say. "All that matters is losing them, now."

Hearing this, Amelia immediately snaps out of it.

"Where are we supposed to go next?" she asks.

"We don't want to lead them to the next card," I answer.

"Should we stop and try to talk to them?" Cleo asks. "Because we definitely should not add a high-speed car chase to the list of events on this trip."

"We won't have to," Logan says, pointing. "There's the freeway on-ramp."

"Their car is going to be way faster than Charvan," Amelia says. "No way we outrun them, even with other cars around. We're going to stick out like a sore thumb."

"Trust me," Logan says, impossibly calm and collected.

Up ahead, a right-hand exit leads to the northbound freeway. Then farther, after the underpass, a left-hand turn leads to the southbound side. Logan gets into the right lane, puts on his right blinker and . . . slows down?

"Shouldn't we be speeding up?" Cleo asks. "They're right behind us now."

Logan doesn't answer, though, his full focus on driving. He stays the course, beginning to exit onto the freeway. Until, at the last possible second, he turns the wheel left. We suddenly go sailing over the median grass. For a moment it feels like we might tip over, but Logan reserved a burst of speed for this maneuver. Once Charvan has straightened out, he lays on the gas pedal and we blast forward safely over the divide.

Turning around, I see Rosa's car charge forward onto the freeway on-ramp, moving too fast to follow our unexpected change of course. Even if she has the wherewithal to stop and reverse down the empty ramp, we already begin to sail through the underpass. Logan then turns us left onto the southbound freeway, driving like a quiet storm. I realize quickly that if Rosa does find some way to follow us, by the time she does we'll be long gone.

Logan proceeds to drive two exits down the freeway before pulling off. He then turns to get onto the northbound side, another brilliantly unexpected course correction. I hold my breath for what feels like ten whole minutes, but when I finally do exhale, it's because we seem to be in the clear. There's no sign of Rosa's Honda anywhere.

"Logan. That was deeply impressive," Cleo says, exhaling audibly as well. "Thank the stars you came back."

I couldn't agree more.

Turn To Page 227

◆ ◆ ◆ ◆

We soon find ourselves at a gas station, refueling in several ways. Logan offered to drive through the night to the final set of coordinates, since he has the energy for it and we don't want to risk being followed again. In preparation, Amelia and Cleo went into the convenience store to compile a makeshift dinner of chips and candy. Though obviously they just wanted to leave Logan and me alone as we refill the tank.

"You know the real reason I came back, right?" Logan says the first moment it's just the two of us. "I needed to see you. To talk to you before it's too late."

Too late for what? I want to ask, but I also know something has shifted in me after today.

"I'm happy you came back. Really," I say. "It's been hard without you. But I need to ask something of you. Something that might not be fair?"

I pause for Logan's approval, but he just waits for me to name my terms.

"A lot happened today that I need to process. So before we talk about what comes next for us, I think I need to decide how I feel first. I need to figure out what I want, on my own."

As I speak, I can't stop Rosa's words from ringing in my mind. Have I really put myself on the sidelines when I belong in the center of the ring?

"That sounds fair enough to me," Logan answers.

"That's not the unfair part. I was hoping that until we decide what to do . . ."

The words feel mixed up, like I'm plucking them one by one from a cyclone.

"If we could just be us, until then?" I finally finish. "The way we were? Even if it's just pretend. Just for a little while, before things change again?"

Emotion strains Logan's face, and a sudden snap of disbelief seizes me. Things used to be so easy between us, for so long. How did we end up here? Is it even possible for us to do what I've asked, or was I just being stupid and selfish? Then again, I remind myself Logan said he wanted this for us once, back on the Isle of Baxter before everything changed.

"I have a lot to say, Chase. That's why I came back," Logan begins. "But if that's what you need, yes, I can do that for a little while."

Logan looks like he wants to hug me, and I desperately want him to, but we don't know what's allowed in this strange new place we've entered. So I try to pull myself off the bench. I step forward and hug Logan.

It feels so good, my chest actually tightens. I press my eyes shut as tears well against the lids, because I'd rather not cry here next to the baked asphalt and gasoline pumps.

"I just need you to know," Logan begins, still holding me, "I did what I did trying *not* to hurt you. Really. I know it didn't work, but I need you to believe that was my intention. That it still is."

Against my will, a couple tears pry loose from my closed eyelids. They wet my lashes and streak my cheeks. I wipe the tears away behind Logan's back, resisting the urge to sniffle.

"I believe that now," I say.

This might not change anything for us, but I know Logan means what he says. Besides, it's not like my own reaction was perfect. I'm sure I stung Logan and that was never my intention, either. I want desperately to hear everything else he has to say, but I also know I really do need to decide what feels right to me first.

I'm thankful we have a long drive ahead of us, because I have to make up my mind very soon. How can time feel so split, abundant and expiring all at once? Either way, I know I need to make every bit of it count.

◆　◆　◆　◆

I end up being the one to drive the final leg to our destination, which feels fitting. We now enter the land of the Sworn—the clear and cutting Corner of Swords, the suit of The Emperor sitting on his mountaintop throne.

The others still doze in Charvan's bucket seats as the sun rises all around us. They need the sleep, but it's almost a shame. The views we now pass approaching this final destination are some of the most stunning of our trip so far.

The Emperor and Death contained the split coordinates for the missing Queen of Swords, which led us to Mammoth Mountain. Logan drove the first six hours of the trip, heading north so that we could actually reach the southbound road that took us into Mammoth. This circuitous route followed the only available roads through the chain of mountains, but it actually worked in our favor. As far as we could tell on our shifts to keep Logan company, we haven't been followed. Whatever we do find at the final set of coordinates, it feels right to be headed up into the sky, to a place of elevation.

The single road leading into Mammoth is breathtaking. It's all sweeping vistas and open fields, half desert and half forest valleys framed by enormous mountain chains.

The view stretches for miles in every direction, and it makes Charvan feel like a sword itself, a white-hot streak piercing the path forward. It's not lost on me as we pass a crystal-clear lake that this is a land suited for all: red deserts and blue waters, green branches and snowy-white peaks.

The hour that follows feels like a holy one, taking in the sights as we come into the more-populated towns lining Mammoth Mountain. It's clearly a summer space riding out its waning days, hiking trails and lake houses breathing their last breaths before giving way to ski season. The GPS puts our final coordinates deep in the heart of the mountain, far beyond the main commercial areas. After another twenty minutes, I come to a long road populated by nothing but forest and winding road. The prospect gives me both a chill and a thrill—what remote corner is Perilli's last card going to bring us to for our grand finale?

It's not until I pull Charvan a few minutes off the main road and up to a set of enormous bronze gates that I finally wake the others.

"Oh my goddess, are we here already?" Amelia yawns, stretching her limbs.

"I don't exactly know what 'here' is, but the coordinates are somewhere up there," I say, craning to look up the winding driveway beyond the gate.

"Well, judging by that, I think we're in the right place," Cleo says, pointing at the top of the gate. When I see what they mean, I can't believe I didn't notice it first.

The top center of the gate is adorned with six wrought-iron swords. These particular swords look like the ones in our deck, simple white blades and a pale blue hilt set with green and red gems on either cross handle. These swords are also arranged exactly like the Six of Swords card in our deck: each pointed tip meets in the middle and the slender blades fan out into a sharp-edged pinwheel.

"The Six of Swords," I say, triggered like an automated assistant. "A symbol of transition, having passed through disorienting obstacles into calmer clarity. A sign of achievement, followed by the need for further curiosity and exploration."

"Can I get an amen?" Amelia adds. "Do those swords look like a pentacle to anyone else?"

"They actually look like a windmill to me," Logan replies.

"If you ask me, it looks like the heart of a compass," Cleo offers.

"No, I know exactly what that symbol stands for," I say, taking my turn. "Can I have the deck a second?"

Amelia hands it to me and I quickly find the card I'm looking for. Sure enough, its symbol also matches the six-pointed shape of the swords on the gate.

"The Star. Representing a guiding light through darkness, one that must be carefully followed. It also stands for achievement awarded, just like the Six of Swords. I never realized how close the relation was between these two cards."

This must mean, one way or another, the Sworn Corner exists up there. To my surprise, a burst of excitement slices away my reservations. Maybe I should know better after everything we've experienced, but despite myself, I cannot wait to see what we'll find at the top.

"Should we just ring the bell on the gate intercom?" Amelia asks.

"I don't think we have a choice." I answer.

When we ring the intercom, no one answers. Instead, the automated gates begin to open slowly inward. There's a camera attached to the system, so whoever let us in must have accepted seeing us. As I drive Charvan forward, the winding driveway is longer than I expect, lined with thick and encroaching trees. I just hope this isn't some kind of Perillian trap—not that we have any other options.

When we reach the driveway's end, we are met with an impressive modern house perched on a cliff overlooking a vast valley, all chrome and wood gleaming in the morning sunlight. As we all begin to climb out of Charvan, I take a deep breath. The air up here feels thinner, but also cleaner. Like the first flushes of autumn fill my lungs, crisp as leaves crunching.

Then the front door to the house opens and a man in a wheelchair emerges. He begins to roll down an entrance ramp toward us, a warm smile on his face. He appears to be in his fifties and his olive-skinned features tell me he's likely a fellow Italian, but his features also strike me as maybe half Filipino? He dresses neatly in a shawl-collar sweater, dark jeans, and tortoise-shell glasses.

"Welcome to the Lianist Outlook Center," the man says, waving as he reaches the base of the ramp. "I've been expecting you."

This line should be a little freaky, but instead it just feels inviting. This man, whoever he is, seems to radiate calm and kind, like a kindergarten teacher. Still, I remind myself not to get too comfortable.

"I'm Brendan," he continues, rolling directly up to us and reaching up to shake each of our hands. "You'll have to forgive the quiet. I'm afraid today I'm the entire welcome wagon. I know you've come a long way, and there's so much to discuss, but we've just finished work on our grand foyer. I'm incredibly excited to show it to someone new. Would you mind following me inside? There are bathrooms and water and some snacks, if you need any."

"Um, I'm sorry," Amelia says first. "But where exactly are we? And how do you know who we are?"

"Shoot, forgive me," Brendan answers. "I'm always getting ahead of myself. It's been just me, myself, and I out here most of the time, so my social skills aren't what they used to be. This is my life's work, the legacy left by my father."

"And do we know your father?" I ask.

"There I go, doing it again!" Brendan laughs. "I'm going to have to get better at these introductions once we officially open. And no, you couldn't have known my father, but you certainly know of him by now. My father was Carson Perilli."

The news spreads across us with an airlock snap. A dozen new questions begin to race across my brain.

"I'll be happy to answer all of your questions as best I can," Brendan continues, rolling back toward the house for us to follow. "You've caused quite the stir, turning up out of the blue the way you have. I must admit, I was starting to think my father's final deck would never surface. I'm sure you know by now he liked his secrets, dolling them out like treasured treats, different flavors for different Corners. None of us have the full picture of his work, not even me. Though I should say, I have no interest in taking your deck. I'm incredibly curious to study it, but I can only imagine the kinds of trials you endured getting here—I myself have found a missing Perillian royal or two in my day. Anyway, I know this means you'll have to take me at my word, but I'm happy to do anything that makes you comfortable."

I turn to Amelia and find her eyes already on me. She nods and I can tell her instincts are saying the same thing as mine: something about Brendan's energy just feels sincere and up-front, especially compared with the other Perillians we've met. Turning to Logan for confirmation, he nods as well. Then we all turn to Cleo, the toughest among us, to find a quizzical look on their face.

"Are you Page Zain?" Cleo then asks.

In response, Brendan laughs.

"An excellent question indeed, young . . . Cleo, you must be? But no, I am not Page Zain. I'm afraid I don't know their real identity, though not for lack of trying."

"Then do you know why we have this deck?" Amelia tries next as we reach the ramp leading to the entrance.

"I think I do, yes," Brendan answers. "But in all honesty, it will be up to you to confirm my suspicions. My father left the last remaining trove of his secrets to be uncovered by the person who turned up with that deck, as I'm sure you've already learned. So if you feel ready, might we begin?"

Brendan casts his eyes over all of us, and once again, we nod along.

"Excellent! I promise your faith in me will not be misplaced. Now, if you'll follow me, I can't wait to show you the Lianist Outlook Center!"

Brendan spins and begins rolling his wheelchair back up the ramp. He turns his head over his shoulder, speaking as we follow.

"I'm the only one among my siblings to develop an interest in our father's work. He started it much later in life, after our mother passed away, and I think they all found it quite odd. I must admit, I pretended to feel the same publicly so that I might continue my father's work in private. If Perillians are anything, they're tenacious. I set myself apart, for obvious reasons. So did my father, in his own way. He only ever sorted two people into his Sworn Corner: himself and myself. He fancied it an exclusive Perillian right. One of his many flaws, if you ask me. Exactly the kind of thinking we're trying to change here at the Center."

"And what exactly is this Center?" Cleo asks.

"What isn't it? A spiritual hub. A charitable foundation. A retreat center," Brendan answers, turning forward as the automatic front doors swing open. "But surely it's better if I show you?"

We follow Brendan inside and find ourselves in a two-story entrance foyer. It's all modern sprawl, gleaming chrome and brass and glass. To our right, a full wall of windows overlooks the incredible vista views outside. To our left, the opposing wall is made entirely of mirrors. The reflections between the two are dazzling, making it feel like we all float on top of this mountain.

Brendan rolls behind a long wooden table, one that has golden letters across its front: *THE LIANIST OUTLOOK.* The tabletop is neatly organized with water bottles and pamphlets and a stack of tarot decks. My eyes lock on the decks because I recognize Perilli's signature artwork right away.

"Not original articles, I'm afraid," Brendan says, catching my eye. "These decks are reprinted from the only complete set of cards I ever got my hands on. I sold that deck years ago to help fund all this, but not before saving prints for reproduction. Your deck there is actually the first authentic Perillian artwork to enter this space in years."

"Can we take one of the decks?" I ask, trying to sound casual. In reality, I couldn't be more eager to pore over another set of Perillian cards.

"Of course. Though we have a ritual here, before you can," Brendan answers, rolling across to the mirrored wall. "You really couldn't have come at a more serendipitous time, though I suppose a proper Perillian would claim the tarot is all about serendipity. We've just finished construction on an interactive introduction to The Lianist Way. No one but our skeleton staff has seen it, since we're not open to the public yet. But I can't think of a group better suited to experience it first, honestly."

Brendan rolls to a doorway, the seams of which are barely visible on the gleaming wall. Registering his motion, an image appears in the center of this invisible door: the Six of Swords. It almost looks like a hologram floating there, but it must be a screen or a projection?

"The interactive introductory hall is designed to explain what our Foundation is all about in tarot form. Engaging in the experience also works as a kind of divination calibration, to let us know where you might benefit most from what we offer here. It's a modern riff on my father's Corner sorting tarot readings."

Brendan looks us over then, the giddiness of his smile feeling infectious.

"So, possessors of Perilli's final mysteries, minor and major. Are you ready to enter The Hermetic Dawn?"

It turns out this interactive experience must be entered into one by one, since Brendan said the readings must be uniquely tailored to each individual. I asked to go first. Logan had his faithful desert, Cleo had their fluid coast, and Amelia had her chaotic forest, so I felt I should enter this clarified peak first—especially after what Rosa said about me on our ride yesterday.

Right now I find myself standing in the main room of The Hermetic Dawn, which is a kind of soundproof studio with several potential exits. In front of me stand two large mirrored panels, each reflecting a different angle of myself in the dim lighting. Before entering, a touch screen had asked me to input some basic information like my name, identifications, hometown, birthday, and a few of my favorite things: blue, spaghetti Bolognese, reading, and my journal. I entered these facts honestly, since I bet Cleo will take their turn to mess with the system for all of us. Besides, something in me really wants to take this experience seriously.

Serene instrumental music begins to play in a major key, and the lights dim as the room registers my presence. A cool breeze of air conditioning hits my arm, then a soothing, agender voice pipes in through some unseen speakers.

"Welcome to The Hermetic Dawn of the Lianist Outlook Center. I'm Waite and I'll be your guide through this interactive experience. All you have to do is relax and listen, then answer my questions when prompted. Before we begin, let me ask, are you familiar with the works of Carson Perilli?"

The lights shift again, and suddenly my appearance in the mirrors follows. I look to my left and see that an image is projected onto my reflection, making it appear like I stand in a living tarot card. I still can't tell if this projection is a hologram or a screen or something else, but it's incredibly cool.

On the left panel I become The Fool, styled in court jester clothes. If I move my hands in the right place, I hold a scepter shaped like an upside-down question mark. Above my Fool head floats the word *No*. Then, looking to my right, the mirror transforms me into the Prince of Swords. I soar through the clouds, away from a city, my sword outstretched like that of a superhero. Above my Prince head floats the word *Yes*.

"Yes," I say, for obvious reasons.

"Excellent," Waite responds. The mirrored panel that depicts me as The Fool then goes dark, while The Prince of Swords panel glows a bit brighter.

"The Lianist Way hopes to take the greatest truth translated through Perilli's tarot and leave behind its elitist elements," Waite continues. "We still believe that knowledge should be earned, but we also believe the right to earn it should be universal—not guarded by gatekeepers. Our aim here is to bring Perillian wisdom out of the shadows and to the masses. Or rather, to those masses who seek it out."

Waite pauses as my Prince reflection fades and two more projections populate the mirrored panels. To my left I see myself as The Magician, wielding a wand in one hand and a cup in the other, then wearing a pentacle necklace on my chest and a sword strapped to my back. To my right I can see myself as The Hermit, cloaked and bearded, standing before a gate guarding stacks of books. If I move my hands in the right place on this projection, a large key appears in my hand.

"The tarot is about a careful balance between the reader and the one being read. The cards you are being projected into have been chosen carefully by our system based on the information you entered. So my question for you is simple at this juncture. Do you have the heart of a Magician or the mind of a Hermit?"

This prompt might sound simple, but I immediately peel back several layers: the keepers of the Minor and Major Arcana, the surreal and the real, emotion and intellect, magic and science, faith and fact . . .

Logan's heart and my head.

◊ "I have the heart of a **Magician**."
Turn To Page 236

◊ "I have the mind of a **Hermit**."
Turn To Page 237

Once I answer, an identical transition process triggers before Waite offers the next guiding steps.

"In many ways, Perilli envisioned a new and unrecognizable 'world to come,' one of digital connection and divisive isolation. He thus believed in preparing his 'Four Corners' differently for that world. However poetic these Corners remain, they have not been effective at much else besides collecting and quibbling. As so often happens, the Corners have not practiced what was preached. Is this because Carson Perilli himself preached openness and thinking for oneself, while in actuality he practiced exclusivity and division? Or is it because the qualities that make each Corner unique can all exist within each of us?

"This choice is not ours alone to make. We here at The Lianist Foundation believe that religions most often proclaim: *I have the answers, come with me and I'll tell you.* In contrast, we believe true spirituality instead proclaims: *You already have the answers, let me help you find them.* Religions can of course harness spirituality in this way, though they so often do not. In this regard, the primary aspiration of The Lianist Way is not to provide the answer, but to pose the question. So, Chase, what do you think about the Corners?"

To my left, my mirrored image populates the Ace of Wands. Seeing myself hold the most potent of wands, I recall it represents the spark of life that lives within the flame of destruction. Then to my right, I become my Major Arcana expression, The Emperor. Seeing myself actually depicted alone on the throne and ready to lead feels especially powerful—but is that how I'm meant to feel, given the information I entered into this reading system?

◊ "We can each individually wield all qualities of the four Corners, like the **Ace of Wands**."
Turn To Page 238

◊ "Each Corner possesses fundamental truths to fulfill, like The **Emperor**."
Turn To Page 240

Once I answer, an identical transition process triggers before Waite offers the next guiding steps.

"Here at The Lianist Foundation we seek to improve upon some tenets treasured in Perillianism, as these in turn were inspired by the nineteenth-century tarot-centric Hermetic Order of the Golden Dawn. Hermit you have become, you have entered one of the most important sequences of this Hermetic Dawn.

"Carson Perilli was surely an insightful artist who had a special way of reading the gorgeous tarot he created. However, Perilli's undeniable connection to the tarot seems to have also made him a bit of a charismatic leader to his many followers. He was thinking of founding a physical center just like this one, but when his terminal diagnosis arrived, he spent the last months of his life devising one final deck that has yet to surface. This was perhaps for the best, since a true cult might have formed under his centralization.

"Accordingly, we have adopted a new name, The Lianist Way, to bridge Perilli's tarot past to its future. Here, there are no leaders and followers. There are only the guides and the curious, two roles we see as fluid and collaborative. So, Chase, what do you think? Was Carson Perilli an insightful man who created an alluring but flawed system? Or could we be wrong—was Perilli truly connected in a higher way to the truth of the tarot?"

The lights shift, and to my left my mirrored image becomes The Hierophant, wearing regal robes and standing before a crowd of eager patrons. Meanwhile, to the right I become the King of Wands, wielding an enormous tree-branch wand and riding over the desert toward a distant pentacle star. It's fascinating—the guardian of uncompromising wisdom versus the champion of passionate conviction, two sides of the same coin.

◊ "Perilli's teachings were wise and accessible, like The **Hierophant**."
Turn To Page 238
◊ "Perilli's insights were prophetic and powerful, like the **King of Wands**."
Turn To Page 240

The now-familiar transition process triggers and Waite continues.

"Chase, it's clear by now how deeply you value individual agency. Taking this path, you might be most drawn to the more practical trails of The Lianist Way. On its most foundational level, the tarot is about peering into ourselves via our potential futures—it's about divination. But Perilli believed true divination meant using the tarot's symbols and predictions to look within ourselves for the answers we seek.

"A profound notion, to be sure, but what does this belief mean in practice? The potential answers can lead you down one of two foundational Lianist trails. The first leads to the development of a unique meditative practice, using tarot readings like this one to identify patrons' truest gifts and center their connection to their intuition. The second Lianist trail involves putting this faith into practice. After all, it does not take Perillian-like vision to see that a time of peril is upon us, a brave new digital world of environmental crisis. This trail seeks to solve the problems of the modern era and the unforeseen problems to come. In this vein, we aim to establish both a think tank and a charitable branch of the Foundation, to enact actual change."

In the left panel, my entire reflection vanishes into the bright and full visage of The Moon. I know The Moon acts as a symbol of mystery to remind us that, even after learning much, we must remain humble and open. Looking to my right, I see myself enter the Two of Pentacles, standing between two stars hanging above diverging streams. The card represents the restoration of balance between opposing forces and reminds us it's best to go with the flow instead of bracing for control.

Considering these "trails" before me, I realize they speak to questions I've held for years, the core of where I feel most undecided. Just what is it that I hope to accomplish? What do I really have to offer? I expect my usual grip of paralysis to set in, because deep down I know I still don't have a firm grasp of the "correct" answer.

However, to my surprise, I feel an unexpected calm settle in the face of this choice. Maybe it's the cumulative effect of this journey, or maybe it's just entering this Sworn space, or maybe it's even Rosa's read forcing me to see myself as I really am . . .

But I suddenly feel comfortable knowing the imperfect answer is the only one I'll ever have.

◊ "I see myself adopting a meditative practice, because The **Moon** reminds me that answering one question simply leads to the discovery of a deeper question."
Turn To Page 242

◊ "I see myself actively making a difference, embracing the harnessed energy of the **Two of Pentacles**."
Turn To Page 246

The now-familiar transition process triggers and Waite continues.

"Chase, it's quite clear by now how deeply you feel the pull of destiny, the power in owning that which you were born into. On its most foundational level, the tarot is about peering into ourselves via our potential futures. A profound notion, to be sure, but what does this mean in actual practice? The answers can lead you down one of two foundational Lianist trails.

"The first views fortune-telling as prophecy, performed by gifted readers like Perilli. We're recruiting those gifted with the skill of tarot divination, as a form of collaborative prayer—a way to deliver messages to and from your spirit guides. We're facilitating conversations with higher powers, whichever one you believe in.

"The second trail leads to tarot readings that focus on embracing future visions and working to actually manifest them. This more psychological practice operates on the belief that fortunes don't come true unless we will them to, empowering the unconscious link between intention and outcome. This style of reading leans most heavily into the physical reactions to tarot readings—sense memory, dreams, and emotions—to devise personal action plans."

In the left panel, the Ten of Cups stack around me in the outline of a house. This feels fitting, since this card represents working with others to successfully build something. Then, looking to my right, my image becomes The Empress. It's odd at first, seeing myself projected as Amelia's Major Arcana expression. Seeing myself this way, I wonder—can I be more bold like Amelia, in the ways I've always wanted?

Considering these "trails" before me, I realize they speak to questions I've held for years—especially the fundamental debate that has always existed between Logan and Amelia. I expect my usual grip of paralysis to set in the face of this choice, because deep down I know I still don't have a firm grasp of the "correct" answer.

However, to my surprise, I feel an unexpected calm settle. Maybe it's the cumulative effect of this journey, or maybe it's just entering this Sworn space, or maybe it's even Rosa's read forcing me to see myself as I really am, but I suddenly feel comfortable knowing the subjective answer is the only one I'll ever have. There's only ever going to be the right answer for *me*—and I have to learn to listen to the inner voice that points toward this answer.

◊ "I see myself learning how to read the tarot as a form of communicative prayer, in the spirit of the **Ten of Cups**."
Turn To Page 244

◊ "I see myself learning how to read the tarot as a form of behavioral therapy, like The **Empress**."
Turn To Page 246

The lights shift, and the mirrored panels dim. I expect my image to transform into another card, a clean-cutting sword or a gleaming prism full of rainbow lines. Instead, the mirrors return to normal, reflecting me exactly as I am.

"You've reached your reading's end," Waite says. "Only you know what you learned from this experience and what you're called to do next. Will you begin to study the Lianist meditative practice? My record of this pathway will soon be over-written, so as always, the choice is yours. Before we part ways, I'd like to leave you with one final pearl of Lianist wisdom. The custom quote selected for you comes from the ever-wise Eckhart Tolle: *It's okay not to know what to do next. The person who cannot enjoy the uncertainty of the journey is going to be in a constant state of negativity and fear. If everything were already mapped out, there'd be no evolution.*"

These new words echo in mind as I stare back at myself. I am indeed someone who thinks and plans, but if I've learned anything on this journey of detours, it's that aptitude is not the same as life experience. The latter is wild and untamed. So what if it were okay to be less put-together? After all, what I love most about Amelia and Cleo and even Logan is their messiness, vibrant and alive.

I feel the urge to thank Waite, even though I know no one is technically there. Just like I know this sudden shift in me isn't so sudden at all—it's been gathering steam every step of this trip. This experience, this hall of crystal-clear refractions, has only sharpened that change. Except now I don't feel quite as terrified by the idea of change. Now, I feel like it might actually stand to work in my favor.

Which means I do know, in the center of myself, what I need to do with Logan before this last chapter ends.

Next, the seams on one of doors across the room lights up yellow, indicating my way out. Feeling ready to finish what we started, I walk through this illuminated exit. When I emerge, I find Brendan waiting for me in a sun-soaked room.

"Chase, one of your friends will be signaled to enter behind you, but I wanted to be here when you exited," Brendan says, smiling wide as ever. "It's important to say that I don't know what you learned or saw in The Hermetic Dawn, but the door you exit through does signal the tone of your reading. I must admit, I'm rather thrilled you were guided through the yellow door. Those who take this path have the clearest point of view."

I can't fight the look of surprise that hits me. *Clearest point of view?* That's not a phrase I'd normally apply to myself.

Then again, this is one new way I'm learning to see myself. So I need to stop confusing the ability to evolve with a lack of conviction.

Turn To Page 248

The lights shift and the mirrored panels dim. I expect my image to transform into another card, a steep-edged cliff side or a colorful gemstone reflecting the light. Instead, the mirrors return to normal, reflecting me exactly as I am.

"You've reached your reading's end," Waite says. "Only you know what you learned from this experience and what you're called to do next. Will you learn the secret methods behind Lianist tarot readings? My record of this pathway will soon be overwritten, so as always, the choice is yours. Before we part ways, I'd like to leave you with one final pearl of Lianist wisdom. The custom saying selected for you was actually coined by one of our own founders: *Worrying about things you cannot control is a natural human function, but it is also a waste of time. All you can every truly control is your perspective and your reactions to the detours that come your way. So, fledgling Lianist, I leave you with this task: every time you have a worry about the future, instead focus on something to be grateful for in the present. It's a small shift, but you'd be surprised how much a tiny shift in perspective can change for you.*"

These new words echo in mind as I stare back at myself, unadorned. I am indeed someone who worries constantly, who loves to control whatever I can. I've been so focused on what I might lose when this chapter ends, it never even occurred to me that letting go of the old things might make room for something even better. I've been so terrified of changing my relationship with Amelia or of losing Logan, but what if I just found a way to be grateful to have them in my life, no matter what?

I feel the urge to thank Waite, even though I know no one is technically there. Just like I know this sudden shift in me isn't so sudden at all—it's been gathering steam every step of this trip. This experience, this hall of crystal-clear refractions, has only sharpened that change. Except now I don't feel quite as terrified by the idea of change. Now, I feel like it might actually stand to work in my favor.

Which means I do know, in the center of myself, what I need to do with Logan before this last chapter ends.

Next, the seams on one of doors across the room lights up yellow, indicating my way out. Feeling ready to finish what we started, I walk through this illuminated exit. When I emerge, I find Brendan waiting for me in a sun-soaked room.

"Chase, one of your friends will be signaled to enter behind you, but I wanted to be here when you exited," Brendan says, smiling wide as ever. "It's important to say that I don't know what you learned or saw in The Hermetic Dawn, but the door you exit through does signal the tone of your reading. I must admit, I'm rather thrilled you were guided through the yellow door. Those who take this path have the clearest point of view."

I can't fight the look of surprise that hits me. *Clearest point of view?* That's not a phrase I'd normally apply to myself.

Then again, this is one new way I'm learning to see myself. So I need to stop confusing the ability to understand multiple perspectives with a lack of direction.

Turn To Page 248

The lights shift and the mirrored panels dim. I expect my image to transform into another card, a rocky plateau or a shiny diamond, hardened and gleaming. Instead, the mirrors return to normal, reflecting me exactly as I am.

"You've reached your reading's end," Waite says. "Only you know what you learned from this experience and what you're called to do next. Will you empower yourself to practice what you preach on behalf of the tarot? Will you work to change your corner of the world in whatever ways you can? My record of this pathway will soon be over-written, so as always, the choice is yours. Before we part ways, I'd like to leave you with one final pearl of Lianist wisdom. The custom saying selected for you comes from the mystic scholar Rumi: *You are not a drop in the ocean. You are the entire ocean in a drop.*"

These new words echo in mind as I stare back at myself, unadorned. I realize I am indeed someone who has thought little of myself, assuming I wasn't what most people wanted. I reduced myself to *Smart Chase*, a useful distraction from the parts of me I thought were dull and plain and ugly. But what if I found a way to look at myself the way Seidon did? Or Rosa? Or even Logan, for so many years? The proof has been all around me, so why am I the last one to see it?

I can't wait to discover what changes for me if I start seeing myself as someone who is a leader, someone who is fundamentally lovable.

I feel the urge to thank Waite, even though I know no one is technically there. Just like I know this sudden shift isn't so sudden at all—it's been gathering steam every step of this trip. This experience, this hall of crystal-clear refractions, has only sharpened that change. Except now I don't feel quite as terrified by the idea of change. Now, I feel like it might actually stand to work in my favor.

Which means I do know, in the center of myself, what I need to do with Logan before this last chapter ends.

Next, the seams on one of doors across the room lights up orange, indicating my way out. Feeling ready to finish what we started, I walk through this illuminated exit. When I emerge, I find Brendan waiting for me in a sun-soaked room.

"Chase, one of your friends will be signaled to enter behind you, but I wanted to be here when you exited," Brendan says, smiling wide as ever. "It's important to say that I don't know what you learned or saw in The Hermetic Dawn, but the door you exit through does signal the tone of your reading. I must admit, I'm rather pleased that you were guided through the orange door. Those who take this path are still the most open to sorting out what they believe and what they have to offer."

I can't fight the look of disappointment that comes over my face. That does sound like me—Chase, ever undecided, even after slicing epiphanies.

But then I force myself to see myself differently. I need to keep reminding myself that remaining open is not the same thing as being undefined.

Turn To Page 248

"If your Hermetic Dawn experience was anything like mine, you probably have lots to process," Brendan continues. "I know I shouldn't be adding to the pile, but I'm afraid I do have a rather exciting offer. Though, first, I must ask—what did you think of the experience?"

"I thought it was fascinating," I say, trying to be honest without getting specific. "And illuminating. I have about a million questions about how it was made."

"Well, I'm thrilled to hear that, Chase," Brendan says, a relieved smile spreading across his face. "Especially since you exited through a very special door. You see, everyone is welcome to join The Lianist Way as members, at whatever level of engagement they choose. But we're being a bit more selective about who we invite to become the first-wave leaders of our movement. And exiting through that door means you passed our Potential Guide metrics with flying colors. I don't know which doors your friends will emerge through, but before they do, you have one final question to answer."

Brendan rolls toward me and reaches into a pocket on his wheelchair. He then holds out two tarot cards, one in either hand. I realize these cards must be from the printed Perillian deck, because their imagery looks both wildly familiar and abstractly different. In his left hand Brendan holds the Six of Swords, arranged with the same symbolism as the gate outside. In his right hand Brendan holds The Star, shining singularly in a night sky.

"Chase, you are officially invited to join The Lianist Foundation as a Guide-in-Training, to fulfill the unique purpose you designated in your Hermetic Dawn reading. I imagine you're back to school soon, but should you accept, you'd be welcome to take weekend web-seminars to fulfill your potential. Then, next summer, you'd have a Guide job here waiting for you. Most importantly, you'd become a vital part of the team building The Lianist Foundation as we open, helping shape our organization from root to branch. We can discuss the full details later, if you choose to take the Six of Swords, our official Lianist symbol."

Brendan holds this card a little higher, glancing down at it with pride.

"However, if you don't wish to join us formally as a Guide, you're always welcome to remain a part of The Lianist Way as a member, either casually or actively involved in the sector you identified. Of course, you're also free to fully move on, taking with you whatever lessons might have resonated. If you choose this trail, The Star is yours to take as a token of the experience."

Looking down at the cards in Brendan's hands, I find I am once again presented with objects that carry heavy meaning. I decide instantly that, whichever card I choose,

I will keep it with me—maybe it can even become my own externalized mantra, like Logan's fidget spinner still in my pocket. After all, this card can symbolize all that I've learned on this trip and all the ways I've grown.

The question now remains: What trail do I think will enable me to continue growing and uncovering mysteries?

◇ I reach forward and take the Six of Swords. I **accept** the invitation to join The Lianist Foundation as a Guide because it feels like I'm meant to belong here.
Turn To Page 250

◇ I reach forward and take The Star. I **decline** the invitation to join The Lianist Foundation as a Guide because I need to continue defining things on my own terms.
Turn To Page 251

I take the Six of Swords from Brendan and the smile that spreads on his face is almost as bright as the sunlight pouring in. And why shouldn't it be? The Lianist Way seems to take the best of the Perillian tarot and expand upon it in the right direction. It feels so similar to the work I've done on myself, I can't ignore it.

"Most excellent," Brendan says, reaching out his other hand to shake mine. "This is the first step in a very beautiful journey, Chase. I couldn't be more thrilled to have someone with your spirit and knowledge on board."

"Can I tell the others about this invitation?"

"That's up to you," Brendan answers. "Out of respect for their privacy, I'll have you wait outside while each of them exits. I don't know if they'll emerge through your Guided door, but at the very least they'll be invited to join as members, in the designations that feel most vital to them. Then it will be time for you all to recover the Queen of Swords."

"What does that mean?" I ask, feeling that familiar tension return.

"You'll learn in a moment, but it basically means a hike. The Queen has been here all along, waiting for you and your friends to arrive."

Brendan then turns, wheeling toward another doorway across the sun-drenched room, where I'll wait while the others exit.

"So you all have one last peak to reach—literally. As it has been said, the journey of self-discovery is like spiraling up a mountain, returning to the same points over and over, just from higher perspectives."

Brendan turns back to look at me as I follow, another grin creasing his face.

"I cannot wait to see what this new perspective brings, now that we've all found one another."

I can't help but smile back at Brendan. Whatever the future holds, I've learned this much by now: sometimes decisions that seem to affect the least in the present have the greatest ripple effects on the future.

Turn To Page 252

I take The Star from Brendan and he sighs. I don't want to disappoint him, but I know that the paths ahead of me lead elsewhere. Especially because, despite what Brendan believes, I don't think The Lianist Way has changed all that much from Perillianism. I don't want to judge—I haven't exactly seen myself clearly for a long time, either. But if I'm going to evolve, I need to forge some new ways.

"I'd still be interested in keeping up with the work you're doing here," I say.

"Right you are," Brendan replies, reaching out his now-empty hand to shake mine. "You'll find The Lianist Way is incredibly flexible, so I do hope you'll stay in touch. It's rarer than you might think to meet bright young people who show such insightful commitment, especially to the tarot."

"Can I tell the others about this invitation?"

"That's up to you," Brendan answers. "Out of respect for their privacy, I'll have you wait outside while each of them exits. I don't know if they'll emerge through your Guided door, but at the very least they'll be invited to join as members, in the designations that feel most vital to them. Then it will be time for you all to recover the Queen of Swords."

"What does that mean?" I ask, feeling that familiar tension return.

"You'll learn in a moment, but it basically means a hike. The Queen has been here all along, waiting for you and your friends to arrive."

Brendan then turns, wheeling toward another doorway across the sun-drenched room, where I'll wait while the others exit.

"So you all have one last peak to reach—literally. As it has been said in the tarot, every ending is a beginning, starting a new cycle of self-discovery at a higher level."

Brendan turns back to look at me as I follow, a sad smile creasing his face.

I nod at Brendan, because I can certainly agree with his sentiment. Whatever the future holds, I try to remember this much—sometimes decisions that seem to affect the least in the present have the greatest ripple effects on the future.

Turn To Page 252

♦ ♦ ♦ ♦

Sweat collects on my forehead as we scale this final mountain trail, but I try to put that out of my mind. Right now there's too much at stake to be distracted by physical discomfort.

Once the four of us are reunited, Brendan reiterated our final task: climb the mountain trail leading out of the house's backyard, to where the Queen of Swords is kept at the peak. He has never made it up there himself, but apparently he sends a trusted friend regularly to make sure his father's Sworn monument is still in place. Brendan also said there would be no trials awaiting us there, but rather one final choice to unearth the Queen. This final task was designed to be as straightforward as a sword, hard-edged and long, but Brendan claimed all that was required was belief and perseverance.

That was an hour ago, and we still have more to climb. Thankfully, Brendan also provided us with hiking gear before we departed. We started with a short discussion of our individual Hermetic Dawn experiences, realizing the type of cards presented among the four of us was truly diversified. However, the others all exited through a pink door, and they just assumed I did as well. This made me uncomfortable, so I still haven't told them about my unique Guide invitation. I don't know why, but it feels like something I should hold on to for myself, for now.

After this, the trail got steep and we lapsed into silence, punctuated only by our labored breaths. It gave me a chance to absorb my Dawn along with the vista below, a stunning landscape of trees and smaller peaks. It's only now, as this view settles, that I know it's time to also settle things with Logan.

I can't say I feel exactly ready, but I'm not sure that matters.

"Think you have the energy to talk?" I ask, turning to him. We've hung back a bit behind Amelia and Cleo, who are practically attacking this hiking trail, kicking up a cloud of dust in their wake.

"Of course," Logan answers. "I've just been waiting for you to be ready."

"Well, being in that Hermetic Dawn experience, something really clicked," I say.

"Me too, actually," Logan says. "Turns out I'm much more of a Magician than I think. Or actually, I'm most like the Queen of Wands."

"Someone who knows themselves well and always walks with honesty. Yes, Queen," I relay, somewhat awkwardly.

Logan laughs, and it's a sound I realize I've missed most of all.

"Yes, and apparently someone who doesn't always think about how my honesty will impact others," Logan follows. "I know you and Amelia seem different in a lot of ways, but I realized you're actually the same in the way that matters, in a way that sets you apart from me. At your core, you both always think about how your actions will impact others, before everything else."

I've never really thought of it that way, but hearing Logan say this, it does feel instantly correct.

"All I mean to say is that I'm sorry for telling you my truth the way I did, even if I didn't intend to hurt you," Logan continues. "I do still love you. Being apart from you this way, it was so much harder than I expected. It terrifies me, honestly."

Logan looks like he might cry, but he carries on.

"I know I promised I'd let you decide what works for you, I just needed to say those things first."

I realize, with a pang, that Logan didn't say he wants to stay together monogamously, the way we were. This one thought rips into me once again, opening another chasm in my chest. However, I force myself to acknowledge this insecure pulse and let the feeling pass through me. Then I choose another thought. I tell myself I am wanted. I am worthy. I am no one's sidekick. Logan loves me for who I am and always has, no matter how our circumstances shift.

Thinking these better thoughts, I feel my decision settle in my gut, the place where my head meets my heart. I might not be sure it's the absolute right answer, but if I trust my instincts this way, how can I ever regret my decision?

◇ "Logan, I think we should take a **break** when we go to college."
   Turn To Page 254
◇ "Logan, I want to stay together and see if an **open** relationship works for us."
   Turn To Page 256

"It's not because I don't forgive you. Or because I don't still love you," I continue, forging forward. "I do forgive you. I do love you. That's why I think this is right. I don't want us to ruin what we have, putting it into the precarious position of being with other people. And if I don't have some kind of clean break, I don't think I'll ever let go."

Tears form in my eyes as I speak, but I make sure I finish saying everything I need to.

"And I think we should let each other go, because we love each other. And because I know, deep down, that can outlast anything. It might not always look the same, but I have faith it'll always be there."

Seeing Logan's face nearly breaks my heart, but that's only because I can see what's written there: he knows I'm right.

"When did you go and get all self-assured on me?" Logan laughs, probably to keep from crying. "Don't tell me it's from Seidon hitting on you?"

I laugh then, too, a nervous release.

"Definitely not," I say. "I can do way better than him. I already have."

Logan reaches out and pulls me into a hug. Here, holding each other on the side of this mountain, we both break down.

"I don't want to do this," Logan finally says. "But you're right. I'm just glad you finally see some of what I've always seen in you."

It feels like my heart literally snaps in half in my chest, a fault line ripping wide open. But then, to my surprise, the crack suddenly feels familiar—like it belongs to me. Someone will love this fractured heart someday, maybe even Logan again. But I'm always going to be the one in charge of mending the tears. There's so much freedom, so much power, in that notion, it almost makes breaking up with Logan bearable.

Almost.

So I kiss Logan and he kisses me back, one last time, for now. I then reach into my pocket and grab the fidget spinner Logan left me, once upon a time.

"Thank you for this," I say, wishing I could put into words how much the little piece of metal meant to me. But then I hold it out for Logan to take back.

"It's yours to keep," Logan says, stepping away.

I shouldn't accept, but honestly I'm grateful Logan wants to leave me this vital piece of him. I wish I had something to give him in return, like the most important page of wisdom collected in my journal bible, but I left it back in Charvan. Then I realize I actually do have something to give Logan. I reach back into my pocket and pull out the Perillian card, the one Brendan just gifted me.

"I was going to keep this card as a reminder of the trip, of everything I've learned along the way," I begin. "But I want you to have it."

Logan accepts the card with a sad smile. The objects we exchanged might carry different weights, but they still feel balanced in all the ways that matter, old and new. And standing here with Logan, I wonder how it's possible to feel full and empty at the same time.

Either way, I know I'll never let this fidget spinner go. Because if some objects are haunted by history, then some others must be blessed by it, too.

Turn To Page 257

"Chase, are you sure?" Logan asks, unable to hide the hope that springs into his voice.

"I'm sure I want to try," I answer. "I'm not sure it will work for me—for us. But there's only way to find out, right? After these past few days, I know this much: I'm not ready to give you up."

"Me either," Logan says, just before he breaks forward to hug me. It feels so right, his body pressed up against mine. He kisses me then, wild and excited.

"I love you, Chase."

"Of course you do," I reply, releasing a bit of nervous laughter. "It has recently come to my attention that I'm a bit of a catch."

"Hell yeah, you are," Logan says, kissing me again. "You know, we'll have to figure out some ground rules. I've been thinking a lot about it."

"We will. We'll figure it out as it comes, until we get it right."

"Wait," Logan says, pulling back. "What happened to the Chase I know, the one who obsesses until he has planned his way to the perfect answer?"

"Oh, he's still in there. But this new Chase wants to be a little more patient."

"Well, I love this new Chase," Logan says. "And maybe he'll love the new Logan, more open-minded and empathetic?"

"I'll have to think on it," I joke, hugging Logan again.

Standing here holding each other, I really don't know if we're built to be open, even these new and improved versions of us. I don't know how this will work, but after our trial separation, I do know we'll find a way to try. Some things are just worth waiting for—usually the same things that are worth fighting for.

Reluctantly, I peel myself off Logan, knowing we shouldn't fall too far behind. Suddenly everything feels charged with potential, even the most familiar things. But before we keep moving, I reach into my pocket and grab the fidget spinner Logan left me, once upon a time.

"Thank you for this," I say, wishing I could put into words how much the little piece of metal meant to me. Still, I hold it out for Logan to take back.

He does, not needing to say another word.

Turn To Page 257

CHAPTER THIRTEEN

AMELIA

THE SUN BEATS down on my face, feeling brighter than ever before. After everything we've experienced it might be easy to feel cloudy or confused, but I only feel clearheaded, like the spotless sky above. Maybe it's this hike, step after strenuous step clearing out the fog. Or maybe it's the fallout of Rosa's reads, altering my own vision of myself. Most likely it's all of it combined, the cumulative weight of this journey pressing me into a diamond.

It really did feel like all that pressure broke something open inside The Hermetic Dawn. I saw so much of myself, vision after vision. The four of us didn't talk about our experiences as much as I expected, but then again, something about it felt so personal. Revealing too much feels like I'd be sharing my bedtime prayers or a birthday-candle wish.

Despite all the cards I saw myself projected into, only one feels stained into my brain: the Queen of Swords, our final missing card. Call it serendipity or call it spooky, but of course I saw myself reflected as the Queen in the Hermetic Dawn experience. That vision has left me with the Sword Queen's conclusion: soon I will be rewarded with something of great value, but also the responsibility of how to wield it. This Queen also represents harsh grace, cutting through truth while also causing destruction. I can't stop thinking about her card quote from the Perillian booklet: *Rules are for peasants, but context is for royals.* It's something Maggie said to us at the start of this journey, but now it feels like it applies more than ever.

Everything feels like it has been building to this point, this peak, this pinnacle. I can't believe Anwar's betrayal only happened yesterday—it already feels like a lifetime ago. In many ways, it was. When he betrayed me in that impossible way, all I could see was the confirmation of my deepest, darkest fears. But today something shifted. Earlier, lying in the back of Charvan while I was supposed to be asleep, I felt the urge to check Anwar's profile. After the way he so thoroughly deceived me, I didn't believe he could have been honest about the story he gave in his letter, about the reasons why he stole the deck.

I half expected to be blocked from Anwar's page, but when I opened it, I was surprised in a very different way. His two most recent pictures were of subjects he never posted before. The first was a photo of him reading on top of a mobile home, calling it his place. The second was a photo of him sitting beside his mom in a hospital bed. I expected to feel fire and fury seeing Anwar's face again, but instead I just felt heavy. It turns out Anwar really wasn't lying about some things, after all. And since betraying me, he obviously felt inspired to show the reality of himself for the very first time.

Even now, I can't help but feel these posts were meant for me. That they were Anwar's way of telling me all the truths he couldn't bring himself to speak out loud. Doing so on social media might not be the best expression, but it's maybe better than nothing.

So right here, on this mountainside, I send my own silent message back to Anwar.

◇ I believe he meant well, even if he didn't do well. I **forgive** Anwar.

Turn To Page 259

◇ He could have handled this situation a dozen different ways. Anwar's actions **revealed** who he really is.

Turn To Page 260

Today I find a way to be the nurturing Empress. If not for Anwar, then certainly for myself, because holding on to a grudge would be like swallowing a sword. However, I must still remember to carry this lesson like a blade across my back.

Whatever damage Anwar caused, I'll prove capable of mending it on my own, alongside the people I love most. I don't need Anwar to feel whole—I never did. So I certainly don't need an apology from him to move on. Maybe next time I'll trust a little less easily, but I will not allow Anwar to rob me of my ability to trust in the first place.

After all, now that I've had a taste, I know there will be others interested in me like Anwar. Better ones. And I owe it to these future loves to be the complete Amelia package.

Especially because one of those people walk beside me right now. And no matter what the cards hold for us, they deserve all of my best energy.

Turn To Page 261

If today is all about the Queen of Swords, then I must embrace the reality that if you betray a queen, you get the chop. Today I must become a more demanding Empress, because I deserve honesty and integrity. Who knows, if Anwar had been up-front with me from the start, maybe I'd even have found a way to help him?

Still, I have to remember what enabled Anwar to deceive me in the first place: my own blinding belief that someone like him couldn't be interested in me. I was so focused on my own insecurities, it never occurred to me to look for Anwar's.

He might not be worthy of my forgiveness, but I will strive to remember what he and Rosa taught me: everyone has broken parts they hide. The only way to mend these parts, however, is to make them known. If nothing else, these two placed me on the path to learning this invaluable lesson.

Then I think: *Hell no.* I placed myself on that path.

And I plan to keep climbing until I reach the very top.

Especially because I owe some honesty of my own to the incredible person waking beside me.

Turn To Page 261

"Pentacle for your thoughts?" Cleo asks, breaking our silence.

We've been hiking so long, I obviously got lost in the loop of my thoughts. Chase and Logan have fallen behind, probably also taking this time to sort themselves out. That spirit seems to be in the air up here.

"You can always hear all my thoughts, Cleo," I answer, smiling over at them. "And I've done a lot of thinking."

I haven't just spent this long morning reflecting on queens and hanged men. I've also spent a lot of time thinking about my last conversation with Cleo, the one where they told me they loved me. Back in Charvan, I didn't just look at Anwar's social media. I spent far more time looking over the doodles Cleo drew of us during this trip. Each one has Cleo and me drawn right next to each other, the way it feels like it has always been.

Except now, these images—our entire relationship—takes on a whole new meaning.

Cleo's confession might have taken me by surprise, but I found once I had a little space to process, I already knew exactly how I felt. The realization cut like a knife, slicing my heart right open.

◇ "I **love you**, too, Cleo," I say, clean and clear. "I belong with you. I think I always have."

Turn To Page 262

◇ "Cleo, in so many ways you're my **best friend**," I begin. "I so badly want to be everything you want, but I don't have the same romantic feelings."

Turn To Page 265

"Wait. What?"

Cleo appears thunderstruck. I know I probably should have built up to this proc-lamation, but some things are meant to be entered into fearlessly. Goddess knows I should have seen this sooner, looking back.

"Be careful what you wish for, huh?" I grin. "You wanted Major Amelia. It seems you've got her."

"But I . . ." Cleo tries to absorb my words. They stop walking almost involun-tarily, as if needing the energy to free up more functions. "I didn't even think you were bi?"

"Well, since you're nonbinary, I'm not sure what identity that adds up to?"

"Pansexual?" Cleo offers.

"I'm not sure what to call it. But what I am sure of? I might not have thought of you in a romantic light before, but once I did, something clicked into place. It surprised me, honestly. But then, very quickly, it didn't. You're the most beautiful, smart, impressive person I know. I'm into *you*, Cleo. That doesn't have to mean anything else, at the moment."

Cleo stares back at me through their purple glasses like they still can't believe what's happening. Maybe it's the undiluted sunshine or the thinning air up here, but everything has taken on a slightly surreal quality, heightened and rosy at the same time. If Cleo can't find the words yet, that's fine. I have plenty more.

"I already chose someone who obviously didn't value me in the end, because I think on some level I didn't know how to value myself. But you, Cleo, you value all of me. You always have. When the voices in my head tell me I'm too big or too much or just flat-out unworthy, you're the one who always sees through me. You're the voice that tells me I'm enough, that I'm beautiful. When I spin out with panic, you're the one to ground me. I know I need to learn to do all those things for myself, but until then—and hopefully long after—yours is the voice I always want to hear."

Tears collect in Cleo's eyes. I didn't mean to make them cry, until I realize tears slide from my own eyes.

"Amelia, always so freaking bold, every minute of every day," Cleo finally says. "You've always inspired me to be brave, to be honest, to speak up. And you've always accepted me, exactly as I am. I just never thought . . ."

Cleo wipes at their eyes, a smile finally spreading across their face as these words seem to settle.

"Is this what people mean when they talk about being with someone who makes them a better person?" I ask, laughing a little. "Because you're the best person I know."

Cleo doesn't answer me. Instead, they step forward and wrap their arms around me. It doesn't matter that we're sweaty from the hike or that it's our first time holding each other when it really means something. Cleo hugs me and it feels like it just fits.

Then I kiss Cleo.

The feeling is hard to describe, except with a word like *home*.

"Is this really happening?" Cleo whispers, resting their forehead against mine. "I don't believe it."

"Of all the strange things we've experienced this trip, this is the part you can't believe?"

"Point taken," Cleo laughs. "Speaking of, I don't think we'll ever see Anwar or Rosa again, but I guess we'll have to thank them if we ever do."

"Um, excuse me?" I ask, pulling my head back.

"I'm not sure I would have spoken up the way I did if they hadn't pushed us," Cleo answers. "So in some roundabout way, they're like our cupids?"

"I think I'll settle for us being our own cupids, thank you very much," I answer. "Watch out world, Clemelia has arrived!"

Cleo steps back, still grinning like a fool. "Absolutely not. That sounds like a venereal disease."

"Ameleo, then?"

"How about we make sure this is really a thing before we start celebrity-naming it?" Cleo laughs again.

"But that's just it, Cleo," I say, making sure to lock eyes with them. "We've already been a thing for years. I just can't believe it took me so long to finally see it."

Cleo's eyes hold my gaze for a moment, then fall away downhill. They never were so great at taking compliments head on. Well, they're going to have to get used to it, with me as their girlfriend.

"Hey, here come Chase and Logan," Cleo says. "Maybe we keep this under wraps until we know they're back on solid ground themselves?"

Seeing the boys round the bend in the mountain trail, my buoyed heart dips. I can't imagine what it must feel like to know, in a matter of days, thousands of miles will separate Chase and Logan from the person they love most. It reminds me that soon Chase won't be just down the street from me anymore, either. Soon, nothing about any of our lives is going to resemble the way things were.

Except for Cleo, I think, turning back to look at them once more. Thank goddess for Cleo, the anchor of my entire life. I just hope I can make them half as happy and self-assured as they make me.

Then, looking at Cleo's shining face, I realize I already have.

Turn To Page 267

I watch as Cleo's face falls, their body deflating like a balloon. Air feels like it leaks out of my own heart, too, now poked full of holes.

Part of me wishes I hadn't been so straightforward, but I promised myself to stop editing my thoughts to spare feelings. Cleo deserves the truth. And I have to learn to be thick-skinned enough to tell people these things, even if I know it's not what they want to hear.

"I think I already knew that, deep down," Cleo says. They look like they want to say so much more, but like words are now dangerous things.

That's okay, because I have more words for Cleo.

"I'm so tempted to accept your love, because it feels so unconditional. But I already chose someone who didn't value me, because on some level I didn't value myself. It would be just as wrong to choose to be with someone because they actually fill that same void—at least, not when I don't feel the same way. And you deserve someone who loves you fully, in every way, for exactly who you are. I wish that person was me, I really do."

Cleo forces a smile onto their face.

"Thank you for not sugarcoating it," they say. "But hey, can you just tell me one thing?"

"Anything."

"Did I ruin our friendship now?" Cleo asks, nearly breaking into tears.

On instinct, I pull them into a hug.

"Never," I say. "Knowing you've seen all my nastiest parts and that you still love me? That's the kindest thing in the world. It doesn't weird me out, I promise. But I do understand if this has to change some things for you."

Cleo sighs, stepping out of my hug. "Maybe some things, once we get to college. But I have a feeling that will happen on its own."

College. I still can't believe, in a matter of days, our whole world is going to change. I'm still so thankful Cleo is going to be on the same island as me when we take this next step, even if there might be some new distance between us.

"Besides, I always want you in my life," Cleo adds. "That will never change."

"I couldn't agree more," I respond. "Though you know, you're totally going to meet someone who worships the ground you walk on. Someone who sees how stylish and beautiful and brave and insightful you are. And I will be cheering that person on every second."

Cleo actually blushes, hearing all this.

"You will, too, Amelia. Just because Anwar was a jerk, it doesn't mean they all will be."

I nod at Cleo. They're right, but I also know how much work I have to do before the next guy comes along. Like, what if every time I feel like I'm not good enough, I tell myself I am? Or what if every time I inevitably fixate on a part of my body I hate, I focus on a part I love instead? What if every time I pull at myself with panic because I'm not perfect, I tell myself it's okay to be a bundle of mess?

If Cleo can see all that in me, why can't I?

Whatever the answers, these are all questions for tomorrow and the next chapters to come. Today, I'm just grateful for my friends, every single one of them.

"Here come the boys," Cleo says, turning to glance downhill. "But hey, before they get here—did I hear you say I'm your best friend?"

"Yes, you did," I say, grinning again. "A person can have more than one best friend, I think. But if it matters, you've got the title. You always have."

Despite the heaviness of this moment, Cleo still manages to smile, shining bright.

"Deal," they say. "Though maybe let's not mention it to Chase anytime soon?"

Turn To Page 267

♦ ♦ ♦ ♦

When we reach our destination, there's no second-guessing we have arrived. First, we come upon a plateau at the peak of the trail that overlooks the sweeping valley below. Standing shoulder to shoulder to take in this view, the four of us all together, I already feel accomplished. It's one truly perfect moment, but it's not built to last. There's too much still left to do.

Next, we gather around what can only be described as a Sworn monument, modeled after The Emperor's symbol. It's a metal throne made of a single sword: the blade points up as the backing, while the cross-guards stick out as armrests. The hilt of this throne-sword then boxes out, likely containing everything we came here to find.

I take one deep breath, looking to the others. Then, with their nods of support, I open the lid to the base box. Inside there is a metal panel, on top of which rests two things: an envelope and a single, face-down Perillian card. Seeing this sitting there for the taking, I look to Chase.

"I know," he says. "It seems too easy?"

"Um, tell that to the very-lengthy hike we just climbed," Cleo replies.

"Not to mention, the only way to access this trail is through Brendan's gated house," Logan adds. "I'll bet that's really the final test to pass, since he'd only guide the deck holder up here."

"You know, you're all getting eerily good at thinking like Perillians," I say. "Here goes nothing."

As I reach down to grasp the final missing card, everything still feels heightened. Half of me cannot wait to finish this, while the other half never wants the journey to end. Half of me feels ready to find the answers I've been seeking, while the other half wants to live in the mystery forever. Somehow uniting all these contradictory parts, I pick up the card and flip it over.

I then gasp out loud.

"Oh my goddess," Cleo exclaims.

"Amelia, isn't that—" Chase begins, not needing to finish.

I automatically reach into my pocket and pull out my Dalet locket. Flipping it open, I reveal the pictures inside, of myself and young Grandma, looking like sisters—and also both looking exactly like the Queen of Swords I now hold in my trembling hand.

Emotion rises in me like steam, flushing and cleansing. I can barely believe what I see. There before me is Grandma, young and regal and powerful as ever. I feel her presence here, as if we have suddenly been reunited. It's like the Hermetic Dawn experience has somehow come to life, springing out of long-hidden history.

"Perilli painted the Queen of Swords to look like Gran Flo?" Logan asks first. "Or to look like Amelia?"

I suppose that's the million-dollar question. Since none of us have the answer, I will myself to turn my attention away from the reflective Queen and onto the envelope still resting in the box. Surely whatever connection Grandma had to Carson Perilli must be explained within? Opening the envelope, I then unfold a few pieces of thick paper covered in handwriting. Flipping to the end, I see an inscription written at the bottom: *Ever thine, Carson Perilli.*

A chill rolls up my spine, thick and prickling.

"Can you read it out loud?" Cleo asks, rising on her toes to try to see.

It's a good idea. I need something to steady myself anyway, otherwise I feel liable to float right off this mountain. So I begin to read Perilli's letter aloud, my voice humming in my chest.

"To you who have found my Queen of Swords, you who I hope is also the carrier of my final Perillian deck. Maybe this letter will mean something to you, maybe it will not. But my intuition tells me it will. It tells me you climbed this mountain for the same reasons you likely braved the fires and swam the oceans and trekked the forests: to earn what you learn. Here on this peak, breathing this rarified air, you have earned the right to learn the story of the Queen of Swords, the truest muse of The Perillian Tarot.

"Once upon a time, a young knight fell in love with a young page. They spent years Coupled, The Moon and The Sun, learning much from each other's differences. It was the first flush for them both, the first bloom of Lovers burning so brightly, their light felt potentially endless. Alas, night befalls all and circumstance pulled the two Star-crossed Lovers apart. However, long after our Tower burned, long after I quite happily married another wonderful woman, long after the birth and maturation of my three children, I still never stopped thinking of that first love: Florence Piccolo."

Speaking Grandma's name forms a lump in my throat. Still, I carry on.

"To my younger self, Flo had been a Magician. She was made of magic, the one who introduced me to the universe of the tarot, who brought me my first deck. But Flo taught me about so much more than the images on the cards—she taught me about the soul of the tarot, about its heart and its history, about the symbols that could open your awareness to your most authentic self. My twenties were lit on fire by this flowing queen and by the tarot itself.

"But as I have already written, flames burn out. I hate to say that my life then settled into the ashes of practicality; the beautiful, fulfilling, exhausting work of building a family. It was only after many years, once my children had grown to leave the nest and I lost my wife before her time—it was only during this time of loss and absence that the tarot called to fill the void. As you likely well know, the last years of my life were devoted to the art of the tarot and sharing this gift I had been given.

"But what of Flo, the first Star in my tarot constellation? We hadn't spoken in a lifetime, but I learned she married another man. She had a child, and then that child also had a child. I never entered Flo's world again, for I was no longer invited. But I always hoped Flo kept the tarot in her heart, that she passed her own gift of wisdom and insight on to those she loved.

"Then I thought: what if she hadn't? What if she needed a reminder, just as I did? When I learned illness would bring me to my own end, I used my remaining time to make one final deck—and I mailed that deck to Flo, out of the blue. As I write this letter, having already set up the missing card adventures and tests that I hope will work wonders, I wonder myself: will Flo be the one to find this letter?

"If it really is you reading, my long-lost first love, just know I am so thrilled to be found by you now. But more likely, if I know Flo, she gifted this deck to one she loves most. I have foreseen much, but it doesn't take vision to see that. From here, this story is no longer mine to tell. I just hope, whoever is reading this letter, you open this final gift I have left for you and use what's inside to continue writing our story. Ever thine, Carson Perilli."

Silence bakes us for some time. Thoughts dazzle in my mind, blinding like sunshine rippling on water. I expect to feel undone, but instead I feel stretched long and thin, like a pane of glass. In my hands I hold the truth, finally.

"Perilli didn't send my grandma the deck because she was some special follower," I say automatically, charged like a battery. "He sent her the deck because she inspired his entire tarot philosophy."

The words might now be obvious, but they need to be stated on this mountaintop. It all makes sense, suddenly. The reason this journey has felt so familiar, so resonant, so tangled. Grandma has been written all over it, from the start. But why did she lie about it? Why keep it a secret from everyone she loved most?

No one speaks for a while, but Cleo does place a hand on my shoulder.

"I don't think that's the end of the story, either," Chase finally says, pointing down at the throne base box.

I look and see there's a latch in the flat panel where this letter rested. Reacting immediately, I pull this latch up and almost laugh when I see what's underneath. Two small chests rest in the base, jewelry-box-sized versions of the one from Coupled Cottage. The left box reads *LEGACY*, while the right reads *PURPOSE*. A quick inspection shows they're both bolted to the base and attached to two tanks, presumably full of some dissolving liquid in standard Perillian fashion.

I also find a long key nestled between the chests, with the Hebrew letter Mem painted on it—just like Perilli's symbol for The Hermit also brought to life. I know above all else that Mem represents water—which means it truly represents flow. Mem is also associated with The Hanged Man, a figure I seem inextricably tied to. You'd think seeing all this would make things feel difficult, especially since it's clear to me by now that opening one box will flood the other.

But really, this choice feels easy. It reflects the direct intention I already set for myself at the start of this trip. So I reach forward without hesitation, knowing exactly what I must choose.

◆ I am **honoring** Grandma's **legacy**, so I use the Mem key to open the Legacy box. **Turn To Page 271**

◆ I am unlocking **personal power**, so I use the Mem key to open the Purpose box. **Turn To Page 274**

I open the lock on the Legacy box, and as I do, I hear the gentle whoosh of water filling the Purpose box. Part of me wants to pry it open before its contents are destroyed, but I fear breaking Perilli's rules might damage both.

Focusing instead on my chosen box, I find another piece of paper inside, folded in three like a letter. It makes me wonder if the other box contained a different letter, now dissolving into nothingness? I tell myself once again: it doesn't matter, because I can't focus on what has been lost. I must focus on what I've found.

So I pick up the letter, and when I see the handwriting there, I gasp again.

It belongs, unmistakably, to Grandma.

My eyes unfocus as I try frantically to absorb the words all at once. I clearly can't read out loud right now, so the others crowd around me, equally eager to read. I then force myself to breathe and hold my hand steady long enough to read this message from my favorite person no longer on the planet.

My Dearest Amelia,

I am told it will likely be you who reads this note, someday. If you have indeed found it, that means you're all grown up. And you will have questions. If I'm not still there to provide these answers, I'm writing them here for you.

When I received Carson Perilli's deck in the mail, I knew exactly what it was. I had heard who he became, later in his life. Why did I keep that a secret from you? Because I had built an entire other life in the many decades since I knew Carson and I knew how reentering Carson's world would disrupt our beautiful life. I suppose you know about this disruption yourself, having entered Carson's world to find this letter.

However, if you indeed came this far in search of answers, you are ready to know the truth. First, I must say that I kept all this from you to protect you. Right now, as I write this letter, you are still a young child. The future Amelia who might read this letter has no doubt grown leaps and bounds. You already absorb wisdom like a sponge, even at this young age. If I leave any legacy to you, I hope it is that you share your gifts and your talent for reading the tarot with the world however you choose.

Because you are not the only legacy that Carson and I leave. And you are not the only one to forge your own path independent of our influence.

When Carson and I were very young and very in love, I became pregnant. Neither of us was prepared to raise a child, so we did the only thing we knew how to at the time: we gave that child up for adoption to a very lovely family. As part of the adoption, neither Carson nor I ever met this child, we never even learned their sex. We gave that child to this family to have their own life, then we built our own lives, divergent as they eventually became. We rarely spoke of this child, but on the occasions we did, we gave them a name inspired by our shared love of the tarot: Zain.

I hope you'll understand why we kept this piece of the past to ourselves— and why I kept the truth of Carson's deck to myself when it arrived at our door. It was for the sake of our family, but also for the sake of this child. I did not want to disrupt the only family they had ever known without invitation. I implored Carson to do the same.

I also hope you'll understand why I struck the following deal with Carson: if he left us alone and allowed me to conceal the origins of the deck, I agreed to teach you about the tarot. That part is easy—I plan to teach you and sweet little Chase, anyway. The hard part has been promising to write this letter for Carson to stash away, as the end to some elaborately constructed hero's journey. He believes you'll find your way to it someday; I imagine he might try to do the same for Zain, despite my protests. My only consolation is that neither of us is supposed to know where Zain ended up.

Carson believes someday you'll want to be a part of this tarot society he is building. I don't know if you'll ever find your way to this secret I've kept, but if you do, it will have been on your own merit. This, of course, is why I left you the deck with all its many mysteries still intact.

You have all the answers you'll ever need inside you, Amelia. I cannot wait to see what you do, watching with pride and love from wherever I am now.

Love, Grandma Flo

I read and reread the letter until the words finally sink in. Once the meaning settles, realizations tumble through my mind. I have a half aunt or uncle out there? This person would be a half sibling to my mom, then also a half sibling to Brendan. This means I am connected to Carson Perilli by blood—and that connection must be the mysterious buyer of Perillian artifacts, Page Zain. Surely, they must have learned who their father was. Or could they have had contact with Perilli somehow before he died, to learn this name? Or, more likely, did they learn this truth similar to how I'm learning it now?

Still trying to sort through all this, I think of Grandma. What must this have all been like for the young version of her painted on the Queen of Swords? It all feels so unfathomable, so distant. But then I remind myself of this much: Grandma always did what was in her family's best interest, to protect all of her children and grandchildren. So despite feeling overwhelmed and shell-shocked, I also suddenly feel fulfilled. In completing this journey, I have learned exactly what I wanted to learn: I finally understand Grandma's place in all this. *What would Flo do?* I know now more than ever exactly how to answer that question.

"Amelia, are you okay?" Cleo asks first, blinking back their own disbelief.

"Yes," I say, meaning it. "I wanted to take this trip to honor Grandma and to learn more about her. We've certainly done that much."

Chase nods, looking as emotional as I currently feel. "It makes so much sense now, why we have the deck. All because of this connection between Gran Flo and Perilli when they were around our age."

I place a hand on his shoulder. Gran Flo might not have been Chase's grandmother by blood, but she was in all the ways that matter most. This discovery belongs to him just as much.

"But where is Page Zain? What do they know?" Chase asks, spinning forward as usual. "Are you going to tell anyone? Are you going to try to find Zain?"

"Zain must have learned about their real parents, but obviously they don't want anyone to know," Cleo offers. "They must have reasons, like Gran Flo."

"Wait, does anyone else see that?" Logan says, reaching into the Legacy box.

Turn To Page 277

I open the lock on the Purpose box and as I do, I hear the gentle whoosh of water filling the Legacy box. Part of me wants to pry it open before its contents are destroyed, but I fear breaking Perilli's rules might damage both.

Focusing instead on my chosen box, I find another piece of paper inside, folded in three like a letter. It makes me wonder if the other box contained a different letter, now dissolving into nothingness? I tell myself once again: it doesn't matter, because I can't focus on what has been lost. I must focus on what I've found.

So I pick up the letter, and when I see the handwriting there, I gasp again.

It belongs, unmistakably, to Grandma.

My eyes unfocus as I try frantically to absorb the words all at once. I clearly can't read out loud right now, so the others crowd around me, equally eager to read. I then force myself to breathe and hold my hand steady long enough to read this message from my favorite person no longer on the planet.

My Dearest Amelia,

I am told it will likely be you who reads this note, someday. If you have indeed found it, that means you're all grown up. And you will have questions. If I'm not still there to provide these answers, I'm writing them here for you.

When I received Carson Perilli's deck in the mail, I knew exactly what it was. I had heard who he became later in his life. Why did I keep that a secret from you? Because I had built an entire other life in the many decades since I knew Carson and I knew how reentering his world would disrupt our beautiful life. I suppose you know about this disruption yourself, having entered Carson's world to find this letter.

But this impact would have been so much deeper than you know. That's because, as you've discovered, Carson painted his Queen of Swords to look like my younger self—and perhaps like you, as you become a young woman. In his letter to me, Carson claimed he had visions of you, my dear Amelia, as the successor to his—whatever we'd call this obsessive society he has built. Carson named you, Amelia, his *Arcere*, his final "mystery solved."

You already know what I believe about visions and fate. I believe Carson wants to use this claim to draw us both into this tarot to further his mythology, as his muse and his chosen one. By now, you know the lengths to which Carson goes to breathe life into his mysteries. After all, how do you draw the line between an informed guess and an intuitive vision?

You are still a young child as I write this letter, and all I want is to protect you. So I struck a deal with Carson: if he left us alone and allowed me to conceal the origins of the deck, I'd agree to teach you about the tarot. That part is easy—I plan to teach you and sweet little Chase all I know, anyway. The hard part has been promising to write this note for Carson to stash away, as the end to some elaborately constructed hero's journey. He believes you'll find your way to it someday. Me, I'm not so sure.

All I am sure of is that if you do eventually follow Perilli's trail, that you do so of your own choosing—not because he or I told you to. I do hope you'll forgive me for lying. I did so not to take agency away from you, but rather to provide it. As you'll no doubt hear me say, I believe the greatest measure of evil is how much choice you strip from others. I didn't want you burdened with anyone's expectations of you. Whatever path you choose, I want you to choose it for yourself. This, of course, is why I left you the deck with all its many mysteries still intact.

It is also why I have shared with you all the wisdom I have accumulated over my life. I don't know if you are Carson's legacy, as he claims. But I do know you are my legacy. I cannot wait to see what you do, watching with pride and love from wherever I am now.

Love, Grandma Flo

I read and reread the letter until the words finally sink in.

Part of me wants to feel sad or upset or doubtful, but knowing what I now know, I just feel fulfilled. I finally understand Grandma's place in all this. I understand what she tried to keep me from and the choice she tried to empower me with, leaving me Perilli's deck. But then I can't help but wonder: have I gained something else along the way, some gift from Perilli—or some curse?

"Amelia, are you okay?" Cleo asks first, blinking back their own disbelief.

"Yes," I say, meaning it. "I wanted to take this trip to learn more about the card and about Grandma, and to learn some things about myself. What more could I ask for?"

Chase nods, looking as emotional as I currently feel. "It makes so much sense now. All of it."

I place a hand on his shoulder. Gran Flo might not have been Chase's grandmother by blood, but she was in all the ways that matter most. This discovery belongs to him just as much.

No one asks the big question, though.

No one asks whether I actually believe in Perilli's calling.

"Wait, does anyone else see that?" Logan says, reaching into the Purpose box.

Turn To Page 277

Logan scrapes his fingernails against the bottom of the box, attempting to grab something lying flat there. Once he pulls it up, we all see it covers a rectangular slot. We then turn to see that Logan has picked up another Perillian card, complete with the Perillian symbol on the back. Logan hands me the card and I flip it for everyone to see. It's a Judgment card, though it's unlike any we've seen before. The usual winged judge figure floats at the very top, but the four corners each bear a drawing of The Hanged Man. Mostly, the card is taken up by writing:

The deck you possess was meant for Flo and her own.
    But as you now know, my own are building something profound.
    You've passed all the tests, so now you face a final choice.
    Do you donate the deck back to its source, to help empower
The Lianist Way?
    Or do you keep this deck that justly belongs to you?

The Hanged Man,
Carson Perilli

Reading this, my brain first flashes to The Hanged Man, which must have been Perilli's Major Arcana expression. The deeper meanings of the card populate my mind, looking at him through this new lens. The Hanged Man represents the debts incurred when we accept the gift of life, to leave the world better than we found it. He also represents turning a world view upside down and being introduced to new ideas. Truer words couldn't be spoken.

Learning this, it turns out I actually have been connected to a Hanged Man all along—it just wasn't Anwar.

Once this meaning settles, I turn my focus to paintings of The Hanged Man. I then see, drawn on his torso, the standard Perillian symbol—but suddenly its truest meaning becomes clear to me. Mem, the head of the P, stands for water—for Flow—but also for The Hanged Man. Then I see the stalk of the P, its upside-down number four, must also stand for the crossed legs of The Hanged Man, which in turn represents the reversal of completion: the incomplete.

So it turns out this Perillian symbol had volumes of its own to speak about the deck and its creators, all along.

"Of course Perilli would write this on a makeshift Judgment card," Chase says, focusing on the more obvious element of the card. "It's the penultimate step in the Major Arcana, one final test of what you've learned on your journey."

"Not to mention reconciling with your past to move forward with your future," I add, as the choice before me begins to crystallize.

"It also means Perilli knew Brendan was going to found The Lianist Way organization," Cleo adds. "I mean, he knew the name, so he had to have had a hand in Brendan's work, on some level, right?"

Hearing Cleo's words, it adds yet another layer to this decision. But honestly, I'm done with layers. I know revelations like this would have decimated an earlier version of myself, riddling me with panic. But now I know that anxiety will always be a part of my life, a season to manage, like the tides changing or the moon phasing. Just like I now know remaining open and evolving through new experiences doesn't obscure who I've been; it only enhances who I'm becoming.

So once again, I know exactly what I need to do.

◊ I **donate the deck** to The Lianist Way, sliding it into the slot.
Turn To Page 279

◊ I **keep the deck**.
Turn To Page 280

It might seem like a decision quickly made, but if this trip has taught me anything, it's how to trust my instincts. This deck has given me so much, but now is the time to share this gift. Some might call it foolish to let go of something this valuable, but I know exactly what being foolish really means.

However, I do decide to save one piece of it for myself. I still hold the Queen of Swords, separated from the rest of the deck. One way or another this deck was never meant to be complete, if only because I deserve to hold this piece of Grandma for myself.

The deck disappears into the bowels of the Sworn monument, and from the moment it leaves my fingers, I feel light. I turn to Chase first, after making this decision. I don't know if he agrees, but either way, he nods at me.

"So what are you going to do now?" Logan asks first, once he senses my dust has settled. "Perilli and your grandma went to some pretty wild lengths to tell you this truth in a private way. So do you want his followers to know about your connection to him?"

As always, the question Logan poses is a good one. Donating the deck was a gesture that doesn't have just one potential meaning. I know I will need more time to process the exact implications of what this means, to unpack this legacy that has been left to me by these two pillared figures.

But for now, I also know what purpose can best honor that legacy.

◇ "Donating the deck is my **introduction** to The Lianist Way, as a founding act. I want to be a part of this new Perillian organization."
Turn To Page 281

◇ "Donating the deck is my **goodbye** to Perilli's world, which I believe is really just filled with smoke and mirrors."
Turn To Page 283

Deciding so quickly might seem spontaneous of me, but I only act swiftly because I know this is the right choice.

"I'm keeping the deck," I announce, turning away from the Sworn monument. "It belonged to Grandma, in all the ways that matter most. Which means it belongs with me, always."

Looking to the others, everyone nods along in support—especially Chase.

"So what are you going to do now?" Logan asks first, once he senses my dust has settled. "Perilli and your grandma went to some pretty wild lengths to tell you this truth in a private way. Do you want his followers to know about your connection to him?"

As always, the question Logan poses is a good one. Keeping the deck was a gesture that doesn't have just one potential meaning. Certainly I kept the deck to use as a tool and a guide, as a conduit of Grandma's wisdom and a way keep having conversations of a kind with her. But this deck carries so much value, so much baggage and attention—so what is my practical intention?

I know I will need more time to process the exact implications of what this means, to unpack this legacy that has been left to me by these two pillared figures. Still, for now, I know what purpose can best honor that legacy.

◊ "Keeping the deck was really an **introduction** to The Lianist Way. I want to help shape this new Perillian organization. Possessing this deck will grant me the influence I need to do so."
Turn To Page 281

◊ "Keeping the deck was really my **goodbye** to Perilli's world, which I believe is really just filled with smoke and mirrors."
Turn To Page 283

This final discovery has clearly unlocked an even more compelling mystery. I don't know where the next chapter in this journey will take me; all I know is that I have to keep following my instincts. The role I have to play uncovering all of Grandma's and Perilli's truths is too important to ignore.

"Well, I think I know what I'm doing next summer," I say, turning to look at Logan, Cleo, and Chase. I then reach down to grasp my Dalet locket, pressing it against the Queen of Swords. Thinking of Grandma, I can only hope she'd be proud of this decision. Something tells me she would be. Really, that's all I need to know.

"We're not quite done with these Perillian adventures yet, are we?"

◆　◆　◆　◆

On our way back down the mountain, Chase and I hang behind. Maybe it's because we're reluctant to let this journey end, but it's probably because we know we need to share this final moment together. The Major and The Minor, the perfect pair, uncovering our greatest mysteries together—the way it has always been.

"Are you all right?" Chase asks first. "That was a lot to absorb."

"Weirdly, I am," I answer, once again meaning it.

"Well, for the record, I'm really proud of you," Chase says, taking me by surprise. There are many other things he could say after everything we've been through, but he chooses these words. They mean everything to me.

"Thank you," I answer. "I couldn't have done any of it without you. And I wouldn't want to. We're a team."

"Always," Chase says, reaching out to grab my hand. "No matter what."

I take his hand, my way of thanking him for giving me the space to make this final decision on my own. Sensing this, Chase then looks like he has something else to share.

"Now knowing Gran Flo was the true founder of Perillianism, it makes sense why they'd want us to join this new foundation," he begins. "I didn't know how to tell you this before, but now I'm glad I didn't, so it didn't influence you. But after The Hermetic Dawn, I actually exited through a different door than you all. Then Brendan invited me to become a Guide-in-Training for The Lianist Way."

I look back at Chase and see the choice he made written all over his face.

- ◆ Chase chose to **accept** the invitation to join The Lianist Way.
  Turn To Page 284
- ◆ Chase chose to **decline** the invitation to join The Lianist Way.
  Turn To Page 285

Something tells me every time I solve one of Perilli's mysteries, it will only lead to another. For now, my next chapter has to be defined by me and not anyone else.

"As much as I hate to say it, this mystical trip is over," I say, turning to look at Logan, Cleo, and Chase. "I think it's time we returned to the real world, huh?"

I then reach down to grasp my Dalet locket, pressing it against the Queen of Swords card. Thinking of Grandma, I can only hope she'd be proud of this decision. Something tells me she would be. Really, that's all I need to know.

"But who knows what kind of trouble we'll get into next summer?"

◆　◆　◆　◆

On our way back down the mountain, Chase and I hang behind. Maybe it's because we're reluctant to let this journey end, but it's probably because we know we need to share this final moment together. The Major and The Minor, the perfect pair, uncovering our greatest mysteries together—the way it has always been.

"Are you all right?" Chase asks first. "That was a lot to absorb."

"Weirdly, I am," I answer, once again meaning it.

"Well, for the record, I'm really proud of you," Chase says, taking me by surprise. There are many other things he could say after everything we've been through, but he chooses these words. They mean everything to me.

"Thank you," I answer. "I couldn't have done any of it without you. And I wouldn't want to. We're a team."

"Always," Chase says, reaching out to grab my hand. "No matter what."

I take his hand, my way of thanking him for giving me the space to make this final decision on my own. Sensing this, Chase then looks like he has something else to share.

"Now knowing Gran Flo was the true founder of Perillianism, it makes sense why they'd want us to join this new foundation," he begins. "I didn't know how to tell you this before, but now I'm glad I didn't, so it didn't influence you. But after The Hermetic Dawn, I actually exited through a different door than you all. Then Brendan invited me to become a Guide-in-Training for The Lianist Way."

I look back at Chase and see the choice he made written all over his face.

◆ Chase chose to **accept** the invitation to join The Lianist Way.
Turn To Page 286
◆ Chase chose to **decline** the invitation to join The Lianist Way.
Turn To Page 287

"So we both want to be a part of The Lianist Way," I say, not surprised. "How could we resist? It's an expression of the tarot we've used our whole lives."

"Especially at a turning point like this one, discovering what we have to contribute," Chase replies. "The old me would have never thought of joining a spiritual organization this way. Though I wonder if college will change our minds about all of this?"

"I doubt it," I answer. "I think college will give us perspective, but doesn't this just feel like it fits? This chance to build something real, a way to share all this fundamental knowledge with the world? I don't know, it almost feels like—"

I don't finish, because the next words I almost speak take me by surprise.

"You were going to say 'like we were born to do this,' weren't you?" Chase asks, grinning

"I was going to say 'meant to do this,' but same difference," I answer, grinning too. "I certainly think we're meant to follow through on the discoveries we made."

"Logan's ears must be burning," Chase says. "Some things really do change."

"Maybe it's more like seasons changing? Different expressions of the same thing?"

"I like that," Chase says. "Kind of like you and me?"

"What do you mean?" I ask.

"If this trip has taught me anything, it's that we're not as different as we used to think. Maybe our personalities, sure. But the things we value, our instincts, how we see the world—that's all the same."

"Two faces of the same coin," I say, emotion stirring in my chest. "Just like Grandma always said."

"Exactly," Chase replies. "Which means a little distance won't kill us. I think maybe it'll only make us appreciate everything even more?"

"And if not, we now have The Lianist Way to connect us," I add. "This new expression of our old ways?"

Chase nods and I smile. I then hook my arm through his as we continue our descent, my partner in turning this final page—and all the pages to come.

Turn To Page 288

"You're leaving all this in your rear view, aren't you?" I ask.

"I wouldn't exactly put it that way," Chase answers. "The tarot is always going be a part of my life—it's the only spiritual center I've ever really trusted. And I am curious about The Lianist Way, but I'm not sure I believe in organizing spirituality this way. Or at least, I'm not sure I believe it's right for me. Besides, I want to leave myself a bit of an open slate for college, to see what else I can discover."

"I'm going to do that, too, you know," I say. "I just want to take all this along with me, in a more structured way. It's a part of me, now more than ever. Especially after this final discovery."

Chase pauses, taking some silent steps before speaking again.

"You know that you're the part of all this I'm taking with me, right? Even if we're not together every day, you'll always be my best friend, Amelia."

Emotion stirs in my chest once again.

"That goes without saying," I reply. "But I'm glad you did, anyway."

The possessive side of me suddenly wants to hold on to Chase, to take this moment in time and freeze it forever. Instead, I allow us to flow forward. This trip has already changed both of us in so many ways. We can never go back to the way things were before, so why try?

"But who is going to think things through for me?" I say, nudging Chase.

"And who is going to take the leaps for me?" he says, nudging me back.

"I guess we'll have to keep doing those things for ourselves?"

Chase hooks his arm through mine, and we walk forward together—even though we know we're about to walk in very different directions. It feels empowering and terrifying at the same time.

"Well, we've certainly learned we're capable of a lot more than we ever thought, huh?" Chase asks.

"Chase," I begin, taking my time with these final words. "I think we're capable of anything we set our minds to."

Turn To Page 288

"You decided to become a Guide for The Lianist Way, didn't you?" I ask.

Chase nods, looking a little guilty. "I mean, I'm still going to college. I probably won't be back here until next summer, but—"

"You don't have to justify it," I interrupt. "I'm walking away because I think it's the best way to keep the tarot alive in my life, especially after this last discovery. But if this is your way of keeping that same tradition, I totally get that."

Chase pauses, walking several silent beats before responding.

"Thank you. It's new for me, the idea of belonging to an organized spirituality. But this feels . . . right. Just like it's new for me to make decisions totally on my own. But I think between you and Logan, I've gotten too used to being someone's other half. I think I need to find the whole version of myself."

It stings to hear these words. My instinct is to clamp down, to keep Chase by my side as my loyal best friend. Instead, I let that instinct flow away. Instead, I remember what my own renewed self is trying to learn: to believe in myself without anyone else's stamp of approval. In an opposite kind of way, it's a reflection of what Chase is striving for, too.

"Maybe Cain was on to something with that whole phoenix motif?" I laugh. "Maybe we do have to burn away some of our old lives to enter the ones we want?"

"Maybe, but here's the thing about phoenixes," Chase replies. "Even reborn shiny and new, they're still the same old birds. They still rise from their own ashes, not someone else's."

Chase turns to me as we continue walking, hooking his arm through mine.

"Some things about us will never change. And for me, that's having Amelia Piccolo as my best friend."

"The Emperor to my Empress," I say, ignoring the urge to classify Chase as the Minor to my Major. That time feels like it has maybe passed.

Chase and I might be setting out on diverging paths very soon, but these paths will always have started in the same place. So I just hope that means we'll end up in the same place, too. Until then, we'll always have this trip—and the tarot we inherited—to keep us connected.

Turn To Page 288

"You're walking away from all this, too?" I ask.

"It feels kind of necessary, doesn't it?" Chase answers. "How are we going to figure out who we're supposed to be if we cling to the things we already know? Besides, I've never really been much for the whole organized religion thing."

"Yeah, the tarot feels more personal to me. But you already knew that."

"You're really okay leaving behind this last part Perilli and Gran Flo left you with?" Chase asks.

"Maybe not forever," I answer. "But definitely for now."

Chase and I catch each other's eyes then, with looks full of meaning. In so many ways, we're cut from the same cloth, despite all the ways we differ. Two halves of the same whole, smoothing out each other's roughest corners. But what happens when you separate these halves? Whether we like it or not, that discovery is exactly what this next chapter has to be about.

"I've been thinking a lot about the Major Arcana's end," Chase says. "How it's all about achieving a new consciousness, a new perspective. But even after shifts like this, you don't enter a new world—you just see the same world differently. I have a feeling the lessons we just learned are lessons we'll end up relearning the rest of our lives, over and over again in different ways."

"Okay, preacher Chase," I laugh, nudging him. "What are you trying to say?"

"I'm trying to say this," Chase says, smiling too. "We always thought of ourselves as two halves of one whole, Minor and Major. But maybe we're really meant to be two wholes, like The Sun and The Moon, existing separately, but always together in cycles. Speaking in non-tarot terms, I just mean that no matter how much we grow and change, you'll always be my best friend."

Emotion stirs in my chest yet again, hearing Chase's words.

"Now you're talking like a true king."

"And you too, my queen."

I lock arms with Chase as we walk. Impossible as it still seems, I start to feel the future arriving, like water staining the edges of paper. Things won't ever be like they were before. But maybe, if we let them, things will be even better?

Turn To Page 288

Sunshine beats down on my face, fiery and free. The four of us ride along in Charvan this one last time, flowing toward home and into the unknown at the same time. "Bittersweet Symphony" plays on the stereo, and nothing could feel more fitting. In this moment, we are a hello that starts with a goodbye. We are sewn tightly together as we prepare to scatter our separate ways. We found the answers we were seeking, but we are filled with even bigger questions.

We are all two things at once, flipped coins and balanced scales.

So what else is there to do but sing along as we hurtle into the four-cornered valley below? I stick my arm out of the open window, letting the air scoop my palm in invisible waves. I think of the answers that burn bright in my brain, waiting to be fully unpacked. I think of Grandma and all she has left me, today and every day. And I think of what she would tell me to do, if she were here:

Enjoy the moment.

"Is anyone else's stomach beeping with hunger like Toky's?" Cleo asks, projecting over the music.

"I definitely wouldn't put it that way," Logan laughs. "But, yes, I am also starving."

"I have two restaurants left on my CleoCraft list, if we want to hit one on the drive back?"

Hearing this question, my eyes shift to Chase. I can tell he has the same instinct to pull a tarot card, to divine one last universal sign as we end this trip.

"What if we just stop at the first place that looks good?" Chase responds first. "One final detour to add to the books?"

Everyone in Charvan reacts with a beat of surprised silence, because this might be the least Chase thing he has ever said.

"I'm in," I say. "Something tells me we'll know the right place when we see it."

These gestures are little, I know. But I also now know how the littlest things can accumulate. Tiny beads of light gathered together, branches and trees, drops and oceans. Single steps that make up an entire journey—major detours, minor miracles and all.

THANK YOU, FIRST and foremost, to Britny Brooks-Perilli, for this enormous labor of love. No one else possessed the vision for what this novel could be, nor the technical know-how and creative spirit to get it made. From concept to proposal to final draft, you've been my champion every step of the way (in a world where champions of interactive and queer fiction are hard to find). For better or worse, you are now forever immortalized as the enigmatic Carson Perilli.

To the other half of this magic equation, my fiction agent, Lucy Carson: you deserve an equal share of gratitude. This thank-you extends all the way back to that first meeting in your office, where you were brave enough to take a chance on representing a relatively unproven author in a totally new genre, all the way through the heartbreaking multiyear creation and submission of a still-unpublished novel, until you ushered us to Britny's doorstep. For every link in the chain, past and future, I thank you for your unconditional support and generosity.

To Amanda Burnett, my friend and TV agent of nearly a decade, I thank you for keeping the faith in me through the years of near-successes, when you had no tangible reason to believe.

To the intrepid team that worked on this newfangled novel, I thank you for your creativity and ingenuity. To Marissa Raybuck, for working overtime to design every aspect of this new format, from cover to backmatter. To Karl James Mountford, for bringing the characters and symbolism of this novel to life on our breathtaking jacket art and interior illustrations. To copy editor Michael McConnell, who felt like an extension of my own brain. To Amber Morris, for deftly handling the production of this novel-puzzle. To Valerie Howlett, Isabella Nugent, and Nicole Banholzer, for marketing and publicizing all this work. And to all the other hands who helped push this novel forward, the ones I don't even (and may never) know about.

To the best friends who Amelia, Chase, Cleo, and Logan were originally inspired by, I thank you for just being you and being in my life. These characters took on a life of their own as they grew and evolved, but you can find their roots in Daniel Denicola, Chase Baxter, Ariel Colangelo, Julia Rubin, Maija Gustin, and Shane St. Hill.

To the few who took the time to read early drafts of this novel, I thank you for convincing me this invented format could actually work on some fundamental level: Chase Baxter, Jessica Goodman, Chelsea Sanders, Jeana Kolson, Stephan Lee, and Kelly Diamond.

To Rosa Van Wie and Brendan Grayson-Wallace, members of the Silver Bay family, I thank you for introducing me to two integral pillars of this novel. Rosa, for reading my tarot cards for the first time on that bay blanket and changing my life forever. Brendan, for sending me that D&D starter kit and hosting my first campaign experience. I'd also like to thank the development executives Lauren Pfieffer and Jamie Fleishman for being the first to believe in my cult-creating and tarot-treasure storytelling prowess on the pilots *Killing Thyme* and *Major Arcana*. You're all now immortalized as the key Perillians named after you!

To the interactive editors who first published my work, I thank you for giving me the space to develop my own unique style of Interactive Fiction (sometimes veering outside house rules). I'd like to thank everyone at Choice of Games, especially Jason Stevan Hill, along with everyone at Tales Fiction and Jessica Delfanti.

To Ned Rust and the James Patterson Team, I thank you for giving me my first internship at Hachette as a college freshman, where I learned so much about the industry and dreamed of someday having my own book to hold. To now be published by Hachette fifteen years later is truly a dream come true.

To my Penn writing family, I thank you for the endless support. Jessica Goodman, host of many lunches to compare publishing notes, from agentless manuscripts to potential TV deals and everything in-between. Grant Ginder, who introduced me to my agent Lucy after a boozy NYC lunch. Kate Myers, my friend-therapist and fellow writing warrior. Mingo Reynolds and RJ Bernocco, ultimate shepherds to all Penn writers, who gave me my career start in LA and who keep me in touch with the next generation of writers.

To all of the mentors and supporters, I thank you for telling me I could do this and shaping me as a writer: John Tricamo, Adrienne Rosado, Max Apple, Valerie Ross, Margo Todd, Paul Hendrickson, Mark Rizzo, Tim McNeal, John Strauss, Jane Ezersky, Lindsay Tolbert, Carmine Gibaldi, and Mary Rita Wallace. I'd like to especially thank dear family friend David Kastan, the very first person to tell me, at age sixteen, that if I worked at it hard enough to develop it, I had the talent to be a writer.

To the generations of tarot wisdom that seeped into this novel, there's an endless foundation of artists and thinkers to thank. I used many decks and guidebooks for inspiration and reference, but a few works remained central to my own understanding of the tarot: David Fontana's *The Essential Guide to The Tarot*; Vanessa Decort's *Sun and Moon Tarot*; and Jason Gruhl, Jonathan Saiz, and Andi Todaro's *The Fountain Tarot*.

I also owe an endless debt of gratitude to Oprah and her *SuperSoul* conversations for so much accumulated wisdom.

To the ladies of High Rise, I thank you for providing the adventures that filled the journals I referenced when bringing these characters to life. You forever have my high school heart.

To my immediate family, I thank you for holding me up when writing felt impossible and for quite literally footing the bill when I couldn't myself. This novel is for you, first and foremost. Kyle, who loves and listens every single day. Mom, who has read every single word I've scribbled since I could lift a pen. Dad, who never lost the faith this would happen for me, not for a single second. Louis and Amanda, who celebrate every little update and who feed me constantly. And Grandma Florence, who lives on in me—and in this novel.

Most importantly, to you, the reader: I thank you for picking up this book. Every novel belongs to the reader eventually, but in Interactive Fiction, the story really becomes yours to have and hold in a unique way. Handle it with care. I hope it will serve you as well as it has served me.

Use this sheet to keep track of your choices and to help calculate *your* unique reader personality profile at the novel's end. This sheet is an optional bonus feature, so no need to fill it out if you're just here for a good read. Each column can represent a new reread, but record your keywords however you see fit!

CHAPTER ONE		
Queen **or** Mother Earth?		
Ocean **or** body heat?		
CHAPTER TWO		
Guidance (compass) **or** help (charms)?		
Learn **or** responsibility?		
CHAPTER THREE		
Fountain of life **or** holy grail?		
Hug **or** response?		
CHAPTER FOUR		
Hold **or** kiss?		
Give the Prince **or** take the Prince?		
CHAPTER FIVE		
Honor legacy **or** personal power?		
Bonus question **or** bring back ?		
CHAPTER SIX		
Calling **or** coincidence? Symbolic **or** invest?		

CHAPTER SEVEN		
Don't believe **or** do believe?		
Tower **or** Hermit?		
Blue door **or** purple door?		
CHAPTER EIGHT		
Forces **or** own making?		
Need some space **or** tell it's okay?		
CHAPTER NINE		
Princess of Cups recovered (blue door) **or** did not recover (purple door)?		
Get intimate **or** check on?		
Magically sprout **or** one truth? Stomach drops **or** tilt head?		
CHAPTER TEN		
A solution **or** learn more?		
With or without **or** same road? Push through **or** keep distracted?		
Tarot history **or** tarot symbols?		
CHAPTER ELEVEN		
Too big **or** be stronger?		
Leave the King of Pentacles **or** keep the King of Pentacles?		

CHAPTER TWELVE		
Magician **or** Hermit?		
Ace of Wands **or** Emperor? Hierophant **or** King of Wands?		
Moon **or** Two of Pentacles? Ten of Cups **or** Empress?		
Accept **or** decline?		
Break **or** open?		
CHAPTER THIRTEEN		
Forgive **or** revealed?		
Love you **or** best friend?		
Donate the deck **or** keep the deck?		
Introduction **or** goodbye?		

NOTES: _____

_____

_____

_____

_____

_____

_____

_____

_____

_____

_____

What Corner has your reading sorted you into?

◇ If the *Prince of Wands was Given* to Cain; the *Princess of Cups was Recovered*; and you *Kept the King of Pentacles* from Rosa, then this suggests you were intuitive, wise, and bold enough to collect all four missing cards intact. You have thus earned the rare right to **Sort Yourself**.

◇ If the *Prince of Wands was Given* to Cain; the *Princess of Cups was Recovered*; and you *Left the King of Pentacles* for Rosa, then this suggests that relationships matter most to you and that you are thinking of others always. You are **Coupled**.

◇ If the *Prince of Wands was Given* to Cain; the *Princess of Cups was Not Recovered*; and you *Kept the King of Pentacles* from Rosa, then this suggests you are willing to experiment via trial and error. While you always advocate for yourself, you also think of others. You are **Repentant**.

◇ If the *Prince of Wands was Given* to Cain; the *Princess of Cups was Not Recovered*; and you *Left the King of Pentacles* for Rosa, then this suggests you are above material possessions and have faith in yourself above all else. You are a **Wanderer**.

◇ If the *Prince of Wands was Taken* from Cain; the *Princess of Cups was Recovered*; and you *Kept the King of Pentacles* from Rosa, then this suggests you work hard for what you want and soldier on to do what is most necessary for your overall journey. You are a **Wanderer**.

◇ If the *Prince of Wands was Taken* from Cain; the *Princess of Cups was Recovered*; and you *Left the King of Pentacles* for Rosa, then this suggests you learn quickly from your mistakes and thus are a keeper of great wisdom. You are **Repentant**.

◇ If the *Prince of Wands was Taken* from Cain; the *Princess of Cups was Not Recovered*; and you *Kept the King of Pentacles* from Rosa, then this suggests you are loyal to your chosen family first and ignore the whims of potentially harmful strangers. You are **Coupled**.

◇ If the *Prince of Wands was Taken* from Cain; the *Princess of Cups was Not Recovered*; and you *Left the King of Pentacles* for Rosa, then this means you acquired none of these three cards intact, but that you think independently and learn from your mistakes—the qualities of a true leader. You are thus singularly **Sworn**.

The Wanderers

The faithful and passionate Wanderers, soldiers and sentinels to protect.

Wands: Fire. Red. East. Summer. Desert.
Spiritual. Passion. Faith. Action. Growth. Goals. Intention.

The Coupled

The loving and creative Coupled, historians and artists to reflect.

Cups: Water. Blue. West. Winter. Ocean.
Emotional. Love. Relationships. Intuition. Connection. Tides.

The Repentant

The grounded and inventive Repentant, scientists and doctors to cure.

Pentacles: Earth. Green. North. Spring. Forest.
Elemental. Physical. Senses. Transaction. Material. Health. Body.

The Sworn

The wise and rational Sworn, guides and mentors to lead.

Swords: Air. White. South. Autumn. Mountain.
Rational. Logic. Warrior. Planning. Analysis. Clarity. Change.

AMELIA

CHAPTER ONE

Queen: Add 1 to *Spontaneous*, Add 1 to *Demanding*
Mother Earth: Add 1 to *Thoughtful*, Add 1 to *Nurturing*

Ocean: Add 1 to *Sensitive*
Body Heat: Add 1 to *Eager*

CHAPTER THREE

Fountain of Life: Add 1 to *Nurturing*
Holy Grail: Add 1 to *Demanding*

Hug: Add 1 to *Thoughtful*, Add 1 to *Sensitive*
Response: Add 1 to *Spontaneous*, Add 1 to *Eager*

CHAPTER FIVE

Honor Legacy: Add 2 to *Nurturing*
Personal Power: Add 2 to *Demanding*

Bonus Question: Add 2 to *Spontaneous*, Add 2 to *Eager*
Bring Back: Add 2 to *Thoughtful*, Add 2 to *Sensitive*

CHAPTER SEVEN

Don't Believe: Add 1 to *Spontaneous*, Add 1 to *Demanding*
Do Believe: Add 1 to *Thoughtful*, Add 1 to *Nurturing*

Tower: Add 3 to *Spontaneous*, Add 3 to *Eager*, Add 3 to *Nurturing*
Hermit: Add 3 to *Thoughtful*, Add 3 to *Sensitive*, Add 3 to *Demanding*

CHAPTER NINE

Get Intimate: Add 2 to *Spontaneous*
Check On: Add 2 to *Thoughtful*

Magically Sprout: Add 2 to *Nurturing*
One Truth: Add 2 to *Demanding*

OR

Stomach Drops: Add 2 to *Eager*
Tilt Head: Add 2 to *Sensitive*

CHAPTER ELEVEN

Too Big: Add 2 to *Spontaneous*, Add 2 to *Sensitive*
Be Stronger: Add 2 to *Thoughtful*, Add 2 to *Eager*

Leave King: Add 4 to *Nurturing*, Add 1 to *Thoughtful*
Keep King: Add 4 to *Demanding*, Add 1 to *Spontaneous*

CHAPTER THIRTEEN

Forgive: Add 2 to *Assured*, Add 1 to *Nurturing*
Revealed: Add 2 to *Honest*, Add 1 to *Demanding*

Love You: Add 1 to *Assured*, Add 1 to *Spontaneous*
Best Friend: Add 1 to *Honest*, Add 1 to *Thoughtful*

Donate the Deck: Add 1 to *Assured*, Add 1 to *Thoughtful*
Keep the Deck: Add 1 to *Honest*, Add 1 to *Spontaneous*

Introduction: Add 1 to *Assured*
Goodbye: Add 1 to *Honest*

AMELIA STRENGTH TALLIES

Which one of the below has the most tallies?
Choose your favorite if there's a tie. This is the first half of your
Major Amelia Type, the greatest strengths you gave Amelia.

Spontaneous Tally:		
Thoughtful Tally:		

AMELIA INSECURITY TALLIES

Which one of the below has the most tallies? Choose your favorite
if there's a tie. This is the second half of your **Major Amelia Type**,
the insecurity Amelia struggled with most.

Eager Tally:		
Sensitive Tally:		

Find your **Major Amelia Type** combo of Spontaneous/Thoughtful
and Eager/Sensitive in this grid:

	EAGER	SENSITIVE
SPONTANEOUS	Passion Empress	Warrior Empress
THOUGHTFUL	Enthused Empress	Wise Empress

AMELIA GROWTH TALLIES

Which one of the below has the most tallies?
This is the way you guided Amelia to overcome her insecurities.

Assured Tally:		
Honest Tally:		

EMPRESS TYPE TALLIES

Which one of the below has the most tallies? Choose your favorite
if there's a tie. This is your **Empress Type,** the tarot expression you
empowered Amelia with most often.

Nurturing Tally:		
Demanding Tally:		

Flip to the Personality Profile of your **Major Amelia Type**
and remember your **Growth Direction** and **Empress Type**!

Obviously *Spontaneous* and sometimes over-*Eager*, the Passion Empress lives by their *heart*. Not afraid to rush into love, the Passion Empress knows that their *openness* is their greatest strength—but also potentially their greatest vulnerability. The Passion Empress is also a fierce *protector*, grounded and able to balance their own instincts against the advice of others.

Balances to Reach

Don't let a love for others turn into a need for validation or approval. Don't let self-assurance turn into stubbornness or confidence turn into impulsiveness. Can see into things deeply, but must not forget to also see widely.

Growth Direction

Assured: Has recognized tendency to be eager to please and has taken steps to harness spontaneity into decisive boldness.

Honest: Has embraced the idea that honesty is the only policy and has begun developing a necessary thick skin.

Empress Type

The Nurturing Passion Empress: An extremely rare rising combination, the Nurturing Passion Empress represents duality—making choices that might seem at odds with one another, but are ultimately complementary.

The Demanding Passion Empress: Doubling down on passion, the Demanding Passion Empress is fierce and decisive as they come. They are strong-willed and inspiring, but must beware their own seasons changing like Mother Nature.

Obviously *Spontaneous* and sometimes over-*Sensitive*, the Warrior Empress lives by their sense of *adventure*. The Warrior Empress knows how to *love* deeply, but also remains grounded in the reality of *responsibility* and *legacy*. A born *leader*, the Warrior Empress also acts as a guide for self-reflection to inspire growth.

Balances to Reach

Don't let a deep well of feeling turn into a thin skin. Don't let a bold and adventurous spirit allow you to outrun that which bothers you. Don't react without thinking first. Anxiety might ensue if proper time isn't taken to process feelings.

Growth Direction

Assured: Has embraced the idea that confidence is queen and knows empowering others doesn't always mean sparing their feelings.

Honest: Has fully recognized their tendency to be sensitive and reactive, so has started processing emotions and is beginning to share them more acutely.

Empress Type

The Nurturing Warrior Empress: The most parental rising combination, the Nurturing Warrior Empress always makes choices that protect those they love. However, a parent's gifts and love can be withdrawn as easily as they are given.

The Demanding Warrior Empress: The most powerful rising combination, the Demanding Warrior Empress makes no compromises about leading with their passions—but they will make compromises for the greater good.

Very *Thoughtful* and sometimes over-*Eager*, the Enthused Empress lives by their sense of *inspiration* and *faith* in things outside themselves: people and higher powers. Able to believe in something greater than self as a way to aspire to greatness, they become a fierce *ally* and *advocate*. The Enthused Empress has an open heart and is a *hopeful romantic*. Knows that wise ones say only fools rush in—but also knows, in the tarot, that a fool is the best thing to be.

Balances to Reach

Don't let a love for others turn into a need for validation or approval. Don't let a deep empathy or a deep understanding for others lead to silencing self. Can see into things deeply, but must not forget to also see widely.

Growth Direction

Assured: Has recognized tendency to be eager to please and has taken steps to speak and act from a place of purpose, always.

Honest: Has embraced the idea that honesty is the only policy and has begun developing a necessary thick skin.

Empress Type

The Nurturing Enthused Empress: Doubling down on enthusiasm, the Nurturing Enthused Empress is as excited and empathetic as they come, but must beware of sacrificing themselves for the sake of others, as it is the most giving expression possible.

The Demanding Enthused Empress: A balanced rising combination, the Demanding Enthused Empress has captured duality, able to be both self-assured and flexible. They must beware of getting too lost in their own thoughts or the thoughts of others.

Very *Thoughtful* and sometimes over-*Sensitive*, the Wise Empress lives by her deep well of inner *knowledge* and *intuition*. Knows the value of a *slow burn*: the best things in life are hard-earned and gained over time. The Wise Empress possesses most *nurturing* nature, always thinking of others and empowering them. Sometimes can allow others to *take the lead* without knowing it, but always follows through.

Balances to Reach

Don't let a deep well of feeling turn into a thin skin. Don't let a deep empathy or a deep understanding for others lead to silencing self. Don't react without thinking first. Anxiety might ensue if proper time isn't taken to process feelings.

Growth Direction

Assured: Has embraced the idea that confidence is queen, especially when paired with a kind heart and good intent.

Honest: Has fully recognized their tendency to be sensitive and silent, so is learning being thoughtful means full expression paired with compassion.

Empress Type

The Nurturing Wise Empress: The most caring rising combination, the Nurturing Wise Empress is as loving and understanding as they come, but must beware of potentially being taken advantage of.

The Demanding Wise Empress: An extremely rare rising combination, the Demanding Wise Empress represents duality—making choices that might seem at odds with one another, but are ultimately complementary. Smart, empathetic, and deeply inspiring, they understand the flow of karma and trust in its force.

CHASE

CHAPTER TWO

Guidance (Compass): Add 1 to *Intelligent*, Add 1 to *Impatient*
Help (Charms): Add 1 to *Intuitive*, Add 1 to *Indecisive*

Learn: Add 1 to *Agency*
Responsibility: Add 1 to *Destiny*

CHAPTER FOUR

Hold: Add 1 to *Intuitive*
Kiss: Add 1 to *Intelligent*

Give the Prince: Add 3 to *Intuitive*, Add 3 to *Indecisive*, Add 3 to *Destiny*
Take the Prince: Add 3 to *Intelligent*, Add 3 to *Impatient*, Add 3 to *Agency*

CHAPTER SIX

Calling: Add 2 to *Destiny*, Add 2 to *Intuitive*, Add 2 to *Indecisive*
Coincidence: Add 2 to *Agency*, Add 2 to *Intelligent*, Add 2 to *Impatient*

OR

Symbolic: Add 2 to *Destiny*, Add 2 to *Intuitive*, Add 2 to *Indecisive*
Invest: Add 2 to *Agency*, Add 2 to *Intelligent*, Add 2 to *Impatient*

CHAPTER EIGHT

Forces: Add 1 to *Impatient*, Add 1 to *Destiny*
Own Making: Add 1 to *Indecisive*, Add 1 to *Agency*

Need Some Space: Add 1 to *Intuitive*, Add 1 to *Impatient*
Tell It's Okay: Add 1 to *Intelligent*, Add 1 to *Indecisive*

A Solution: Add 2 to *Intelligent*
Learn More: Add 2 to *Intuitive*

With or Without: Add 2 to *Impatient*
Same Road: Add 2 to *Indecisive*

OR

Push Through: Add 2 to *Impatient*
Keep Distracted: Add 2 to *Indecisive*

Tarot History: Add 2 to *Agency*
Tarot Symbols: Add 2 to *Destiny*

Magician: Add 1 to *Intuitive*, Add 1 to *Patient*
Hermit: Add 1 to *Intelligent*, Add 1 to *Confident*

Ace of Wands: Add 2 to *Intelligent*, Add 1 to *Agency*
Emperor: Add 2 to *Intuitive*, Add 1 to *Destiny*

OR

Hierophant: Add 2 to *Intelligent*, Add 1 to *Agency*
King of Wands: Add 2 to *Intuitive*, Add 1 to *Destiny*

Moon: Add 2 to *Patient*, Add 1 to *Agency*
Two of Pentacles: Add 2 to *Confident*, Add 1 to *Destiny*

OR

Ten of Cups: Add 2 to *Patient*, Add 1 to *Destiny*
Empress: Add 2 to *Confident*, Add 1 to *Agency*

Accept: Add 4 to *Destiny*, Add 1 to *Intelligent*
Decline: Add 4 to *Agency*, Add 1 to *Intuitive*

Break: Add 2 to *Intelligent*, Add 2 to *Confident*
Open: Add 2 to *Intuitive*, Add 2 to *Patient*

CHASE STRENGTH TALLIES

Which one of the below has the most tallies? Choose your favorite if there's a tie. This is the first half of your **Minor Chase Type**, the greatest strengths you gave Chase.

Intelligent Tally:		
Intuitive Tally:		

CHASE INSECURITY TALLIES

Which one of the below has the most tallies? Choose your favorite if there's a tie. This is the second half of your **Minor Chase Type**, the insecurity Chase struggled with most.

Impatient Tally:		
Indecisive Tally:		

Find your **Minor Chase Type** combo of Intelligent/Intuitive and Impatient/Indecisive in this grid:

	IMPATIENT	INDECISIVE
INTELLIGENT	Crusader Emperor	Scholar Emperor
INTUITIVE	Catalyst Emperor	Council Emperor

CHASE GROWTH TALLIES

Which one of the below has the most tallies?
This is the way you guided Chase to overcome his insecurities.

Patient Tally:		
Confident Tally:		

EMPEROR TYPE TALLIES

Which one of the below has the most tallies? Choose your favorite
if there's a tie. This is your **Emperor Type**, the tarot expression you
empowered Chase with most often.

Agency Tally:		
Destiny Tally:		

Flip to the Personality Profile of your **Minor Chase Type**
and remember your **Growth Direction** and **Emperor Type!**

Obviously *Intelligent* and sometimes *Impatient*, the Crusader Emperor is assured in their *problem solving* ability. Knows exactly what they want to *achieve*— but can become pushy or arrogant striving for it. *Action*-oriented, the Crusader Emperor is a beloved *leader*, especially because they don't always see themselves that way. Perhaps hard to get close to, but once trusted, fully *embraces* others.

Balances to Reach

Don't let a superior talent become a superiority complex. Have patience and don't force others into your way of things. While there is unique value in your talent, remember you have so much more to offer as a well-rounded being. Can love deeply, which can lead to deep wounds—but always remember you can heal these wounds.

Growth Direction

Patient: Has recognized tendency to be impatient, has taken active steps to give others more grace and extend that same grace to self.

Confident: Has begun believing in self calmly instead of always striving to prove self arrogantly, an act only fueled by doubt.

Emperor Type

The Agency Crusader Emperor: Doubling down on intelligence, the Agency Crusader Emperor is as strong and decisive as they come. They must remember leadership can turn into authoritarianism when the throne becomes too isolated.

The Destiny Crusader Emperor: A potentially volatile rising combination, the Destiny Crusader Emperor combines a fierce belief in self with a belief in a fateful higher power. They must beware being blinded by any static beliefs.

Obviously *Intelligent* and sometimes *Indecisive*, the Scholar Emperor has the impressive ability to *study* endlessly and is adept at seeing the finer *details*. Understands *complexity* and *nuance* more than most, but sometimes feels stuck or unsure as a result. Never suffering fools, the Scholar Emperor always thinks with their head first and makes the *smartest* moves, forever a student of the world. Perhaps hard to get close to, but once trusted, fully *embraced*.

Balances to Reach

Don't obsess too much about always making the "right" decision. Let go of perfectionism, because you are enough as you are. When feeling overwhelmed or paralyzed, trust your gut feeling. Can love deeply, which can lead to deep wounds—but always remember, you can heal these wounds.

Growth Direction

Patient: Has embraced the idea that thinking things through isn't about being stuck or paralyzed, but rather patience is an art of stillness and focus.

Confident: Has recognized tendency to be indecisive and has taken active steps to trust and believe in own voice, having more to offer than just one facet of self.

Emperor Type

The Agency Scholar Emperor: The most intellectual rising combination, the Agency Scholar Emperor believes all answers can be found with enough attention. They trust in their judgment, but must beware the things they cannot always see.

The Destiny Scholar Emperor: A balanced rising combination, the Destiny Scholar Emperor has captured duality more seamlessly, able to be both rational and faithful, objective and subjective, studious and commanding, scientific and spiritual.

Very *Intuitive* and sometimes *Impatient*, the Catalyst Emperor really is a *seer* into souls. *Understands* people and knows how to *inspire* them, but also might overstep boundaries to coerce them. Always willing to *learn* and *grow*, but also knows what is best for most. *Cares* about others deeply, especially loved ones.

Balances to Reach

Don't let leadership turn into dictatorship. Self-assurance will often lead to confrontation, so be sure not to lash out at those who disagree. Learning to center self and slow down will be essential for future mental health.

Growth Direction

Patient: Has recognized tendency to be impatient, but has begun to use deep understanding of others to lead to an understanding of self.

Confident: Has begun believing in self calmly instead of always striving to prove self arrogantly, an act only fueled by doubt.

Emperor Type

The Agency Catalyst Emperor: A balanced rising combination, the Agency Catalyst Emperor believes in the power of emotions and connections. However, they never lose sight of the real and believe that truest power comes from individual action.

The Destiny Catalyst Emperor: Doubling down on rising intuition, the Destiny Catalyst Emperor understands the power of human connection. Possesses a keen sense for all the higher powers, but can be blinded by the singularity of this vision.

Very *Intuitive* and sometimes *Indecisive*, the Council Emperor is the most *supportive*. Understands *nuance* and also has *reverence* for higher powers and those with wisdom. Can sometimes feel overwhelmed by input, but capable of processing and sharing the most *profound* truths. *Cares* about others deeply, especially loved ones.

Balances to Reach

Don't shrink self to fit the mold of others. Be sure of the things you believe in, because they have likely been arrived at after much council and consideration. Revere the words of loved ones, but never more than your own.

Growth Direction

Patient: Has embraced the idea that thinking things through isn't about being stuck or paralyzed, but rather patience is an art of stillness and focus.

Confident: Has fully recognized tendency to be indecisive and has taken active steps to trust in own voice, letting support of loved ones embolden instead of overwhelm.

Emperor Type

The Agency Council Emperor: An extremely rare rising combination, the Agency Council Emperor trusts in their own voice as much as the voices of their trusted peers. A subtle leader, they are entrusted with the safety and well-being of others.

The Destiny Council Emperor: The most intuitive rising combination, the Destiny Council Emperor has the keenest ear for hearing what others cannot. They are always asking: Are you contributing more than you're taking away?